FATED
TO THE
WRONG
WOLF

STOLEN MATES DUET

SARAH SPADE

THE FERAL'S CAPTIVE

INTERNATIONAL BESTSELLING AUTHOR
SARAH SPADE

THE FERAL'S CAPTIVE

SARAH SPADE

ONE
FATE

ate sucks.

Rearing back my foot, I kick the baseball-sized rock in front of me. The toe of my worn leather boot connects with it, shooting it sky-high. The rock flies a good thirty feet before it pelts the thick trunk of a hickory tree in the distance. I hear the thud, my inner wolf yipping at me when the bark splits and the ancient hickory groans.

I wince. Fate still sucks, but the tree didn't deserve that.

I know better than to treat the forest with disrespect. A member of the Sylvan Pack since birth, I've lived along the edge of these woods for the last twenty-six years. They're almost as responsible for me as our Alpha is.

Probably more since I'm nothing but a delta.

We have at least fifty-six packmates at last count—fifty-eight if Kara had her twins—and there's definitely a hierarchy. Alpha is at the top. Beta is next. Our Omega doesn't have the dominance that the higher-ranked wolves do, but her role as peacemaker for the pack is essential so she's up there; of course, being the younger sister to our Alpha doesn't hurt, either. Gammas are the older wolves who have earned a peaceful retirement after protecting the pack. Then there are deltas. Regular rank-and-file packmates, deltas make up both the bulk and the base of the hierarchy.

Of course, among deltas, there's a hierarchy of our own. Some deltas are members of Bishop's pack council. Others are patrollers; protectors who are responsible for keeping the borders of Hickory secure. We have deltas who are cooks. Who teach. Who sew. A couple of deltas are tasked with leaving pack land and mingling with humans, buying the supplies we need as a community.

And then there's me. Quinn Malone. I… I'm just a delta.

I used to have a job. I fulfilled a purpose for the Sylvan Pack. Jokingly referring to my duty as stylist/groomer, I was the one my packmates came to when they needed a haircut or —after one memorable tumble through the blackberry bushes with his mate—they had canes and tangled thorns all up in their fur. I'd needed my clippers that day, and Frankie's wolf had a bald ass for a week after that.

But that was before.

Something similar happened to Sofia. I should've anticipated my fate after seeing hers, but I hadn't. That was my fault.

Sofia is the female half of our Alpha couple. Bishop's mate, she came from the River Run Pack on the East Coast where she taught the local pups math and science. When the Luna whispered her name to Bishop during his Alpha ceremony five years ago, he sent for her, and she accepted his mate bond. They performed the Luna Ceremony during the full moon that followed, and, once they were fully bonded, she was no longer a plain, boring, nobody delta like me.

Her dominance level didn't change by mating Bishop, but her rank sure did. From the bottom to the top, she couldn't be a math teacher anymore. Being the Alpha's forever mate was a full-time job of its own.

So is being the Beta's mate, I've discovered.

That's supposed to be me, but it isn't, and I'm still shit out of luck when it comes to my place in our pack after all this time —and all because of the Luna and her twisted idea of Fate.

Six months ago, I smiled at Weston Reed, the Beta of the Sylvan Pack. I'd done it a hundred times before. We were friends, growing up in the same age group, even though being a born beta wolf meant he was a much higher rank than us deltas. I knew that, one day, West would succeed our old Beta, Harris, and it didn't hurt to be buddy-buddy with him while he still rubbed elbows with the rest of us.

Truth be told, I'd always been drawn to him, but friendship was all he could offer so I took it gladly. For as long as I could remember, he had been together with Helene, our pack's Omega. And while their official relationship ended about three years back when Helene was promised to the future Alpha of a neighboring pack, West… he didn't get the memo.

He's been trying to convince her to choose him over Rafael ever since. Still is even now.

I was on his side when the pronouncement first came. As much as I had a crush on West, he loved Helene. I knew that. Anyone with eyes could see that. I thought she loved him, too. She didn't have to leave Hickory when Rafael eventually became Alpha if she didn't want to. She could reject him and choose West instead.

She refused. Pack gossip said that she was content to wait until Rafael could claim her by shifter tradition. That she had decided to accept her fated mate. It also said that Helene gently suggested that West do the same.

But *he* refused to do that—and, six months ago, when I smiled at him and, suddenly, something snapped into place, our goddess whispering to me that West was *mine*... he still refused the idea of taking any mate other than Helene.

Worse, he *rejected* me.

He rejected the idea that *I* could ever be the female meant for him.

Oh, not with words, though. That's not West's style. He's never been cruel. He just pretended that he didn't feel it when a bond sprang up between us, and because he's the Beta, the rest of the pack did the same.

One problem: ignoring the bond doesn't mean it isn't there.

Following his lead, I stayed away, too. I didn't push him. I gave him the space he needed to work out his feelings for Helene before he did what nearly every other shifter did and claimed his fated mate as his own.

But Fate sucks, remember? And West is the rare wolf who seems to be able to fight her pull.

I just wish *I* could.

Even worse, the pack still considers me his mate. Does it matter that West doesn't? Nope. The Luna says I'm the Beta's mate, so I am.

You know what that means?

No one comes to me for a haircut anymore. They don't want to bother the Beta's mate for something so trivial, and now Gregory is the new pack stylist.

I've gone from a flirtatious she-wolf needing to fight off

interested males to basically being the shifter version of a freaking nun, only without a wimple. None of the males treat me like a prospective mate anymore. Why would they when they already believe I'm taken?

Worst of all is how when other packmates need West, they come to me as if I hold any sway over him. Then they apologize when I point out that they'd have better luck going to Helene.

I was understanding in the beginning. As much as I was over the moon to discover I was meant for West, I knew he loved Helene. I just thought… maybe he could love me, too.

But, once again, I was wrong.

Ugh!

I don't kick another rock, but that's only because I still feel guilty for striking the tree before. This is my safe place. The clearing on the edge of pack territory where I can go to bitch and rage and get out all of my frustrations before I go back to Hickory where all I have to look forward to are pitying looks.

They all know I'm the rejected mate. The one cast aside. West never had to say it, but it's obvious.

And that makes it so much harder to take.

ONE OF THE DOWNSIDES TO BEING THE BETA'S FORGOTTEN mate? If I'm gone too long, West won't even notice—but someone else in the pack will.

I lose track of how long I was sitting on the grass, absently weaving flowers into my hair. I used to keep it short, usually shoulder-length, but in the last six months, I let it grow. I guess I lost the taste for cutting even my own hair, and now the deep black strands go nearly past my boobs when I'm standing up.

Hiding out in this clearing isn't new to me. I've been coming here since I was a randy teen and I needed a place to meet up with shifter males who wanted nothing more than a good time. I've never been the type of virginal, holier-than-thou she-wolf who wanted to wait until I took a mate. Shifters are earthy creatures. Sex is a biological urge. And, fuck it, it just feels amazing when done right.

I haven't been laid in six months. That's my longest dry spell since I started crooking my finger at horny males, inviting them to join me out beneath the hickories. Maybe that's why I'm feeling kind of twitchy all of a sudden.

My skin feels like it's stretched over my bones. Letting go of the wildflower I plucked, I rub my neck. A bird sings in the distance. My shifter's ears tune in. I hear… I hear…

Rustling?

The twitchy feeling turns into something else. Unless I'm imagining it, it's like I feel eyes on me. Like someone's watching me.

But who? There aren't many who come this far. Most of my packmates prefer to stay close to the cluster of cabins where we each have our homes. The pack circle is there—the cleared area with picnic tables where we can meet and talk and eat together—and it's within reach of the Alpha cabin where Bishop lives with Sofia.

I've brought plenty of males here over the years, but none recently. And those who know that I consider this part of the woods mine would never approach without permission. This is my territory, and a male encroaching on a possessive she-wolf learns very quickly how far she'll go to protect what's hers.

Especially because I never would've found it if it wasn't for West.

Before he was the Beta, he was another shifter who

enjoyed exploring the woods. He showed me this spot years ago and I immediately proclaimed it as mine. He didn't mind; he already had his own. While I came out here for the peace and, later, the privacy, West always visited a grove on the far borders of Hickory where countless types of wildflowers grew; similar to the ones that are growing by me, but more plentiful. It was a thing he had with Helene. Whenever they were separated during the time they were a couple, he'd bring a flower back for her.

They're not a couple anymore, but he still does it. I used to think it was cute. These days, though, I get a funny feeling deep in the pit of my stomach whenever I see him from a distance, stalking toward the Omega cabin, a stem clutched between his fingers.

I did a few weeks ago. Just like now, I'd sensed someone near a few seconds before my wolf started to whine once she recognized West's. He was in the woods, and he found me on my own, even stopping to say hello for the first time in ages… but all I could focus on was the flower in his hand.

Is that who is out there now? Should I go look?

Will my battered heart handle it when I see him holding another flower for Helene?

This isn't the first time I've longed to get up and run to West. Once again I'm sitting here, wondering if I should work up the nerve to head upwind and confront him in his own private sanctuary out in the woods.

It's getting harder to resist. I have to remind myself that he's chosen Helene, and I'm better off by myself—even if I'm not.

So, yeah. That's my big secret. My dark shame. I pretend like it doesn't faze me one bit that my fated mate follows another female around like a besotted puppy dog. On the rare occasion one of my old friends tries to see how I'm doing, I shrug and say that it happens. If the Luna got it right every time, there would be no rejected mates. No broken bonds.

Heck, one of the biggest cautionary tales in the shifter world is Jack "Wicked Wolf" Walker, a cruel Alpha who—at one time—ruled almost the entire West Coast of shifters. He turned his pack into a haven known as the Wolf District, and he lorded over it with an ever-changing retinue of Betas—and no mate. His fated mate rejected him before he bonded her to him, choosing to mate the Alpha of a nearby pack instead.

It's an open secret. While the Wicked Wolf was still the biggest threat on the West Coast, every shifter knew why he went through she-wolves the way I used to go through males. After losing his fated mate, he didn't want to choose another. He was happy by himself, and he was one of the most powerful—and feared—Alphas in the whole Luna damned United States until a challenger finally caught up to him and he lost everything except for his head.

I try to tell myself that I could be like the Wicked Wolf. Not the sadistic bastard part, but a shifter who doesn't let the pain of a jagged bond stop them from living life to the fullest.

Unlike me...

Another rustle and, so soft I'm not sure it's real, an animalistic snuffling sound that has my wolf cocking her head.

I take a deep breath, trying to see if I catch a familiar scent. I'm out here so often that I can recognize the wild wolves that visit, the prey animals that skirt around our territory, even the other shifters who take a break from pack living by passing through.

Is there a whiff of sandalwood?

I exhale. Nope.

Nothing. I get nothing. Everything is the same as usual.

And that makes the weight of the stare on me even weirder…

Brushing my hands against my jeans, I rise up from the ground. The sensation that someone is close by is only growing stronger. I can't shake the feeling that I'm being watched.

Maybe it's a packmate. Maybe it is West. Maybe it's someone—or some*thing*—else entirely.

Whatever it is, I don't like it.

I'm not scared, though. Please. I'm a wolf shifter. There's nothing out there I can't take.

Well, maybe not a vampire, but you have to be much more dominant than me to take on a vampire. Good thing you can scent one of those undead corpses from a mile away. Between their icy auras and the scent of blood and rotten meat that clings to their supernaturally beautiful forms, they'd never get close enough to Hickory before the whole pack would work together to take them down.

Still, scared or not, I've been out here too long. The last thing I need is Bishop sending West after me again. It's always super awkward when I have to talk to him. We have an unspoken agreement to pretend we're strangers most of the time, and whenever we don't, it's fucking terrible.

Just like it was a couple of weeks ago when I hated the azalea he held almost as much as I wish I could hate *him*.

But I don't. I *want* him.

He doesn't want me.

And there's not a damn thing I can do about it.

Purposely giving my back to whoever—*whatever*—might be out there watching me, I start to stalk back toward Hickory. It isn't long before I leave that strange sensation behind me. By the time I cross back into the inner border of pack land, I've forgotten all about it.

I want to go straight to my cabin. Despite having a decent enough afternoon by myself in the woods, I'm not in the mood to deal with any of my packmates today.

Who knows? Maybe I'll feel like being social tomorrow. Not likely, but you never know.

Of course, that's when I hear someone call my name from off to my side—

"Quinn!"

I freeze.

The voice… it's familiar and, for a split second, hope fills my chest. And, sure, his aura marks him as a delta, and he doesn't smell like sandalwood like West does, but I'm so far gone over my fated mate that I'm willing to be delusional until I turn toward him and see—

"Tucker." *Crap.* "How've you been?"

His smile is blinding. Something about Tucker Madden always reminds me of toothpaste commercials I see on television. He has bright white teeth, gleaming golden eyes, and dark blond hair styled in soft waves. Like all protectors, he has a lean body that I know intimately.

From the heat in his eyes as he looks me up and down, he's thinking the same thing about me.

"Missing you, but other than that I'm alright. I've been thinking about how much fun we used to have. Good times, huh?"

"Yeah. Sure."

"I was also thinking… it's been a while. You know. You and me. Maybe we could have some fun again? Go visit that spot in the woods you like? I know it's not too far. And it's real nice and private."

Ah, Luna. As if I need another reminder that I'm single as fuck. With West making his rejection obvious, the males I used to fool around with still see me as a sure thing—but they're the only ones.

Funnily enough, even they left me alone for the first few months. West is our Beta, and he has the respect of the entire pack. I'm his fated mate, and they figured he'd come to his senses eventually and accept that.

But he didn't. In so many different ways, he continues to reject me. To reject our bond. Tucker coming up and reminding me about old times isn't an insult to West so long as the Beta acts like I'm nothing to him. Tucker is just a horny male shifter who wants to get his rocks off, that's all.

And he probably guesses I'm the hard-up she-wolf who might say yes to his offer because he doesn't try to be coy or sly at all when he says, "I'm going on patrol after dinner, but that gives me a good hour. I was heading out to take a walk in the woods now anyway. You want to join me?"

A walk in the woods... every adventurous shifter in Hickory knows what that's a euphemism for.

I should. The longer I stew over a male I can't have, the more bitter I'm becoming. Maybe a quick romp with another packmate is just what I need to get my mind off of West.

But I can't. As insane as it sounds to want to be loyal to a male who doesn't want you, if I sneak off with Tucker, it's almost like I'm cheating on my fated mate.

Speaking of—

My wolf yips when she senses him. The little hairs on my human arm stand up, almost like I've been shocked by a tiny jolt of electricity. I instinctively know where he is and, shifting my stance a few degrees to the right, I look over Tucker's lean shoulder.

And there he is.

Weston Reed, the Beta of the Sylvan Pack.

My heart stutters in my chest. I'd always thought he was good-looking before. Since the bond appeared, he's more than that.

He's *breathtaking* to me.

West isn't as conventionally handsome a male as Tucker is. He wears his dark brown hair cut short, and his eyes are unusual for a shifter. Normally dark grey, they only turn gold when he's lost control of his emotions. Since that's almost never for a disciplined beta wolf like West, I've only ever seen it happen twice: the day we recognized each other as fated mates, and when he discovered that Helene was fated to belong to Rafael Cruces once he took over his pack.

West isn't alone. Though it takes a second for me to stop staring at his profile, I force myself to look away from him. Even before my gaze lands on the beautiful, blonde Helene Dupuis, I knew exactly who he was talking to.

The look of pure adoration on his masculine features made it obvious.

My heart aches. There's no other way to describe it. My fated mate is right there, barely twenty feet away, and I've never felt farther apart from him.

And wouldn't you know, I'm also not alone.

My heart still aches while my stomach sinks.

I shake my head. "Maybe some other time, Tucker."

Tucker follows the direction of my stare, making a soft sound of understanding when he sees West and Helene together.

"Yeah. Well, you know where to find me." He reaches his hand out to pat me on the shoulder. I try not to wince when he pauses, only an inch separating us, careful not to actually make contact. "Until next time, Quinn."

He couldn't touch me. West is over there making goo-goo

eyes at Helene, Tucker wanted in my pants two minutes ago, and once he noticed the Beta nearby, he couldn't even touch me.

Until next time?

Yeah. I don't think there's going to be one.

TWO
POISON

Sometimes I wish that West would just reject me completely.

It's easy enough. Up until the moment we perform the Luna Ceremony and get her blessing, all it takes is one half of a promised pair saying the words with meaning: "I reject you." *Boom.* The bond snaps, and though I'll have lost any chance of ever having my fated mate, at least I wouldn't be existing in this state of constant ache.

I know he doesn't mean to give me hope. He never has. In his own way, the Beta is being a decent wolf. He knows how much it'll hurt me to hear the truth so he just doesn't say it.

He doesn't have to.

As Beta, he's the second highest-ranked wolf in our pack. Bishop is first, and though we have two other budding alphas living in Hickory, West ranks higher than them because of his title. He's Bishop's right-hand wolf, the only one—besides Sofia—who can look Bishop in the eye without immediately baring his throat in submission. All of our fellow packmates follow his lead. As soon as he pointedly ignored the fact that the Luna paired us up, so did everyone else.

As far as the Sylvan Pack is concerned, West rejected me in every way that mattered—except actually setting me free.

I must be a fucking glutton for punishment. I walk around like a pariah, the topic of whispers and rumors that they know me and my wolf can hear. They feel pity for me, but they also wonder why I don't just leave.

Sometimes I wonder the same exact thing.

Hickory is my home. I was born on this land, and until the Luna upended my life, I planned on dying on it. My dad did—a victim of a challenge against another delta that he didn't win—and my mom, unable to live without her lifemate, who followed soon after.

I was twelve when all that happened. The rest of the Sylvan Pack rallied around me, giving me time to mourn, but also making sure I didn't want for anything. If I walk away because I can't have the one male meant for me, it's like I failed or something. I've never given up when things got hard. I'm stubborn to a fault.

Petty, too, I admit. If I have to live with the urge to go to West every single day, I'm not gonna make it easy for him to get out of doing the same. He's gonna see me. I know what an unfulfilled bond feels like. No matter how much he loves Helene, it's hard to beat Fate.

Am I hoping that he might wake up one day and realize what he's been missing out on? Not really. Maybe at first I did. If so, it was short-lived.

Am I waiting for Helene to leave Hickory for her promised mate?

I… I might be.

I'm not sure what that says about me. I never wanted to be

another she-wolf's sloppy seconds or a male's second choice. During my wild early years, when I was exploring my sexuality without the pesky complications of settling down with a mate, I had half the males in my age group sniffing around my tail. All I had to do was run into the woods, content in the knowledge that an interested male would chase.

Not West. Never West. He's always been hovering over Helene.

No one knows when she'll be leaving the pack. As our Omega—and the Alpha's beloved younger sister—Helene will stay in Hickory until her promised mate performs the Alpha Ceremony, taking over the Gravetail Pack. Only then will they perform the Luna Ceremony that will bond them together, and West will finally have to accept that he can't have the mate he wants.

Will he come crawling back to me?

I don't know.

Will I be waiting for him if he does?

I… I don't know that, either.

Another reason why I wish I could just get rid of this pull I feel for him. After the last six months of pity and need and loneliness, there's a good chance I would jump him the first time he acted like he wanted to be with me.

A she-wolf's gotta have some pride, right? When it comes to West Reed, I'm pretty sure I don't.

Ugh.

He won't do it. He won't snap our bond. Why? I have no clue. But six months after we both recognized that we were fated, all he's done is grow colder, more distant, while focusing all of his intention on a female he can never have.

And me? I spend all of my time on the edge of Hickory. Still near enough to the pack that I don't accidentally become a lone wolf, but with enough space that I can shake off the mantle of being the Beta's rejected mate.

There are other options. If Helene *did* forsake her own fated mate and choose West, our bond would break. Even less likely, I could choose another male. Since my packmates would never dare try to steal their Beta's mate—though, as Tucker proved the other day, fucking me is okay, but mating me is definitely a no-no—and I have no intention of leaving Hickory, I'm gonna have to just suck it up and get used to being the pack outcast.

It's like I've got a scarlet letter on my damn chest. Only, instead of Hester Prynne's A, I've got an R.

R for rejected. Yippee!

You know, I've heard rumors about a Luna-touched female with the gift—or curse, depending on your point of view—of breaking bonds with her little finger. One touch and, so long as one of the mates was willing, it was as though it never existed.

As much as it must suck to be her, if she's real, maybe I should see if I could track her down. With West content to go on as if our bond doesn't exist, she might be the best chance I have.

I'm just thinking about which of my packmates might know more about the mysterious Luna-touched female when, suddenly, a very familiar aura wraps around me. Just like the other day when I was talking to Tucker, I sense him before I pick up his scent, and by the time I turn to find West walking toward me, all I can think is: Mate. *Mate. Maaaaate.*

As handsome as ever, his face is an expressionless mask. I can't tell if his thoughts are running along the same lines as mine or if he was even expecting to run into me like this in the first place.

I peer closer. There's a look in his eye I recognize. Shortly after Bishop proclaimed him as his Beta—and long before I realized he was my fated mate—I used to tease him that it was his "business" look.

Wonderful.

"Quinn. There you are."

As if he's surprised to find me. Whether he wants to admit it or not, with our bond open, he's as viscerally aware of me as I am of him. It wouldn't have taken much to know that I was sitting on the front porch of my cabin.

Unless... unless he keeps our bond closed on his side. It takes a lot of effort to cut off a mate, and it would probably be more uncomfortable than leaving it unfulfilled, but it *is* possible. I don't do it because, really, what's the point?

Is that what he's doing to me?

I don't ask. I can't. Honestly, I'd rather not know the answer.

Instead, I shrug. "Yup. What's going on? You need me for something?"

Please need me...

He nods. "I know you spend a lot of time out among the hickories and the oaks on the edge of our territory." Gee... I wonder why. "Some of our patrols have picked up a few unfamiliar tracks recently. No scent, and that's what's weird about them. You should probably stick closer to the heart of pack land until we figure out what's going on."

My heart stutters against my ribcage. I don't want to read too much into West coming to warn me personally, but...

"Are you telling this me because you're the Beta and I'm a packmate, or because—"

West's perfectly chiseled jaw goes tight. "Because I'm the Beta and I have a duty to every wolf in Hickory."

Right. Message received.

So we both know where we stand. As if I wasn't already aware.

I offer him a mock salute. "Will do. Thanks."

West nods. His dark grey eyes travel over the fake smile I pulled on my face. For a second, I think he wants to say something else. I'm almost begging him to.

He doesn't.

With another nod and a short wave, he turns on his heel and starts to walk away. Probably going to see Helene again.

I wait a moment. When he doesn't turn to glance over his shoulder at me, I think about West's warning—and then I completely blow it off.

I'm not worried about there being a threat in the woods. True, I could've sworn I felt someone watching me the other day, but nothing happened. If it was really that big of an issue, Bishop would forbid any of us from heading out there instead of just giving us a warning. He'd amp up pack patrols on the edge of our territory, too.

Besides, I'm scarier than anything else that could be out there. I'll be fine.

And if this is my own way of saying, "Fuck you," to West without it being a challenge, then that makes my decision to retreat to the woods again that much sweeter.

***

THE BEST THING ABOUT BEING A DELTA? I'M NOT IMPORTANT enough that I can't slip away without one of the higher-ranked packmates noticing.

If I'm gone too long, they will. Our pack is strongest when we're whole. Bishop takes his role as Alpha seriously. If he can't account for all of us at any given moment, it sets off his wolf—and that usually sets off West.

It's bad enough I ran into West a couple of weeks ago, carrying another Luna-damned flower for his precious Helene. No doubt in my mind that it was an accident, and that he only stopped to talk to me because his wolf spurred him to. With all of Hickory between us, he can usually avoid me. When we're that close? Even he isn't strong enough to resist the pull. Part of the reason I call bullshit on his warning me about the woods earlier today. Sure, he's the Beta, but any other protector could've done the same thing. It didn't have to be West.

Of course, then I remember how, after I ran into Tucker a few days back, I saw West watching Helene with such open adoration—the Omega the only one worthy of him showing any hint of emotion toward—and I realize I'm still fooling myself.

Come on, Quinn. He's just one male. One dick. If he can beat Fate, so can I.

Right?

Well, not in the last six months I haven't…

Our tie has another downside besides the fact that it rules me: if I'm missing for too long, Bishop will definitely send West in particular to find me. Neither of us wants that. He'd be able to, too, and not only because he's the Beta. Mates can find each other by following their bond to the other end; unless it's closed off, of course. It's how I know that, whenever he's not busy with his pack duties, West spends all of his free time outside of Helene's cabin, waiting for her to give him a moment of her attention.

Me? I spend mine in the woods.

That afternoon, as I move soundlessly through the trees, I rub my chest with the heel of my hand.

It's getting worse. Can't deny it anymore. The jagged edge of our neglected mate bond… it *hurts*. At this point, if I could use my claws to gut myself open and rip it out, I would. Anything has to be better than walking around with the sting of rejection as my constant companion.

Usually just being close enough to take in West's scent soothes it for a little while. Talking to him, hearing his voice… it helps.

Not today, though.

When I get to the small clearing I consider mine, I plop down on the ground. My legs are stretched out in front of me, I'm leaning back on my hands, my eyes cast toward the sky. The caps of leaves on the crowded hickory trees block out most of the sunlight, leaving a few stray beams filtering through.

I exhale roughly. It's not much, but at least I find some peace here.

Later, I'll look back and accept that everything that happened next wouldn't have if I'd only swallowed my pride and listened to West's warning. But I didn't, and by the time I discovered there was some merit in it, it's too late.

A big, black wolf has stalked out of the woods about twenty feet away from me.

I only noticed because his eyes are a vibrant gold, and as shadows fell around me, their shine caught my attention. I never scented him. Never heard him. I don't know where he came from or how he snuck up on me, but it doesn't matter. He's here.

Lips parted, I breathe in deep, sampling scents. Big mistake. Something burns the back of my throat.

I choke.

Wolfsbane.

No wonder I didn't catch his scent before his eyes flickered in the distance. No wonder the pack patrol found prints and no other trace. Wolfsbane can cover up anything except muddy prints.

He's not a real wolf. I hadn't thought he was, but the wolfsbane gives him away. That's a shifter out there. The wolfsbane makes it worse. He's not only a stranger, but he has to be an enemy. No supe with good intentions carries wolfsbane on them.

And that's when his aura rushes at me. It took a few seconds, thanks to the wolfsbane messing with my senses, but I can't miss it now.

He's a shifter—and he's an alpha. Explains why he's so huge.

The way his gaze is locked on me also explains why he's here.

I have no clue what the hell he wants with me, but there's no denying the predatory gleam in his gaze as he pads closer.

He's moving slowly on purpose. He doesn't want to spook me. He's treating me like prey and, Luna, does that rankle.

I hop to my feet. He pauses, then continues to stalk forward.

My first instinct is to shift. I run faster as a wolf. His every move screams he's ready to take off if I do, and I'm not sure I can waste the precious seconds it would cost me to explode out of my clothes and change shapes.

I'm still a wolf whether I'm in my skin or not. I know these woods like the back of my hand. I know every member of the Sylvan Pack. The black wolf is undeniably a stranger. So he tiptoed up to the edge of our territory. I can lose him, then make it further into Hickory where the rest of the pack can help me.

That's what we do. When push comes to shove, we help each other.

I bolt. Just like I figured, he comes racing after me.

I can make it. Weaving around the trees, taking the quickest path back toward Hickory, I can lose him—

Nope.

With all of his brute strength, the wolf barrels into my legs. It's a cheap shot. I'm lucky he didn't snap a bone with his impact, and when I go flying before landing on my belly in the dirt, all of the air is knocked out of me.

A second later, his wolfish body is covering my human one.

Shit. I knew he was big, but pressed against me, I realize he's *massive*.

What *is* he?

He looks like a wolf, but he sure doesn't act like one. Wolves rarely give pursuit when they're hunting. They prefer to ambush their prey.

Then again, isn't that what he's done to me?

Once I'm down, I figure it's worth the split second of vulnerability. The force of my shift will tear my clothes off of my back, but the supernatural magic inherent to our kind will also push him away from me if only for a second.

That might be all I need to get away from him. My wolf is much squirmier than my human form. Faster, too. Shifting now should give me the best chance of escaping him.

I'm quick. He's quicker. As if he expected me to change shapes once he got a hold of me, he grabs my scruff between his fangs. Though, as a shifter, I only have sex when I'm in my skin, never my fur, there are some primal memories I can't deny. A wolf on top of me, his fangs pinning me by the scruff?

He's mounting my wolf.

No fucking way.

He's an alpha. Not as strong as Bishop—as if anyone could be—he's still twice my size and probably triple my power. He must've thought I was an easy target.

If so, he was wrong.

I jerk my head. His fangs rip through my skin. Ignoring the pain, I whirl on him, snapping my fangs back, trying to bite any part of him I can reach. I'm especially partial to any dangly bits. An unknown wolf attacking me on pack land? I have every right to defend myself, and if he ends up castrated, he'll learn that even a low-ranking delta she-wolf has claws and fangs.

I lock onto his foreleg. Blood gushes into my mouth. Swallowing it greedily, I tear.

Feel that, asshole!

The wolf growls. Instead of trying to get me off of him, he pushes against my fangs, feeding me more of his fur, his muscle, his blood.

I choke on it. Breathing through my snout, I refuse to let go.

He shifts. I'm ripping human flesh now, but I don't care. In fact, without the fur in my way, I'm sure I'm doing more damage.

Why isn't he fighting to be free? Or fighting back? From his aura, I can tell he's an alpha. Just because I'm defending myself, it doesn't mean that he won't take this as me answering his challenge. By shifter law, he can put me down without any consequence. He's certainly strong enough to. Failing that, bastard could force me to submit. He's too dominant for me to ignore.

I'd never win.

Only… he isn't. He's willingly allowing me to gnaw on him as the heat of his naked body pushes me to the ground.

I stay in my fur. I need my fangs to be at their sharpest, I need my jaw to be strong, and I need to keep my naked human body away from the monster erection digging into my back.

That's not the only thing I feel poking me.

Still clamping down on him—now that he's human, his foreleg is now his upper arm—I jerk in time to see he has something in his other hand. I don't know where he got it from. Clothes never survive the shift so it's not like he pulled it out of a pocket. Jewelry that's been charmed might, but he's not holding a necklace or a bracelet.

That's a shot. The vial is filled with a viscous, silvery grey liquid that shimmers against the glass casing—and he's buried the needle part of the injector past my fur.

I know what that is, too.

Mercury.

Quicksilver.

Poison.

Before I can react, he uses his thumb to press down on the plunger at the top of the injector.

Fucker.

It's not enough to kill me—he'd need pure silver to do that—but quicksilver isn't just a poison. It's also a sedative. Pour a couple of drops in a drink and it'll do something funny to a shifter's beast. Shoot one with an injection of the stuff and I'm gonna be on my ass before I know it.

He runs his fingers through the fur on the top of my head, obviously pleased with himself. His mouth reaches one of my ears. I flick it angrily, but that doesn't stop him from leaning closer.

"Remember," he whispers in a gruff voice, "it didn't have to be this way."

As the quicksilver worms its way through me and I start to go under, I suddenly remember something I should never have forgotten.

Real wolves will rarely pursue prey. But give a wolf shifter the chance?

He'll *always* chase.

I also realize something else.

There's no escaping him, either.

THREE
CHAINS

My eyes flutter open.

I already know something is wrong before I'm completely awake. As a shifter, my senses are usually firing on all cylinders. My nose can tell me almost as much about my surroundings as my sight does. My ears, too.

None of them are working right.

My nose is stuffed up. Supes don't get sick like humans do, but this is what I think it must be like. It's as if someone shoved a wad of cotton up each of my nostrils because I can't smell a damn thing.

Same with my ears. Everything is dull. I move a little, and I hear something heavy sliding across the floor, but it sounds like it's coming from far, far away.

The room is dark and, except for me, it's empty. There's one window, high above my head on the wall at my back, and it's closed. Shades are drawn, letting in a sliver of light, so I know it's still daylight out there. Normally the meager light would be enough for me to make out every detail—but it isn't.

The most I can see is that the room is made up of four solid grey cinder block walls with a single dark brown door breaking them up. If I didn't know any better, I'd think it looks like some kind of cell.

And that's when I remember.

The quicksilver. The black wolf.

The chase.

My senses are trash. Now that I remember that I was dosed with quicksilver, it makes sense. Quicksilver is a sedative, but it also cuts a shifter off from their wolf. It wears off in time. Based on how… how *human* I feel right now, I can tell it hasn't yet. My wolf is eerily missing.

And that's not all that isn't quite right.

Wherever I am, I'm laying down on a blanket that's protecting me from the hard cement floor beneath it. I jerk up, and that same sound from before follows my movement. I feel heavy, too, like whatever I'm dragging is attached to me.

Uh-oh.

I look down.

The first thing I notice is that I'm human again. Last I recall, I was in my wolf form, but the human arms and legs I'm looking at are undeniable. Of course. With the quicksilver coming between me and my wolf, I would've reverted back to my human form in order to contain my beast.

The second thing?

I'm not naked.

Not that I would prefer to wake up without any clothes on in an unfamiliar room. Considering I had shifted during the attack, I *should* have. My clothes are a mess of tattered remains in the forest while I'm here, wearing a slinky, dark red dress that covers me all the way down to the middle of my thighs.

No bra, no panties, but at least my tits aren't hanging out. Small victories.

Then there's the tiny matter of the third undeniable thing…

I've been chained to the bare wall behind me.

Each of my ankles has a shackle on it. A length of chain—from the faint crackle I sense coming from them, I know they're made from silver, just like the shackles—is attached to each one, threaded through a sturdy-looking ring screwed into the cinder block over my head.

I don't scream. He's already proven that he sees me as his prey, and no matter what his intentions are, I'm still as much a predator as he is. My heart might be racing, my stomach tight and queasy as the reality of my situation sinks in, but losing my head won't help me get out of it.

Think, Quinn. Focus.

Okay. First things first. I can't reach my wolf. I can't rely on my shifter's senses. I still have a brain.

What happened after I was out? That's something to worry about.

Rubbing my thighs together, I'm relieved to find that I don't feel any tenderness or pain. On the plus side, my mysterious captor might've dressed my naked body before chaining me to a wall, but he didn't force himself on me.

Yet.

Once I pay closer attention to the shackles on my ankles, I no longer expect him to.

I already knew he was a shifter. He appeared on the edge of Hickory as a black wolf before turning human. The chains only reinforce my belief.

A human in the know might still be stupid enough to go for steel or iron chains if they wanted to trap a she-wolf. At my full strength, I could snap those easily; they'd never hold me. Only silver could, but even if they were tipped off to one of a shifter's few weaknesses, I'd expect them to wrap me up in them, not caring if they burned the crap out of me or not.

I'm just a captive, right? Depending on what they want with me, so long as they keep the chains away from my goods, what does it matter if I suffer in other places?

But the person who locked me up in these chains? They were careful to keep the silver from my bare skin. The chains are stretched out and positioned far from me so I wouldn't accidentally brush against them while I was unconscious, and there's fabric padding between me and the silver shackles.

I might be trapped. The silver might weaken me further.

At least I'm not being burned by it.

Just in case, I give an experimental kick. The chains swing, then go taut, but they don't break. Even when I can tap into my wolf again, I don't think I'll be able to snap them. The silver is too powerful.

Crap.

Now, I'm not pissed about the chains. Not really. Maybe a human chick would be, but us supernaturals see things a little differently. While I don't know exactly why he took me captive, I can't deny it wasn't smart of him to lock me up. He doesn't know me. He doesn't know how I'll react. She-wolves of my rank are still vicious and strong when we're backed in a corner, and that's exactly where I am right now.

I've also heard stories about shifters on the edge of going feral who chose the chains for themselves. Usually they're alphas, but most dominant shifters have a close call or two. I did. When I first understood—really understood—that West was rejecting our mate bond, I wanted to lash out. It didn't get so bad that I needed to be restrained from taking out my pain on him, but it was rough.

So the chains? The chains I can understand. But the quicksilver burning through me, keeping me from getting in touch with my wolf?

He never should've done that.

I'm a shifter. You hurt my wolf, you hurt my soul. And you'll pay for it.

Unfortunately, attacking the black wolf who ambushed me is out. Even before the quicksilver, he was too strong for me. I either need to outsmart him, or get the heck out of Dodge before he realizes I'm awake.

I look down at the chains holding me back again and wince.

This is gonna hurt, isn't it?

Supes, as an advanced species, are powerful. We're long-lived, have amazing regenerative properties, enhanced strength and speed, and the ability to form mate bonds; a vampire has their beloved while a shifter can find their fated mate or choose one to bond with forever. When humans know we exist, we're respected and revered.

All that power comes with a price. As strong as we are, we're not invulnerable. While each type of supe has a few weaknesses specific to their race, we all share one: *silver*. It's deadly to supernaturals. In small amounts, it's like acid against our skin, and a drain on our abilities. In larger amounts, it doesn't need to be a weapon to kill us, though a silver stake, blade, or bullet will certainly do the job.

I'm hoping that the quicksilver he shot me with is enough to temper my wolf's reaction to the real stuff. I'm still a shifter, but with my wolf out of my reach, maybe I can try to break the silver chain without too much damage.

It's worth a shot.

Reaching down by my leg, I grab the nearest length of chain and yank.

As soon as the silver touches my skin, it begins to sizzle. I bite back a scream, gritting my teeth as I tug. I won't give him the satisfaction of hearing me yell. I'd much rather he come back to this room only to find a set of snapped chains and me already gone.

Serves him right from trying to steal me, I think, and seething past the agony, I tug again.

IT WAS A GOOD PLAN. IF ONLY IT WORKED.

I've burned almost all of the skin from my fingers for nothing. The silver chains are as unbreakable as they were when I first came to, only now I'm pissed off, my hands feel like acid has bitten through most of the flesh, my throat is raw from the screams I refused to let out, and, to cap off my shitty, shitty day, my aching, empty stomach is starting to grumble.

I'm a little bit worried, too. The reality of the chains has sunk in. The padding beneath the shackles makes it obvious this isn't some kind of sick torture play—my captor doesn't want me to suffer needlessly because of the silver in the chains —so that means he wants me in one piece.

Not only that, but he wants me in one place. He went to a lot of trouble to get me here, so he must have a reason.

And I'm pretty sure I know what it is.

Realistically, there are only a couple of options. We're shifters. We fight. We fuck. We feed. Life is about survival, making sure the pack is safe, and our future pups are provided for. We feel things more strongly than the cold-blooded vampires, or even humans. Our wolves, at their core, are just like their counterparts in the wild. We see things in black and white; there are no shades of grey.

There's no denying the black wolf took me. Whether he targeted me on purpose, or I was just the bonehead who went to the edge of Hickory that day on my own, he brought me here. The quicksilver sedated me before, and is still subduing me now. The chains make it impossible for me to escape.

He wants me here. It doesn't take a genius to know *why*.

He's a male. I'm a she-wolf. His aura reads as alpha, though it's pretty different than Bishop's level of dominance. I'm a delta with just enough spunk to put up a fight against him, proving that I'd be a good protector to any pups I might have.

How much do you want to bet he wants a mate and I'm the lucky gal he's chosen?

It's a lone wolf thing. All shifters belong in a pack or a clan or a brood. Wolves are the most notorious for needing to be among their own kind. Sometimes, if one of us goes out on our own, we start to forget how to act like a shifter.

Some rely more on their human side. Others go wolf. With our wolves in charge, pesky things like right or wrong—or letting another shifter know you're interested instead of just straight up *taking her*—fall to the wayside. He might not know how much he fucked up.

That's okay. I'll make sure to tell him.

Even with these chains I have the advantage. He wants something from me, and I want to get the hell out of here. If he really wants me to mate him, he'll try to prove himself to me. I can work with that.

Unless he's a feral.

When it comes to the broken shifters, more wolf than man,

there's no guessing what they'll do. They are as vicious and cruel as they are territorial and protective. A feral might force a female, then tear out her throat in an attempt to mark her as his.

Worse, he might force a female, then tear out her throat because he'd gotten what he wanted, and she was a casualty that didn't matter once he finished.

I shiver at the thought. I can handle anything but *that*. Being rejected, catching the attention of a lone wolf on his own, even walking away from the Sylvan Pack if that's what I decide to do. But a feral?

I'd be better off slitting my own throat. At least I would save myself from anything else a twisted feral shifter might come up with.

No. He can't be feral. Ferals are rabid, untamable wolves walking around in their human shape. They're ruled by their urges. If he looked at me and wanted to mate, he would've fucked me in the woods just outside of Hickory.

The black wolf that stalked me was methodical. He knew exactly what to do to take me down, and he capped it off by injecting me with quicksilver. That takes planning. Precision. Human reasoning.

He has to be a lone wolf. One aching for a female of his own.

Shame he chose me.

And once he finally shows his face again, I'll make sure he knows it.

He's somewhere near. As the hours pass, the quicksilver is finally beginning to work its way out of my system. I can't reach my wolf just yet, but I'm able to rely on some of my shifter's senses.

My nose recovers first. Breathing in deep, I catch notes of a male scent overlaying everything in this room—including me. The chains carry his scent. The dress I'm wearing is entrenched in it. *I* kind of smell like him, and when I trace the most potent source to my hair, I wonder what that's about.

Did he pet my hair when I was unconscious or something?

His musk lingers everywhere. It seeps in under the door. It hangs in the air. I don't hear him, but his scent keeps renewing. He's near, and, after a while, I get annoyed that he's left me here to rot.

He fucking kidnapped me. The least he could do was make sure that his quicksilver didn't stop my heart and kill me after he dressed me up like his own personal doll.

The longer I'm in here, the easier it is for me to be angry instead of worried. I need someone to take it out on, and he's the perfect choice.

"Hey!" My voice is rusty from not using it. I clear my throat, then try again. "Hey, you! I know you're here! You can't leave me like this!"

He can. Of course he can. But I'm sure as hell not gonna make it easy on him.

"Where are you? Let me out of here!"

No answer. I didn't expect one, but I let out a full-throated shout that irritates the entire length of my poor esophagus. At least it makes me feel a little better to get that out.

I'm a she-wolf. While I admit it was a shock to realize that I've basically been put in a cage, I'm not going to sit here like some damsel in distress. Maybe if he realizes that I'm a complete pain in the ass, he'll think better of keeping me.

Hey. It's a thought, and one I perk up at.

I can do that.

Just as I'm about to start shouting again, a new scent mingles with that of the wolf. Once it hits me, my mouth waters as my stomach grumbles loudly, and it's all I can think about.

Meat. Beef, if my nose is right. I think it's steak.

Why do I smell steak?

I want steak.

If he's cooking himself dinner while I'm chained to a wall, I'm going to lose it. If I didn't already want to break free, the promise of a steak has me just about ready to see if I'm strong enough to snap my chains yet.

I glance at my fingers. Thanks to the quicksilver, my regenerative properties aren't as fast as they usually are. My palms are covered in pale pink blisters—better than the angry red ones from before, but barely—and my fingertips are tender.

Damn it. Better wait.

Frustrated, I kick out my legs, putting the chains as far away from me as possible. The blanket beneath me is soft and luxurious, but I'm still lying on the floor. I need to get up. I need to move.

I also have to pee. Something I'm going to have to deal with sooner or later, though I'm not above pissing in this dress if I have to. He wants to put me in this room? I'll mark it as mine if he doesn't let me use the toilet.

It's a win-win. He either has to deal with me marking my territory, or he has to unchain me so I can go to the bathroom. If he thought he was going to get some docile female out of this, he chose wrong. He needs an omega like Helene.

Damn it, why didn't he go after Helene?

I know the answer to that. Li'l Miss Pack Princess would never be caught out on her own. And if she was? Both the

Alpha and Beta would be on the black wolf's ass so fast, he'd be nothing but a pile of fur and guts by the time Bishop and West finished with him.

And then there's me. If I want out, I'll have to free myself.

I will. Bet on it.

Another couple of minutes go by. Without a phone or a watch or a damn clock on the wall, I have no idea how many. Could be five. Could be thirty. With the scent of cooked meat teasing me, it feels like forever before I hear something on the other side of the door.

Suddenly, it eases open.

It wasn't closed all the way. When I noticed it before, I'd thought it was because he just hadn't bothered on his way out. The silver chains make it so that I can't get out of this room unless I gnaw off my ankles and I crawl out, and if I tried, he'd be after me before I got that much further. I'd put money on it.

Maybe that's true. Could be. When the door inches inward, I discover the real reason.

Wolves don't have opposable thumbs.

With his height, he'd be able to reach the knob if he stood up on his back legs, but he'd never be able to turn it with his paws. The black wolf from the woods uses his head first, then the brunt of his shoulder to push the door in.

He's just as big as I remember. I'd thought my panic made him seem huger in my memories. Nope. The black wolf is probably the largest shifter I've ever seen, except for maybe Bishop.

Alpha. Right.

His golden eyes have that same insane gleam as before, too. As he pads into the room, they're almost flashing as he turns his unblinking stare on me. A muffled grunt is probably his idea of a greeting.

Wait… muffled?

He has something in his mouth. It takes me a second before I realize that he has a hunk of meat hanging from between his clamped fangs. A quick sniff reveals that it's the steak I caught cooking before.

The black wolf is walking right toward me. Any bravado I had earlier fades when I see that his eyes don't just look insane. They look *hungry*.

And he's staring at me.

"Who are you?" I ask, scooting back on the blanket. It's fluffy and thick, the only hint of softness in this gloomy, dark room. It shifts when I move, following me. "Where am I?"

He doesn't answer me. Of course not. In his wolf form, the most he can do is communicate with howls, yips, grunts, and snarls, none of which will tell me what's going on.

But the way he crosses the room before he spits the hunk of meat out of his mouth, dropping it in front of me?

That does.

FOUR
STEAK

Oh, Luna. He's got to be kidding me.

"I'm not eating that."

The black wolf grunts again.

Too bad. "I mean it. Get that away from me. I'm not touching that."

Acting as though I didn't say a damn thing, he has the nerve to nudge it closer to me with his snout.

Despite how hungry I am, I flip him the bird. Probably not the smartest move when I'm guessing I know exactly what he wants with me, but I don't care. If he thinks I'm going to accept food from him, he's crazier than I already think he is.

He curls his muzzle over his fangs, showing off his canines.

The fact that he's walking around in his fur, baring his fangs at me, just makes me more pissed off. It's a shifter thing. If I'm in my skin, he should be, too.

"What's the matter? Come on, tough guy. Use your words. Answer me. Who are you, and what do you think you're doing?"

He growls.

"Sorry"—I'm not sorry—"but that shit you pumped into me is cutting me off from my wolf. I have no idea what you're trying to say."

It's a lie and we both know it. I don't need my wolf to translate when it's obvious. He wants me to eat the steak.

I absolutely refuse.

As if the padding around my ankles isn't enough, I can't deny what this strange wolf is after. In shifter culture, food has a very important meaning. Parents provide for their pups until they come of age. Even if you're separated from your folks before then, it's the Alpha's responsibility to make sure that none of us go hungry; that's why Bishop and Sofia make sure there is breakfast, lunch, and dinner ready for any and all packmates, no strings attached.

And, of course, there are mates.

As a she-wolf, if a male offers me food, it's a precursor to mating. Simple as that. Not just fucking, either, but it's his way of initiating a relationship that might eventually become permanent.

The first time I saw West pick out the thickest, most perfectly sauced chop during dinner before plating it and offering it to Helene in front of our packmates, I knew that I'd never have him. There were plenty of other clues in the beginning—the most significant one being the way his gaze often passed over me as though I wasn't there—but that was the one I couldn't deny.

It wasn't bad enough that he was basically begging for a minute of her attention. Even knowing that the Luna picked me for him, he tried to feed Helene.

She's the Omega of the Sylvan Pack. Considered almost like royalty among our kind, she's always been prized, protected, and coddled. The only one allowed to feed her—apart from her promised mate from the Gravetail Pack—is Bishop. As both the Alpha of her pack and her big brother, there's no sexual intent behind it, so Helene can accept food from him.

When West offered her that meal, he was saying: *I will protect you, I will feed you, and you'll want for nothing if I'm around.*

Of course, Helene gently refused him, and instead of eating the chop himself—or throwing it my way in an act of pity—West disappeared into the woods, tossing the food to the wild wolves that sometimes visit our pack.

Did that stop him from trying again? No. At least once a week West still tries to feed Helene, and the more he did it, the more I felt the eyes of my packmates on me as if watching to see how I'd react. That's why I stopped eating with the pack. Over the last six months, I've gotten used to grabbing my plate and heading back to my cabin instead of sitting down to a pity party of one.

I can't believe this shit. The first time a male shifter propositions *me* with food and it's a lone wolf who stole me away from Hickory. If I eat this meat, I'm basically telling him I'm interested—and that I don't mind what he's done.

Yeah, right. Not in this lifetime.

The black wolf is watching me unblinkingly. After a few tense seconds, he taps his front paw against the floor. The claws clink. I cross my arms over my chest. He chuffs, then scoots the steak closer to me with that same paw.

What is wrong with him? Not only have I already refused his meal, but I'm obviously in my human form. That means my human brain is currently in charge. As a wolf, I have no problem hunting a deer or a rabbit, then eating the bloody meat raw, ripping it right off the bone. As a human? All I keep thinking about is how dirty his paw is, how he had the meat in his mouth, and how he keeps dragging it across the floor.

He finally gets it. When I turn my nose up at his offering again, he pads away from me. He moves slowly, his head hanging as if trying to figure out what to do next, and I only hope he'll leave me the hell alone so I can figure out what *I'm* going to do.

The black wolf doesn't. Instead, he crosses the room, then lowers himself down into the corner opposite of me. He folds his back legs beneath him, stretching out his forelegs. His golden eyes locked on me, he settles his muzzle on his legs, almost like he's settling in for a good, long wait.

Oh. I see. He's gonna lay there until I accept his steak.

I snort softly. Good luck.

Even if I don't know exactly why he thinks his tactics are going to work, I understand *what* he's doing. A lone wolf is still a shifter, and I've spent twenty-six years around my male pack-mates. I don't think there's a more stubborn creature on the planet—except, perhaps, a she-wolf who's been wronged.

However, there is one thing I don't get. If he really is treating me like a prospective mate, why is he giving his wolf control? While a mating would never work unless both halves of each shifter were in agreement about their future mate, our wolves are easy to convince. If a mate is attractive, a good protector, a good provider, and a good parent to any future pups, our wolves will be on board long before our human halves are sure.

That's why so many shifters wait to find their fated mates. Whether the Luna pushes us together, or we just sense it like how I was always drawn to West even when he was dating Helene, it's hard to deny a fated mate. There's usually a moment when the pair just clicks, and both halves know they're looking at their forever.

Unless, of course, you already chose your mate. Then you can reject Fate, hoping that the mate of your heart would choose you back.

And when she doesn't, all three of you are left heartbroken and alone…

I bite down, pushing thoughts of West out of my head. I've gotta stop thinking about him. As soon as the quicksilver started to fade earlier, I purposely cut West off from my side of our useless bond. If I keep letting him back into my head, it'll only be a matter of time before I slip up and he can sense something's wrong, no matter how closed off his side is.

How long have I been gone? Long enough that my pack has noticed I'm missing from Hickory? I'm not sure, but if it is, they'll turn to West to find me. They'll have to. Between the wolfsbane and the quicksilver, my captor covered his tracks. And that's assuming he carried me out of Hickory. If the lone wolf had a vehicle, it'll be impossible to scent me unless they know where I disappeared off to.

Considering I have no idea where I am myself, the odds of them finding me are pretty much nil—unless West tracks me using our fated mate bond.

I can't let that happen. If West did come, it would only be out of a sense of duty.

And if he didn't come…

I know he doesn't want me. I know he's rejected me in every way except telling me bluntly that he'll always choose Helene over me. I know that, if I want a mate of my own, it'll be one *I* choose.

But I'm still tied to West. If he abandons me to a lone wolf because I'm nothing to him, I don't think I'd be able to survive that last level of rejection. No. It's better to deal with this situation on my own.

After all, I got myself into this mess. I'll get myself out, too.

Talking to the black wolf is like talking to a brick wall. I'm not going to make any progress there. I need him to shift.

But he doesn't, and not because he can't.

I know he's able to shift to a human form. I didn't get a good look at him before, but my wolf latched onto a human arm at one point when he was trying to subdue me. His naked body seared my back right before he jammed that needle past my fur.

He spoke. In a raspy, hoarse voice that followed me into unconsciousness, he spoke to me, trying to make it seem like getting shot up with quicksilver was my fault for resisting him.

For that alone, I snag the slab of meat from the floor. It's just like I guessed. Barely seared, it's mostly raw, and it squelches against my grip. I can see the fang marks from where he carried it in his mouth to me.

I might be hungry, but I'm not *that* hungry.

The wolf lifts his head when he notices I've finally reached for the meat he gave me. If I eat it, it's a clear sign that I'm accepting his attention. At the very least, I'm telling him that he might've ambushed me and chained me away from my pack, but that's okay since he brought me food.

I'd rather starve.

I fling the steak across the room, aiming for the black wolf. It hits the wall about two feet higher than where his head is. The slap echoes, then the steak thumps as it lands between his ears. He flattens them against his skull before he shakes his whole head roughly, tossing the battered steak to the floor.

The black wolf looks at the steak, then at me, then back at

the steak. I think me throwing the meat finally got through to him because, instead of trying to force it on me again, he digs in. In a matter of bites, it's gone.

Good for him. At least one of us enjoyed it.

———

AFTER THE DISASTER WITH THE STEAK, I DON'T THINK HE'LL come back for a while. He leaves the same way he came, in his wolf form, though he doesn't drag the door behind him when he goes.

Almost immediately, I scent more food cooking. I can't imagine that he's making it for me after I refused the steak, and I figure that the meat he scarfed down hadn't been enough for such a big brute. It must be for him—and I believe that until a looming figure appears in the open doorway not much later.

With a surprised gasp, I finally get my first good look at my captor in his human form.

Luna damn it. It would be so much easier if he was hideous. A beastly male might have to resort to stealing a she-wolf for a mate, but one glimpse of him and I begin to second-guess everything that's going on.

Because this wolf? He's way too good-looking for me.

He's handsome in a rugged way that's so different than West, but still enticing to me and my wolf. Though I can't quite shift yet—probably because of the silver chains—I can sense her rousing deep inside of me, and her head jerks up when he stalks into the room.

His skin is the soft bronze shade of someone who earned the coloring from hours in the sun. Considering he's wearing a pair of low-slung jeans and nothing else, it's easy to see his tan is unbroken. His thick, shaggy hair is the same color as his pelt, his eyes a shade darker than his wolf's.

He has broad shoulders, a sculpted torso, and a patch of dark hair on the height of his chest; it's also the color of his fur. As he moves into the room on soundless, bare feet, the light flickers against something, and that's when I notice that he has a golden necklace around his thick throat. Two charms hang off the chain: a white sliver of who knows what, and a slender golden cylinder about three inches long.

He has a plate in each hand. Learning from before, he brought me a steak, but it looks like it's medium this time instead of super rare. French fries are piled high next to it. On the other plate, there's a mound of bacon higher than the fries, and a few pieces of lettuce mixed with tomatoes that might generously be called a salad. He has a glass of water tucked under his muscular arm and—

I blink, then blink again because I can't believe what I'm seeing.

He has a bite mark on his upper arm, just above his bicep. *My* bite mark. I can see the imprint of every one of my fangs, plus where I tore the skin as I was fighting for my freedom. It's not still bleeding, but it's nowhere near as healed as it should've been. Actually, depending on how long I've been stuck in this room, it should be way gone by now.

But it's not. And that… that's almost as weird as a half-naked shifter bringing me a meal.

Handsome or not, I can't let him get away with this.

I glare up at him. "What do you want with me?" As if I didn't already know. "You have to let me go."

Like he did when he was a wolf, he pretends not to have heard me. Instead, he lowers himself to a crouch, placing both plates down on the ground. The glass tucked under his arm is next.

Once he's done, he cocks his head. Then, for the first time since he tackled me, he speaks.

"Will they come for you?"

His voice is as gruff as I remember it. More than that, it's deep, so deep it does something to my insides.

Or maybe that's because I can't stop glancing at my bite mark staring out at me from his upper arm…

I shake my head. I mean it to clear the unwelcome thoughts inside my mind, but he takes it as my answer.

"Good. You're mine now. It's better that they forget about you. I won't let them take you from me anyway. And if they try? I'll just go after you and take you back with me."

Wait—*what?*

Forget the fact that he misunderstood. Forget the fact that, despite how low I rank in my pack, I know that Bishop would never abandon me.

He thinks he can keep me here just because he wants to?

"You can't do this," I snap at him, kicking out at the nearest plate. Thanks to the weight of the chain and how short it is, I can't really reach it, but my big toe brushes it. The pile of bacon scatters on the plate.

He frowns when it falls before his attention is back on me.

"That's what you say."

I don't like how he put it like that. "Okay. What do *you* say then?"

"That I already have." He points at the steaming plate of food. "Now eat before it gets cold."

No way. I might've been hungry before, but I've totally lost my appetite.

"You can't keep me here," I insist instead. He has to

understand how insane he sounds. "You misunderstood me before. They will come. My mate will get me."

He will. Out of a sense of duty if nothing more, if I open up our bond, West will come and get me.

My captor's eyes flash angrily. "Mate?" he says. "What mate? I will be your only mate."

"You can't be. I already have one!"

Yeah… in retrospect, that was probably the worst thing I could've said to him while he was trying so desperately to feed me.

I knew that's why he wanted me. For me to be his mate. I already knew that. The chains, the blanket, the food… in his twisted way, he was providing for me. He brought me here to be the plus one to his lone wolf.

Thing is… wolves mate for life. If I already have one, I can't be his.

So what if me and West will never be? Technically, I have a mate—and it isn't my captor. He had to know that. Every shifter within miles of Hickory knows about me and West.

Too bad me pointing that out sets him off way worse than I ever would've expected.

With a roar, he just… he loses complete control. There's no other way to explain it. He snaps. Shoulders hunched, eyes a blazing gold, he lunges. Not at me, thank the Luna, but across the room.

Swinging wildly, he bashes his fist into the nearest cinder block he can find.

Something cracks. Since the cinder block wall is still standing strong, I think it might be his hand—or paw, really.

Because that's a fucking paw at the end of his wrist.

I don't know what happened to him, but he's shifted into some form of monster I've never seen before. He's still on two feet, his arms covered in fur. So is his chest. Terrifying fangs jut from a twisted mouth, and his cheekbones look sharp enough to cut paper. His tanned skin seems stretched over bulging muscles. His arms are too long, hanging forward, and those are definitely claws attached to his paws.

What the…

Shifters have two forms: the one that mimics *human*, and the one that mimics *wolf*. Two-legged or four-legged, but never anything in between. Our fangs don't elongate like vamps do, and while our nails tend to grow like claws, they're still recognizable fingernails.

Not him.

He's engaged in some kind of terrifying partial shift: half-human, half-wolf, and all something straight out of a horror flick. This? This is what unaware humans think werewolves look like. This mangled creature with patchy fur, a broken body, claw-tipped fingers, and a mouth full of fangs.

Even more amazingly, he didn't lose his clothes. Not that I was looking forward to seeing his jeans explode into tatters as he went from man to wolf, but that's what happens. If you don't strip before you shift, your clothes are toast.

After a few more furious punches, he prowls around the room, his muscular, animalistic form pushing against the seams on his jeans, but he stays covered.

At least now I know why he didn't bother with shoes or a shirt. They never would've made it.

The partial shift lasts for about thirty seconds more, though it seems like an eternity. He doesn't come at me, instead spinning to the other side of the room where he punches the cinder block wall enough times that his furry knuckles are shredded and the rusty tang of blood perfumes the air.

As I fold myself into a much smaller target, huddling in my corner, I suddenly understand why he hasn't acted at all like I've expected him to.

He's not a regular shifter. He might be a lone wolf, but that's not all.

Feral, I realize. He is a feral.

And I'm in deep, deep shit.

FIVE
FERAL

This isn't just some shifter who decided they liked the smell of me, or who mistakenly believes that I have any worth to my pack just because the Luna said I was supposed to be with the Beta. Sofia would've been a better target if he was going after Bishop, and if he wanted to bring West to his knees, Helene is the she-wolf he needs, but neither of those two was dumb enough to leave the heart of pack territory.

Up until now, I really figured him for a lone wolf. Not common, but not unheard of. Since shifters are a mix between human and beast, our instinct is to search out a pack and make a community of it. It takes a lot for a shifter to willingly live on their own—and more for them to turn feral.

Packs stabilize a shifter. It keeps our two halves in sync. We *need* the balance. Ferals are what happens when the dark side of both halves takes control. Between the wolf's single-minded focus to survive above all else and a human's capacity for viciousness and evil, a feral shifter is almost as dangerous as a rogue bloodsucker.

The only thing *more* dangerous?

A feral alpha wolf.

Like my captor.

His dominance is undeniable. As a broken wolf, it was easy to ignore it; with the quicksilver running through me, my senses were dull. But almost all of that shit is out of my system now, and in his human shape, it pours off of his hard body.

As the urge to submit to him hums through me, he pulls it back. The aggression. The rage. The dominance. He finds control—and that, more than anything else, is terrifying to me.

He makes no mention of how he lost it in the first place. Following his lead, I clamp my mouth shut. He just flicks his wrist hard enough to re-set it, then points down at the plates again.

"Eat."

I gulp, but I still can't bring myself to accept it. Especially now. "No, thanks."

I lost my nerve. Sue me. It's easy to be brave when I thought he was a lone wolf who's been out of touch. But a feral? One wrong word and I can trigger him. I have to be careful.

But, oh, he doesn't like me being overly careful, does he?

With a scowl, he says, "Eat or I'll pin you down and force you to. Your choice."

One look in his golden eyes and I know he'll do it, too.

What else can I do?

"I will," I tell him, "but only if you accept that it's because I'm starving and not because I'm letting you feed me."

"You'll eat because you have to." Reaching behind him, he pulls a fork out from his pocket and sets it down on the floor.

No knife, but even if he gave me one, I'm not sure I'd be strong enough to use it on him. "And I'll make sure you're fed no matter what I have to do."

It's not a 'no'. Deciding that means he agreed with my stipulation, I lift the first plate onto my lap, then grab the fork.

Growing up in a pack, I'm used to having an audience when I eat; to shifters, eating alone in our cabins is weird since we often have communal meals. Even so, I've never had a male watch me do so with such intense interest. His arms crossed over his chest, bare feet planted in front of me, the feral is witness to every single bite I take. When I finish one plate, he shoves the next at me, then plops the glass of water within my reach.

It's delicious, though that has to be because I *was* starving; shifters need to eat constantly to replace the calories we burn when we shift, and I've already missed a few meals. Regardless, I refuse to thank him. Why should I? Bringing me here makes me his responsibility. Feeding me is the least he can do.

Once I'm done, he gathers up the plates, grunting in approval when he sees that they're just about licked clean.

If I wouldn't be spiting myself more than him, I'd stick my fingers down my throat and hurl everything I just ate out onto the floor. Of course, then he'd probably decide that I didn't deserve to have my hands free. My legs are chained. What's stopping him from locking up the rest of me?

Better not chance it.

As if he's thinking the same thing I am, he piles the dishes by the door, then comes back to me. Crouching down so that we're on the same level, he holds out his hand.

"Arm."

My initial instinct is to refuse. Unfortunately, I make a mistake. Feral or not, he's still an alpha. His dominance rolls over me, and I might've been able to withstand it if I hadn't glanced up.

Our eyes meet. With my hold on my wolf tenuous at best right now, I can't resist the power in his golden gaze.

I submit. Thrusting out my right arm, I'm not able to look away from him until he's cradling my arm with his hands.

It's only after I do that I realize just how dangerous that was. Prolonged eye contact with a dominant shifter is usually a sign of a challenge. Even if I didn't mean it, a higher-ranked wolf might take it that way. He must really think of me as his future mate because any other alpha would've at least snapped their fangs at me.

And that's not counting what a feral is capable of.

Take my arm for example. The strength in his grip tells me that he could easily snap my bone. The gentle way his fingers stroke the crook of my elbow is a sign that—for the moment at least—he won't.

I should've realized he had an ulterior motive. While still stroking me with one hand, he reaches up to his chest. His fingers grope for the cylindrical charm hanging off of his golden chain. Tugging the bottom part, it pulls free, revealing a loaded shot about two inches long.

Well, now I understand how he got me last time. The charm on his neck isn't some kind of decorative pendant like I first guessed. It holds another injection, and if the cylinder was charmed to survive a shift, he'd be able to carry a shot full of quicksilver whether he was in his wolf form or his human form.

Oh, yes. This feral is very, very tricky—and more dangerous than I already believed.

He moves the quicksilver shot toward my elbow, his intentions obvious.

The only reason I don't jerk away is because he could still snap my arm if he wanted to. Doesn't mean that I'm not going to try my best to stop him from shooting me up a second time.

"If you do this," I snarl, letting the edge of my wolf into my tone before she's cut off from me completely again, "I'll only hate you more than I already do for taking me."

Still holding onto my arm tightly with one hand, he uses the other to caress my cheek; the injection is tucked beneath his fingers. When I jerk my head out of his reach, his eyes gleam, but the notable insanity in them dies down almost immediately.

He leans in. The heat of his skin nearly sears mine as the edge of his jaw brushes against me, the stubble on his chin burning my cheek. His grip on my arm tightens further an instant before I feel the prick of the needle.

"Having you here with me is worth your hate," he whispers into my ear as he presses the plunger. "Now sleep, and we'll try again tomorrow."

I'm already dropping. With this new dose mingling with the quicksilver already in my veins, it hits me harder this time around. My eyes flutter closed as he wraps me up in his arms, laying me out on the blanket beneath me.

My last thought—*if I'm lucky, there might actually be a tomorrow*—runs through my muddled brain, and then I'm out again.

Feral dickhead.

A LONE WOLF WOULD NEVER HURT A FELLOW SHIFTER, especially one he was trying to mate. My worth is in my body, and an interested male would try to prove he was smart and strong and a fierce protector so that he could earn access to it.

But a feral…

A feral is unpredictable.

An intelligent feral like my captor is even worse.

He has just enough hold on his broken mind to protect me from the silver chains while also injecting me with quicksilver to keep me under control. That says he doesn't want to hurt me, but he also isn't willing to let me get the upper hand. I'm his captive until he gets what he wants—or until I find a way out of here.

Or he kills me in a fit of rage. Can't forget that.

I think of West again. He is so calm. Contained. He would never lose control like that beast did and—

Shit. I check my bond. The block I threw up yesterday is still there, and I only hope that it held while I was sedated.

Even if it didn't, I'm betting he wouldn't pay any attention to me until he was forced to. Once someone noticed I was missing—and the tattered clothes and destroyed shoes I left behind are a pretty big clue I was forced to shift in a hurry—Bishop would use West to try to track me down. I'm just about sure of it.

I can't let him come after me. I can't let any of my pack-mates try to find me. Right now, so long as the feral thinks of me as his, I'm as safe as possible. After the way he fucking lost it after I mentioned that I already had a mate, he'll see any other male as a rival. And that's assuming he doesn't know that West is the male I was talking about when I threw it in his face that I already have a mate.

What would he do if my fated mate came to rescue me after all? He already said he'd go after me, but he might challenge West, too. While I know that the Beta of the Sylvan Pack is a strong shifter, he's not an alpha. He's definitely not a feral.

He'd never survive.

If the feral challenged him, West would fight. I'd have to live the rest of my life knowing that he died because a feral decided he wanted me for a mate.

There is no other choice. I have to stay.

Besides, I also have to admit that *I* can't fight my way out of this because if I accept that West could never, then I'm definitely shit out of luck. Sure, he let me get away with biting him in the middle of him abducting me. Something tells me that that was my one freebie and I shouldn't expect another.

Sitting up slowly, refusing to let my growing frustration pull me under, I realize I don't know how long I was out for after he dosed me with that quicksilver shit again. Longer than last time, I bet, since my shifter senses aren't as muted as before; either that, or I'm recovering from the poison faster. It's light outside once more, but that doesn't mean anything since my cage is still dark and gloomy.

I've got the same wine-red dress on. The same chains on my feet. I'm laying on the same blanket as... yesterday? I'm gonna go with yesterday. Another one, as silky as the dress I'm wearing, is spread out on top of me.

Shifters run hot. A heavy blanket would've made me melt, even if the room carries a chill. The flimsy, silky covering is closer to a sheet than a comforter, and it's perfect.

Of course, the thoughtfulness just pisses me off. I fling the covering from my body, scooting it away from me with the heel of my foot, then glare at it.

I'm pissed, but I'm also starving again; however long it's been, it's enough that my hunger's returned. So has the need to pee. A quick check down below reveals that he still hasn't taken advantage of me being sedated, plus I managed to keep from pissing myself while I was out.

I'm just beginning to think that I'll have to start marking

this room after all when, suddenly, my captor walks into the room.

He's in his skin, which is a good sign. He's carrying two more plates and another glass of water. That's even better.

"Breakfast," he growls.

I planned on being cautious. Careful. That lasts as long as it takes for the feral to set down the plates, the glass, and slowly rise up from his crouch. As he does, his hand reaches to his crotch. The way he adjusts himself, whistling in a breath as he pushes against his junk, draws my attention to that spot.

Oh. Wow. Either he's bigger in the dick department than any male I've ever seen, or he's already sporting a woody in there that's equally as impressive. That bulge is huge, and his sensitive hiss is a sure sign he's aroused.

Uh-uh. Nope.

I haven't forgotten the way he pinned me down in his fur before shifting back to his skin.

I point dead at his chest.

"If you try to mount me again, I'll rip off your dick."

He has the nerve to look surprised that I made such a threat.

"I would never do that." He frowns as he dips his head. A hunk of black hair falls forward into his face. "That's not why I brought you here."

Yeah, right. He calls himself my mate, he's hard as a rock as he walks into my new cage, and he expects me to believe that he doesn't have sex on his mind? And, sure, maybe he's not going to force me to mate him or anything like that. He probably has grand ideas of *seduction*, of making me choose him.

Maybe if he hadn't drugged me, I might've.

Now?

Good luck.

"Same goes for my mouth. Put your cock anywhere near my mouth and I'll bite it off instead." I snap my blunt human teeth in warning. Never underestimate a ticked-off she-wolf. We don't just threaten—we promise. "You might've taken my claws when you cut me off from my wolf, but I still have these."

"The quicksilver is for your protection. You shouldn't have struggled."

Asshole. He's really going to blame me for putting up a fight when an unknown wolf was stalking me?

I kick out a leg, making the silver chain rattle. "What about these?"

A shadow passes across his face. "Those are for mine."

Smart feral.

Since he seems more chatty today, I decide to keep the conversation going. "What's your name?"

No answer.

I'm not surprised. He wouldn't tell me yesterday, and he point-blank ignored me when I tried to find out where I was or what he wanted with me.

Does that stop me from trying another, more brash tactic?

Nope.

"How long do you plan on keeping me here?"

A muscle tics in his cheek. "You already know."

I didn't, but I could guess. Shoving the idea that he plans to keep me here with him forever far, far away, I open my mouth to ask another question when a low rumbling sound fills the quiet.

He's growling at me again.

I close my mouth.

"No more talking." He points at the food. "Eat. Now."

Then, crouching down a few feet away, forearms resting on his thick thighs, he stares at me. It's clear he plans on staying right there and watching to make sure that I obey.

I have no choice. Last night proved that he'll get his way in this. I tell myself that it doesn't mean anything. That I'm only using the food for fuel. It doesn't matter. I have to eat it, and I do.

When I'm done, he moves into me again, staying low so that we're on the same level. This close, I can either look into his golden eyes or stare at the bite mark on his upper bicep that I gave him.

Bicep it is.

It was half-healed yesterday. I wanted to see if it was gone or, like me, he was having a hard time regenerating. I'll admit, it was a deep bite, but even a feral should've been able to shake off the damage I did to him after a few hours.

And that's when I see that the wound from yesterday is still there as a noticeable silvery scar today.

He took my bite and kept the mark.

That… that can't be good.

He's still wearing jeans. I can't tell if he's hiding any other scars or marks beneath them. One thing for sure, the rest of his upper body doesn't have a single blemish on it—except for my bite.

Due to our regenerative properties, a shifter can keep any mark we want, but it has to be a conscious thing otherwise we heal completely. Scars have two meanings: either a memento from a fight that was significant enough to leave a reminder of it behind, or a mating mark.

As I stare at him, he closes the remaining gap between us. Starting at the hollow of my throat, he takes a deep breath. He's sniffing me, and he trails his nose along the column of my neck, the edge of my jaw, the curve of my ear, before burying his face in my hair.

It's a little bit greasy. It's kind of flat from where I slept on it. He groans under his breath anyway, then slowly inches away.

I'm too stunned to come up with any kind of comment—until he pulls a tiny key out of his front pocket and reaches for the nearest shackle.

"What are you doing?"

"Bathroom," he explains. He makes quick work of the lock, popping it open without ever brushing against the silver. He turns to the next. "You must need it by now."

I do, but I'd rather my bladder burst than admit it. "I guess."

Just goes to prove that he isn't intimidated by me at all. He removes both shackles, leaving the fabric padding wrapped around my ankles in place. I can see now that it's been taped together so that it stays there. The fact that he doesn't also take the padding off says he plans on chaining me up again.

Joy.

He hovers over me as I slowly stretch out my legs, then climb to my feet. Between the quicksilver and the chains, I'm not all that sturdy. No wonder he doesn't think I'm a threat. In this state, a pup could take me on and win.

That makes me angry again. Good. Hopefully the fury can burn through the quicksilver faster, letting me rely on my wolf to make me strong again.

After taking a steadying breath, purposely ignoring him, I scoop the mass of my greasy hair over my shoulder, trying to stretch out the crick in my neck.

Behind me, he starts to snarl. The pitch is low, but it grows and grows until I can no longer ignore it.

I mean, a strange feral is making threatening sounds at my back. Of course I'm going to spin around. My instincts have me throwing my hands up in a vain attempt to protect myself.

He scowls. "Don't be afraid. I won't hurt you."

"I'm not afraid," I lie. My heart is pounding. He can probably hear it. "I just don't want a feral snarling behind me."

I wait for him to deny it. Either the snarling part, or the feral.

He doesn't.

Instead, he frowns. "Couldn't help it. You moved your hair and I saw that my bite was gone."

"Bite? What bite?"

He gestures to the back of his neck, then gives me a pointed look so I know he means mine.

I blink. Hang on… does he mean when he had me pinned in the woods? When he sank his fangs in my scruff, holding me down so that he could jab me with the quicksilver shot?

That bite?

CHASE

My fingers fly to the same spot on my neck. I probe it gently, letting out a sigh of relief when I find that the skin is completely healed.

He growls under his breath.

"Stop that," I tell him, though I keep any heat from my voice. Don't want to set the feral off. Gotta keep it cool— though a girl also has to have her limits and I'm already way past mine. "And of course it's gone. I'm as much a shifter as you are. Obviously I heal."

"Yeah? So do I," he grunts before he shifts his shoulder, drawing my attention back to the silverish-white fang marks standing out in sharp relief against his tanned arm.

Don't freak out, Quinn. The unstable shifter is wearing your bite like a badge of honor he's earned, but don't freak out.

I shake my head royally. "You deserved that, you know. If you kept the scar, that's your business, but I'm not going to apologize for biting you. In fact, give me the chance, and I'll do it all over again."

"And I'll keep that one, too. I'll keep any mark my mate wants to give me."

Don't freak out…

"I'm not your mate."

His expression darkens. I'm not sure how I know, but I'd put good money down that he's thinking about the unbroken skin on my neck. "Not yet. But you will be."

Right. I give him my back as I leave the room. Keep dreaming, dickhead.

Aware that he's right on my ass, I pause as I get my first glimpse of the space outside of my cell. It's a narrow corridor with a flight of stairs at the end. No windows, though a few weak overhead lights flicker down on us. I expect to head toward the stairs, but he moves in front of me, guiding me to a door built on the other side of the hall.

He opens the door, gesturing for me to go inside.

The bathroom looks new. A sparkling toilet is gleaming. A porcelain white sink is perched on the wall with a wooden cabinet built beneath it. He even has a perfume-free bottle of soap on top of the sink.

I step inside. He doesn't.

Interesting.

"Do I get privacy?" I ask him.

With another dark look, he says, "For now."

After the way he seemed to think I would've kept his bite as some kind of mate mark on my skin, I'm not too happy to hear his answer. *For now…* at least he's not going to follow me into the bathroom just then.

With a feral captor, I'll take what I can get until I can finally find a way out.

For the next two days, that's our routine. He brings me a plate of food for breakfast, lunch, and dinner before he disappears into a different part of the house to sleep. He unchains me after every meal, leading me to the bathroom at the end of the hall so that I can do my business and wash my hands.

I peeked in the cabinet. I found a toothbrush, toothpaste, and extra toilet paper. I helped myself to all three. If he cared, he didn't say, and I feel a lot better with my mouth clean.

After my bathroom trips, he brings me back to my basement prison. I hope that he'll decide that I've been well-behaved enough to go without chains, but I guess I'm not that good of an actress.

I still snap at him. I badger him with questions he won't answer. He feeds me, and at least twice a day I try to refuse the meals before I eventually give in.

One time, I got frustrated at how he'd rather stare at me than take the chance to get to know me. I tossed my fork at him.

I didn't mean to stab him. Honest. Not gonna lie and say that it didn't make me happy that my wolf lent me the strength to fling it like a spear, but I hadn't meant to hit him hard enough that the tines lodged in the muscle of his pec.

Of course it did. He still goes without a shirt. The bite mark on his shoulder mocks me every time I see it.

I flinched when the fork got stuck. But my captor… he just smiled, then pulled it out of his chest with a firm tug. He offered it back to me, his blood still slicking the tines, and it was all I could do not to hurl up my hamburger patty.

Definitely not the reaction I was expecting.

Something's different about him. I can't put my finger on what it is and that makes me suddenly wary. When dealing with a feral, *different* doesn't mean *good*.

He's a little more quiet this evening. At breakfast, he didn't give me my daily dose of quicksilver, though he put the chains back on me before he left my room. I think it was a test, and one I failed because I spent way longer than I probably should've trying to break the chains again. I couldn't shift, but my wolf was prowling around inside of me, yipping her encouragement.

It didn't work. When he came back with lunch and saw that my hands were destroyed, he dropped my food before storming out again. I figured I had pissed him off enough that he'd leave me to eat in peace. Nope. He came back seconds later with a salve that healed me up in no time.

It was my turn to scowl. I would've been healed before long. I didn't need his help.

I didn't know what to do with it when he gave it to me so readily, either…

Now it's dinner, and apart from taking my hand in one of his massive paws, checking it out before he pressed a fork against my palm, he's sat in the far corner, watching me again.

Routine, right? I eat my food, then shove the empty plates away from me. Knowing what comes next, I put my ankles in his reach so that he can unlock the shackles.

I was trying to skip a step. As if he'd ever let me.

He sniffs me like he usually does. I guess I don't pass the test this time because he tells me gruffly, "You need to shower."

"What's the matter? Didn't think that I might start to be a little ripe after three days of being stuck down here?" I snap.

"The sink only does so much, and I didn't see a shower stall in the bathroom."

His jaw goes tight. "I have to bring you upstairs."

The last few days, I came up with a plan. It wasn't foolproof, but it was the best I had.

Step one: get out of the room.

Step two: get out of the basement.

Step three: get out of this place.

I jiggle my leg. "Let's go."

I'M ALMOST A LITTLE DISAPPOINTED AT WHAT I FIND ON THE other side of the stairs. I expected blood and bones, ripped furniture, claw marks slashing through everything. He's a feral, after all, and if he lost control, I thought his home would reflect that.

It doesn't.

In fact, it looks like one of the cabins we have in Hickory. He has an unlit fireplace in his living space, a couch big enough for him to curl up in his wolf form—and, based on the amount of fur covering it, he *does*—and a television that doesn't even have a single crack in it.

I feel cheated.

The few windows I see are closed. He has his shades drawn, as if the light outside hurts his feral eyes. Every inch of his space smells like him. Apart from mine filtering up from the basement, it's the only scent here.

I'd guessed he lived alone. Now I'm sure of it.

He lets me get a good look around before telling me to go ahead. Smart feral. He must've seen me eyeing the door that would lead to the outside.

There's only the single floor, not counting the basement below. Behind one closed door is a kitchen, he explains, and another is a bedroom. The last one is a full bath.

Thank the Luna. A shower.

I walk inside. He follows me in.

That's new. Every time he's led me to the bathroom before, he's left me to do my business in privacy.

Not now.

He closes the door behind me. In the back of my head, I remember the way he said, "for now," like that when I asked about privacy. It implied I wouldn't have it for long.

Yup. Looks like the clock ran out on that one.

Especially when, in a throaty voice, he tells me, "Take off your dress. Get in the shower."

Does he think I won't do it? Is that it?

Please. I'm a shifter. So long as he keeps his paws to himself, I don't care if he sees me.

I raise my eyebrow. It's the right one, with a tiny nick where the hair never grew. It looks like my eyebrow is split in half, and it's something I always had. Males seem to like it, and that's how I got into the habit of raising that one instead of the other.

I like to show off. Always have. Besides, in a pack, nudity doesn't mean anything. How can it when we always come back naked when we shift from fur to skin? The only time it matters is if there's sexual attraction—which is exactly why I'm surprised he's demanding I strip.

Handsome as he is, it's hard to be attracted to your captor. There's no denying that he's got it bad for me, though. I mean, he stole me from my pack to be his mate. Yeah. He wants me.

Call me petty, but I have no problem showing him what he'll never have. Especially since I'm sure he's already gotten more than an eyeful after he dosed me with quicksilver the first time and I shifted back from fur to skin.

Still…

"Don't forget what I said. Look all you want, but if you get too close…" I hold up my hand. My wolf gives me her claws. I slash at him. "Got me?"

"I won't touch you," he grumbles, moving around me at a quick clip, turning the shower on. Water streams down, splashing off the porcelain tub. "Not until you ask me to."

So. Never, then, huh?

Good.

He sidles past me again, moving in front of the door. He blocks it, so I can't leave, then turns his sculpted back on me.

What's that about?

"Why the back?" I ask. "You already saw everything I have to offer when you took me."

His shoulders hunch. "Didn't."

I know he's not pretending that he didn't straight-up wolfnap me. "What was that?"

"Said I didn't." He keeps his back to me as he adds, "I covered you with a blanket when I put you in my truck. Kept you covered when I pulled the dress on over your head. I never looked."

Oh. That's… actually a bit surprising. I could tell he hadn't touched anything more than my back, my arms, my shoulders, and my hair, but I expected he would've at least gotten a nice, long peek first.

"Why? Don't you like my body?"

His hands turn into fists. He tightens them, then flexes his long, claw-tipped fingers before rubbing the side of his thighs. "Yes," he finally says. "Too much. But I'll earn my first glimpse. I won't steal it."

"Really?" For some reason, his newfound nobility pisses me off. "You mean like you stole *me?*"

"I had to."

Uh-huh. Sure.

I give him two minutes before he's sneaking a peek.

There's no mirror in here—just another toilet, a sink, and the combination shower/tub—so, if he does, I'll notice. He won't be able to catch my reflection in anything. No. He wants to see the goods, he'll have to turn his head.

I pull the slinky red dress up and over mine, dropping it to the bathroom floor. It pools like blood at my feet.

His posture goes stiff, but he refuses to turn.

Taking my time pulling the shower curtain away from the tub, I push my ass out, waiting to see if he's going to look. I'm not so sure if I should be relieved or offended that my feral seems to be a complete gentleman.

Shrugging my shoulders, I step beneath the spray. The second the warm water hits my skin, I forget all about him. I tug the curtain closed, then focus entirely on how good it feels to be clean again.

He has shampoo, conditioner, and a bar of soap waiting for me. I make quick use of the shampoo, gleefully rinsing his scent out of my hair when he clears his throat and says over the echo of the shower spray, "Chase."

I call back, "That another threat to chase me down if I try to leave, tough guy?"

He's silent for a moment. "It's my name."

Oh. Never would've guessed that.

I grab the bar of soap, lathering my belly. If he wants to be friendly, I might as well give it a shot.

Hey. What can I say? This shower has put me in a much better mood.

"I guess it's finally time I tell you mine," I tell him. "I'm Quinn."

"I know."

My fingers bite into the edge of the soap bar. There goes my good mood. "You know?"

"Yeah. I know."

My stomach drops. For just a few moments here, I'd forgotten that I was his captive. He picked me, he drugged me, he stole me. He decided I was his mate. He locked me up.

Of course he knows my name. And after only three days of treating me like his personal pet, he deigns to give me his.

I grit my teeth, grateful for the thick shower curtain. If he could see me now…

Making quick work of the soap, I lather up, then rinse the rest of my body. I finish with the conditioner. As much as I want to linger because it helps wash away the last of the fog left behind from the remains of the quicksilver, I turn off the shower.

After wringing the water from my long hair, I shove my hand out. "Towel?"

He places one in my grip.

I wrap the towel around me, covering up. I've lost the taste for showing off. Just then, I need to make sure he's not watching me.

And he isn't.

I've never dried off so quickly before. I end up doing a shit job of it because the dress is sticking to my damp skin when I hurriedly pull it on over my head. Doesn't matter. With my newly formed plan running frantically through my mind right now, I can't risk Chase figuring out what I'm thinking.

How strong are his alpha senses? I don't think he can tell when I'm lying, but does he know when I'm plotting?

I'm about to find out.

"Hey, Chase?"

The big feral shudders. He obviously likes it when I say his name. "Yes?"

"I'm covered. You can look now."

He slowly turns on his heel.

I react.

Taking the towel still in my hand, I throw it in his face. It blinds him for a split second, but that's all I need. I hurry forward, plowing him in his junk with the point of my knee. As a howl tears out of his throat, I fold my hands together, then swing up at his jaw.

I don't hold back. Swinging with all of the pent-up aggression I have, I connect. His head shoots over his shoulder. I feel the reverberation of my hit all the way up to mine.

He stumbles, then drops to his knees. It's too much to hope I knocked him out. At least he's seeing stars.

And I have my chance.

Leaping over him, I dash out of the bathroom, running right for the front door. He roars again, and I pour on the speed. To escape the feral I just pissed off, I'm going to need it.

I never make it.

I get to the door, at least. I throw it open and even manage to get a few steps out onto the wraparound porch before he catches up to me.

One arm goes around my neck. The other wraps around my waist. The dress rides up as he pulls me back against him.

His chest is hard—and so is his cock. I can feel his erection through his jeans, prodding me in the ass as he secures me in his hold.

Looks like violence turns him on, doesn't it?

I huff as I sag against his hard chest. *Feral.* I should've known.

I don't fight Chase. I had my chance, and though I got him down, I just wasn't fast enough.

That's partly my fault. I might've been if I hadn't been stopped short by the rusty, tangy scent of blood and rotten meat that permeates the forest outside of his house.

"Phew." He's conveniently left my arms free. I use both hands to cover my nose. "That's awful!"

For the first time, I'm grateful my nose is still a bit stuffy. How much worse would the stink be at full strength?

Chase leans down, his jaw pressed against the side of my head. "Now you see why I keep the windows closed."

"Where *are* we?"

To my surprise, he actually answers. Then again, with that stink, it's undeniable.

"My land is just off of Sacre Coeur."

Sacre Coeur. It's the French name for one of the infamous cities that every local shifter has heard about. It might mean 'Sacred Heart' to those who don't know better. I'm not one of them. I know exactly what Sacre Coeur is—and it's nowhere as nice or pleasant as its name suggests.

I whirl on him. Just like I thought. *Vampires.* "That's a Fang City."

Chase nods, a hint of a satisfied smirk tugging on his lips. He's won this round, and I hadn't even known we were playing. "Even if you find your way out of the woods, you'll never survive the vampires out there. Not without me."

Suddenly, I realize what that white crescent moon-shaped charm hanging off of his golden chain is: a vampire fang. It's a pass that gives its wearer some protection from the vampires that make up the nearby Fang City.

I can't believe it. My captor is a shifter who lives on the border of a notorious vampire settlement. Our sworn enemies, and he's their neighbor.

"You're not just feral," I breathe out. "You really are insane."

His eyes spark, a vivid gold that only highlights just how right I was. "Ah, Quinn… it's about time you figured that out."

SLEEP

Chase doesn't use the chains on me again.

What's the point? He's proven that he's stronger than me, faster than me, and he put me in a small cabin in the middle of the woods where no one would ever look for me.

Because it's surrounded by vampires. You know. A shifter's ancient enemy.

Supernaturals are technically at war. Vampires versus shifters, it's referred to as the Claws and Fangs war, and it dates back to the animosity that's existed between our races since the beginning of time. It's not a constant fight, but every few centuries or so, a skirmish flares up and we battle ruthlessly.

The last real fight was two hundred years ago. It was easier to hide the truth of supes from humans then, and the bloodshed went down in human history as another of their wars; Luna knows they have plenty. Since then, we live in a constant state of wariness.

After the last real battle, the Alpha of the main pack

involved met with some of the surviving vamps. They decided that the only way to prevent future casualties was for wolves and vampires to keep their distance. Wolves formed packs on secluded tracts of lands far from humans, and vampires—who needed humans for their blood—created vamp-run communities called Fang Cities.

Led by an elected leadership known as the Cadre, Fang Cities are havens for vampires. They run the town, protecting their kind and keeping shifters out. Any humans living within their protected borders—whether they know about supes or not—are also under the Cadre's protection. If you defy the leadership, you die. They're kind of like the vampire version of an Alpha in that way.

No one challenges the Alpha and hopes to survive except, perhaps, another alpha wolf.

I thought Chase was insane. I mean, you can't be a feral and have your sanity intact. That was one of the defining characteristics of *being* a feral. But purposely choosing a cabin that butted up against a town full of vampires? It would be crazy even if he didn't have some kind of agreement with the local Cadre.

Which he does.

I was right about his necklace. By wearing it, he can come and go in Sacre Coeur without any vamp going after him because he's a shifter. Once he realizes I'm not going to fight him again, he explains how he got it.

His land borders the edge of their settlement. Because vampires are almost as fanatical when it comes to patrolling their territory as us shifters, the head vampire—the leader of the Cadre—has some of his bloodsuckers roaming Chase's woods.

That's how he earned his necklace. By keeping to himself

and allowing the vampires to come onto his land, he was given the fang.

And look at me. I don't have one. A fact he points out when he mentions that, if I get caught by a vampire, they might drain me first, ask questions later.

It's not even just the vampires that have me reluctantly following him back inside the cabin. Any hope of a quick escape dies an ugly death once I know where I am. Sacre Coeur is near enough to Hickory that I've heard of it. Too bad that *near enough* just means it's not on the other side of the country. In our fur, it's a good couple of hours away. A car might shave off some of that time, but Chase's woods are just as dense as mine. Anyone approaching—or escaping—the cabin would have to go on foot eventually and risk being caught by vamp patrollers.

Good thing I kept myself closed off to West even as I was breaking for the door. It was bad enough when I was trying to protect him from only the feral. Now I have an entire town of vamps loyal to Chase to worry about…

I expected the chains. Actually, considering I just kneed an aroused feral in the nuts, I expected retaliation.

At the very least, I expected to see him turn into that monster again.

He doesn't. Chase just leads me back inside, then guides me down the basement stairs again. I flop myself down onto my blanket, leaving my ankles free for him to reach. I still have the fabric padding wrapped around them. They're pretty much soaked. So used to having them there, I guess I didn't bother removing them for my shower.

Wonderful. Putting silver shackles over wet fabric… that's not gonna be comfortable.

To my surprise, Chase doesn't grab the shackle. He

reaches for my ankle instead, using one of his claws to slice the padding in half. He does the same for the other. For a second, I wonder if he's gonna slap the shackle on without it so I can feel the silver, some way to make me pay for attacking him, but he doesn't do that, either.

Rising up, kicking the chains away with the side of his bare foot, he moves them away from me.

"No more chains?" I ask.

He shakes his head. "No need."

He's right.

"But I have to stay in the basement, right? On a blanket, like a dog. You just showed me that I'm more stuck here than I thought. Can't I at least get a bed?"

Chase's expression turns thoughtful. Holy shit. Did that actually work?

I'd meant what I said. Now, that doesn't mean I've given up on getting out of here. I haven't. I belong back in Hickory, and I refuse to stick around this feral just because he got lonely and decided to take me home with him. Since he has, though, I figure I should make the best of a bad situation.

He makes sure I eat. He finally let me shower. Sure, my hair is quickly drying into a tangled mess since I don't have a brush, but maybe I can work on that one later. For now, I really, really don't want to sleep on the floor again.

If I have to, I'll shift into my wolf. It's been days since she's been free, and I can already sense her begging to come out now that the quicksilver is gone and I'm not wearing silver chains that weaken the both of us. I know she wouldn't mind curling up on the floor. Still, I'd prefer a bed.

Chase rocks on his heels. His hands slip into the back pockets of his jeans. "You won't leave me? If I bring you upstairs… you won't go for my cock again? 'Cause that hurt, Quinn. I didn't like it."

Whoa. The grumble in his voice when he says 'cock' like that… it shouldn't be anywhere near as sexy as it is. He's my feral captor! I shouldn't think he's sexy at all! But, come on. I'm only half-human. His mind might be broken, his sense of right and wrong way off, but he's a hunk of a male who hasn't worn a shirt the entire time I've known him, and he seems more upset at the idea I might try to run out on him again than the fact that I tried to break his dick with my knee.

An apology is on the tip of my tongue before I remember: *Hello! Captor!* I swallow that back, then say, "I won't."

"Promise me." His eyes light up. "Vow to the Luna you won't leave me."

I hesitate. I didn't plan on running out before I came up with a foolproof plan to bypass the vampires, but if the opportunity presents itself…

A vow to the Luna isn't unbreakable. However, good chance I'm already on her shit list because me and West haven't bonded yet. Do I really want to risk pissing off our goddess? Maybe she'll erase the tie I have to West and decide that a feral loner might be a better mate for me. What would I do then?

I mean, he might be convinced. I'm not.

"Chase—"

"Tonight," he amends. "Vow to the Luna you won't leave me tonight."

Okay. I can do that.

"I vow it. But only if you vow you won't try to mark me again."

I'll only heal it, and that'll just bring out the feral. None of us wants that.

His expression shadows. I wait to see if he'll refuse, but I should've known better.

I gave him a promise. He wants to prove himself. Of course he'll give me one back.

"With the Luna above as my witness, you have my word."

Good.

***

THE BLANKET HE PROVIDED FOR ME WAS SOFT ENOUGH WHILE he kept me tucked away in the basement. That's nothing compared to the oversized, overstuffed mattress that I plop onto after Chase leads me to a bedroom.

The whole space smells of him. Besides the bed in the middle of the room, a blanket that looks like the twin to mine in the basement on the floor, and a single dresser, it's pretty empty. No knick-knacks. No photographs. The walls are bare, the windows closed and covered just like the rest of the cabin.

If his scent didn't overlay the room, I'd think it was a spare one no one used. There's no personality in here. No sign that anyone actually sleeps in it unless you count the blanket in the corner.

When I asked him if it was his room he was giving me, he ignored the question. Instead, he gestured for me to sit down on the bed.

I do, and then I watch him warily as he begins to pace. The room's big enough that I don't feel crowded by him, but it pays to stay on guard. If he snaps and lunges, I don't see anything I can use as a weapon, so I decide to crawl under the bed if I have to.

Something's wrong with him. Him being on edge has *me* on edge. I don't get it. He wasn't even this agitated after my escape attempt earlier and that was after I aimed for where it hurt the most.

When I can't take it any longer, I snap at him. "For the Luna's sake, can you either sit the fuck down or get out? Your pacing is driving me crazy!"

Chase freezes on the opposite side of the bed from me, his head shooting my way. His predatory gaze narrows, locked on his prey.

On *me*.

Smooth, Quinn. Because antagonizing a distressed feral is a genius plan. Way to go.

I clear my throat. "I mean, there's no reason for any of that. I promised I'd stay. Lock me in if you feel better. I don't care. I'm tired and I want to go to sleep. You should go to your room"—which is probably this one, but he didn't confirm it, so I'm gonna play dumb—"and leave me to it."

When he starts to stalk around the far side of the bed, I have a hard time believing it was that easy. Turns out that's because I'm right. Chase doesn't leave the room. Instead, he lowers himself to the blanket tossed in the corner.

He stretches his legs out in front of him, looking like he's making himself comfortable.

Oh, come *on*.

"Really? Are we really doing this?"

"What? I just thought I'd sleep here."

"On the floor."

He nods.

"With me sleeping in the bed over here. By myself," I emphasize.

He nods again.

I jerk my chin at his lower half. "In your jeans?"

His gold eyes flare, turning molten. Shifting against the

blanket, his hand covers the button. His claw scratches at the metal as he fiddles with it. "I could take them off if you want me to."

I walked right into that, didn't I? "No, thanks. You can keep them on."

He nods, letting his hand fall to the side. He'd expected that answer.

Chase goes quiet. The eerie way he stares has me grasping for some way to break the silence. One of us needs to fill it, and from experience, I know it won't be him. But since he seems a lot more talkative lately, I figure it's about time I get some answers of my own.

"Hey… can I ask you another question?"

"You can ask me anything, Quinn."

Really? He might live to regret being so agreeable.

"Okay, then. Why am I here? And I don't mean in this bed. I mean *here*. With you."

Chase's big body stiffens. His jaw clenches. Typical. "I already told you that."

"Because you want a mate." He's made that clear from the moment I came to in his basement. "Why me, though? Was it because I was by myself in the woods that day? If it had been any other female, would you have grabbed her instead?"

He shakes his head.

I'm just about to call 'bullshit' on that when he says, "It couldn't have been anyone else. You're the only female that visits those trees."

How does he know that? He's right… but how does he know?

I scoff at him. "Big deal. My scent's all over the place." So I might've marked the clearing as my territory a few times. It's a shifter thing. When my wolf is out, she can't help it. "That's how you know."

Chase shakes his head again. "I know because I watched you for almost nine months. You were always alone. Me, too. That's part of the reason I picked you. If we were together, we wouldn't be lonely."

I'm not lonely. I mean, I *wasn't* lonely. I had a pack.

And a mate.

I'm smart enough not to mention West. If Chase can be believed—and I can't think of any reason why he couldn't—then he was watching me *before* the Luna picked me for our Beta. As if I need another reason why the feral is out of his head thinking we could ever be together. If we were meant to be, the Luna would've made him my fated mate instead of West, right?

Nine months... I really don't want to believe that. Nine months he watched me and I had no idea? What kind of patrols did Bishop have checking out our borders? No one knew he was out there? What the hell?

That makes me think of something else, too. He stalked me both before and after I found my fated mate. That was six months ago. What happened between then and now that he only just decided it was time to bring me to his cabin?

And what about him? Ferals aren't born, they're made, and usually after a tragedy so terrible, it breaks their mind. What happened to Chase to make him like this?

I open my mouth. Think better of what I'm going to ask. Close it.

Chase notices.

"Quinn? If you have something to say, say it. Don't hold back. Never hold back with me."

Holy shit. Leaning toward me, one knee folded, a brawny arm curved around it, the big feral is pleading.

Surprised as I am by that, I can't stop myself from blurting out, "Do you have a mate?"

Okay. Say I believe this. Say I fall prey to freaking Stockholm Syndrome or something and I stick around long enough that even a feral starts to look enticing. As a she-wolf who's already been rejected by her fated mate, if there's one thing I absolutely refuse to do, it's get involved with a male who is only settling for me because he can't have who he really wants.

I don't realize how much I'm suddenly invested in his answer until Chase immediately says, "Yes. *You.*"

Ah, Luna. Maybe I should've explained better. I know he's convinced that I should be his, but even if he did choose me for reasons of his own, what about his fated mate? Has he found her? While lower-ranked wolves could go their whole life never being told who their fated mate was, most alphas are blessed by the Luna with a name long before a mate bond snaps into place. It usually takes place during the Alpha Ceremony, but not always.

Now, a lone wolf wouldn't have an Alpha Ceremony. Does that mean Chase doesn't know his fated mate?

Is she out there somewhere?

Would a feral who went to so much trouble to take me captive reject me just like West did?

I huff in frustration, unable to articulate what I'm feeling just then. "That's not what I mean, Chase."

"I know what you meant."

I give him a pointed look. "Then answer my question. You said you would."

"I did. You're the only mate I've ever wanted, Quinn. The only one I've ever had. When you finally agree to stay with me forever, I'll claim you as mine, and there will be no one else for either of us. Forever."

If only I could believe that. He might, but I can't.

"You could walk out that door tomorrow and meet your fated mate. What then?"

"Fuck Fate."

I blink. For someone whose personal motto is "Fate sucks," that's a little harsh, even for me.

"What? What's wrong with what I said?"

"Nothing."

It's his turn not to believe me. "It's true. Fuck Fate. We make our own fate, for good or for bad. Just like we make our own choices. And I choose you."

It's not blasphemy, but it's pretty damn close.

Most shifters revere Fate almost as much as they worship the moon. It's why I was shocked when West refused to acknowledge our mate bond. If it was up to me, I would've locked him down the same night I recognized him as my fated mate. Not because I loved him. I didn't. I still don't. At least, not any more than I did when I thought of him as an old friend. But shifters believe that the Luna can do no wrong, and a fated mate is a wondrous gift to have. I might not love him now. If the Luna paired me with West of all other males, there had to be a reason. I'd learn to love him.

He never gave me the chance.

I admit, as much as I would've hopped into West's bed if he let me, I can't deny that it irks me to have my choice taken away. As a delta, I'm at the bottom of the pack. My whole life, I never got to choose anything. First, my parents were in charge, then the packmates that rallied around me after they were gone.

Bishop, of course, makes decisions for the whole Sylvan Pack daily.

Just when I was on the cusp of maybe making a choice for myself—if I didn't take Tucker as my first lover after West rejected me, it could've been another shifter—I had that taken away by a feral who thought *his* choice was more important.

Fuck Fate, sure. But fuck dominant wolves who think they can control me.

I'm Quinn Malone. I can take care of myself.

And I won't give up until I've proven it.

UNFORTUNATELY, TONIGHT'S NOT THE NIGHT THAT I GET TO.

I thought that Chase would get tired of staring at me from his place on the floor. Why, when he's done nothing to give that impression at all, I have no clue, but I was ready to wait him out.

An hour of silence following our last awkward conversation was about as much as I could take.

I point-blank asked if he really planned on watching me sleep all night long. His only answer was a solemn nod as he placed one leg over the other, crossed his arms over his chest, then rested his head against the wall at his back.

I should've guessed.

Well, at least I have the bed.

I expected it to be harder to fall asleep. It annoys me that it isn't. With Chase watching over me, instead of suddenly developing a bout of insomnia, I'm out within minutes—and unless he slipped quicksilver into my dinner hours earlier, it has nothing to do with being sedated.

My sleep isn't unbroken for long, though. At some point in

the middle of the night, I hear a noise that has me stirring. I fight to stay asleep as long as I can, and it isn't until I lose the elusive grasp on unconsciousness that I realize what it is.

It's Chase, and he's whimpering.

Leaning over the side of the bed, I see a dark, shadowy shape on the blanket. My shifter's sight is strong enough to see that not only has Chase fallen asleep, but he reverted to his fur either before or after he did.

His destroyed jeans are ripped up and tattered, scattered on the floor. At first, I wondered if he shredded them off while I was sleeping, but no. I've seen ruined clothing like that before. He shifted while he was dressed, and now his jeans are toast.

I've heard of something like this happening before. Sleep-shifting. It isn't something we usually do once we're out of puphood, but it's a sign of a shifter losing his hold on his other half.

In other words, it's something a feral does.

He's not snarling, though. He's completely his big, black wolf, instead of that partially shifted beast I once met. As his wolf, Chase is curled up on his side, one of his back legs jerking, almost like he's running in his sleep.

Or in his nightmares.

A pang hits me right in the chest. Before I know it, I'm sliding across the sheets, moving toward him.

Another whimper escapes him. This one sounds pained.

I can't leave him like this. Pulling my blanket over my head, pretending I don't see him suffering… I can't do it.

That leaves me one other choice—and it might just be the dumbest thing I ever do.

As I remove the silky red dress, folding it up so I don't ruin the only piece of clothing I own right now, I remind myself that he hasn't flipped out again like he did my first night here. Not when I refused him. Not when I went for his balls. Not when I ran.

In fact, the only time he turned feral like that was when I mentioned having a mate. So long as I don't bring West up, I can almost convince myself he's just another male wolf. Maybe even just another packmate.

Wolves are pack animals. Us shifters have the same mentality. The same instincts. We thrive better when we're part of a community. I've lived alone for years. I was never lonely, though. Our cabins are built close enough that we take comfort in knowing our packmates are near.

With the Fang City surrounding Chase's land, there isn't another shifter around for miles—except for me. Maybe… maybe he wasn't just looking for a female to fuck. Maybe, when the feral inside of him decided it needed a mate, it was just looking for someone who would be there so he wasn't alone anymore.

If we were together, we wouldn't be lonely…

I'm here. For better or for worse, despite how I got here, he's not alone. I'm here.

Before I think better of what I'm doing, I shift from naked skin to sleek brindle fur. Once I'm on four legs instead of two, I curl up next to Chase, joining him on the floor.

With my wolf in charge, I can pretend I haven't laid down next to the insane, broken, possessive bastard who thought stealing me from my pack and making me his captive was a way to win my heart. I'm just doing what I would do for any other packmate.

So long as I give my word to stay with Chase, we're a pack of two. That's all. That's why I'm doing this. Not because it pains me to see him suffering when I might be able to do something to help him.

Here's hoping that I don't get attacked in the process…

The moment I lay my muzzle on his back, his whimpering stops. His choppy breathing slows. His back leg settles down, no longer jerking in spasms.

My wolf curled up with his, Chase calms down almost immediately. After a few seconds, he sighs before he falls into a deep sleep.

And all because I'm near.

Oh, yeah. I don't know what that means, but I'm guessing it can't be good.

EIGHT

KISS

There's no sign of Chase—in his skin or his fur—when I wake up again the next morning.

That's a good thing. Honest. I don't feel a sting when I realize that he slipped out from beneath me, leaving my wolf to sleep on the blanket all alone.

Nope. Not at all.

I don't want to be the support she-wolf for a feral. It's better this way.

And maybe if I tell myself that enough, I'll believe it.

Blowing a frustrated rush of air through my snout, I slowly climb back to my four legs. His fresh scent lingers in the room so I know he hasn't been gone long. Cocking my head, I see if I can sense him nearby.

It's been days since he dosed me with any quicksilver. I had already slowly gotten used to his aura while I was chained in the basement. Without anything affecting my senses, his dominance is like a beacon to me. When he's not with me, I can usually focus and pinpoint where he is in the cabin.

Before, it was vague directions. Now that he's allowed me to see the rest of his home, I have a better guess of where he is.

Kitchen. Why am I not surprised?

If he's prepping another meal for me, he'll be back soon. I might've been willing to strip in front of him yesterday if only to show him what he'll never get from me. That was yesterday, though. Something changed after I curled up next to him. What? I'm not so sure, but I do know that being naked around Chase isn't a good idea.

The silky red dress is still folded on the side of the bed where I left it. For a heartbeat, I almost decide to stay in my fur. That's how much I don't want to put that dress back on. I might've been able to shower. The dress hasn't. It's rank, especially to my wolf's nose, and a reminder of the days I spent chained.

Only one problem. If I don't shift back, I won't be able to communicate with Chase. After last night, my wolf also has a bit of a soft spot for his. I let her stay in control and who knows what'll happen.

Nothing my human half wants, I bet.

Another wolfish sigh before I quickly shift back to my skin. Snagging the dress, I yank it on again. It looks shorter than before, though that could also be me becoming more aware that I still have no bra, no panties, and what amounts to a slip to cover my body up from a wolf who has made it clear he wants me.

After I'm dressed, I think about what I'm supposed to do next. Now that he's sure I'm not going to run again—as far as he knows—Chase told me I had free rein of the house. It's so different from how he's treated me since he first brought me here that I don't know how to feel about that.

Should I go find him? What kind of signal would that send? The fact that I have the urge to track him down in the kitchen has me going a little queasy. I don't chase males. They chase me.

In the case of my feral, I mean that literally.

I sit down on the edge of the bed, gripping the mattress until the desire to find Chase passes. It's easy to get distracted when the scent of eggs cooking floats into the bedroom, followed by the crackle and hiss of bacon sizzling.

I can hear him moving about somewhere down the hall. Well, not Chase. He's pure predator, soundless on his bare feet, but the pans clanging and the dishes clinking let me know where he is and what he's doing.

When the noise stops and he moves closer, I scoot further back on the bed, crossing my legs and shaking out my bedhead a split second before he walks into the room.

Why did I do that? That's something the old Quinn—before the mess with West—would've done. I liked attention. I liked attention from males in particular. And though I already have it from Chase otherwise he wouldn't have bothered to take me, I put myself in a pose that makes me as attractive as possible without even realizing I've done it until it's too late.

Chase has a prowling walk. Sometimes he stalks, sometimes he stomps, but he usually prowls on the balls of his feet. He's doing that now as he steps into the room, a plate in one hand, a glass of orange juice in the other, and a plastic shopping bag hanging off of his wrist. He's back in jeans. Still no shirt, but at least I know it's a new pair since the remains of the ones he fell asleep in are still scattered on the bedroom floor.

He stops short when he sees me. A soft rumble builds from

deep in his chest as he falls back, regaining his balance just in time to keep a drop of OJ from spilling to the floor.

I grin. "Morning."

Chase clears his throat, erasing the rumble. He hasn't blinked yet, his fierce eyes locked on the thigh I'm flashing him. "Uh. I brought you breakfast."

I uncross my legs, then cross them so the left one is on top now. His nostrils flare, his expression hungry—and I don't think it's for breakfast. "Thanks."

He holds the plate out to me. I notice he has a white-knuckled grip on the edge of it, but he passes it easily. The juice, too.

I plop the plate down on the bed. I take a sip of the juice.

His gaze tracks my swallow.

I hide a smile behind the glass. And, okay, I know I'm playing with fire. I can't even explain why I'm doing it.

It's fun, though. I deserve a little fun after the last five days.

When he reaches behind him, muscles on his forearm flexing as he grabs the fork he has for me, the shopping bag bobs. Chase gives his head a little shake, staring down at the bag. I think he forgot he was carrying it.

After he hands me the fork, he shimmies his hand, removing the bag. He holds that out to me next.

"What's this?"

"For you," he says gruffly. "I meant to give it to you before, but I didn't think you'd take it.

I open the bag. It's stuffed with clothes.

Brand new *female* clothes.

I start pulling them out, stomach going tight as I get a better look at them.

"Where did you get these?" My flirtatious teasing utterly

disappears as it hits me what this might mean. He could've left the cabin and I *missed* it. I have to ask: "*When* did you?"

"I bought them at the store when I got you that dress."

The dress I've been wearing for almost a fucking week. He's had clothes all along.

What?

Chase reaches up, scratching the back of his neck. If I didn't know better, I'd think he looked ashamed. But why would he? As long as he gets what he wants, why should he give a shit how his captive feels?

Any good feelings I developed for him when I found his wolf whimpering last night are gone. But then... then I notice something.

They're not my clothes or any other females. The only scent clinging to them is Chase's. They're clean at least, but they're also new. Like brand spanking, still has the tags on *new*. They're definitely not mine.

But they look like they are.

I have a t-shirt just like this one. Same color and everything. These jeans are the style I prefer. And that skirt... when I still believed I might be able to turn West's head and make him want me instead of Helene, I styled my hair, did my make-up, and wore a skirt that looks like that one to go see him at his cabin.

He didn't even let me inside.

As I marvel at what else is in this bag, Chase is talking somewhere over my head.

"I couldn't risk letting you go back to your pack to get your own clothes so I bought you some of the items I saw you in the most. I hope you like them."

Good going, Chase. Like I need the reminder that he was watching me long before he stole me away.

No underclothes in the bag, I notice. Why I am not surprised?

Still, I recognize what this is. It's a peace offering. I'm so sick of the silky red dress, I accept it.

"I'm going to the bathroom. Don't follow me."

He doesn't. I almost thought he would. Chase stays in the bedroom while I go to the bathroom. After I do my business, I decide to wear a pair of jeans and a yellow t-shirt that sets off my eyes. And if it shows off my nipples, too? Oh, well.

Once I'm dressed, I pat down my hips. How he got my exact size, I have no clue, but I feel so much better now that I'm out of that dress. Look better, too.

Chase seems to agree.

The moment I enter the room again, he immediately starts for me.

"What are you doing?" I don't back away. If I do, he'll only chase, and I kind of want to see what his intentions are. Especially since… "You've got that look in your eye again."

"What look?"

"The hungry one."

"That's because I am."

Holding my position, I gesture to the abandoned breakfast cooling on my plate. "Have mine."

He shakes his head roughly, his shaggy hair dancing as he prowls closer. "Not hungry for food."

Oh, boy. "Chase—"

His shake was rough, but when he closes the gap between us, his hands are gentle as he cups my cheeks with his palms.

"Don't be afraid, Quinn," he rumbles.

The heat of his breath fans the flyaways framing my face. I tilt my chin up. "I'm not."

Should I be? Oh, yeah. He's twice my size, a million

times more dominant, and I can't allow myself to forget that he's a feral. Even so, it's been so long since a male looked at me like that. Longer since one touched me as if I was precious.

He brushes his nose against mine. "Good," he whispers before he slants his mouth over mine.

His lips are softer than I thought they would be. It's like his gentle touch. I expect the feral to always be rough, but he isn't. He's tentative, almost as if he's afraid I'm going to refuse his kiss.

Maybe I should. I don't. Instead, I part my lips and invite him inside.

Once he's sure of his welcome, Chase deepens the kiss.

Before I know it, his hands are at my waist. Slowly, he begins to skim up my side. His claws lightly scratch my skin. The tiny shock of pain makes me realize that he's slipped his hands beneath my shirt.

Do I mind?

I… I don't think I do. How can I? My hands are clinging to his back, pulling him against me.

I want *more*.

There's an awkwardness to his kiss that tells me that he's unpracticed. I guide him, stroking his tongue with mine, leading him so that it's more enjoyable for us both.

He breaks the kiss first. I get the vibe it's because he really doesn't know what he's doing and he needs a few seconds to recover before he goes in for another kiss.

That was my mistake. I gave a feral the benefit of the doubt—and that was after I willingly let him kiss me.

He buries his nose in the crook of my shoulder, right where it meets my throat. I'm used to this. Chase has this weird thing about taking my scent into his lungs. He hasn't done it since yesterday morning, and I figured he was making up for lost time.

Nope.

The light scratches on my side were erotic enough that I didn't stop him. But the way his fang drags across my neck like that? Or how it pierces my skin?

There's no way that was an accident.

Fucker *bit* me!

The hazy cloud of lust settling over me is gone in an instant. With one rush shove, I push Chase away from me. If he'd expected my reaction, I never would've been able to move his feet. Good thing he wasn't expecting it.

Chase slams against the door, rattling the whole damn frame. He drops, catching himself time to land in a crouch before he jumps back up to his feet.

I'm bristling with rage. "What were you thinking?"

"Quinn—"

Nope.

I can't believe it. I can't believe I let down my guard like that.

I'm a fucking *moron*.

My hand flies to my neck. When I find a trickle of blood there, I snarl, then show Chase the red slicking my finger. "Did you try to mark me?"

It wouldn't take. I'm already willing it to heal, so it's not like he left any damage. But he tried to, and that's all that matters to me right now.

"It was an accident," he says gruffly. His eyes are wild, his hands clenched into fists. His whole body vibrates, like he's dying to touch me again but the big, bad wolf knows better. "I never meant… Look, I told you. I want to *earn* you. I won't mark you until you ask me to. You have to believe me."

No I fucking *don't*.

Some alphas can tell when someone is lying. Deltas can't. What I wouldn't give for that ability right now because the expression he's pulling makes me want to believe that maybe —just maybe—he's telling me the truth. But why would he? I have to remember that he's proven again and again that the only thing that matters is that he gets his way.

Not this time.

I cover the scratch. Something warns me against letting him see me heal it even as I snap back in the heat of my temper, "I will *never* want you to bite me."

I was right. Chase doesn't like that, not one bit.

It's as if a flip's been switched. His features twist, going from wounded to territorial in a heartbeat. "You're mine!"

This shit again?

"No. I'm not. And don't you yell at me like that." As he looms in front of me, I continue to stand my ground. Forming my own fist, I shoot out my pointer finger, jabbing him in his heaving chest. "Pro-tip, Chase? Females don't like males who bite them without permission and then yell at them when they get called out on it."

Thank the Luna that my words seem to sink in. He's the one who backs off. Chase is hanging his head, obviously holding onto his control by a thread.

He swallows roughly. I watch his Adam's apple bob with a pointed glare.

And then he sighs. "I need you with me, Quinn. I don't know how to be with females. You're the only one I've ever wanted… it was my wolf. My wolf told me to do it."

"Yeah? Well, tell your wolf that you can't just take me away from my pack and think that I'll jump at the chance to stay with a male I barely know." Or let him fucking *bite* me.

He dares to meet my angry gaze through the shaggy hair flopping forward into his determined face. "You'll get to know me in time."

Right. Like he learned all about me without me having any idea he was out there, watching. Too bad only one of us is an obsessed stalker, and it isn't me.

My hands go to my hips. "It's not that easy, Chase—"

"Why? Because of *him*?"

Did I think that he was holding onto his temper? His sanity? Yeah. That doesn't last.

Something crunches. It doesn't take long for me to realize it's Chase's bones. His shoulders widen, then hunch over, his fingers cracking as they begin to change into fucking *talons*.

He hasn't shifted to that beast all the way yet. It's close, though. His skin stretches, his cheekbones jutting out. His eyes have gone even wilder.

And all because he brought up West.

He doesn't use his name. He doesn't have to, and I'm not even sure if he knows it. When he was stalking me, he saw me with a male, and even as broken as he is, Chase would've been able to sense that West and I have a connection; everyone does, though my packmates pretend they can't. To Chase, the Beta of the Sylvan Pack is a target—because of me. If he thinks I'm meant to be his mate, then West is his rival. That's how ferals think. Everything is black and white.

Chase wants me.

West is, technically, my fated mate.

No West. No other male to claim Quinn. If his wolf is riding him as much as it seems he is, then there's one simple solution to his problem: eliminate the other male.

No.

"It's not about him," I say hurriedly. "It's about me and you. Leave him out of it."

Chase growls. My wolf yips. I clamp my jaw shut to keep from doing the same.

"You're trying to protect him from me." Well, yeah. Obviously. "*Don't,*" he commands. "He doesn't deserve it."

That's where we'll have to disagree. West doesn't deserve to have a feral's rage directed at him all because he had the bad luck to be my fated mate.

"Stop this. I don't like the way you're acting."

I don't raise my voice, purposely staying as calm as possible as he continues to loom in front of me. I'm not afraid of him. Not really. If there's one thing I'm sure of right now it's that Chase won't hurt me. Now, if West suddenly appeared, he'd probably lunge for him, but I'm as safe as can be.

Still, I don't want him to completely snap. Right now, Chase is still with me. He's talking. He's not prowling around or smashing his fist into the wall. I have to keep him on the right side of his sanity or else I don't know what'll happen next.

Luna damn it. When did this become my responsibility? Just like this morning, I don't want to be in charge of him. I want to respond to his rising aggression because, as a delta, the alternative is submitting—and if he really was my mate, he wouldn't use his dominance against me. He'd understand that we're equals, and that, as his mate, I should come first for him.

That realization pisses me off even more; I shouldn't have to hold back because I'm afraid of setting him off more. He's still on the edge of going feral, and while I won't be the one who gives him a push, this is exactly why—despite his attempts at peace offerings earlier—I could never be a feral's mate.

With a wave at his still heaving bare chest, I tell him in a firm yet gentle voice, "Take a step back, Chase. Get your shit together. You want me to be your mate? Here's another hint. This"—I wave again—"isn't attractive."

He throws his head back and roars.

I refuse to react. When the echo dies down, I raise my eyebrow at him. "That's not, either, tough guy."

Too far. I tried my best to reason with him, one shifter to another, and I think I went too far.

Chase's paw curls into a fist. "He doesn't want you." *Thud. Thud. Thud.* He beats himself in the chest. "I do!"

Oof. They're only words. Chase didn't hit me with his fists. Doesn't matter. I stumble back anyway, almost like he *did* strike me.

Wow. Just when I was beginning to think that he might not be so bad, he comes out with this bullshit.

Like I don't know that? Like I've spent the six months blissfully unaware that I was rejected? It's not a surprise to me that he knows—if Chase really did stalk me for nine months, there's no way he wouldn't—but did he have to throw it in my face like that?

At least he realizes it.

His hand falls to his side—and it is a hand again. The crazy gleam in his feral's bright golden eyes fades as his expression darkens. Sucking in a breath, he plants his feet, as if he wants to go to me but he accepts that he can't.

Bowing his head, chin to his chest, hair falling forward and covering his eyes, Chase rasps out, "I didn't mean that."

Yes. He did.

My laugh is hollow. "What? You're just telling me something I already know. West doesn't want me. He's made that clear. Still a dick move rubbing it in. Is that what I'll have to look forward to if I stay? Should I be grateful that you decided to make me your captive? Is that it?"

His head jerks up again. There are red welts on his chest from where he smashed it with his fist. "No. I brought you here because I had to have you with me. I'm a selfish bastard, I know that, but I thought—"

"What? You thought that, just because my mate doesn't want me, I'd be happy to accept you as a… a… what? A consolation prize?"

"No!"

"Then what is it, Chase? Why me? I'm nobody."

He swoops in. Brave bastard, approaching a she-wolf who's on the edge herself. He's quick, too. Before I can dart out of his reach, he has me in another embrace.

His hand goes straight to my hair. His claws thread through the strands, stroking me softly as he murmurs, "You're somebody to me, Quinn. You always will be."

He says that now. I know from experience that a male will say anything to get a female on all fours. Why would this feral be any different?

"Yeah?" I say daringly. "Then prove it."

"I will. I vow it to the Luna. I'll do whatever I can. Give you everything I can. Everything you want."

If only I could believe that. "Let me go home. That's all I want."

Chase's hold on me tightens. "Everything but that."

Yeah. That's what I thought.

NINE
PESTO

Thank the Luna for locks.

Oh, how the tables have turned. I went from being chained to a wall in Chase's basement to locking him out of the bedroom he gave me. When he realized that I needed some time to cool off, he left me alone. The second he was gone, I turned the lock.

He's gone for ten minutes. Maybe twenty. It wasn't enough time, and when I hear him padding back down the hall, I throw a nasty look at the closed door.

Chase tries to open it, muttering a curse under his breath when he discovers it's locked.

I smile, only because he can't see me through the door. When he rattles the knob, I school my face into my best pissed-off expression again.

"Let me in."

"No."

"Quinn—"

"Do I get to go home?"

Another rattle is my answer.

"Thought so. Until you decide to let me go, you can stay out there."

"This is my room."

I knew it!

"Too bad. You gave it to me. No take-backs. Sleep in the basement." I huff at the closed door. "Way I see it, it's your turn anyway."

"If that's what you want, I will. We need to talk first."

"No, thanks."

"Quinn. If you don't open this door, I'm coming in anyway."

"Go right ahead."

The knob turns again. With one quick jerk, he breaks the lock.

I should've known better than to dare him like that. Despite this being a shifter's cabin, there was no way any of the locks inside of here would be strong enough to withstand a determined male shifter.

He lets himself in. His eyes flicker over to the bed, but if he expected to find me waiting for him like I was before, he's sorely mistaken. I'm standing across from him, hands on my hips again, a warning on my face.

He scowls when he sees the food I still haven't touched. "You didn't eat your breakfast."

"I wasn't hungry."

"Be angry with me. Luna knows I deserve it. Kick me out of our room—"

"It's my room now," I remind him. "And I already did."

"If you need your space, I'll give it to you. But you will eat. I won't back down on this, Quinn. Kick me, scratch me, throw a sucker punch my way... that's fine. But don't go hungry because I fucked up again. Please."

I wish he was still the gruff, grunting wolf from a few days ago. When he talks to me like this, when he pleads...

"Why are you like this?"

His jaw goes tight. "Feral?"

"Confusing."

He opens his mouth, then closes it with a *click*, fangs hitting each other.

Good. I'm not done.

"I'm still a fucking prisoner here," I point out, "but you want to take care of me. You bought me clothes. You promise me things I want, things I can't have. I don't know what you're playing at, but it makes it harder for me to hate you for what you've done to me."

Chase's expression goes blank at my confession. After another moment when he just stares at me, unable to find the words, he finally nods. "I don't know. But I can't let you go. I'm sorry."

If only he really was. Maybe then I'd get to go back to Hickory after all.

I KNEW HE WAS INTELLIGENT. I MEAN, HE HAD TO BE. SOMEHOW he was able to watch me for nine months without anyone knowing. Think about it. It wasn't just me he concealed himself from. He managed to evade the entire Sylvan Pack, including our Alpha and Beta, the entire time. It wasn't until he was ready to make his move to take me that Chase slipped up at all, and, honestly, I wouldn't put it past him to have done it on purpose for reasons only a feral would understand.

The wolfsbane helped. I'd gotten him to admit that he rubbed his wolf in a whole pile of the stuff before he approached our territory. It had covered up his scent. He didn't have any excuse when it came to his aura, though he did confess that it's only as strong as it is when his feral's close to breaking free. So long as he held back his wild side, it was easier for him to hide.

I asked him how he was able to do that. He refused to answer. He has a tendency to do that whenever I bring up his being feral.

I understand. Still, so much for *you can ask me anything, Quinn*, right?

He's smart, but he's also capable of learning. When I threaten to fling the plate of cold eggs and limp bacon at him like a freaking frisbee if he doesn't leave me the hell alone, he makes another strategic retreat. And, this time, he stays in the kitchen for the rest of the day.

I slam the door behind him. Lock's broken, so he can get back in any time he decides to. At least the loud noise makes me feel a bit better.

I stew for a little while, then begin to regret that I chose the bedroom to make my stand. If I kicked him out of the living room, I could've watched television to pass the time. There's nothing to do in here.

Figuring he lost any rights to privacy when he kidnapped me, I snoop through the room. That takes like two minutes. He has a closet full of jeans with maybe three or four t-shirts hanging off to the side. Nothing under the bed. He has a dresser, but that's empty, too, except for a sweater that looks suspiciously familiar.

I shake it out, scowling when I see the hunter green sweater I lost last spring. I'd forgotten it during one of my trips out in the woods. When I went back later to retrieve it, it was gone, and I thought one of the local wolves grabbed it for their den.

A wolf grabbed it all right. A big, black one.

Funny that he gave me an entire bag of new clothes and neglected to mention he had one of my old sweaters tucked in his dresser drawer.

That makes me angry again, and I pace around the room, cursing Chase and his heavy-handed belief that his desires trump mine. Who does he think he is anyway?

Ugh!

What makes it so much worse is that, around midday, the air begins to smell of food again. I can't quite place what the aroma is. It's a mixture of so many delicious scents that tease my hungry belly. I ended up eating the bacon in case I need some fuel later on, but that's nothing compared to a shifter's metabolism.

I'm hungry, and still pretty pissed, and I stay like that until Chase is knocking on the door, announcing that dinner is ready.

I've got two choices: I can either go hungry the rest of the night or suck it up to accept the food from Chase. He might think it's another gesture that proves I'm his, but I think of it as a necessary evil to keep my wolf strong.

I throw open the door, expecting him to have my plate ready. Not that I'm spoiled and he should. It's just that, since I've been here, that's how he's served me.

His hands are empty.

"Funny, Chase. What? Are you expecting me to apologize or something before I can eat? Because I'd rather starve."

"You know I won't let that happen." We've gotten past his early threats of holding me down and force-feeding me. The edge of his rough voice tells me that he doesn't need to threaten me again. I've been warned once. Next time, he'll just do it. "But, no. I've been thinking about earlier. I apologized, but you obviously didn't believe me. Words are cheap. I'll prove it. Come with me."

I almost refuse. He didn't use his dominance against me to order me to go with him, so I technically *could*. I've grown used to being around him, and him being a feral does something strange to my wolf. She doesn't react like he's an alpha. Despite his aura, she doesn't have the urge to submit to his like she does Bishop or even West.

I don't know what that means. Choosing not to examine it too closely, I think about telling him to fuck off—and that's when one of the food scents reaches me.

Holy shit. He has pesto out there. I can scent the basil and the garlic over the other aromas, and it sings to me.

Luna, I love pesto.

I shrug, trying not to drool. "I was getting hungry anyway."

It isn't just pesto.

I'm gaping at the circular wooden table he has stowed in the corner of his kitchen. Like, mouth open, eyes wide, nose twitching, full-on gaping. My wolf is up and bouncing around inside of my chest, eager to dig her snout into all that food.

Not gonna lie, so am I.

I can't believe it. My nose tells me that my eyes aren't lying, but I'm struggling to accept it.

Every single one of my favorite foods is laid out on his table.

I might be able to explain away some of it—I don't know anyone who doesn't enjoy a good spaghetti with pesto, or cheesy bread—but when you add the chicken enchiladas next to the venison steak, plus the meatball soup and a slice of caramel cheesecake… I can't pretend this isn't meant for me.

None of this stuff goes together, except for in my belly.

The clothes are one thing. Him telling me that he decided he wanted me nine months ago is another.

Realizing that Chase learned enough about me that he knows my favorite *foods*… that he spent all day cooking them for me as his way to apologize…

My stomach twists. I'm starving, and I'd chow down on every single one of those dishes, but I can't.

He… he really means it. He really wants to make me his mate.

This isn't just a meal or even an apology. It's a feast fit for a fucking proposal.

Food has a special meaning for shifters. Apart from how accepting a meal is the same thing as accepting a prospective mate's interest, it's part of our love language. It's also part of our community. In packs, shifters eat and talk together. It's a communal affair.

That's why it's been so hard for me lately. With West's rejection earning me the pity of every packmate in Hickory, I stopped eating with the others. When I couldn't face the others, I'd cook for myself in my cabin, always quick meals just to choke something down when my hunger outweighed the ache I felt at being ignored.

Chase isn't ignoring me. He's watching from the corner, his hip cocked against the stove as he waits on bated breath for my reaction.

I don't think he ever guessed I would burst into tears.

They're tears of frustration, and the first I've shed since he brought me here. Because this? This is proof that he won't be moved. He's going to keep me here with him. Unless I reach out to my pack and risk them facing off against a feral—because Luna knows he'll turn into the monster if I try to go—I'm stuck. He won't let me escape, and if by some miracle I do, he'll come after me.

And that's if the vampires don't get me first.

Chase pushes off of the range, stalking toward me. "Quinn? Are you… are you crying?"

I use my wrists to rub roughly at the tears. "It's nothing," I lie. "The food looks amazing."

"Fuck the food. You *are* crying. Come here—"

He moves to grab me.

I spin out of his reach, backing up until I hit the wall. It's instinctive. I just… I don't want him touching me right now. "I said I'm fine, Chase. Leave me alone."

"What's wrong?" He stops dead in his tracks. "What did I do?" he demands, suddenly panicked. "How can I fix it? Tell me."

He can't, and I look away.

"I knew it. I'm doing this wrong. I've done it all wrong." Out of the corner of my eye, I watch as Chase runs his fingers through his hair, an anguished expression on his face. "I've fucked this up from the beginning."

He drops down into a crouch, cradling his head. "I had a plan. I was going to take this slow. It's just… a few months in, when I finally was ready to make my move, I followed you to your pack land. To the cabins, and the other wolves were there. I thought it would be easier on you if I said you were mine when you weren't alone. I didn't want to scare you, Quinn. But then I heard the rumors. About the Beta… I saw you with him. Your"—he takes a deep breath, then spits out the word—"*mate*. Approaching you, introducing myself… I couldn't wait, knowing someone else had a claim to you, even if they weren't following up on it. So I started to plan. I watched you. I watched him. I watched you watch him… and then, when I caught you two talking in the woods a couple of weeks ago, I knew… I had to do something."

I can't believe this. I can't believe this is happening. That Chase is actually being open and honest with me at last, and that he's confirming what I guessed all along: he *did* stalk me these last nine months. In the woods, in Hickory… he was there.

And I had no idea.

My mouth is suddenly dry. I don't know what to say or how to act. Am I scared, or is this what I've been waiting for? All I've wanted is to know *why*. Any maybe I still don't, not yet, but this is something.

I know that it really was *me* he was targeting.

"You took me." My words are soft. I'm daring him to deny it as I say, just a bit louder, "That's what you did."

"Yeah." He shakes his head in remorse, though the glimmer in his eyes when he looks up at me says he doesn't regret it one bit. "I took you." The glimmer dies. Anguish returns. "And now you hate me."

The pain in his voice cuts like a damn knife. Especially since the truth is that I don't actually hate Chase; his actions maybe, but not he male. He's too broken to hate. It wouldn't be fair.

I exhale roughly. "I don't hate you. Don't get me wrong," I add when his expression quickly shifts to one of hope, "I'm not your biggest fan right now. But I don't hate you."

I can't. Don't ask me why. He's certainly done enough to earn my hatred. I still can't hate him.

The hope fades. "I don't know what part of me led me to treat you like this. When you've done so much to help me without even being aware of it… I was selfish. I saw something I wanted. The idea another male had a claim to you made me crazed. I couldn't stop myself. I could blame it on being feral, but my wolf and human halves were in agreement. I had to have you, Quinn."

"But you knew about West." He made *that* clear. "You knew he rejected me. I might have been watching him"— Chase's cheeks go hollow as he sucks in a breath—"but you should've seen him watching Helene. We don't talk." As painful as it is to admit that, it's true. "I've had like ten conversations with West total since I found out who he was to me. That day in the woods you mention… it was a pity chat. Nothing more."

"And the day he warned you from going into the woods on your own?"

Ah. So he was spying on that conversation, too?

"You mean the day you kidnapped me?" I toss back.

The feral is a mess of emotions right now, barely hanging onto his control, but he has no shame as he nods. "Yes. That day."

"He was only doing his duty. Beta, remember?" And if I find out that he knew I had a stalker and never clued me in, I'm gonna go furry on his ass. One upside to his wolf being drawn to mine? It wouldn't necessarily be a challenge, would it? "Now, I'm not saying I want you back. It's just… he's my fated mate, but he's not *mine*. You acted like a creepy fucking stalker for nothing. You could've said 'hi'."

Chase slowly rises up from his crouch. His voice drops,

imploring me. "Fate is a powerful thing," he tells me. "Everyone knows he can't have his omega. When he finally realizes that... when he accepts his fate... he'll turn to you. I thought that's what he was doing that day in the woods with the flower when you were talking. Didn't matter that it wasn't. My wolf needed you. I needed you. I had to bring you home with me."

"But why?" For days now we've danced around the topic. If Chase really wants me to believe that he picked me for some reason and not just because I was the only she-wolf he could get his claws on, he needs to explain himself. I have to ask: "Why me?"

"I didn't mean to go feral."

That doesn't answer my question at all. And, until I know *why me*, we're fated to go around in circles just like this.

"No one does," I say drolly. "But I don't care about that. You did this. You made these choices. I... I can't take this anymore, Chase. Be honest. What the hell do you want from me?"

I expect him to walk away. He does that. When I ask a question he doesn't like, it's time for him to leave. He always returns, as though he can't stay away, but he goes.

Not this time.

Instead of walking away, he takes a few careful steps toward me. Once he's within reach, towering over me, he says, "It started with your scent."

TEN
DEAL

"My scent?"

"When I become that… thing, I'm ruled by instinct. It's not my wolf in charge or my human half. It's something different. Something I can't control. If I have an urge, I act on it. If I'm hungry, I feed. If I feel threatened, I kill. And when I caught a scent on the breeze that had me going hard, all I could think about was getting the owner of it beneath me so that I could rut until I'd spent all my lusts."

I go still. He… he can't mean me, can he?

One look at him and it's clear. He does.

"I've never felt like that before," he continues. "I admit, I didn't fight the urge. I searched for the scent and I found a beautiful she-wolf sitting beneath a tree, playing with the flower in her hands. She was plucking it, singing a song under her breath…"

That does sound like me. Sometimes I would pick a flower, then play the old "he loves me, he loves me not" game as I tore off its petals. When I was younger, it would help me decide which male I would take out for a romp. Then the Luna picked me for West, and I stopped playing the game. It kind of loses its allure when you have to change the words to "he loves *her*, he loves me not".

"Are you telling me your feral side is what chose me?" I ask. "Not you. Not your wolf. But your feral beast?"

"All three of those are me, Quinn. We all want you. But being feral… I haven't been like this all that long," he admits. "Barely a year. It's still hard for me to understand what… *how* I ended up breaking in the first place."

It's the first time he's ever mentioned it himself. I'd have to be a fool to let the chance pass me by without saying anything.

I tilt my head just enough that I'm meeting his gaze. He can consider it a challenge if he wants, though I'm pretty sure he won't, as I ask him, "What happened?"

As if he purposely misunderstood me, he says, "I was a lone wolf first. I had my cabin here, but I spent more and more time in my fur. I should've known then that I wasn't right. I was too late, though. I changed into my other form for the first time and, after that, there was no going back. I'd never found a female that enticed the beast. I didn't know what would happen, and I was terrified."

Me, too. Just the idea of that hunched, patchy, snarling monster coming upon me when I was alone in the woods is pure nightmare fuel. The big, black wolf was bad enough.

"I couldn't stop him, though. At least, not when he had your scent." Chase pauses, then takes a hesitant step toward me, closing the meager gap between us. When I don't try to bolt past him, he takes another. He's slowly caging me in. We both know it. As long as he keeps talking, I'll allow it. "It was your voice. Your scent drew me to you, but then I heard your voice."

Look at that. Talking to myself in the woods might've saved me from being mounted by a feral. And all the times after that, too, most likely. Ha. To think I was worried my packmates might think West's rejection was making me lose my mind…

"My voice," I say, returning to the conversation. "That stopped you from trying to mate me then?"

"That's the truth of it. Something about you… hearing your voice calmed me down. It used to take hours for me to shift again. After hearing you sing, I still wanted to go to you, but I was a wolf again, not a monster. Mating was a want, not an uncontrollable need. I couldn't let myself hurt you." He moves into me, completely caging me in with one arm while laying the back of his other hand against my cheek. "I never will."

The funny thing is, I believe him. Even when I kneed him in his dick, then sucker-punched him, the most he did was wrap me up in his arms so that I couldn't lash out at him again.

"Nine months, Quinn. Whenever I had the chance, I ran from my cabin out to Hickory, hoping that I'd get the nerve to approach you. Every time I saw you from a distance, scenting you, hearing you… I got better. I almost introduced myself to you six months ago. But then…"

We both know why he didn't. Six months ago was when I found my fated mate—and it wasn't Chase.

This close, I can see how tight his jaw goes. A muscle tics in his cheek, his eyes lighting up. Just the thought of West is bringing out the beast, even as Chase tries his hardest to hold him back.

He does. It's obviously rough, but as he stares unblinkingly into my tear-stained face, he does.

After a few moments, he shudders, then lets out a soft breath that warms my forehead. "It didn't change anything. You were still the only thing I looked forward to, the only thing that kept me sane. I found out about the other male after he already made his choice, and I worked toward taking you before he changed his mind."

He's so close to me, I can hardly move. When I shake my head just enough to disagree with him, my hair whispers against the wall at my back. "You don't have to worry about that. He won't."

"Don't be so sure about that."

I am. "He chose Helene. Our Omega. He isn't mine."

"You keep saying that. But let me tell you something, Quinn. A half bond can only last so long. I've seen it happen. One day he was going to wise up and he'd claim you. I would lose you before I ever had a chance to find out why you affect me like this. I couldn't let that happen. And every time I saw you together, I was more sure that I had to do what I was planning to do. My mind was made up, and not a moment too soon." Those golden eyes are gleaming with insanity. "You were together that morning. I was there. I heard him. He was trying to keep you from me. I had to keep you first."

Ah. He must be talking about the afternoon he took me, when West came over to warn me about the presence in the woods. After his subtle rejection, I can count the number of times we were together on maybe two hands.

So Chase really was there in Hickory that day, too?

I swear, if I ever get back, I'm going to have a word with Bishop about our shit security...

"I had a choice of my own. I could take you with me, or I could kill your male before he could claim you." At that confession—and the way I suck in my breath—Chase draws away from me. "I figured you'd prefer the first option. I don't want to hurt you. I fell in love with you that first day in the woods, and my feelings for you have only grown. You know I'm an alpha wolf. We're persistent, possessive bastards. I'm feral, too. I can't change that. You're the only one who can tame my beast, and I really am sorry. This isn't the way I wanted us to happen, but I can't change the past. I can only make up for it in the future.

"Stay with me, Quinn. Not because I chained you, or because you don't want to face the vampires. Stay with me because no male will ever treat you better than I will from this moment on."

He has such an intense look on his ruggedly handsome face that I can't come up with an answer for him right away.

I just stare back at him, but the more he meets my stare unblinkingly, the more I understand that he's absolutely serious.

I glance behind me at the food on the table. I fucking knew it. This totally is his version of a proposal, isn't it?

He's waiting for me to say something.

"Chase…" I sigh. "I can't promise you forever. If that's what you're asking me for, I can't do it."

"Then don't promise forever. Promise that you'll stay just a little bit longer. But you'll have to let me try to prove that I'm the male for you."

"How long would I have to stay?"

"The Luna will rise in a little less than three weeks. If I haven't convinced you to choose me by then, I'll let you go."

Chase might be a feral, but I've had the same thought since the beginning: he's a very intelligent feral.

I'm not saying I'm going to mate Chase. If I did that, I'm basically condoning how he's treated me from the moment I discovered him watching me nine months after he started. But the kiss did something to make me forget West if only for a few moments—something I never would've thought was possible before now—and lying down beside the black wolf had gone a little way to soothing something sharp and jagged inside of me.

He's broken. I'm broken. Maybe we can't fix each other, but hopefully we can't fall apart any more.

"And if I choose to go?"

"Then I'll just ask you to chain me up before you go. You'll be able to get away, and no matter what happens when I become that thing, he won't be able to get to you."

Fair enough.

"Okay. Until it's the next full moon, I'll stay with you."

It's not technically a lie. I have every intention of honoring my agreement—unless the perfect opportunity to escape presents itself.

Then all bets are off.

His lips split into a grin that turns him from ruggedly handsome to downright gorgeous. "Sit down. I'll grab the plates and utensils, and we can eat together."

Together. Oh, boy. It would be the first time, too.

Welp, I already agreed to this insanity. I might as well get a good meal out of it.

"Sure, but touch the pesto and you're losing a paw."

He chuckles as he moves past me toward the cupboard by the sink.

And I realize something. His chuckle? That was another first from Chase.

He wasn't kidding when he said he'd take any chance to prove to me that he was the right male for me. The food was just the beginning, and he's only playing hardball from there on out.

I'm ready for him.

Assuming I won't get to escape him, my new plan is to run out the clock while using my undeniable attraction to Chase to find a way to forget all about West. I only have to make it until the next full moon before he'll let me go back to Hickory. If I'm lucky, by then I'll have finally gotten over West. Let Helene have him. I'll find a mate of my own, bond with him, and my fated mate bond with West will be nothing but a bad memory.

That can't be Chase. No matter how much he believes that we belong together, he's still a feral alpha wolf.

Of course, if our goddess blesses him with a bonded mate during the Luna Ceremony, that might be enough to keep him turning feral again…

That's just a guess. I don't know for sure. He tells me that, the closer we get, the more sane he feels, and I want to believe him. At the very least, he certainly seems like he's better than he was.

Even so, I'm not going to tease him because I don't know how his feral side will react; no matter how much he swears being around me calms his feral side, even he acknowledges that he's not whole, and I can't risk him turning on me. I won't let him fuck me, either. I haven't been with a male since I discovered West was my fated mate. I've finally admitted to myself that my days of casual sex are behind me, and the next time I let a male inside of me, it'll be because he's my forever mate.

I expect Chase to push me on that point. After all, I said I would give him until the next Luna to see if he can convince me that, even if we're not fated, we have some kind of tie between us.

To my surprise, he agrees that sex is off the table for now unless I'm the one who chooses to initiate it. Since I know that he's not the type of male who will mate just for the sake of the act, I won't do it. It might feel good for one night, but I have no doubt in my mind that he'll try to turn it into forever.

Luckily for me and my libido, it's not as easy as that. Say I forget myself for a moment and decide that Chase might be the perfect wolf to break my celibacy streak. Just having sex doesn't create a bond; otherwise I'd have at least ten mates of my own already. No. All matings have to be blessed by the Luna.

A bond can only be finalized on the night of the full moon, when the Luna is out. The couple has to mate—obviously— and they have to wear each others' mark. Some mates bite each other. Others use their claws. So long as they choose to keep it, the scars turn white. If the Luna accepts the mating, a bond snaps into place.

Don't want a bond? Don't fuck on the night of the full moon, and don't go crazy with your claws or your fangs. It's as simple as that when you're a low-ranking member of the pack.

Now, Chase is an alpha wolf, but he's not an Alpha. He doesn't have a pack; before me, he was a lone wolf. Only Alphas and their mates have to turn the Luna Ceremony into a spectacle for the rest of the pack. It's a way to welcome the female half of the Alpha couple into our tight-knit community, and to show every packmate that the Luna blesses their mating.

Of course, the rest of the ceremony takes place when the couple is alone, but the marks they each wear are a symbol of their lifelong mating.

Hey. Who needs wedding rings when a mating mark truly says *forever*?

Chase wears my bite on his upper arm. I haven't forgotten his reaction when he realized that I healed his bite on my neck. He truly wants to make me his mate. Sleeping with him when I have no intention of spending the rest of my life with a feral is just out of the question.

That's not the only boundary we set up.

We each have one that's non-negotiable. Chase refuses to talk about anything that happened to him before he first chanced upon me in Hickory nine months ago. I refuse to talk to him about West, and when he asks me in a puzzled tone how my fated mate could ever choose another over me, I add Helene to the list.

Once that's clear, our battle of wills is on.

He wants to prove he's the right male for me. I need him to understand that he doesn't have a chance.

And then he does something that is one hell of a blow to my resolve.

ELEVEN
FLOWERS

The bloody stink of hundreds of vampires permeates the woods outside of Chase's cabin.

Phew. I thought it was bad the other day when I ran face-first into the stench. My nose must've still been a little off because this is *worse*.

My wolf puts her paws over her snout. I do the same.

Chase chuckles. "You'll get used to it."

Yeah. Maybe if I chop my nose off.

Since he's watching my reaction closely, I reluctantly let go of it. Blowing air through my nostrils, trying to erase the stink, I settle on breathing through my mouth.

Better.

I toss my hair over my shoulder, looking around. My ears are cocked, searching for some sign that we're not alone. Unless I hear a footstep, there's a good chance a vampire could sneak up on me since relying on my nose is out. I'd never be able to pinpoint one vampire when they're all I smell.

I don't think anyone else is out here. Chase's senses are

much keener than mine; if there was, he never would've invited me to go out for a walk with him. He'd probably toss me in the basement if we had visitors.

Instead, with his hand planted on the small of my back, he guides me around the side of his cabin.

His palm is like a heated brand through my shirt. The first time he touched me like that, I slapped his hand off of me. Since then, I've gotten used to his casual touches. I promised I'd give him a chance to court me, to be my partner in the mating dance, and though I haven't let him kiss me again, I can tolerate a caress here or there.

It's been a couple of days since I gave him my word that I would stay. There are moments when he looks at me as if he can't believe I'm here; there are others when he's watching me darkly, already envisioning me walking away. I'm just glad he mentioned the chains. Something tells me that, despite *his* promise, I'll need them when I decide to go.

If I decide to go.

I've been gone from Hickory for more than a week now. Every day, I check on my bond with West. It's still there, though I'm finding it easier to block off. Where was this ability six months ago? It's almost like I suffered for nothing. Whatever happens with Chase, at least I know how I'll survive seeing West with Helene.

They say distance makes the heart grow fonder. For me, I've had the opposite effect. I don't know if it's because I've purposely blocked him so he can't find me, but the idea of the two of them together doesn't hurt me as much as it used to. It's getting easier and easier to push him out of my head the longer I'm out of Hickory.

Now I just need to find a way to push him out of my heart and soul—

I blink. It's an insane idea, and one that I've had a bunch of times since I made my deal with Chase. I couldn't believe I came up with it in the first place. The fact that it keeps popping up in my brain? Maybe… maybe I should try it.

I mean, hey, if putting enough distance between us has finally lessened the sting of West's rejection, what would an affair with another male do?

I could do worse than Chase. At least he's devoted to me. Sure, you could say *obsessed*, but that's not a bad thing for our kind of supe. When a shifter male threatens to challenge and kill a rival to claim a mate, it's considered romantic, as long as the she-wolf wants him back.

Do I want Chase?

I didn't. I swear I didn't.

I blame him. He said he would prove himself to me. So far, he's giving it a good go.

And all his efforts pale in comparison when he guides me around his cabin, down a dirt path that leads further into the trees that surround his home, and into a clearing filled with—

"Flowers," I breathe out.

He's at my back. I don't see him, but I can sense his heat as he moves into me. With one hand on my shoulder now, the other settles on my waist.

He sounds nervous as he says, "It's the Quinn Malone Memorial Garden."

"Memorial?" I echo. My words sound faint to my own ears. I'm too stunned by what I see. "But I'm not dead."

His husky chuckle sends a shiver down my spine. "Memorial because each one of these flowers reminds me of you. They're *my* memories."

"Oh."

What else can I say?

There are hundreds out here. Some are recognizable types —daisies, carnations, roses, tulips—while others are the wild-flowers that spring up around Hickory. Those flowers are native to our land. Most of the others aren't. This is definitely someone's garden.

"I planted the first flowers after I found you. Those… the two bunches of roses over there, because your lips were red and your eyes were yellow. I thought they would be all, but I just… whenever my need for you got to be too much, I'd run from the edge of your pack land all the way back to my cabin. Some of these are ones I carried back between my fangs, roots attached. Others I bought from a human-owned florist down in Sacre Coeur."

Using his grip on my shoulder, he directs me to look at some pale pink posies. "You had a blouse that color on the day I planted those."

Again he moves me. He points at a yellow-petaled wild-flower with a brown center. A brown-eyed Susan, one of the wildflowers that's shaped like a daisy, and is perfect for "he loves me, he loves me not". "You liked those. I saw you weave them in your hair sometimes. I tried to relocate those the most."

He did. Among the garden, I see at least twenty brown-eyed Susans that are everywhere in the woods surrounding Hickory.

Whoa. For the first time in a long time, I'm actually speechless.

Back home, West is known for bringing Helene a flower every time they meet as a token of his affection.

But Chase?

He gave me a whole garden.

Behind me, he's humming in anticipation. He's waiting for my reaction.

He desperately wants me to like what he's showing me.

You know, I should've guessed something was up when Chase pulled a worn, thin t-shirt over his head. It's a pale grey, cotton shirt, but it's been washed so many times, I can make out his pecs and his nipples and the dusting of hair at the top of his chest through the material.

It's the first time I've seen him wear one. I still don't have any shoes, and I'm beginning to think there isn't a force on Earth that'll get Chase to wear them, so we had headed out together in our bare feet. It's not so unusual. Shifters have thick calluses to protect our human feet while our wolves have pads. I could run without noticing the rocks or sticks, though you really appreciate a good boot when you accidentally step in a pile of shit someone left behind.

Trust me. I know.

And, sure, Mitchell said it was from a wild wolf lurking nearby, but I have my doubts about that...

The shirt was the first sign that something was up with Chase. The way he kept reaching for me, fiddling with my hair, absently stroking his fingers through the dark strands as if he needed to remind himself that I was still there was the second sign. It was like he was working himself up to something.

I guess he was. He finally invited me for a walk, and here we are.

I can't believe it. I don't know what to say.

So I don't say anything.

Spinning in his arms, I grip Chase's shirt, tugging him down so that his mouth is near mine. The material tears. I wince, but he doesn't seem to notice; if he does, he doesn't care. Now that our mouths are only a few inches apart, Chase swoops in, taking my lips with his.

Uh-uh. This kiss is mine.

I take control. Nudging him back with my nose, I tilt my chin so that I can suck his bottom lip between my teeth. I nibble it lightly, and when he groans, I slip my tongue into his mouth.

Chase shudders. His hands cup my ass, pulling me into him. I can feel the heat of his erection poking my lower belly and that just spurs me to kiss him harder.

When we finally break apart, he leans his forehead against mine, his hands on my shoulders bracing me.

"Reject him, Quinn. He doesn't deserve you. He doesn't deserve your heart."

"Do you?" I whisper, my voice as rough and ragged as his panted breaths.

"No," he says honestly, "not yet. But I won't give up until I do."

I press my hands against his chest. He doesn't realize that, with this garden, he pretty much has.

But reject him?

Reject West?

I feel like an idiot, but as often as I wished he would just put me out of my misery and finally cut the tie between us, I never realized that I could do the same. Probably because he's so much higher in the pack than me. Would it even take?

It did when the Wicked Wolf's mate rejected him, but she was an omega. They exist outside of the hierarchy of the pack for the most part. I'm just a delta.

Is it possible for me to reject the Beta?

I don't know. But it's definitely something to think about.

Another week goes by, and Chase continues to do his best to take us deeper into the mating dance.

Luna help me, I let him.

At first, I had to keep reminding myself that this was never my choice. I didn't want to be here, and he basically conned me into staying for a couple of extra weeks. I did, making up every excuse to myself why I didn't try to find some way to escape, and it's been days since the idea even crossed my mind.

Eventually, I had to admit that I'm holding a grudge against something he can't help and I'm being just a little unfair. I still don't know what turned him feral, and courtesy of the boundaries we set, I don't ask.

He's done nothing but treat me like I'm the best thing that's happened to him. He's changed, too. He hasn't grunted in a week. He doesn't growl. The panicked look in his eyes when he walks into a room before he finds me there doesn't come as often lately.

He hasn't gone feral again, either. He insists it's because of me. It's a heady responsibility, but I've learned that a sane Chase is one I can't help but like.

I just… I guess I'm struggling with understanding why, of all females, he chose *me*.

If I'm being honest, if Chase showed up in Hickory in his skin, he probably could've had his pick of any of the single she-wolves there. Between his wolf being an alpha, his body looking like it was sculpted by one of the masters, and his eyes promising wicked things when they're not being used to threaten, no one could resist him. I certainly wouldn't have been able to.

Even knowing that he has his… issues, I don't think I can now.

The night after he showed me his garden, I invited Chase to sleep in the bed with me. I hadn't meant to do it. I've grown used to him sleeping on a blanket on the floor. He always fell asleep in his jeans. On two other occasions after the first time, I woke up to find his black wolf whimpering. Shifting to my wolf, I joined him on the floor.

He was always gone again when I woke up.

That night, right when he was about to make his bed on the floor, I cleared my throat, then patted the empty spot next to me.

I realized then that I trusted him, at least when it came to having him near while I was vulnerable. I didn't need to threaten his dick again. He would never touch me intimately without my permission.

Of course, when he joined me in bed and I pressed my body into his side, Chase nearly choked on his breath when I willingly touched him. Emboldened by his reaction, I made sure it was okay if I touched him a little more.

He told me before to think of his cabin as mine. Same with his room.

That night, he added his body to the list.

I had free rein to explore it, and Luna did I. To be fair, after a couple of nights of me playing with Chase, I told him he could touch me, too.

He kissed me as if I'd given him some great gift. The way he stroked my belly before palming one of my tits was so reverential, I began to wonder how I was ever going to walk away from this male.

Plus, I'd finally gotten my hands on his dick. No way was I leaving until I got to take a ride on that sucker.

Did that mean I was thinking about taking him up on his offer? Staying with him forever and becoming his mate? I wasn't convinced just yet. Bonding with Chase would completely erase my tie to West, which would save me the trouble of figuring out if I can reject him instead, but then I'd be mated to him for life.

Was I ready for that?

No. And until I changed my mind—*if* I changed my mind—sex was still off the table.

For now, at least.

That's the problem with the Luna. Our goddess wants her wolves to take mates. She wants us to fuck. At its core, mating is about creating pups. It's about building families and continuing our species. In order to encourage shifters to procreate, something about the Luna appearing high in the sky turns a shifter's sex drive up to eleven.

Throw in a promise of a mate? It cranks up to twenty.

It's worse for males. At least, that's what I heard, though I take it with a grain of salt since it was usually my prospective lovers telling me that so I'd fuck them under the full moon. As long as I didn't let them mark me, it was just a good time, so it didn't matter.

Of course, after I found out West was my fated mate, I realized the need surrounding the Luna's arrival is pretty bad for females, too. I burned through a ton of batteries using a vibrator to keep me satisfied these last six months since I found it nearly impossible to turn to another male while West was still my Luna-given mate.

As a shifter, I know the Luna's cycle intimately. Already the need is clawing at me, and I still have six days to go until she's full. That means I have six days to make my decision because, if I do stay here, I'm going to fuck Chase. Already I feel like it's inevitable.

And though he vowed never to mark me until I agreed to let him, would he be able to control himself during mating? Or would his feral take over and, like he told me once before, decide to *rut* me until all of his lusts are spent and I'm his forever mate?

I don't know, but at least I have a few more days to figure it out.

TWELVE
BETRAYAL

After breakfast, Chase leaves the cabin. We're running low on groceries, and since he insists on serving me at least three home-cooked meals a day, plus snacks, he needs to restock his supplies.

I discover where he gets everything from. Using the same truck that brought me from Hickory to Chase's territory, he drives into Sacre Coeur and loads up the bed with everything he might need for a few weeks at a time. He went through it all faster with me here, so he needs to head back earlier than he expected.

I offered to go. Not because I'm itching to visit a Fang City—I'm *not*—but because I figured Chase would never leave me on my own. He doesn't say it with words, but I can tell that he still expects me to vanish anytime he takes his eyes off of me.

If my choice is between being chained again or seeing where the vampires live, I'll take a ride into town.

Surprisingly, Chase doesn't choose either option. He doesn't want to risk me being around vamps, and he already said he'd never chain me up again. This might be some kind of test on his part, but he lets me stay in the cabin by myself.

It's lonely without him. I don't realize how much I've grown used to his aura brushing up against mine until he's out of the reach of my wolf.

He swears he'll only be gone for a couple of hours, max. When I get tired of waiting—and it's only been about twenty minutes or so—I decide to visit the garden out back. Chase made sure to let me know that it was close enough to the cabin that it was safe from any vamps who might be patrolling nearby so I could go there without him.

I lose track of how long I'm outside. Despite the vampire stink that, surprisingly, I *have* gotten a little more used to, my wolf preens being surrounded by nature. Having all of these flowers around me, it's like a little slice of home.

I have trees. I have wildflowers. For the first time in so long, I'm content again. I'm not hiding in the woods to avoid the pitying looks back in Hickory. I'm sitting in the grass because that's where I feel the most at peace.

The only thing that would make it better? Was if Chase was with me.

When I feel a prickle against the back of my neck, I know that he's home again. Since he doesn't know I'm out here—and after a trip to Sacre Coeur, he might not be able to sniff past the vampire stink to find me—I climb up from the grass, then jog back to the house.

I'm actually kind of surprised by how much I miss him, and how much I want to see him again. Just the thought of seeing what he brought back for me has me moving faster. He'd promised me a gift for leaving me behind, and if there's one thing I know about him, it'll be something meaningful.

I enter through the front door, expecting to find him

waiting for me there. Nope. He's in here, I can sense him nearby, and I follow his aura to our bedroom.

Chase is pacing back and forth, muttering under his breath. So consumed by what he's doing, he doesn't even realize I've walked into the room until I call his name.

"Chase?"

"Quinn!" His head shoots up. A second later, he's lunging at me. "Where were you?"

He grabs my arm. It's not rough, but it's not a gentle caress, either.

What the hell?

I try to shake him off, immediately going on my guard. This isn't like the Chase I've come to know. "Let go of me."

He doesn't.

"You were gone. I couldn't scent you."

"Of course not. It stinks like fucking bloodsuckers out there, remember?"

His eyes are wild. I don't think he's listening to a word I say. His grip tightens. "I thought you left me."

"Why?" I shake my arm again, still trying to break out of his hold. I don't like the way he's looking at me right now. "You should've known better. I said I would stay. At least until the Luna appears again."

"You were lying to me."

I freeze. "What was that?"

Alphas know. It's just one more thing that makes them different than the other ranks of wolves. An alpha wolf instinctively senses when someone is lying to him.

I knew that. Not many shifters do, but the Alpha of the Sylvan Pack never hid that from the rest of us. Our old Alpha, Xavier, was open with that skill, too. Then, when he was younger, Bishop made a game of it among the shifters in our age group.

Chase is a born alpha. He might not have a pack, so he isn't a capital-a Alpha, but that doesn't change his rank. I guess… I just thought he didn't have the skill because he was feral. How many times have I lied to him? Whether on purpose or not, I must've done it a bunch of times. Did he ever call me out on it? No. So I thought he didn't know.

I was wrong.

I grit my teeth. I don't deny it, because he'll know that, too, but I do tug on his arm. "Does it matter? I'm still here. I stayed. Now, let go of me before I make you."

He does. Finally releasing me, he whirls away. I expect him to lash out, maybe punch the wall. He doesn't. He threads his fingers through his hair, leaving track marks with his claws, before he turns on me again.

"I need you, Quinn." His voice is soft. Broken. "When I thought you were gone… I don't think I can survive without you."

He might have to. "You barely know me."

The look he gives me just then calls me a liar without him saying the words.

He's right. Stalker or not, I have to admit he does know me.

The truth of just how much is in the clothes he bought me, everything in my size and close enough to my style that I probably would've picked out a bunch of those pieces myself. It's in the foods he prepares, and how often he serves me meals that are my favorites.

It's in the flowers out back that I was looking at just to be close to Chase while he was gone.

It's in the new pair of shoes laying on the bed, and the

expensive shampoo and conditioner set I mentioned preferring in one of our conversations.

See. A meaningful gift, just like I thought, all because he *does* know me.

Just like I've gotten to know him.

His chest is heaving. At his side, he's fisted his hands. Chase is on the edge of his control, and all because he'd convinced himself that I left him.

I think about what he just said. I don't want someone to *need* me. I want them to love me. To *choose* me.

Maybe… maybe this is the best I'm going to get.

Back in the Sylvan Pack, I'll never be mate material. Not when the pack gossips will always whisper that I belong to West. The way that males like Tucker and Eddie proposition me for a quickie in the woods… that's all I'll ever be good for.

Chase isn't perfect. He has his flaws. I mean, for Luna's sake, he's a feral! And, sure, he hasn't gone off the deep end since my first night in his cabin. The threat that he might is always there.

Only one thing can tame a wild feral wolf: his mate.

It's something I've been trying to ignore for two weeks now. He's been so good since I've been here, so different, and he whispers at night it's because of me. It's like how he's convinced it was Fate's hand that had him running past Hickory the day he found me. Even then he knew I could calm him. If he claims me as his mate, I might just be able to tame him.

He wouldn't go feral again. It's a weight on my shoulders I don't need, so I've purposely avoided dwelling on that fact.

I can't now.

What if… what if I gave him what he wanted? Instead of waiting for him to take it, like how he took me from my home,

I can offer it to him. It's not like he'd be my first. I mean, I've actually grown to like him which is more than I can say about some of the other males I've fucked.

This isn't a sudden impulse, either. While I was sitting near the garden, I kept thinking about it over and over again. Whether I want to be his mate or not is one thing. I definitely want to mate him at least once.

Why not now? Maybe it'll prove to Chase that there's a reason why I stayed.

I move into him. It takes all the courage I have, meeting his stare head-on and stepping close to an alpha that is bristling with unbridled emotion.

"Chase?"

He gulps. Something about the change in my tone has him watching me warily, though I can sense the lust and desire pouring off of him. He wants this as much as I do. More, actually.

"Yes?"

"Remember how we agreed you wouldn't even mention sex until I initiated it?"

His Adam's apple trembles. I watch it bob as he swallows roughly before grating out a very fierce, "I do."

"Well…" I open up my arms to him. "Consider this me initiating it."

That's all the permission I have to give him.

Chase falls on me. He buries his face in my hair, breathing deeply, before dropping his mouth to my neck. His hands are at my waist, holding me against him, though he leaves me a little room to work when I take a firm hold of his cock through his jeans.

Just like I expected, he's already hard. I'm ready for him, too. When he inhales deeply, then groans against my skin, I know he can tell. My arousal fills the room the same way his is a crackle in the air.

I flick open the button on his jeans with my free hand. He starts to suck at my neck, lapping at my skin, almost like he's tasting me. It feels so good, I tilt my head further, baring my throat to him in an instinctively submissive gesture.

My fingers reach for his zipper. His erection pulses against my palm.

His fangs sink into my neck.

I go motionless. It's a prey response, and one that pisses off this predator. But that's nothing compared to the realization of what Chase has just done. I initiated sex. I wanted to mate him. This was going to happen.

I had good intentions. And all that got shot to hell when he *bit* me.

This isn't a graze or a scratch. This isn't an accident. This is a male marking his female, making it so that every other shifter knows she's taken.

But he *promised* me...

Releasing Chase, my hands slam into his chest. I don't care that it's going to rip his fangs out of my neck. Using all of my sudden fury, I tap into my wolf and push him as far away from me as I possibly can.

He's strong. Too strong. Unlike the last time, I only get him a few feet away from me.

It's enough.

He freezes, like a deer caught in headlights. "Quinn, I... I don't know what came over me."

I do.

"You promised." My voice is low. It's full of agony and betrayal and rage. "You *promised*."

For a moment, I see the Chase I know. The horror that fills

his expression, the remorse in the depths of his golden gaze. My blood dribbles down his chin, and he wipes it away with a shaky—

Paw.

Shit!

It all happens so fast after that. His body crunches, his fangs grow longer, and his eyes lose any semblance of rational thought. He darts out his tongue, lapping at my blood that stains his lips, before throwing his head back and howling.

It's a song of need. Of lust.

Of possession.

I know then that Chase is too far gone. The beast has taken him over, and I'm not his mate. Not really. He might wear my bite on his skin, but I just refused to let him mark me. He bit me before I even got his zipper down, so it's not like we had sex to take off the edge. Besides, without the Luna being out to bless any mating, a bond won't form.

He loves me, though. He told me so.

He said he'd never hurt me.

I hold out a hand. Like his paw, it's also shaking. "Chase? Can you hear me?"

The feral lowers himself into a crouch.

Shit. I take a step back.

He pounces.

I turn and run.

It was in the way he held his hunched body. A split second before he moved, I was already going. I bolt through the exit to the bedroom, pausing only long enough to throw the door closed in his face.

I expect him to follow right behind me and I'm not disappointed. From the smash that happens, then the crash, I'm pretty sure the feral ripped off the bedroom door before throwing it down the hall.

Crap, crap, crap.

Chase isn't thinking. That thing… that isn't my Chase. He told me before that, when he's completely feral, he loses any conscious thought. The beast runs on instinct and urges. After I flipped out on him for trying to mark me, leaving him with his button undone and his heavy erection pushing against his zipper, it doesn't take a genius to figure out what he's after.

Me. He wants me.

Fuck that.

I throw open the door that leads to the basement, thundering down the stairs. I don't bother being quiet. I *want* him to know where I've gone.

I won't let him touch me again. He'd never forgive himself if he did in this state. I don't think I could forgive him, either.

In that moment, I don't even know if I can get past him biting me after he promised he wouldn't.

He accused me of lying. Maybe that's true, maybe I did plan on escaping at the first chance I got, but I didn't. I stayed.

He lied to me. Well, turnabout is fair fucking play.

I duck into my old room in the basement. There's only enough time for me to throw myself in the corner hidden in shadows before Chase comes thundering after me. He races into the room, but I'm ready for him.

He's huge, but I've been underestimated my whole life. Just because I'm a regular old shifter, nothing special, everyone thinks that I need someone to take care of me. Screw that. I can take care of myself.

I throw my body at Chase. Knowing that I'll get only one shot at this, I aim for his knees.

The element of surprise is the only thing on my side.

Chase would never expect me to attack him which just goes to show that maybe he doesn't know me as well as he likes to think he does. I'm still the same Quinn Malone that responded to a strange wolf encroaching on my territory by running first, then wheeling around to fight back.

That's what I do right now. To me, it's not fight or flight. It's a mixture of both.

I already ran. Time to throw down.

Or, better yet, throw the feral down.

Leading with my shoulder, I slam right into his knees. The force of my hit is enough to send the both of us flying across the room. Chase slams into the cinder block wall first, taking the brunt of the impact.

Just like I hoped.

When he's a feral, he can take a lot more damage than when he's in his skin or his fur. He's not invincible, though, and I made sure to hit him hard. Between me and the immovable cinder blocks, it's enough to stun even Chase. He collapses in a heap.

I make my move.

Running to the basement wasn't a mistake. Chase might've thought it was—with one high window and only one door, it was like heading straight toward a dead-end—but even in my panic and my sense of betrayal, I knew exactly what I was doing.

The chains are still down here. Even after he gave his word that he wouldn't use them on me again, he admitted he kept them in the basement in case I ever needed to use them on *him*.

Like, oh, maybe now?

There's no time to treat them with an extra layer of padding like he used to do for me. While the shackles are silver, and so is the length of the chain, the inside of the ankle cuff has been gilded. The gold doesn't completely shield the power of the silver—that's why Chase insisted on the fabric padding for me—but it'll offer him some protection.

It has to be enough. With my blood continuing to trickle down my chest, a stark reminder that Chase did this to himself, I grab the nearest shackle. Still open from the last time he unlocked it from me, I hurriedly attach it to the easiest part of Chase I can reach.

It's his wrist, and the shackle closes easily around it, snapping closed with an ominous *click*. It's looser than it would be on his ankle, but it's still tight enough to keep him in place.

My hand is already blistered from where I grabbed the shackle. I'd barely held it for five seconds, and the damage is almost enough to make me forget about the ache in my shoulder.

Almost.

Once he's trapped, I don't waste time hanging around. He was still huddled on the ground when I ran out on him, though the howl he lets out when he finally comes to again and sees what I've done shakes the whole fucking cabin as I dash up the stairs.

Welp, I think he just noticed that I trapped him in chains…

Good. Not only is this the payback I promised myself I'd get those rough days when all I knew was that I was a feral's captive, but only being chained by one shackle isn't that bad. Who knows? Maybe the sizzle and burn of the silver shackle will be a good enough reminder that, even if he believed I lied, so did he.

He said no pressure. He agreed to no sex unless I initiated it. And maybe I had, but I never once invited him to *mark* me.

So what if he wears my bite on his skin like a brand he's earned? To me, that's not a mate mark. That's a battle scar from when he attacked me, nothing more.

I can still feel the sting of his fangs sinking into the point where my shoulder meets my neck. Using the one drop of energy I can spare, I focus on beginning to heal his bite.

Only then do I head for the front door. Without a second look back—or even a second thought—I rip it off the hinges, then dash out into the darkness.

The sound of the feral's furious roar chases after me.

Ignoring that is easy. He's in the basement, and it's not as loud as it could've been.

Ignoring the pang in my heart that hurts so much worse than Chase's bite?

Yeah. That one's a little bit harder…

THIRTEEN
VAMPIRE

t's dusk. Not so dark out that I have to rely on my wolf's eyes to see, but the woods are gloomy. Unfriendly. The vampire stench doesn't help.

It surrounds me. Any resistance I built earlier is gone. The weight of the bloody aroma is heavy on my shoulders as I sprint through the trees.

I'm in my skin. I thought about letting my wolf take the lead, but since I have nothing but the clothes on my back to find my way home, I'd rather not run around butt-naked if I don't have to. Shifters don't mind nudity. Humans… they definitely do.

Of course, if it's the better option, I'll shift. For now, I'm moving at a quick clip, anger at Chase spurring to run faster. Now that it's his turn to be chained up, I know he can't come right after me, but he will eventually. I just have to be back in Hickory before he does.

Then, once I let Bishop know that he needs to train the pack patrol better, Chase will never get to me again. And if I feel a pang at that thought, it's nothing. Just a stitch in my side from not having run in so long…

I pour on the speed, desperate to outrun the thoughts in my head. For some reason, every instinct inside of me is telling me to turn around. To go back to him.

Am I insane? Is Chase rubbing off on me? I always knew I was a broken she-wolf deep down, but this is nuts.

I can't go back. I left. I've made my choice. I have to deal with it.

Later, I'll blame what happens next on how I was more focused on what I left behind than where I was going—or who I might run into. By the time I realize that I can sense someone closing in on me from behind, and that they carry the stink of the undead with them, it's too late.

I try to escape my vampire pursuer anyway, silently chastising myself as I tear a path forward.

What were you thinking, Quinn? He warned you about the woods! He warned you that this was as much vamp land as it was his. Chase said I'd never survive it out here without him.

Luna damn it, I think he's right.

I'm flying through the trees. Vampires don't have wings, but somehow the corpse following me has kept up. Worse, he jumps out in front of me when I least expect it, as if I made a circle or something instead of fleeing straight.

Vampires are beautiful. It's just a fact of life. I've never heard of an ugly one since their supernatural looks have long been a lure for them to snare their human prey. They need to feed, and they need to compel the non-supes to let them. Sure, they could just take the blood, but it's easier to return to a donor when they *want* you to feed on them. Good looks and charm go a long way to hide what monsters the bloodsuckers truly are.

The male who jumps out in front of me is no exception. His skin is perfectly creamy, without a single imperfection to mar it. His hair is golden blond, tousled in careless curls, with one stray curl falling forward, centered in the middle of his line-free forehead. His cheekbones are chiseled, his mouth full and sullen.

The pout becomes a smile when he sees me, panting and obviously afraid.

He's a vamp. I'm not an idiot.

I'm *terrified*.

"Look what we have here. Pretty little donor." His voice is eerily seductive. I shiver. "I caught your blood on the air. I already knew it was sweet, but you… this is my lucky day."

Are you kidding? Desperately ignoring the hungry look on his otherworldly features, I think about what he said? He could scent my blood? How—

It hits me. Chase's bite. I'm still wearing the blood on my skin from Chase's bite.

Damn it!

"I guess I never expected it to belong to such a female. Pretty enough to eat, you are. Such a shame you're one of *them*."

Them. A shifter. He knows what I am.

Worse? His eyes are red.

Ah, crap.

Every pup learns the rhyme: *When a vamp's eyes go red, run or you're dead.* Red eyes mean that a vampire is either a rogue— the vamp version of a feral—or in the throes of bloodlust.

I'm lost out here. Apart from this beautiful monster, I'm also alone. The air stinks of blood, but it's pouring off of the male standing right in front of me. He's already fed tonight.

Does that stop him from targeting me?

Not even a little.

I make it five running steps before he's on me. His arms wrap around me like steel bands, lifting me up off of the ground so that my neck is right at his mouth.

"It doesn't have to hurt," he tells me in undisguised glee. "For one of your kind, I'll make sure it does."

Sick bastard. His fangs sink into my neck like a pair of knives stabbing me. With his first pull, it's like fire has flooded my veins as he sucks my blood. I scream, hating myself that he got a reaction out of me, but it *hurts*.

Which is exactly his point.

Shifters aren't used to pain. We heal too fast, and even when we come into contact with silver—something that is deadly to us—it's bearable until it *isn't*. Suddenly, I completely understand why vampires are our ancient enemies. With their bite, they could bring even an alpha to their knees.

I'm no alpha. I'm a delta, and I'm about to fucking die in these woods in the arms of a vampire and there isn't a damn thing I can do about it.

I shouldn't have run. Almost delirious, I realize that, if my fate was to be bitten tonight, there's only one male I want biting me.

Chase.

With the vampire's arms squeezing me tighter than an anaconda, his fangs digging deeper into my neck as he takes deep pulls that have me crying out in pain, I can't help but cling to the memory of Chase like a lifeline.

Even when he was a feral, he never turned on me. When he bit me, he was kind. Gentle. He lapped at my skin, marking me with a reverence we reserve for the Luna.

And while I had no choice but to leave him before he did

something one of us would regret, I probably shouldn't have taken off so recklessly into the woods.

It hits me then. Really hits me. I'm about to die. This vampire is too strong. He's draining me right now. My wolf is almost feral herself, desperate to do anything to survive, but my human half is no match for him. And all I can think about is Chase.

It could've been so different. *We* could've been. So hung up on the idea of a fated mate, I thought I needed West. I don't. All my life, I've known that Fate—in the form of our goddess, the Luna—would have the final say when it comes to my life. That includes everything: my pack, my rank, even my forever mate.

I hate it. I always have. It's why I've rebelled since I was a pup. Whether it was taking to the woods to be alone, or accepting as many lovers as were willing to fuck me, or eating in my cabin while the rest of the pack was in the pack circle… *I* wanted to choose. I want my life to be *mine*.

It's why I fought so hard against Chase. No matter how much I felt for him and his situation, and Luna knows if things had been different, I probably would've wanted to jump him from the beginning… he chose me. I didn't choose him.

So why did I follow along with the idea of West being my fated mate for so long? That's not me. That's not Quinn Malone. For the last six months, I've been agreeing to something that I would've normally shot my middle finger at, wishing that West would give up the mate of his heart and fall in line because Fate said so.

Why would I want him to do that? I like West. We've always been friendly, and though I was drawn to him, I knew he belonged to Helene. That hadn't changed.

So why had I?

I've heard that your life flashes before your eyes when you're about to die. Not me. I see things oh so clearly, even as my vision begins to grow spotty.

I don't want West. I never did.

As for Chase…

I wish things had been different. At the very least, I wish we had made it to the Luna. I would've loved to know what decision I'd have gone with if I stayed.

My legs are weak. I suspect that I'm only on my feet because he's holding me up. The vampire is still feeding, and I don't know how much more blood I can stand to give him before I'm fully drained.

How will my feral react when he finds my lifeless body in his woods? He's already broken. I think this… this might shatter him.

I'm so sorry, Chase…

A familiar aura brushes up against me. For a second, I think this is delirium brought on by blood loss. I left him chained in the basement. No way he could've figured a way out already *and* tracked me down. It's impossible. It has to be.

But what if it's not?

If Chase is out there, I'm not going to just roll over and become this vampire's meal. I can't believe I submitted to him as much as I did. He's strong, sure, but I'm a fucking shifter. A Luna damned she-wolf.

With my last burst of strength, I tear my neck away from his fangs at the same time as I bury my elbows in his gut. The vampire—too complacent, and probably drunk on my blood—isn't expecting it. He grunts, and I rip myself out of his loose hold.

I break free, putting a good ten feet between us as my hand clamps over the brutal bite he left on my throat. Vamp bastard got the right vein because he tapped me like a fucking fountain. Hot blood is gushing past my fingers, pooling on my shoulders before dripping down my back.

I glare at him.

What a messy eater. I've never been this close to a vampire—before Chase, I've rarely even left pack land—but you'd think that a bloodsucker would know how to feed without having it stain his lips and dribble down his chin.

His red eyes are shining, almost like his irises are filled with blood. His grin widens, revealing his fangs. They're almost three inches long.

His voice has gone thick and throaty as he demands, "Give me more."

He doesn't do that weird super fast gliding thing like before when he first captured me. Instead, savoring my fear and my pain, he stalks toward me.

Asshole.

I stumble back, relying on the last of my wolf's strength to keep me moving. "No fucking way! Leave me alone, you freak!"

"I'm not a freak," he sniffs. Oh, great. I've offended one of the undead when I'm barely staying on my feet. "You are. And you're a trespasser here. Worse, you're a *dog*. I'd put you down for that crime alone, but your blood... it sings to me. I think I'll have another taste. If you're lucky, I won't drain you completely. Then maybe you can think of a way to convince me to keep you."

If I wasn't half-dead from the 'taste' he'd already taken, I'd snap out a kick to his legs, or maybe aim for the bulge those leather pants of his aren't doing anything to hide.

Some way to convince him? Yeah. It doesn't take a genius to figure out what the corpse is thinking. He might have a hate hard-on for shifters, but that won't stop him from sinking his fangs in my neck again or shoving his cock inside of me.

I'd rather fucking die.

The aura brushes against me again. It's like a caress, and one that bolsters me and my wolf. Deep inside of me, she throws back her head, singing a sweet song to her mate.

My bond with West is wide open. In a rush of panic after I ran from Chase's cabin, I demolished the block I'd kept up these last couple of weeks. I wanted West to find me. I wanted my pack to know where I was. With Chase chained in the basement, I could finally escape—so long as I made it out of these woods. I wanted them to know I was alive.

And if anything happened to me? I wanted West to sense it so that the pack could stop wondering where I'd disappeared off to.

Is my wolf singing for West? No. He never could've made it from Hickory so soon, plus I haven't felt an answering tug from him since I opened it. That's not surprising—distance does play a factor in how a bond reacts between promised mates—but the wolf mine is calling to isn't a sleek grey wolf.

It's a big, black behemoth.

"Chase?" I whisper.

His aura pulses, so incredibly dominant that it nearly brings me to my knees.

It doesn't, though. It wouldn't. Alphas can make any other shifter submit, but not their mate. Instead, his aura lends me strength, and I put a few more feet between me and the vampire threat the second before I instinctively sense his approach.

He's here.

He's found me.

And though he's in his skin—and not his feral beast form,

either—the look on his face is fierce and wild as he leaps into the woods, landing in a crouch that shows off his powerful torso.

"Get away from her," Chase snarls, spit flying as he stares down the vampire. "She's no trespasser. She's my mate."

Maybe it's the blood loss after all, but my wolf definitely thinks so.

I don't know how he got here. Unless he kept a key to the chains in the pocket of his jeans or… or he swapped out the injection stores in the cylinder on his chain for a key instead… I don't know, but he's here, and I've never been more glad to see my feral in my life.

The vampire's whole demeanor changes. Chase is at his back, and he quickly palms his crotch before reacting.

Silly Quinn. I thought he was going to face off against my feral. Nope. As if he senses he needs some leverage, he flies toward me, putting me back in that iron-tight hold before I can blink.

Chase lets out a warning rumble.

The vampire smiles as he turns so that we're facing him—and Chase can see that he has an arm around my waist, his hand at my throat.

"Wilder. I didn't know she was yours."

Chase's last name is Wilder? Any other time I would've laughed at how fitting that was, but I'm half-drained. Barely standing. If it wasn't for the vampire still holding me close as though he's using me as a shield, I think I would've dropped already. Blood loss isn't as bad as a heavy dose of quicksilver— at least I can still tap into my poor, whimpering wolf—but it's a close second.

Chase circles him, growling softly under his breath.

The vampire moves in sync with him, dragging me as he

goes. My head is feeling kind of woozy, but I'm still coherent enough to realize that my instinct was spot-on. The vamp is using me to protect himself from my furious feral.

"You knew this was my land," Chase says at last. "You knew she carried my scent—"

"I never—"

"Don't deny it," growls Chase. "She sleeps in my bed. Lives in my cabin. I stroke her hair to soothe myself so don't you fucking insult me by pretending you didn't recognize that she belongs to me. And you *bit* her."

His soft chuckle tells me that the vamp's given up on pretending he's innocent in how he treated me. How can he? My blood's still flowing!

"You're right," he says, digging his fingers into the virgin side of my throat. It's better than him poking his bite, but not by much. "I did. And I'll do it again."

"You'll die first!"

The vampire pauses. "Is that a challenge? You dogs… you do so love a challenge. If it is, I accept. Last male standing gets the female for their own needs. What do you say, Wilder?"

I don't know what Chase is going to say, but I think the vampire is a moron.

This vampire might know enough about shifters to recognize me as one, but not enough to realize that you *never* come between a male wolf and the female he claims as his.

Good. He deserves whatever's coming to him when Chase rasps out, "I accept."

When the vampire sets me aside, promising to finish what we started as soon as he's done, it's all I can do not to laugh. He's signing his own death warrant and he doesn't even know it.

He opens his mouth, making sure Chase can see his long,

pointy fangs. He flexes his fingers, his fingernails sharpening into claws. And then he grins.

Sick bastard.

Chase obviously agrees. His golden eyes flashing, he lets his feral beast out in a heartbeat. Bones crunch, deadly claws of his own unsheathe from his newly formed, furless paws, while fangs thicker than the vamp's—if not as long—jut from a crowded mouth.

He snarls, and the vampire flies at him. The sound their bodies make when they collide rattles the whole damn woods.

In reality, the fight doesn't last long. What seems like an eternity is probably only three or four minutes tops, but in a challenge? That *is* an eternity. I go light-headed from holding my breath in worry, silently cheering Chase on so that I don't distract him.

Did I think the air couldn't stink more of blood? I'm wrong. As soon as the two males collide, fangs flashing, claws slashing, bones crunching as they try to rip each other apart… the whole forest becomes covered in blood. The vamp stink grows worse, but Chase's blood joins it.

The scent of his blood makes my wolf insane. Only knowing that it's against pack law to interfere with a challenge keeps me on the edge of their battle. Even if a vampire isn't aware of our traditions, breaking them might be the one thing that Chase will never forgive me.

I can't help him.

Good thing that, nearing the end of the fight, I realize that he doesn't need my help. He's as battered as the vamp, but Chase wants the win more. I almost wonder if he let the vampire get some nasty hits in just so he could maneuver him into a better position because, as soon as Chase locks his hands around the vampire's throat, his muscles bulge and he not only snaps the vampire's neck. He turns it into a stump!

The second the vampire is *dead* dead—and having your head ripped clean off your shoulders is a pretty good sign you're not gonna come back from that—Chase drops the head, kicks the body aside, then staggers toward me.

Right before he reaches me, he drops. Panic welling up inside of me, I throw myself down to my knees. He's on his, slumping forward, and through the patchy fur that covers his bare chest, all I see are gaping wounds and smears of blood.

Chase killed the vampire, but it hadn't been easy.

"Chase? Are you okay?"

At the sound of my frantic voice, the big idiot starts crawling on his knees toward me. His one hand is tucked to his torn-up chest, but he uses the other to gesture for me.

I hobble toward him.

He hooks his arm around me, pulling me against his body. Blood—the vampire's and Chase's—covers my clothes. I don't give a shit. I wrap my arms around his middle, just grateful we're both alive.

He's murmuring something into my hair. It's unintelligible over his choppy breathing. Before long, I realize he's not saying words, but making soothing sounds to calm the both of us. Bowing over my body, he laps at my ripped throat, cleaning out the vampire's mark on my skin. Half-feral, half-Chase, he's gentle as ever as he tends to me, mere seconds after ruthlessly decapitating a vampire.

Some girls like flowers. Luna knows I do. But to protect me? To keep me safe?

Is there anything sexier than that?

I want to tell him I'm sorry. That he shouldn't have bitten

me, but that I shouldn't have run away. That I didn't truly believe he'd always come for me until he did.

I want to ask him how he found me.

But I don't. As I shift in his arms, deciding it's my turn to tend to his wounds, to make sure that my protector isn't too injured, I begin to notice all of the gouges, the claw marks, the scratches, and the bites that cover him.

Vampires are nasty fighters. They have claws and fangs, too, just like us shifters, but they can access them in their two-legged form in a way that most shifters can't. Alphas have more control over their bodies than regular wolves, but Chase didn't rely on his alpha side. He nearly went full-feral to fight that vamp, and he barely won.

Once I take stock of the wounds on his chest—some of them slowly beginning to close over—I see why the fight was as close as it was.

Picking up his hand, careful not to jostle it when he doesn't hide his wince, I stare down at it in horror.

"Holy shit, Chase! Did the vampire do this to you?"

"No." His voice is harsh. Choppy. He still answers me. "I did that."

His hand is mangled. *Chewed.* The bones are crushed. The skin around his wrist is burned through, angry, red, and raw.

And I remember. The shackle.

The silver.

With a guilty pit forming in my belly, I admit that the silver explains the burns. But what about the rest of his hand?

My voice is a shaky whisper as I ask, "What did you do?"

"I needed to get out of the chains," he explains, as if attempting to gnaw off your own hand to get out of a shackle is the most rational thing in the world. "You were scared. I had to get to you."

I *was* scared. Terrified, actually, once I realized I had a vampire on my tail.

But how did he *know*?

My wolf yips, trying to get me to understand. I'm still feeling muddled. I have no idea what she's trying to tell me.

I'd opened up the bond I shared with West, hoping he might sense me on the other end and know that I was in trouble. That I needed help. With Chase in chains, I thought it was safe. He wouldn't be able to fight West, and I might be able to find the escape I've been looking for.

Only Chase found me first.

"How did you know?"

With his good hand, he pounds his bloody chest. "I felt you. In here."

"Like… like a bond?"

His eyes gleam, and I know that's exactly what he thinks it is.

"It's been there since the beginning," he says gruffly, daring me to argue. When I don't, he adds, "I told you. Fuck Fate. I chose you. My wolf did, too. Everything I am… everything I'll ever be… it's always been yours. I was just waiting for you to notice."

Oh, believe me.

I'm definitely noticing.

FOURTEEN
DINNER

Chase doesn't have a phone in his cabin.

I already knew that. He made it clear when he removed my chains for the last time. A loner by choice even before he turned feral, he had no friends. No family. It was like pulling teeth to get him to admit as much—though I kind of guessed already—and he only did to point out the fact that he very rarely had contact with the outside world.

Translation: no one would hear me scream.

He has no one to call, so of course he doesn't have a phone; I don't, either, since mine is somewhere back in Hickory, I'm sure. To let Henry know that he had to kill the vampire that attacked us, Chase would have to head into Sacre Coeur and meet the leader of the Cadre at his office in person.

He heads out the morning after. He refuses to go until he's sure I'm completely healed, and I do the same for him. By the time he carries me back to the cabin, both of my bites are gone. Smartly, he doesn't mention the one he gave me, only fussing over the one I got courtesy of the vamp.

Chase takes a little longer to heal. He really did a number on his hand, and that's not counting the injuries he got fighting a vampire hopped up on shifter blood. I made him take a shower so I could see how bad they were when the blood washed off. When I saw they were worse than I thought, I made him lie down.

My feral alpha was as submissive as a kitten. He went straight to bed, and I searched the bathroom for the salve he had that would speed up his healing. It was the jar he used when the silver of the chains burned my skin the time I tried to snap them. I figured, if it worked on silver, it might work on vampire bites, and it did.

Score one for Quinn.

By morning, he was healed up, too. There was no delaying it at that point. He had to go see Henry.

He assured me they have a good working relationship. I still don't quite understand why Chase would've chosen to live just off of a Fang City in the first place. At least, with the fang around his neck, I knew he would be safe when he meets with Henry.

I stayed behind. Of course I did. Chase wants to protect me, and there's no denying that I'm the one that vamp targeted. He doesn't want it to happen again. Neither do I.

That's why, after Chase sets out, I decide to stick inside of the cabin. I would've liked to visit the garden, but considering what happened the last time I did—Chase going feral, me going on the run, the vamp biting the shit out of my neck after Chase already had—it's probably a better bet to stay inside.

Chase wasn't sure how long he'd be. It all depended on Henry's busy schedule and when the Cadre leader could fit him in. He promised that, at the latest, he'd be home by dinner.

Taking him at his word, I figure out how I'm going to spend the day so I don't go crazy worrying about him telling the most powerful vampire nearby that he killed one of his.

I'm going to cook dinner.

Way I see it, it's my turn to feed him. I think of it as a thank you for saving my life, and if he wants to read more into it, well… he wouldn't be wrong.

The kitchen is stocked. The pantry is full. He has a freezer full of every kind of meat a shifter could want. I pick out a beef tenderloin, then grab a bag of potatoes to start peeling.

I'm not the quickest cook. I make a disaster in the kitchen, and it takes me twice as long because I try to clean up as I go. At least I'm sure it'll be somewhat tasty when it's done. Plus, Chase is a little later than I thought he'd be, so that gives me enough time to let the tenderloin rest when it's done.

I made mashed potatoes and asparagus as a side. I toasted pre-made rolls in the oven and left a crock of butter out to soften. I'm just setting the rolls down on the table with the rest of the food when I hear the front door to the cabin open.

The stink of vampire filters in first, though it's almost immediately replaced by Chase's musk. His alpha aura reaches out to caress my skin, as if he's searching for me.

I give him a hand. "In the kitchen!"

Apart from looking exhausted, he's in one piece. I sniff. He doesn't have any blood on him.

That's a good sign.

"How did it go?"

"Henry understood. That's all that matters. Nolan came on my land and he targeted my mate." He pauses, waiting for me to argue with him. His eyes spark again when I don't. "We both know I had every right to kill him for biting you. He won't retaliate."

I blink. "Retaliate? Was that something that might've happened?"

He doesn't say anything. He just stares at the spread I have out on the table.

"Chase?"

"I… don't worry about it. Everything's fine."

If he says so. He's too preoccupied with the food. I'll just have to get more out of him later.

For now—

I wait for him to ask me about the meal. When he doesn't, I gesture for him to sit. "As you can see, I just finished cooking dinner for you." Not us, Chase. *You*. Hint, hint. "Sit with me. Let's eat. I mean, you've got to be hungry."

"I'm starved," Chase admits. He hesitates, and when he glances over at me, I swear I see hope burning in the depths of his golden eyes. "You cooked this? For me?"

"Yup." He's still standing there. "Aren't you going to eat?"

"Actually, I wanted to talk to you about something first."

"Oh." I try to hide my disappointment. I should've guessed cooking for him would lose any meaning after how many times I reminded him I was only eating because I had to. "Yeah. Sure. Food can wait."

Chase's gaze roves over my face. I don't know what he sees there, but it has him sitting down and reaching for the fork. With intense focus, he starts shoveling the food into his mouth.

I stifle a short giggle, irrationally pleased that he's tasting my food. "Slow down. You're going to choke."

"Can't," he says around a mouthful of potato. "It's too delicious."

"Eh. It's passable."

"You made this for me. I've never had better."

Oh. My cheeks warm as I flush in pleasure at his compliment.

Okay, then.

I join him at the table, taking a seat across from Chase. I go to make my own plate. Before I can grab it, he stops chewing and immediately takes the plate out of my hand. He's not rough, though he is determined to take it off of me, so I let him have it.

Chase swallows his mouthful, then starts piling food up on my plate. I watch as he picks the largest piece of tenderloin left on the serving dish before scooping out some mashed potatoes meticulously. He grabs one roll, thinks better of it, then reaches for one just a shade more golden brown.

No asparagus, I notice. I've given up wondering how he knows when he does shit like this, but I *hate* asparagus. I only cooked it because it was in the fridge so I figured it was something Chase liked.

After placing the plate in front of me, he slides the rest of the asparagus onto his own plate. He eats it all.

As I eat like a normal shifter who isn't trying to gorge themself and get sick, Chase slows down. He matches my pace, the two of us having a companionable meal. I can still sense that he has something he wants to talk about, but he waits until we're both done with dinner, the dishes soaking in the sink, and the two of us sitting on the couch together before he mentions it again.

"Is it okay? Can we talk now?"

He looks so solemn, I can't help but tease him. "Hey… what's up with the long face? You're not breaking up with me, are you?"

Chase looks away.

What?

"Shit. I was kidding. What…" I move so that I'm standing in front of him. He still can't quite meet my eye. "Chase. Look at me."

A horrible suspicion slams into me as our eyes meet. My hand flies to my mouth. Between the gaps in my fingers, I say, "It happened, didn't it? When you went to the Fang City… you found your mate."

I always knew it wasn't me. I knew he had to have one out there.

Holy shit. Was it a vampire?

"I thought it was so weird that you'd want to live by vampires. I mean, it reeks, but you don't seem to mind it. I guess that would make total sense if you're supposed to be the mate of one of those fucking corpses. See! I knew it! All your talk of choosing me, of wanting me… you found her, didn't you? Is she pretty? Oh, Luna. And I fed you—"

Okay. I might've jumped the gun a little there. Chase's mouth had fallen open while I ranted, but since he didn't stop me, I kept on going. I probably wouldn't have stopped if it wasn't for the way that he finally breaks free of his sudden paralysis, hurrying toward me and placing his hands on my shoulders.

"Quinn."

"She's probably blonde, like Helene. With dainty little fangs and—"

"*Quinn.*"

I gulp. "What?"

"I didn't meet any other females, especially not a vamp one. And I'm not breaking up with you. You're mine. Until you walk away from me, you'll always be mine. That.. that's not what I wanted to talk about."

"Then what did you?"

He lets go of my shoulders, putting some space between us.

"Chase?"

"Look, I know I've fucked this up since day one. Every time I think I'm getting better, I inevitably screw up again. Like last night. I'm not doing it on purpose. Being an alpha… my wolf is strong enough to take what I want, and my feral side tells me I should. But I want you so bad that it means nothing if you're only here because I'm bigger than you or because I'm more dominant. You were right before. I'm not your mate. I'm only your captor."

He *was* my captor. That fact won't change.

But, when I was hiding from the vampire, it was Chase I thought of. It was Chase who I wanted to find me.

He said he would come after me. He did.

"You were," I begin, "but now—"

He gives his head a sharp shake. "I'm still feral. Last night proved that. I want to say I won't lose control again. I want to promise I won't bite you again. But I did that, and no matter how much I want you to trust me… to love me… to *choose* me… how can I expect you to do that when I can't even trust myself?"

"It's not you. It's the feral—"

"It's me. If you knew what made me like this…"

I take his hand in mine. "Then tell me. Help me understand."

Because he might've said he wasn't breaking up with me, but this ain't my first rodeo. This sounds like a textbook dumping speech.

It's not you, it's me…

Chase squeezes my fingers. And then, after a shuddering breath, he begins to speak.

I listen without a sound—or judgment.

"I was born into a small pack on the West Coast. The Wilder Pack. There were only ten of us, and I was the only one who was a true alpha from the time I was six. They couldn't let a six-year-old run the pack, obviously, so our Beta stepped up. My dad refused to leave our land, so we stayed. I always knew I'd take over when I got older, but power is a heady thing. Dane didn't want to give over control to me. He wanted to keep it. I let him. I was only fifteen. I didn't care. He did. He tried to push me from the pack, telling me a young alpha needed to see the world.

"I didn't know he was trying to get rid of me. He wanted me to leave. I left because it was Alpha's orders. At least... I told myself that because I didn't want to admit that my wolf was chafing against having to listen to a less dominant leader. It was better to be on my own."

I nod. I know exactly what he means. Almost everyone in the Sylvan Pack was more dominant than me, so maybe not that part, but being on my own? I was as much of a lone wolf as I could be while still staying a packmate.

Taking heart in my nod, Chase leads me over to the couch again. Once we're seated, he continues.

"I spent months away at a time, but I always went back. Until... one day, about a year later, they were all gone. No," he corrects, "not gone. *Dead.* My whole pack was wiped out by a single rogue vampire that stumbled on their territory." He pauses, then glances at the closed window. "He was from Sacre Coeur."

I gasp. "No."

"Yes. It took me three years to find him. All I had was his

stink mingling with the blood of my family. Blood and death…
it wasn't easy, but I was determined. I was nineteen when I
tracked him to the Fang City, but I'd been a lone wolf all that
time. I wasn't strong enough to fight him. So I bided my time,
staking this land out as mine."

Still holding onto my hand as if it's a lifeline, he uses the
other to gesture around him. "I built this cabin. Brick by brick,
board by board. I had money. Everything that belonged to my
old pack was mine, and I used it for my vengeance. I bought
this land, so the vampires couldn't expand past their borders,
and I built this cabin with the goal of one day finding a way
past the vampires so that I could slaughter one of their own."

He says he was nineteen. The male in front of me is in his
late twenties at least, if not his early thirties.

"Did you?" I whisper. For the young alpha he was, I
desperately hope the answer is yes.

"No."

Damn it.

He sighs. "The Cadre knew I was here. They knew what I
was doing. They let me build the cabin, and they allowed me
to test their borders. I think… I think I amused Henry. That's
a rarity to someone as old as he is, and because I did, he left
me to it. He's a good judge of character, Henry. He knew I
wanted revenge for something. He guessed I planned on
attacking his city. He would've stopped me if I tried, but…"

His voice trails off. I can sense how much this is costing
him, finally telling me the truth of his past, but as much as I
need to hear this, he needs to say it.

So, with another squeeze, I wordlessly encourage Chase to
continue.

He does.

"It was one vampire who destroyed my pack. A rogue who

was good at pretending he was sane." Chase scoffs. "Kind of like me. He was responsible. Not the humans who live in the Fang City for supernatural protection. Not the vamps just living their lives. One male. I couldn't hurt the others. I just wanted *him*.

"Henry found out who I was hunting. I don't know how, and I've never asked. It was a couple of years after I finished my cabin. I'd given up hope of finding my parents' murderer, but I stayed because I couldn't go back home. Then, one day, the leader of the Cadre showed up on my doorstep. Henry found the rogue, and he had him executed. He brought me his head, then he gave me his fang." Chase pats the vampire fang hanging off of his chain. "We made our deal that day. I got my revenge. If he wanted to share my territory, I was more than happy to. But…"

Somehow, I knew there would be a 'but'. "But?"

"But there was a problem. Henry killed Lucius for me. I got my revenge. I was satisfied. My wolf… wasn't."

"Oh."

"I thought losing my pack was the worst thing that could happen. I was wrong, Quinn. Do you know what really is? Apart from losing a mate, that is?"

I shake my head.

"Losing the last of my humanity."

And… there it is.

"That's how you became feral," I say, understanding the point of everything he just told me. "Your wolf didn't get to avenge his fallen packmates."

"I managed to stay sane up until about a year ago. It was fighting a losing battle. For years, I could feel my wolf twisting, changing, breaking. Eventually, my outside matched the way my wolf felt. After that, I could *only* feel when that… thing was in control. When that happened, I ran from here. I ran and I ran, and I didn't stop running until the time I passed the outer limits of a wolf territory and the most enticing scent stopped me in my tracks."

The whole time he was talking, Chase would only look at me for a split second before he glanced away. He stared at his lap. He stared at our joined hands. He looked over at the doorway to his cabin or watched the empty fire grate.

Just then he meets my eyes again. And, this time, he keeps his gaze on me.

"Rainwater," he whispers. "You smell like rainwater and hope. You smell like the home I lost, and the one I would've done everything to have again." His chest rises, then falls with the force of his exhale. "Even make you a feral's captive. And now you know it."

His expression says he believes that, now that he's told me his truth, I'll get up and leave him.

I tried. It didn't take.

Hey. I'm a shifter. I'll always see things differently. My wolf was smitten almost from the beginning. Chase won her over with his plotting, his dedication, his show of strength, and the way he proved that he could take care of me.

My human half took a little more convincing. But after I saw the garden… Yeah. I didn't stand a chance.

He was so sure he could convince me to stay. Damn it, he was right.

"Okay."

He leans back, taking in my whole face. "Okay?" he echoes.

I shrug. "Hey. You said to give you until the Luna. Just because you broke your vow, doesn't mean I'm going to break mine."

He opens his mouth.

"Me running from you doesn't count. You were feral, and I was pissed off from being bitten. Not either of our finest moments."

Chase exhales softly. "Do you mean it? Could you… do you think you might choose me? Someday?"

I'm still holding his hand. I lift up, pressing my lips to his heated skin, enjoying the way it makes my feral alpha rumble. "I think I might be able to do that."

FIFTEEN
SANDALWOOD

id I think that Chase seemed different in the days following him first bringing me to his cabin? That's nothing compared to the change that comes over him after I give him one last chance to prove himself.

At least, that's what he thinks he's doing. Me? I'm pretty much a done deal.

He chose me. As a wolf, a man, or some twisted combination of both with piss poor self-control, he wanted me. How could a she-wolf who desired nothing more than to be loved put up a fight against *that*?

He won me over slowly. A couple of weeks might not seem like slow to a non-shifter, but it is. We usually know our mates instinctively—whether they're given to us by the Luna or we choose them on our own—and if I hadn't been so hung up on West, maybe I would've seen what was right in front of me all along.

I fell for the broken male who lost everything, yet who could still touch me as though I was more than that.

The Luna is almost completely full. Four days until she's at her peak and any shifter couples could perform the Luna Ceremony and receive her blessing and a bond. Unless something goes terribly wrong between now and then, I might just be a mated she-wolf in a couple of more days.

Do I tell Chase that? Nah. Though I've basically gotten past his way of courting me in the beginning—he's a feral, and I finally understand that part of him will probably always be whether we have a bond or not—I still get a little pleasure making him squirm.

Besides, nothing ever goes right for me. I guess, deep down, I'm still waiting for something to go wrong.

Two days after the vampire attacked me, I'm afraid it does.

We're sitting in the living room. Though Chase has a television, he rarely uses it, and I kind of commandeered it over the last couple of weeks. He doesn't have internet or streaming services like we do back in Hickory—something I will be changing ASAP—but he gets a couple of basic cable channels.

It's after dinner. He's sitting on the couch, bare-chested as always, while I'm curled up into his side. The warmth of his skin does more to heat me up than the fire we lit earlier. It's cozy. Homey. My wolf is dozing, content to be so close to her mate, while I breathe in Chase's intoxicating musk.

I feel safe with him. Something I never would've believed after his ambush, but I do. He's my protector. I can let down my guard with him because I know that Chase never will.

So when his body goes hard and tight, stiffening beneath my cheek? I notice.

I glance up at him. His cheeks are hollowed. His nostrils are flaring.

His golden eyes have that warning gleam I know so well.

I sit up. "What's wrong?"

He doesn't deny it. Instead, placing one hand possessively on my thigh, he grates out one word: "Vampires."

"What?"

"I sense them. They're on our immediate territory." He narrows his gaze, concentrating. "At least two. I sense a female and a male, but there could be more. They're heading this way."

I'm not even a little surprised that he can tell. Bishop is like that, too. An Alpha imprints on their pack and his territory, all the more reason I still have trouble understanding how Chase was able to infiltrate Hickory without even Bishop knowing.

Then again, maybe he did. One of an Alpha's main jobs is to make sure their packmates are protected. If he sensed Chase stalking me and could tell that he was no danger to me, maybe he let him. Could be.

When it comes to Chase, though, I don't doubt his instincts. We might be a pack of two now, but he's lived on this land for almost twelve years. He knows every inch of it the same way that I could navigate the woods of Hickory blindfolded if I had to. If someone is trespassing out there, he'll know it.

He looks pissed, but not surprised.

"Were you expecting visitors?" I ask.

He shakes his head. "No. I talked to Henry. I told him what happened. Nolan attacked my mate. He forfeited his life when he bit you. Even if he hadn't challenged me, by vamp law, I could take his head."

Pack law is clear like that, too. I'd wondered if the vampires would be ticked off that Chase killed one of their own, but he assured me that that wasn't the case.

So what are vampires doing here?

When I ask Chase that, he squeezes my thigh, then rises up

from the couch. "I don't know, but I'm going to find out. Stay inside the cabin. I'll be right back."

I nod. "You better, or I'm coming after you."

Despite the fierce look in his eyes, his lips curve. He loves it when I show concern for him, even if it's pretty much unnecessary.

With a stolen kiss to the top of my head, Chase heads out of the room. He disappears down the hall, returning less than a minute later. He's tugged on a t-shirt, pulling his necklace out so that the fang is on display. As always, he's barefoot, but he must have decided this meeting is important if he's gotten dressed.

Or maybe that's because I might've mentioned just how much I love his chest—and how a possessive she-wolf doesn't share. If there's a female out there, like he guessed, he wouldn't let her see what belongs to me.

And doesn't that just make me all warm and fuzzy inside?

After pausing to lay his hand on my shoulder, assuring me without words that he'll be safe, Chase heads out the front door. I feel his slipping aura and know that he's racing to meet the vampires before they make it to the cabin.

Like he said, he isn't gone long. Five minutes, maybe, and my wolf stops her pacing as she cocks her ear. I do the same. Chase isn't bothering to step lightly as he returns to the cabin.

I wonder why.

He pushes the front door in, waiting at the entrance. I run my gaze over him, exhaling when I see that he looks exactly the same as before. No bite marks, no slashes. I sniff softly, sampling the air. No more blood than the stench floating in through the open door.

He doesn't step inside. That's weird.

"Chase? Who was out there?"

"Giorgio and Louise." His brow furrows. "Cadre vamps."

"What did they want?"

"Henry needs to see me. He has something he has to tell me, but he couldn't come in person. He sent two of his top vamps to let me know. I'm supposed to head down to Sacre Coeur right now."

It's already dark. I can see the faint beams from the nearly-full Luna shining down behind him, silhouetting Chase.

"This late?" I ask.

"Yeah." He's frowning now. "I have to go. He knows what I am. He knows what kind of wolf I am, too. He didn't order me to see him. He asked. Cadre vamps don't ask. I have to go."

Following on the heels of Chase killing that Nolan vamp? He does. I know he does. He has a truce with Henry, and the challenge didn't change that, but what if he ignores this request for a meeting?

"Do you want me to go with you?"

His jaw tightens. I know what his answer is going to be even before he says, "No. I need you to stay inside of the cabin. You'll be safe here, and I'll be back before you know it."

I get up from the couch. He's clutching the doorjamb with one hand, but the other reaches out toward me. He does that a lot. If my scent attracted him and my voice lulled his savage beast, the touch of my skin and the feel of my hair against him is enough to keep him in complete control.

Right now, I get the feeling he needs that.

I step into Chase. His free hand closes around me in a hug.

"I'll be safe." *I'm not leaving again.* "Will you be?"

His chin is resting on the top of my head so I feel it when he nods. "Of course. When I have my Quinn waiting for me, nothing can stop me from getting back to her. I told you when

I first brought you home with me. I will always come for you, no matter what."

He did.

I used to think it was a threat. Now I know better. It's a promise.

I kiss the t-shirt material stretching between his sculpted pecs. "I'm holding you to that, Chase."

———

I'M NIBBLING ON MY THUMBNAIL, TAPPING MY FOOT AGAINST the floor as I wait for Chase to come back.

I won't go to bed without him. I could try, but it would be pointless. I have this growing sensation that something bad is about to happen. I'd rather stand in the living room, waiting for his eventual return.

The television is off. The noise was only bothering me before. The quiet is driving me crazy, too, but at least it can help me pick up on any sounds outside. Between that and Chase's alpha aura, I should be able to sense him when he's almost back.

An hour goes by, give or take. I don't know. Using his last trip to Sacre Coeur as a guide, it's nowhere near long enough for Chase to head into the Fang City, have an emergency meeting with the head of the Cadre, and come back.

So why do I hear soft footsteps approaching the cabin?

I go still. He told me that the vampires would never dare come this close to his house. The only reason Nolan was able to pounce on me in the first place was because I left Chase's immediate territory without a fang to protect me from the vampire's thirst.

My wolf is up, prowling around. She heard it, too, and she's growling softly under her breath.

And that's when a familiar scent breaks through the vampiric miasma outside. Despite the closed door and the shut windows, it finds me.

Sandalwood.

West.

It's impossible, but also undeniable. It's not just the scent. Now that I've locked on it, it wraps around me, making my wolf stop in her tracks. It's not alone, either. A handful of other scents—all of them familiar—are mingled with his. Packmates. I can't decipher whose is whose, but I know them.

Am I hallucinating?

The doorknob turns. Without a knock, the door pushes in, and I'm standing in the perfect spot in the middle of the living room to see the males standing on the porch.

There are four of them, actually. One in the lead, three forming a triangle behind him. Tucker. Joey. Darrin.

And, of course, West.

"Quinn?" Like always, his voice is clipped, his expression closed-off and chilly. While relief comes from some of the other males out there, I don't sense any from West even as he says, "Thank the Luna. We found you."

My jaw drops. For a moment, I goggle at him, before I blink rapid-fire a couple of times.

Nope. He's still standing there on the porch in front of me.

I take a step back into the safety of the cabin. "West? What are you doing here?"

"Isn't it obvious? I've come for my mate."

"Your *what?*"

West looks around as he steps into the front room. The other three hang at his back. "Where is he? He's a smart male,

I'll give him that. He hid his scent well in Hickory, and he covered up yours and his with the blood and death that surrounds these woods. It took us hours to track you, Quinn. Where is he? I want to face him."

He says face him. I know shifter males. He means *kill* him.

"You have to go," I say, barely able to hide my panic. "Before he sees you. You have to go."

"Not without you."

No.

I grab West's sleeve. The other three are his backup and, honestly, no real concern. I focus on the Beta. "Go. Now." I tug on his sleeve. "I'll stay. I'm fine. Go back to Hickory and let Bishop know not to worry about me."

Did I think that that would convince West? Maybe if I didn't sound like I was freaking out, it might've.

He disentangles his sleeve from my grip, announcing, "Look at her. She's too afraid to leave him." West pulls me into his arms, tucking me under his chin. His hand ghosts over my hair. "Ah, Quinn. What did that bastard do to you?"

I don't answer. I can't. He's not listening to me, and I'm still in shock that he's here. That he called me his mate.

He's touching me, too. I would've given anything a few weeks ago to know what it was like to find warmth in his arms, but now I feel nothing but an iciness in the pit of my stomach. My wolf is pacing back and forth, snapping her jaws, confused. She senses West's wolf, recognizes him as someone she should respect, someone she should want to be with, but he doesn't smell like *mate*.

Because he isn't Chase.

West takes my silence as confirmation that something bad did happen to me. And, maybe if he found me two weeks ago, I would've agreed. Being drugged, being chained... it sucked.

But I understand why Chase did it. He was desperate. He thought I was his mate. He would've done anything to keep me with him.

Wouldn't I have done the same if I was dominant enough to make a beta wolf mine?

If I could have chained West up to take him away from Helene, I would've. Now? I want to ask him why he's here. I'm not his mate. I'll never be his mate. He made that clear when he rejected me six months ago and let our bond grow jagged between us before I discovered how to cut him off myself.

Until I went ahead and opened it up while I was fleeing Chase...

Uh-oh.

No wonder they think he's done something to me. The bond was open when I was running, but I'd been angry then, only wanting to let my packmates know that I was alive and I was on my way home. It was still open, though, when the vampire attacked me.

Even if West kept his side of our bond closed, no way he could've missed my reaction to the pain as Nolan bit me, or how absolutely terrified I was when I thought the vamp was going to kill Chase.

He came. I don't know why, since every one of us knows I'm not his true mate, but he's here.

And he brought help.

There are four of them. West, Tucker, Joey, and Darrin. One beta and three deltas. None of them is an alpha wolf— thank the Luna that Bishop had to stay behind in Hickory when these four set out—but they're all part of the Sylvan Pack's inner circle. They're protectors, each one of them, and fierce fighters.

So is Chase. If he discovers that four of my old packmates

came to his cabin to bring me home, there will be no holding his feral side back. Four on one odds aren't great, but I've seen him destroy a vampire. He could take them on. He might even win, which means that these four will die.

If they don't, Chase will.

I can't let that happen.

Pulling away from West, I clutch his shirt with trembling fingers. "West, you don't understand—"

"Sh. It's okay, sweetheart." *Sweetheart?* What the fuck? "You're safe now."

I was safe before.

"West, please—"

He ignores me. Chase… he would never, but West does.

Turning to the others, he's not just West anymore. He's the Beta of the Sylvan Pack as he gives them an order. "Take Quinn back to Hickory. I'll stay here and take care of the wolf."

What? No! This is exactly what I was afraid of all along. In the beginning, I didn't want the feral to destroy my fated mate for the sole crime of Fate giving him to me. Now? I don't want to see West die for the same reason. He never wanted me. I don't know why he's here now, but despite how my relationship with Chase has changed, I know he'll always see West as a rival until we have a mate bond between us.

The Luna is still four days out. We have an undeniable connection, sure, but it's nothing like the bond I share with West—and Chase knows it.

"He's a feral," I blurt out.

West exchanges a look with Tucker. Tucker nods, and West's cold, controlled expression cracks just enough to be noticeable.

"That explains everything," he says, more to the male

wolves than to me. "Did he hurt you?" That one's for me. "Did he… force you?"

What?

"Are you asking if he fucked me?"

He blanches. He probably didn't expect me to put it out there like that. Clearing his throat, not quite meeting my eyes, he says, "Yes."

"He didn't." That's the truth. Chase is so desperate to make sure that he doesn't accidentally bite me again that the most we've done the last two days is kiss. "Not that it's any of your business, but he didn't."

West's grey eyes glimmer. They don't quite go shifter gold, but I see the emotion he's trying to hide before he says, "You're my promised mate, Quinn. My intended. It *is* my business."

No the fuck it isn't. One look at his handsome face, though, and I can tell it's not worth arguing with him over it. Something has happened since I was stolen from Hickory, but now is not the time to ask about it. With these four here, I can't risk Chase coming back to find our unwanted visitors.

I have to leave with them. I'm one delta she-wolf facing off against four of her much more dominant packmates. Even if West wasn't the Beta, I would never be able to refuse them if they insisted on me walking out of that door.

The most I can do is get out before Chase challenges them. Because he will. I know he will.

I can't let that happen.

I'm no damsel in distress. I never have been. Even when Chase had me chained up in the basement—something I will never, ever tell these wolves since they already expect the worst —I didn't shy away from him. I distinctly remember threatening to rip off his dick if he got any sick ideas in his head.

But West is used to an omega female. If Helene had been taken captive by a feral, how would she act?

I throw myself back at West, wrapping my arms around his waist. He stiffens for a moment before closing his arms around me.

Purposely putting a tremble in my voice, I whisper, "Don't leave me, West. Don't stay behind. I don't want any of you to. You came to bring me back to Hickory. Let's go. Let's go now, all of us."

West sucks in a breath.

Did it work? Luna, please… please please please let it have worked.

"Of course, my mate. If that's what you want."

Yes!

"It is." I sniffle for good measure. "I'm ready."

"You heard her. Come on. Let's get her out of here before that feral monster returns for her again."

I'm not his mate. The way West so readily gives in to my theatrics… I know then and there that I'm not his mate, no matter what he's saying now. Because, as a dominant shifter male, no way in hell would he walk away from challenging Chase. If he thought of me as his, he would make the feral pay for what he did. His own wolf would need it otherwise he would never be satisfied.

Just like how Chase's wolf needed vengeance on the rogue that decimated his pack, West's should hunger for revenge on the feral who stole his mate away from him.

But he doesn't want it. Despite his words, he's not here because I'm his mate. He's here because he feels like he should be, and as the Beta, it's his *duty*.

Good. Because I'm not his mate, either.

Not anymore.

Now I just have to hope that Chase really meant it when he said he would always come for me.

And that he doesn't take it as the ultimate betrayal when he walks into the cabin, discovers I'm gone, and inevitably recognizes one of the male scents lingering in his space as West's.

SIXTEEN
BISHOP

don't know why I thought they'd come on foot. I mean, I knew that Chase had used a truck to travel from Hickory to just outside of Sacre Coeur. Considering the last my packmates knew was that I was missing, then I was running, then I was hurt, and finally terrified, they had no idea what they were going to find when West followed his half of our bond to me.

Especially since I threw up a block as soon as I remembered to. For all they knew, closing it off meant I'd succumbed. No wonder they all looked at me like they'd seen a ghost when the door flew open and I was standing in the middle of the room.

Joey and Darrin are murmuring to each other. With West hurrying me through the woods, Tucker taking the lead to clear the path, I guess they thought that their bringing up the rear meant that I couldn't hear them.

They're wrong.

I can pick up their concerns for me. None of them are

alphas so they can't tell what part of what I said was true and what was a lie. With the exception of West, I've slept with every other male here. It was no big deal at the time, and I don't regret it one bit. Still, knowing how free I used to be with my affection, they both doubt that my feral hasn't spent the last two-plus weeks screwing me senseless.

It doesn't help that I carry his scent on me. On my skin, on my clothes, on my hair… there's no denying that he's touched me and I've touched him. For Luna's sake, Chase and I sleep in the same bed. I was living in his cabin. Of course I smell like him!

Before, my packmates pitied me because they knew my fated mate rejected me. Now they feel sorry for me because they're sure I've been a feral's chew toy since I've been missing.

Let them think what they want. I've never really cared what other wolves thought about me before, and after the last six months, I've developed a hard shell. So long as we get out of here before someone gets hurt, I don't care. I'll go back to Hickory like they want, I'll explain everything to Bishop, and then I'm gone. If Chase doesn't come for me first, I'm going back to him.

And not just because I promised I'd stay until the next full moon…

They came by car. I'm squeezed between West and Joey in the backseat, with Tucker and Darrin up front. Smart. I've seen Darrin drive before. Guy's got a lead foot and a need to find adrenaline wherever he can. He drives like we're invincible instead of simply supernatural.

We're back on pack land before midnight.

I can't wait to hop out of the car. Being around four male shifters has rubbed my wolf so raw, I have to keep my teeth gritted to keep her snarls from escaping me. What used to signal *safe* to me is a big, honking neon *danger* sign. They're too close and it's almost all I can do to resist the urge to unsheathe my tiny claws and slash at them to get them to back away.

West... he's too close. He's not quite touching me anymore, though this is the closest we've been since we recognized the mating bond springing up between us. This nearness has my stomach flip-flopping—and not in the good way.

When Joey starts to ask me for details about what happened with the feral, West silences him with a look. Heeding the Beta, Joey shuts up, but I know he's not only just curious. He's dying to know what happened. They all are. But West is the highest-ranked shifter in the car and they follow his lead.

It's an awkward, quiet ride back. I almost scream out loud just to break up the tension. The only reason I don't is because my packmates—all of them except West, that is—are watching me closely as if they expect me to do just that. They expect me to break.

I just want to go to sleep, wake up, and discover I'm curled up next to Chase.

Before, all I wanted was to get away from him. I was dying to get back to Hickory, even though I knew West wouldn't be waiting for me. Now he's here, he's bringing me home, he's calling me his *mate*... and I just want to be back in the cabin in the woods, with my garden and my male.

West didn't bring me a flower, I realize. I was missing for just about three weeks and he showed up like my knight in furry armor—and he didn't bring me a flower.

If I was Helene, he would've.

Surprisingly, that realization... it doesn't hurt anymore. It's just fact. He can call me his mate all he wants, but I know where his heart truly lies. It's where it always has been: with a beautiful omega she-wolf who I was jealous of for way too long.

Which makes my decision to skip out on my old pack as soon as possible a sound one.

The Sylvan Pack is based in the woods; it's how we got our name after all. The original pack didn't go for grandiose names. We live in the woods, we're the Sylvan Pack. The majority of our forest is made up of hickory trees? Boom. Our community is known as Hickory. The heart of pack land is in the center of the circle where our ancestors first built their cabins? It's the pack circle.

On the edge of our land, on the side closest to the local human town, is where the pack council keeps the cars we all share. Fittingly enough, it's the pack garage, and Darrin drives us there. Once we all hop out of the car—and I mean that literally, I'm so ready to get away from their auras—we jog the rest of the way back to Hickory. I have two males on each side, as if they expect me to be attacked again.

Yeah, right. First of all, if Chase attacks anyone, it's not going to be me. Secondly, even if he's made it back to the cabin, I'm hours ahead of him. I don't expect him to drive. Knowing him the way I do, he'll go feral and run the entire way here.

I just hope I can intercept him in time before he decides to challenge my whole pack.

Four on one… I give Chase the edge. Dozens on one? With Bishop involved in the fight because, technically, I'm still one of his? And with West suddenly insisting on calling me his mate?

My feral is strong. He won't survive that.

I can't let anything happen to him. I *won't* let anything happen to him.

Too bad it's not going to be my choice.

All I want in life is to get to choose. When we cross into the inner border of Sylvan Pack territory, I move a few steps ahead, running in the direction of my cabin. As much as I wish I was still with Chase, I miss my home. I miss my stuff. Maybe… maybe this was a blessing in disguise. While I'm here, I can pack up everything I own so I can bring it back to Chase's cabin. Really make the place our home.

West moves ahead of me. Shaking his head, he tells me, "Not there, Quinn. Alpha wants to see us."

At that, the other wolves break off from me and West. Now that they're back, they have cabins of their own to go to, and they did what they were instructed to do. They brought me back to Hickory.

Seems like it was West's job to bring me before Bishop.

The porch light is on in the Alpha cabin. We don't enter through the front, though. That part of the cabin is saved for Bishop and Sofia, plus the pups they'll have together one day. As a packmate, I'm allowed to visit Bishop at any point during the day—when he's home—and when that light is on at night, but only if I approach the back of his cabin where he keeps the den.

In a shifter pack, the Alpha's den is a safe place. We can bring any concerns to the Alpha there, knowing that he'll listen to what we have to say. Pack councils have their meets here, too, and if a she-wolf wants to talk to our Alpha female, Sofia is known to make the best cappuccino ever as we chit chat by the fireplace.

Tonight, Sofia is standing beside her mate as West opens the always unlocked door to the den before ushering me inside.

She smiles when she sees me, relief flooding her softly

rounded face. "Quinn… I'm so glad you're home. We were so worried about you. Weren't we, baby?"

The Alpha nods.

Bishop Dupuis is the opposite of his sister. While Helene is fair-skinned, slender, blonde, and beautiful, Bishop is a hulking, tanned male with dark brown hair, a full beard, and a hard look in his dark gold eyes.

He's also a male of few words. Chase might've grunted a lot while he was struggling to keep his hold on his feral side, but Bishop? He's the big, strong, silent type. Before Sofia mated him—when he was still the future Alpha instead of the leader of our pack—West usually did the talking for him. Despite Bishop being five years older than West, they've been best friends for as far back as I can remember, and West was Bishop's right-hand wolf long before he was named Beta.

I always thought it was interesting that West always knew what Bishop was thinking. Just then, as the two males look at each other, I get the feeling it goes both ways.

West lets out a breath. "You were right. The prints we found belonged to a feral. He's the one who took Quinn."

Bishop frowns.

Sofia lays her hand on his forearm. Her pretty hazel eyes flicker over my face. "Oh my Luna… are you okay? I can wake up Ginnie, if you want. She can check you over, if you need her to."

Ginnie is the pack healer. I shake my head. "I'm fine. I just… if it's okay, I'd really rather go to my cabin. It's been a long night. Maybe we can talk again tomorrow?"

Bishop furrows his brow. His alpha aura slams into me like a gust of wind during a thunderstorm. I almost stumble.

Wow. I forgot what it was like to be around an alpha who has no problem using his dominance against me. I hadn't even dared to meet Bishop's eyes—I was focusing on his forehead, instead, so he didn't take any accidental eye contact as an inadvertent challenge—but the urge to bare my throat is so strong, I cock my head to the side, letting my sheet of hair fall over my shoulder.

Sofia slaps Bishop's arm. It's more of a gentle love tap, but it does the job. He reels in his aura enough that I can straighten again.

West hasn't moved. He's just standing there, like he's a soldier at attention.

Then again, he's the Beta. That's kind of his job.

Bishop jerks his chin at West.

He nods.

Sofia helpfully translates for me. "I think that's a great idea. West can bring you back to your cabin, Quinn, so you can get some rest. If you feel up to it, we can talk tomorrow."

Fingers crossed I'm gone by tomorrow.

I don't say that, though. I don't say anything that Bishop can tell is a lie.

So I just nod. "Thank you."

***

WEST FOLLOWED ME THE ENTIRE WAY HOME.

I couldn't shake him. No matter what I said or did, he refused to leave my side. He didn't throw the *m*-word around again, but he made it clear: Bishop and Sofia thought he should stay by me for the time being, so that's what he was going to do.

I drew the line at inviting him inside of my cabin. The Alpha couple didn't say that I had to, and it's a relief to bid him good night before closing the door in his face.

Bet he never expected *that*, huh?

The next morning, I meet with Bishop again. West knocks on my door, bright and early, to tell me that the Alpha wants to see me. He walks me over, then leaves me at the den, mumbling something about returning for me later.

That throws me. Not only doesn't West *not* mumble, but since when do I need a freaking bodyguard while in Hickory? Do they know that Chase will come after me again? That it wasn't a fluke he took me in the first place?

Or is something going on with West that I just don't understand?

Hoping it's the second one, I let myself into the den where Bishop is waiting for me.

Sofia had gone with Ginnie to check on Kara's twins— who were born while I was gone—so she misses the meeting. Fun for me, right? Without his mate to speak for him, I get to have a heart-to-heart with the Alpha of the Sylvan Pack.

It isn't so bad. He apologizes for letting Chase get that close to me in the first place, and when I point-blank ask him if he knew there was a shifter watching me, his only answer is, "I didn't know he was a feral or I would've stopped him before he took you."

Alphas. They do what they think is best for the pack, and he begrudgingly admits that he hoped I might reciprocate the strange shifter's attraction to me. He understood that I was his Beta's fated mate—something he respects since Sofia is his— but his parents were a chosen mating. He knew firsthand that they worked out, just like he knew that I'd never be happy with West.

It's weird. He makes it a point to tell me that. Not that West will never want me—which I already knew—but that I won't be happy settling with his best friend.

And it's not like he's trying to get me out of the picture so that West and Helene can finally be together. I asked. I have no shame, and it was so strange to have a one-on-one conversation with Bishop, I just went for it.

No. Helene is still promised to Rafael of the Gravetail Pack.

And West? Up until he came running to Bishop with the news that he finally felt me on the other side of his bond, he was still hoping that Helene would change her mind and choose him.

That's when he told Bishop that, if they found me alive and brought me back to Hickory, he would make me his forever mate as soon as I was willing to perform the Luna Ceremony with him.

That… that brought our little chat to a screeching halt. I didn't believe him. Bishop's my Alpha, and I almost accused him of being full of shit. If he could keep something like a strange wolf stalking me for nine months from me for all that time because he thought it was for the best, who knows what his motives are now?

Turns out? He was telling the truth.

Know how I know?

That night, after I managed to slip out of the Alpha's den on my own, heading out to my favorite spot in the woods, then dashing back to my cabin when I smelled sandalwood on the breeze searching for me, West finally tracked me down.

And it's not like he didn't know where I'd be. Since my forcible return last night, I've had more eyes on me than ever before. Each and every one of my packmates is dying with curiosity over my abduction, plus the patrollers are watching me so closely, it's like they expect Chase to show up in the middle of Hickory to claim me or something.

He hasn't yet. I try not to let it bother me that it's been twenty-four hours since I've seen him last—more than enough time for him to finish his business with Henry, discover I'm gone, then come for me—and there's still no sign of him.

I'd had high hopes when I went out into the grove. I know his scent now. Even if he rolled around in a tub full of wolfsbane, it doesn't matter. I'd recognize him anywhere.

But he hasn't come for me yet.

West did, though.

When I peek out of my window and see him on my doorstep, I almost want to call out, "Nobody's home." It would be pointless, since his wolf would've told him I'm inside even before my voice would've confirmed it, but I don't want to see him right now.

I also don't think I have a choice.

Pulling open the door, I cock my hip against it, barring him from coming inside. "West. I thought you didn't have to watch me when I was safe inside of my cabin."

A flush rises high on his tanned cheeks. Bulls-eye. I knew Bishop had them keeping a close eye on me.

"Can I come in?"

I pretend to think about it for a moment. "I don't think that's a good idea," I say honestly. "Why don't you tell me what you want out here first?"

He clears his throat. "Very well. I've come to ask you if you'll accept me as your forever mate? The Luna chose us for each other, and I know I... might not have reacted to that news as I should've, but I did a lot of thinking while you were gone." Gone, he says. Not missing. Not abducted. For Luna's sake, he sounds as if I was on a three-hour cruise or something, not living with a feral for three weeks. "I shouldn't have tried to go against Fate. The Luna rises in three days. Will you have me then?"

I can't help myself. I laugh.

A month ago, I would've done anything to have Weston Reed standing in front of me, asking to be my mate.

But that was a month ago.

"No," I tell him when I can finally stifle my laugh. "Of course not."

I don't think he could've been more stunned if I shifted on the spot and my wolf went for his cock with her teeth. "What?" It's not a stammer, but it's pretty close. "You're refusing me?"

If that's what he wants to call it. "Uh, yeah."

"Why?"

Why? Is he fucking serious? "Um, maybe because you spent six months ignoring me? Rejecting me? That ring a bell?"

A flash of shame shatters his composure. It breaks my heart for him.

"West," I begin.

"No. You're right. I shouldn't have done that. If anything, I should've released you from the bond as soon as I knew I couldn't go through with finalizing one with any other female."

Couldn't. Not wouldn't. Just like I knew all along… he didn't have a choice any more than I did. Only his choice was about giving up on his heart's mate while I just wanted to get out from under the thumb of Fate.

We both did, I guess.

And it wasn't me. Any other female unlucky enough to get between the Beta and the female he really wanted… she would've been treated the same way.

Good thing I'm Quinn Malone. It sucked, but I dealt with it. If I hadn't been paired with a male who didn't want me, would I ever have been free to fall for Chase? Probably not.

In a weird way, he actually did me a favor.

It's time I do one for him.

I clear my throat. "Weston Reed?"

His grey eyes flash golden. I think he knows what's coming. "Yes?"

I take a deep breath. "I reject you."

The bond snaps. Just like that. No muss. No fuss. It's just… *gone.*

West exhales softly. "Thank you, Quinn."

I wink at him. "No problem. Honestly, if it had occurred to me sooner, I probably would've done it before. I guess… I guess I just didn't think it was right for a delta to reject the *Beta* of the pack."

He snorts. I haven't heard him do that in years. "Please. Everyone knows that the hierarchy is bullshit half the time. Sure, Bishop is in charge, but the rest of us? It doesn't mean anything. Even the smallest delta can be strong. Look at you. You survived a feral."

As if on cue, a howl splits the night's sky. It sounds closer than the source probably is, and if I was inside my cabin with the door closed, I don't know if I would've heard it as loudly as I do, but it stops me before I respond to West's comment with a retort.

That's okay. I forgot what I was going to say anyway.

Because that howl? I *know* that howl.

Chase.

He's here.

West's head whips around. "What the fuck was that?"

Ah. There's the West I remember. Not the cold-hearted

Beta who pretended I wasn't there and who spoke so prim and proper, but the guy who was handsome and funny, and who cursed like a drunken sailor when it suited him.

He would never be a good mate to me. Hopefully, one day, he'll find someone to make him forget Helene the way that I found Chase.

The echo of his howl makes my heart thump fast and, I kid you not, my panties damp.

That was a possessive howl. His wolf is shouting, *Mine.*

And he's here for me.

I grin. "It's my mate."

SEVENTEEN
MATE

ased on his howl, I can tell what direction he's coming in from. I don't even think. I just bolt out the door.

West is *quick*, damn it. He lashes out his hand, snagging me by the wrist before I've made it two steps past my doorway.

"Quinn, wait—"

No waiting. I have a feral out there who doesn't know what happened to me. Can Chase catch my scent from that far? I'm not sure. Considering he's heading toward the clearing where I've spent so much time, he should be able to tell that the most recent layer of my scent is from this morning and not three weeks ago.

Then again, I'm pretty sure his feral side will be in charge.

Will the beast be rational? Doubt it.

Will he tear past the hickories and the wildflowers, racing for the heart of pack land where my cabin is? Probably.

Will he challenge any wolf he sees?

Oh, yeah. You can bet on it.

I have to go. I'm the only one in the Sylvan Pack who can calm this raging feral. If he scents me, if he sees me, if he hears my voice… I can keep anyone from being hurt tonight.

I absolutely refuse to let anyone get hurt because of me.

"I love him," I blurt out. It's the truth, too. I love Chase, and if anything happens to him, I'll never forgive myself. "Let me go!"

West does.

"I'll lead him away from the pack," I yell back, already running toward the trees. "Don't let Bishop send anyone to hurt him!"

Does he hear me? I don't know. Will he listen? I'd like to think so.

Will I do whatever I can to save Chase?

Yup.

I run. Out of Hickory and through the woods, I sprint. As soon as I make it to the edge of our immediate territory, I shift. My wolf will give me more speed and I'll need it if I want to get ahead of Chase and guide him to a spot where it's safe for us to reunite.

If there's one thing I know, it's this: if I run, Chase will come after me. He doesn't just ambush. He pursues.

And I'm counting on him to.

I know when he picks up on my scent and realizes that I'm nearby. His howl turns into a mournful whine, then an echoing roar. If I wasn't absolutely one hundred percent sure that he would never hurt me no matter what form he took, I might've dashed back to Hickory and prayed that my packmates would protect me.

But I don't. I keep running, and when the big, black wolf suddenly appears behind me, I push my wolf to go faster.

He lunges for me.

I zig.

He snarls.

I zag.

He doesn't give up. There's no reason to. As if the primal part of our wolfy brains has taken over both of us, we continue the chase.

He's never that far behind me, and though I could lose him easily if I wanted to since I know the woods outside of Hickory far better than he does, I don't *want* to lose him.

He still needs to feel like he earned me, and I need to make sure we're as far away from pack land as possible.

Then we'll both get what we desire.

When I feel like we've put enough distance between us and Hickory, I pretend to stumble over a rabbit hole I could've easily avoided. It gives Chase the chance to overtake me and he does.

Yes.

He catches me, tackling my wolf to the ground just like I thought he would. I land in my fur, taking the hit a lot easier than if I was in my skin. Chase lands on my back. With his instincts riding him hard, I know he'll go for my scruff.

I shift. No wolf, no scruff. All I am is a willing female who got mega turned on during the chase, and as soon as my arousal hits him, I'm betting he shifts, too.

If he doesn't, I'm screwed. Well, no. The opposite, actually. Shifters don't mate in their fur, and if I'm in my skin, Chase will either shift with me or his wolf will back off.

Of course, there's a third option. He might turn into that beast form where he can barely speak and he's ruled by his urges. On the plus side, I know from firsthand experience that, as a feral, he's two-legged with a cock that grows hard.

Is it a technicality?

Maybe.

Will I let him fuck me?

I think I might.

He's still Chase after all, and I have to believe that, even as a feral, he loves me enough to be gentle.

When I feel the pulse of his shift on my bare skin, I can't bring myself to turn around just yet.

"Quinn… Oh, Luna… *Quinn*. I thought you were gone. I thought you left me."

His voice is broken, but it's human.

I glance behind me. I have to. Know what I find? A very naked, very *aroused* Chase is on his knees behind me, clinging to my thighs, holding onto me so he can keep me from running from him again.

Good thing I have no intention of doing that.

He chased me. He caught me.

He won.

"I would never," I tell him, reaching back to stroke whatever part of him I can find. I touch his forearm, and he jolts. "I want you to know that. What happened… what you think happened… it didn't. I didn't want to leave. I was coming back to you. I just… you said you'd always come for me. I was waiting."

"I'm here." He sounds a little calmer. Like being near me is enough to soothe his beast—and it is, isn't it? "I will always come. Choose your male, I'll still follow you. Because I chose you and I can't let you go."

"Then don't."

"What?"

I wiggle my ass, just in case he didn't notice that we're both completely naked. "I don't just want you to hold on tight. I want you to get as close to me as possible. Take me. Claim me.

Make me yours, and then you'll know that, no matter what, I *want* you to chase me."

You know, I thought I'd have to work harder to convince him. Nope. As soon as I wiggled my ass at him, he was already mounting me from behind.

"I'm sorry, Quinn. I can't… I have to."

"That's fine, baby. I want you to."

"It's that *thing* in me. I can't fight him—"

And… that's where we have a problem.

I immediately drop to my belly.

Chase lowers himself down, too. I can see his arms bend from my angle, and I scoot out from under him before he can pin me on the grass.

"Quinn?" His voice is a confused grunt. He's winning the battle against his feral side, but I don't think he'll be completely victorious until he finally feels like he's claimed what is his. "I thought…"

Good thing I'm ready to help him with that.

Only… we're in this together. I never want Chase to look back on our first mating and regret it. If he mounts me from behind while blaming his feral side, he won't see my face. He won't know that I want this as much as he does. That even if his instincts are hard to ignore, I don't want him to ignore them.

There's only one thing to do about that.

Using the tip of my foot, I push him back. He's on his knees, cock pointing straight up at the sky. It's even more impressive when I have him this way.

Oh, I'm going to enjoy this.

Looping my arms over his shoulders, I climb up on his thick thighs. My intentions are obvious. There's no denying what I'm about to do.

So that he never doubts that we're in this together, I need to claim *him*.

But he's an alpha. A feral. Some males can be touchy when a female takes them like this instead of her assuming the usual face-down, ass-up position.

Just in case, I check with him. "This okay?"

"The only female I've ever wanted is sitting on top of me. We ain't got a stitch of clothing on between us. Her arousal is making me dizzy, and it's all because of me." He pauses, suddenly unsure. "It is for me, right?"

I nod.

He shudders. "It's more than okay, Quinn. I'm yours. I've always been yours. If this is what you want to do, that's fine with me. I just… I need to know you're mine."

I climb off of him. For a split second, his face twists in an expression I can't quite see even beneath the moonlight, it's that dark, but he gets control an instant later. He obviously thought I was rejecting him, but if that's what I want, he'll let me.

Look at that. My feral finally learned to let me make decisions on my own.

Good boy.

I jerk my chin at him. "I am. Now get on your back."

He looks puzzled but he doesn't even question me. He immediately lays flat on his back.

It's not the full moon. The Luna won't be out for three more nights. Though I called him my mate to West—and Chase is, now that I've finally released West from the bond I clung to for way too long—he won't really be mine until we perform the Luna Ceremony.

Does that mean I plan on waiting?

Not even a little.

While he watches me closely, I get down and straddle him until the weeping head of his cock is pointing straight up at my pussy. An inch, maybe two separates the tip from my entrance. I have one hand on his chest, bracing my weight as I rise up on the balls of my feet so that I'm crouching over him.

I've seen his chest heaving before. I've seen him out of control. I've seen him go absolutely still.

Somehow, Chase is doing all three at the same time. It's like he's waiting for me to change my mind, climb off of him again, and sashay away back to my pack.

"You're mine," I tell him, lowering myself just enough that the head of his cock brushes against me. "I'm yours. The Luna can bless our mating another time. Tonight, I make you my mate. And you can't stop me."

"I never would."

"Good."

I'm so fucking wet, he slides right off of me, though his audible moan makes me eager to let him feel that sensation again. I put my weight against him, pressing his impressive length against his taut belly. Sliding back and forth, I make sure to spread my wetness all over every bit of his hot and heavy cock.

Chase's eyes are glowing in the darkness. He slams his head back against the dirt, clutching the grass with his fists. I realize that he's trying his best to stay still only to hurt himself when it gets too much. I can't have that. He needs to feel as good as I do, and though pleasure sometimes is so intense it can be painful, I don't want him banging his head.

"Stay still," I tell him, my voice coming out throaty. I press down on his cock again, making sure he can feel my heat. Chase moans, and I grin. He didn't move at all.

Good.

As a reward, I reach down, taking each of his hands in one of mine. I use my thumbs to knock loose any stray blades of grass he yanked out, then press his searing palms to my aching tits.

"If you need something to hold onto," I purr, "why don't you give these a try?"

"Luna, Quinn… you're so fucking *soft*."

"Mm. You like that?"

He bobs his head, his fingers roving over each of my breasts. "Very much, yes."

I lift myself up off of him, careful to make sure he doesn't lose his grip. I shouldn't have been worried. He's not letting go of my tits for anything.

"Maybe you'll like this better," I tell him, reaching between our bodies again. I'm soaked, his cock is slick with my wetness, and as I angle him so that he's lodged firmly inside of me, gravity takes over and slowly, slowly I sink down on top of him.

Once I'm fully seated, our groins touching, I take a second to adjust to the fullness of Chase inside of me and *squeeze*.

He just about chokes.

"How was that?"

"Unh… yes. This… this is very good, too."

I wink at him. "Got one more trick for you, tough guy. You think you can keep up?"

"I think you're trying to get your revenge and kill me, baby, because I don't know if I'm going to survive what else you've got in store for me. But, Luna, what a way to go…" A bead of sweat forms on his brow. "Try your worst."

Oh, I'm in trouble. A male who is playful during sex? That's my *dream*. Add that to a cock that stretches me out in all the right places?

I already planned on keeping Chase. Now I dare anyone to try to take him away from me.

Bracing my hands on his sculpted torso, I push against him, using the leverage to rise up off of his dick. Not entirely, though. Just to the point where it's only his head still inside. With a chuckle, I tell him, "Remember that you said that," before I let my full weight fall back on top of him.

Chase screams.

"Good?" I ask, double-checking.

"Do that again and I'll give you whatever you want."

How can a girl resist? "Okay."

He doesn't scream this time, though he does moan. I like it so much that I pick up the pace so that he'll do it again. Before long, I develop a rhythm that has Chase knocking his head against the ground once more. He stops when I slow down, though he keeps his hands right where I put them no matter how fast I ride him.

I don't think he's blinking. It's like he wants to witness every time I bounce up and down on his cock, so he's watching me closely, taking it all in. I think I'm doing the same. His look of awe mingled with the sounds I'm tearing out of him is doing one hell of a number on my ego. It's never been so boosted.

I've never felt so worshipped before, either. It's a heady feeling, only surpassed by the look of wonder and despair that flashes across his face when he realizes he's about to come.

"I… I don't think I can last much longer," Chase grunts, kneading my tits with so much force, I'm just about there with him.

"Stay with me just a few more seconds," I tell him. "Almost… almost there."

He nods, as if his words are failing him. Like all of his concentration is on doing what I asked.

He's an alpha who will take commands from this delta, in a moment where things like rankings and dominance don't exist, and I've never felt more powerful.

Still riding him, moving as fast as my hips will allow to increase the friction against my clit rubbing against his groin, I let go. It's harder to keep such close contact without me grabbing onto his waist, but I need my hands.

I doubt Chase agrees since I use them to shove him off of my tits.

"Hey!"

"Sit up, Chase," I tell him. My words come out choppy. He says he's close. Well, so am I. "Grab my lower back so that you're sitting up and I'm still on your lap."

Does he know what I'm doing? Maybe. His brow is creased, though maybe that's because I'm still working his dick. I squeeze my inner muscles to punctuate my directions, breaking him from his notably stunned spell.

Shifting his upper body, rising up so that he's sitting, I let out a squeal. This new position hits me at a different angle that has my orgasm coming on fast.

But first—

I swoop my hair over one shoulder, then tilt my head to that side. "When you're ready to go," I tell him, "let yourself go. But this is it, Chase. This is your chance. If you want to bite me, I'm ready. If you don't—"

I don't know why I thought he might refuse. I haven't even finished the alternative before he strikes like a damn rattlesnake, biting me at the point where my shoulder meets my neck.

It stings for a second, but I expected that. I mean, he's

bitten me before, and that was nothing compared to a vampire making me his dessert. There's something different in this bite, though. Maybe because I know it's for real, that I'm keeping this one, that it will forever be a sign of the love I have for this male… it's different.

And I immediately start coming from the force of it.

I'm not the only one. Removing his teeth gently so that I have a perfect mark instead of a tear, Chase holds on just long enough before he starts bucking up in me wildly, shouting my name to the sky as he finds his release.

That's okay, I'm yelling, too.

Good thing I led him on a chase out of Hickory, I think as I start to come down from the height of pleasure. With the both of us being screamers, none of the pack would get any sleep tonight…

I WAS READY TO SPEND THE REST OF THE NIGHT RIGHT WHERE we landed. With Chase curving his body around me, my beloved hickories arcing high over our heads, I've never been so content. We're not on pack land, so I thought it would be fine.

And that's when Chase takes my hand in his.

Thinking he's just insatiable, I expect him to place my palm on his cock. With him being the big spoon and me the little one, there's no missing the fact that he's already recovered from our first momentous claiming—and the second.

I'm still humming inside of my skin. My wolf preens that Chase is choosing us again already. With him buried to the hilt inside of me, it's the one time both halves of me can enjoy this magnificent male. She's game. I'm a little sore—six months of celibacy will do that to a girl—but I don't mind. If he wants to mount me again, he's more than welcome to.

Or I can mount him again. That was fun.

Mm. Maybe he can take me while we're both on our sides and that way I can fall asleep as soon as my next orgasm crashes over me…

I'm just about to ask what he thinks when he moves my hand. It isn't down toward his erection, though, like I expected. Instead, he brings it up to his nose, then takes a deep sniff that has him growling under his breath.

Uh-oh.

How could I have forgotten?

"You smell like *him*."

Him. Right.

West.

Crap.

"He grabbed my hand. That's all, Chase."

He sniffs again. Starting at my palm, he trails his nose all the way to my armpit. Probably not the most pleasant for him after all the sweating I just did, but I guess I pass tonight's sniff test because he starts grinding his cock against my ass. I can't tell if it's an involuntary reaction because my scent turns him on or his way to initiate sex so that he can get more of his scent on me to replace the one spot on me that West touched.

Considering he's jerked my hand higher, burying it into his sweat-soaked hair, covering me with his scent as he slips his cock between the cleft of my ass, I'm going with that second one.

I widen my legs just a little in open invitation.

He stops. Damn it. He was getting so *close*.

"Chase."

"You said he grabbed you. Why did he grab you?"

Single-minded male. I should've known.

Fighting back a frustrated sigh, I admit, "He tried to stop me from going to you when I heard your howl. I wasn't going to let him stop me, and when he realized I was going to you no matter what, he let go. I didn't have to break his hand or anything."

I thought that would appease him. At the very least, he seems pleased to hear how desperate I was to get to him. He starts rocking again, slower this time, as he grates out, "No one keeps us apart. Next time I see him, I'll kill him."

I'm not surprised. Can't let him kill my ex-almost mate, but I'm not surprised that that was his reaction.

I wonder... will a quick handjob distract my murderous mate? It'll kill two birds with one stone: transferring the overpowering musk of his innate scent to my hand while also making him feel good. Then we can forget all about killing West.

Hmm.

Won't know until I've tried.

Jerking my hand out of his loose hold, I reach all the way down, taking firm command of his cock. He immediately starts moving again, thrusting into the circle I form with my thumb and my forefinger.

"Quinn..." He's panting. "If you think... unh... you can control me... oh... with sex..." He shudders, and though I can't see what's going on behind me, I feel it when his come spurts out, getting on my hand. He falls forward, one hand landing on my hip in a possessive brand. "You're absolutely fucking right."

With my back to him, I don't have to hide my smile. "Don't kill him, Chase. For me?"

He stiffens. Unfortunately for my libido, it's the rest of his body this time, not his cock. "Because you still love him?"

I snort. "Please. I never loved West. Not like that. I never got the chance to. He's loved Helene for like ten years now. He was my friend, and, sure, the Luna thought he should be my mate, but that didn't mean I loved him. I just figured I might in time."

"But you don't?"

Letting go of him, I spin in the grass, moving so that we're facing each other. His hand fell when I moved. As soon as my position changed, he put it right back there. It's almost as if he can't let go of me for a single second.

I look into his bright gold eyes and I know it's true.

Just like I know how to soothe his worries.

"How can I love him?" I nip his bottom lip. "Mating is for life, Chase. I rejected the bond I have with West—"

"You did?"

I nod. "Yup. And you know why?"

He swallows roughly. He shakes his head.

Luna save me from overly thick males.

"Because I love you. I choose *you*. You asked me if I could. Well, I did when I rode your cock. Remember? Like an hour ago?"

Chase rumbles deep in his chest. "I remember."

I raise my scarred eyebrow at him. "You sure? 'Cause, if you want, I can refresh your memory."

This close, it's my belly that notices it when his dick starts stirring again. It twitches, then leaps, prodding me just above the curls that cover my pussy. If I didn't know any better, I'd think the damn thing has a mind of its own, already seeking my entrance.

Not that I mind. And when Chase takes me up on my

teasing offer, lifting me up and guiding his length back inside of me, I give myself a mental high-five for coming up with this plan to distract him.

It won't last, though. So I snapped my bond with West earlier tonight. I told Chase the truth: that I love him. That I chose *him*. I have his mark on my skin. Even now I can feel the itch of it turning to a scar that I'll never erase.

But until we're fully bonded, he'll think of West and his wolf as a rival. Even though we're not in Hickory, we're close enough.

West is *too* close.

I don't want to risk Chase going feral again. And though the idea of wearing him out through copious amounts of mind-blowing sex has a certain appeal, I gotta sleep some time. And while I trust him when it comes to me and my safety, it would be cruel of me to insist on staying nearby the Sylvan Pack when it would make things so much harder for Chase.

Especially since we have a perfectly good cabin waiting for us.

I ride Chase again until we're both falling apart in each others' arms. Then, at my urging, we shift. Kind of have to. Chase ran all this way as a big, black wolf, and my clothes are scattered ruins somewhere on the edge of Hickory.

One day soon I'll have to go back to clean my old cabin out; I want my stuff and I won't leave any of it behind for good. Maybe once we're fully mated and I can bring Chase with me to show my feral mate off to the rest of the pack, I will.

For now, with both of us in our fur, we head in the direction of Sacre Coeur.

We've got a long night of running ahead of us. At least we're going home together.

EIGHTEEN
CHOOSE

Three nights later, I'm standing on the front porch of our cabin when Chase sneaks up behind me. He makes not a single sound as he approaches. He doesn't need to. I've always been able to sense him. It's just… now more than ever.

He rests his palms on my shoulders, moving his head so that his beautiful mouth is right next to my ear. "What are you looking at, my Quinn?" he murmurs.

As if he has to ask. But since he did so nicely, I point up at the sky.

The Luna shines down on the forest in front of us.

His grip tightens on me. It doesn't hurt; he vowed he'd never hurt me, and I believe him implicitly. In fact, when Chase loses just enough control that the points of his sudden claws dig into my shoulders, it's all I can do not to let out an audible moan.

After I accepted his bite that night outside of Hickory, I'm not worried about him marking me anymore. Not while I'm the proud owner of twin crescent-shaped fang marks that created a beautiful silvery-white scar at the point where my shoulder meets my neck.

Once the Luna blesses our mating tonight, the mark will turn pure white. Our bond will forever be unbreakable.

Chase Wilder will be mine forever.

For the last two days, ever since we returned to the cabin, we've hardly been off of each other. It's like Chase needs to be constantly assured that I'm open to him whenever he wants me to be, and I already knew that it got me off to be desired. All he has to do is growl softly, whispering how much he wants me—*wants* me, not *needs* me—and I'm already growing damp and ready for him.

Today was different. As if we knew what was coming, we managed to stay apart from the moment we woke up in bed together. Chase took a drive into Sacre Coeur to buy more supplies when he found his control failing. I cooked him another meal that he devoured while eating me up with that hungry look of his.

We watched some television, both of us sneaking peeks toward the window, waiting for the Luna to rise.

Chase doesn't keep the shades drawn anymore. The windows stay shut—I don't think I'll ever get used to *eau de vampire* wafting past my nose like that—but he doesn't mind letting in the sun now that I'm here with him. It was his feral side that was sensitive to the sunlight, but the longer we're together, the easier it is for him to restrain his beastly side.

I thought mating him would make him a former feral. I asked him when he first made it back to the cabin, but Chase admitted that he still felt the urges. He said it with defeat, as if he thought that I might change my mind about staying with him if he couldn't shake that part of him.

Silly feral. To prove to him just how unfounded his fears were, I dragged him into the shower so that we could rinse off after our long run, then I sank down on my knees in front of him to worship his cock.

Yeah. He doesn't doubt that I'm hot for him anymore.

At least, I thought so, until he says in a hesitant voice, "Are you sure about this?"

Oh, Chase. He's not going to stop worrying until the Luna Ceremony is done and we're forever mates. Then again, this male will probably worry for the rest of our long lives together.

That's fine. I'm up for the challenge.

Does that mean I'm going to make it easy for him, though?

Ha. Not a chance.

I swivel my head on my neck, giving him an incredulous expression. "Luna knows I am. What about you? You want to call this off, let me know." I twitch my lips, going from incredulous to teasing. "I might be able to find another male to do this with tonight."

Chase lowers his hands from my shoulders to my waist. When I first met him, a tease like that would've triggered his feral side. He would've shouted that I was his, maybe even thrown a couple of punches at a cinder block wall.

The new and improved Chase?

Fucker *tickles* me.

I squirm. I've always been incredibly ticklish, something he learned early on when we first started to play with each others' bodies. Lately, it's his secret weapon. He tickles me and I wiggle, and eventually he gets me in a new position that he can enjoy. Once I'm full of him, pleasure usually replaces my ticklishness, so we both end up winning.

Too bad we're not naked—yet. All I can do is try to avoid

his questing fingers, curling up as I turn into Chase, giggling against his bare chest.

"Okay, okay. You win."

He drops his lips to my mark, pressing an open-mouth kiss there. "You gonna threaten me with another male, Quinn?"

"Well—"

He tickles me again.

I squeal and bite his nearest ab.

Chase shudders, all playfulness gone.

His aura grows thick with arousal. He was already hard when he approached me—I could feel his cock pushing through his jeans as he stepped up to my back—but this is different. He already wears my mark. I got him to admit that he was pleased when I fought back the day I met him because he got to keep the scar to prove that, no matter why I'd done it, I marked him.

Of course, I wanted to give him a mark that didn't represent me trying to flee from my captor. I did that last night, taking a chunk out of that gorgeous tight ass of his. I'd waited until he'd finished to roll him over, massaging his cheek before I bit it, leaving a mating mark that was just for the two of us.

Courtesy of a shifter's amazing recovery time, he was already erect by the time I chose my spot. Probably because of the massaging, or because I point-bank told him his ass was mine and I was marking it so he always remembered that.

Poor guy. I don't know if I was his first lover. I never asked, and he pointedly refuses to ask me about any of my previous males. We chose each other. That was all that counted. We didn't have to be the first, just the last. Either way, he's definitely out of practice. It doesn't take much for me to make him go off, and he just about *exploded* when I marked him.

Fair enough. I don't think I've ever come so hard in my life as when he bit me that night in Hickory.

Tonight's the night of the full moon. Lust and promise and *forever* are hovering just out of our reach. To make what we have final, all he has to do is claim me beneath the moon. That doesn't necessarily mean out in the wild—in our bedroom would work just as well—but we're shifters.

Why shouldn't we claim each other wearing nothing but the moonlight on our skin?

"Do you have your necklace?" he asks me.

I know exactly what he means.

It was a gift from Henry to Chase in celebration of our mating. He'd claimed me as his in front of Nolan, and later told the head of the Cadre the same thing: that I was his mate. Mates are sacred to all supes, shifter or vamp. As a sign of an apology on behalf of the Cadre, Henry had one of his vampires retrieve Nolan's severed head. He broke off one of his fangs and had a necklace made for me.

Giving it to Chase as a peace offering wasn't the only reason why Henry had sent those two Cadre vamps up to our cabin. While doing their patrol, they reported seeing four unfamiliar wolves running in a diamond formation. They told Henry who called Chase down to see if he knew anything about that.

Of course, he didn't. He had no idea that West, Joey, Tucker, and Darrin had followed West's bond to the area and were searching for some sign of me. He's smart, though. Putting two and two together, he took the necklace from Henry, thanked him for the heads up, and arrived back at the cabin just in time to miss us leaving.

I found out why it took him so long to come after me. He actually put himself back in the chains for the night so that he didn't show up at Hickory and slaughter the four males—and the rest of the pack if he had to—to get to me.

See? I knew I had good reason to worry. But, on the plus side, my feral's getting better and better. Even Chase admitted that the old him would've followed his instincts and gone after me. The new Chase? He knew that I'd never get over him hurting one of my packmates. He waited until the urge to attack became a determination to get his mate back before he came for me.

And, Luna, am I glad he did…

With the necklace, he doesn't have to worry about another vampire bothering me if I go anywhere in our territory without him. He's even willing to bring me to visit Sacre Coeur now that I have a fang that's an added layer of protection.

As for shifter rivals, he has none. Any wolf who might be interested would look the other way as soon as they saw the mating mark on my neck. After tonight, it'll show every other male that I'm a happily bonded she-wolf.

I can't freaking wait. Dipping beneath my shirt—one of a set of cheap tees that Chase bought for me when I complained I was going through my new clothes too quickly—I snag the golden chain, lifting it up so he can see the fang hanging there. It's charmed, too, just like his. When I go from my skin to my fur, my clothes might be destroyed if I don't strip first, but I'll have the necklace wherever I go.

"You ready, Quinn?"

Excitement floods through me at the way his deep voice dropped.

Breathlessly, I nod.

His eyes flash. "*Run.*"

It's instinctive. My feral growls for me to run and I don't

even stop to tear off my shirt or shuck my jeans. I shift on the spot, letting the tatters of another outfit rain down behind me. My wolf is already streaking away from him, my tail going horizontal at my speed.

My mate lives up to his name. I run. He chases.

But I'm as eager to make him mine as he is, so while the chase is fun, so is what happens after it's done.

Together, we sprawl out under the moonlight as Chase claims me for once and for all.

Look at that. I started out the feral's captive. Now I'm the feral's mate.

No.

As our bond snaps into place, the Luna bathing us both in her silver glow, I dig my claws into his back as he empties himself inside of me. And I think to myself, this feral alpha is *Quinn*'s chosen mate.

For the first time in my life, I finally got to choose.

EPILOGUE

WEST

I t doesn't matter how far away Quinn is from me, or that she released me from our bond when she rejected me three nights ago. Whether she stayed in Hickory or she followed her heart to that small cabin outside of the Fang City… it doesn't matter. When she performs the Luna Ceremony with that feral of hers, I still feel an echo of it.

I expected it to be a relief. One of the many weights off of my shoulders. In a way, it is. For the first time since I met her golden gaze across the crowd that fateful day, I don't have my wolf torn between circling the dark-haired delta and lying down at Helene's feet, offering his throat up to her, begging for her to show me a lick of attention.

In other ways, it's like I'm a failure. A complete fuck-up. The Luna meant for me to make Quinn mine, but I couldn't. Not while Helene owned every inch of my heart and soul already.

I've loved her since I was a pup, too young to understand the yearning I felt for her. This isn't fate. It isn't ordained by our goddess. This is just a male knowing in an instant that he's found his female.

But she isn't mine. Helene is promised to another, and when her alpha mate comes calling, I know she'll go. She believes it's her duty, that no matter how she might feel for me, she'll become an alpha's mate.

Unless… unless she becomes a beta's bride.

My love for her is the biggest open secret in the pack. It's the same reason why I never had to outright reject Quinn, turning her into an outcast; unfortunately, I did anyway. She always knew she'd only have half a male at best if we went through with our mating. She'd own my body, and my wolf would be the perfect mate to hers, but could I ever love her as much as Helene?

No. It was harsh, but reality, and when I accepted that, I knew I could never accept Quinn as mine.

For nine years I believed that Helene would always be. I imprinted on her with our first kiss, and I waited for the day the Luna would inevitably mark us as fated mates. For alphas, the Luna usually blesses them with the name of their mate during the Alpha Ceremony; sometimes they learn it as a future Alpha, like Rafael did. As a beta, I just thought I had to wait until I came of age.

Didn't work like that. I was twenty-seven before I heard the Luna's whispers, but it wasn't Helene's name echoing in my ears.

And it wasn't Helene that my body responded to in that moment like it had a thousand times before.

When my cock went hard for Quinn the first time, it was an utter betrayal. By then, I already knew that Helene was promised to Rafael, but I'd resigned myself to waiting for her to wake up and choose me. To love *me*.

To claim me the same way I would've killed to make her mine…

Wolves have a reputation of mating for life. Fuck if I know if that's true or not, but shifters? We do. Once you perform the Luna Ceremony, have claiming sex, and leave a mark, the only way out is death. Even then, if I thought all I had to do was wait out her mating and challenge Rafael, I might. But a mate bond doesn't necessarily snap after death, and most mates don't survive it when theirs died.

If I challenge Rafael and win, I might lose Helene anyway.

As if I have her now…

She loves me. Though she hasn't said the words back to me since we were twenty-four and foolishly oblivious to the way life works in a pack, Helene *is* my life. She loves me, but she won't betray the promises she already made. She won't betray the Sylvan Pack and the alliance we have with Gravetail.

She loves me, but she'll never betray Bishop—

"*Fuck!*"

The curse bursts out of me. At the same time my fingernails lengthen and thicken, my claws unsheathing. My shoulders hunch, fangs burning my gums, begging to turn the canines into something sharper, something more fierce and wild and untamable.

Just then I understand what might drive an honorable male to become feral. The weight is lifted, but all that does is remind me that I'm still suffering.

At least Quinn isn't anymore.

She's set me free. No challenges—though her feral would've if she hadn't gone to him before he reached pack land—and no regrets. I gave up on the life we might've had the second I realized that I still loved Helene more than I was willing to bend and accept a fated mate bond. Quinn chose her mate, and though some part of me will forever wonder *what-if,* the way she laughed at me when I offered to bond with her was the right move.

We were fated, but she wasn't mine. I didn't choose Quinn—I chose Helene. I'll always choose her.

Once upon a time I thought she chose me, too. And it doesn't matter that I know why she won't.

I still turn into a fucking wrecking ball as I take out all of my frustration, my fury, my *need* on the tree in front of me. I scratch and I claw, shredding the bark until I reach the pulpy inside. The behemoth shakes under my attack, but I keep on going until I've turned my claws into nubs, blood trickling down my fingers, pooling in the lines of my ripped-open palms.

Sweat drips from my brow, stinging my eyes. I need the pain. Without it, I feel the ache of Helene's continued rejection, plus the emptiness where Quinn used to reside in my chest. She deserves her happiness. If I accepted our bond—if she fucking settled with me like I asked her to—she would've been as miserable as I am. As possible as it was, I did love her. I wanted what was best for her.

It just… it wasn't me, damn it. It would never be me.

I keep going. The hickory can take it. It's covered with gouges from all the other times I just couldn't keep control, and though it shudders, it'll be here the next time I need an outlet for my grief.

It's the only one I have.

My claws will heal. So will my fingers and my palms. Using my forearm to knock back a loose strand of hair, swiping the sweat slicking my forehead, I fold my fists, pummeling the other side of the tree. Flesh tears. Blood sprays. A drop lands on my lip and I lick it, savoring the tang.

More.

If any of my packmates saw me like this, they'd be running to Bishop. Alphas are the only ranks in a structured wolf pack that are allowed to momentarily lose control like this. With all the aggression built into their bodies, if they didn't blow off steam from time to time, they'd explode. Betas… we're the righthand wolves. The calm and steadying ones. Those responsible for bringing our Alpha back from the brink for the good of the pack.

Mates do that, too, but Luna knows I don't have one. Rejected by one, loved then released by the other, the only thing that calms me is knowing that my chosen mate loved me once.

I swear to our cruel goddess, she loves me still.

Helene refuses to say the words. From the moment it became obvious to the pack that Quinn was my fated mate, she stopped me from telling her the same. We were both meant for others, she whispered the night she tried to tell me goodbye, and it was better that we leave it at that.

Better? I'd asked. Better for fucking *who*?

Not me. And when I saw the regret in her pale yellow eyes, I knew that Helene was as trapped in the idea of a fated mating as I was. Only, I loved her enough that I made a conscious decision to reject Quinn, leaving her free to choose her feral.

If only my female would choose me, I could make her that happy. I know I could.

There's still time. Glancing down at my hands, my chest heaving as I struggle to get my control back, I see that my shifter healing has already started to kick in. The smaller cuts have closed over, the larger gashes beginning to clot. Dried blood has left my hands sticky. I quickly wipe them on the flattened grass, trying to get rid of some of it. My packmates will still scent it on me, but we're shifters. Blood usually comes with the territory.

Rising up, I run my ruined fingers through my sweat-soaked hair. I shove it out of my face, tilting my head up to look at the sun streaming through the trees, the early light of dawn shining on me. The Luna must've swapped places with it while I was getting some of that out of my system.

It's morning now.

My wolf is hungry. My stomach is twisted—it usually is—but I'm not an idiot. I need food, and I also need to show my face around the pack so that they know their Beta isn't suffering from losing his mate. It doesn't matter that I ache for Helene, or that I was happy for Quinn to choose another male instead. Shifters live and die by the grace of the Luna, and if the Luna blesses us with a mate, we're not supposed to disagree. It's one thing to choose a mate before we find the one meant for us, but to reject them for another? The way my packmates see it now, Quinn rejected me for her feral.

Good. Though I know I came off like I couldn't give a shit about Quinn's feelings, I did. I'd rather be the rejected Beta than the prick who kicked a poor delta while she was down. I can take the hit. For a while, she had to, but if I could've made any other choice—if I could've turned my fucking heart off and put Helene behind me—I would have. But I couldn't, and I have to live with that.

That's my choice.

Bleeding for Helene? I'll do it gladly.

Waiting on the sidelines, hoping against hope that maybe she'll see me again?

If that's what it takes.

I exhale. It's rough, a full-body shake, and then I'm West again. I'm the Beta of the Sylvan Pack. I'm Luna-damned untouchable, answering to only two others: my Alpha and my heart.

Glancing around, avoiding the added destruction to my tree now that the urge to hurt has been sated for the moment, I tap into my wolf and look out into the distance. Shimmering with dew, I see a flower that would look perfect nestled in Helene's beautiful blonde hair.

I can't say I love her. She won't let me.

But I can show her.

Loping past the closely grown trees, I pluck the flower from the dirt, then twirl the stem between two blood-stained fingers. My claws are halfway regenerated, and by the time I stop by Helene's cabin on the way to meet with Bishop, they should be completely healed.

She doesn't need to know that I still visit the edge of Hickory to work myself over in order to feel *something*. This is where the best flowers grow on our territory, and I'll never visit her without one.

And maybe… maybe she might realize she has a choice to make after all.

CHASE
AND THE
CHAINS

A STOLEN MATES SHORT STORY

SARAH SPADE

CHASE
AND THE
CHAINS

SARAH SPADE

CHASE AND THE CHAINS

CHASE

You'd think that, after twelve years on my land, the wretched stench of hundreds of vampires living nearby wouldn't bother me as much as it does.

Probably because I need it as a reminder. With the meaty, rotten, *corpse* stink hitting me every time I walk out my door, I can never forget.

Even if I wanted to avoid it or get used to it, I *can't.*

Gotta give Henry credit. The only parcel of land available for me to claim back then is downwind from the Fang City. In Sacre Coeur, humans and vamps live together, with an impenetrable border surrounding the city; impenetrable, of course, unless you've got a vamp fang in your mouth or one hanging off a chain that you'd been gifted. Any supe with a nose and a brain would steer clear of any Fang City. It isn't worth the trouble.

And then there's me.

Even when the wind is still and the stink doesn't travel all the way to my cabin, I can feel the vampire's cold, dark, dead magic on my skin. Alpha shifters are tuned to danger by design —and, though I lost my pack when I was sixteen so I've never been an actual Alpha to one, it works the same for any wolf born with an alpha's rank and dominance. Alphas are created to protect their packmates. I might've failed once, but even as I wear the fang that belonged to the bastard bloodsucker who killed my family, I live by one adage: keep your friends close, and your enemies closer.

Supernaturals are a ticking time bomb. I know that better than anyone. Though I came to Sacre Coeur an angry teen, looking to get revenge on the whole damn Fang City for the pain I was feeling inside, I finally realized that not every vamp was bad. Not every human was an annoyance.

Not every supe was damaged.

Lucius was. When he chanced upon the small pack I grew up in, he'd tripped so far into the hazy bloodlust that he went from vampire to rogue. He targeted the Wilder pack because we were shifters, and because he could.

I spent three years searching him down. At nineteen, I did. I wasn't feral then, but a lone wolf—and, undeniably, an alpha.

When I tracked Lucius to Sacre Coeur, claiming the territory as mine, Henry—the Cadre leader—couldn't ignore the shifter stubbornly prowling along the edge of his city. At the beginning, I challenge every bloodsucker insight, demanding they bring me Lucius so I could have my revenge.

As a peace offering, Henry did just that. He executed the rogue, bringing me his head and his fang.

Vamp justice. It's not for everyone, but I'm a supe. The fang hangs around my throat to this day, a sign I accepted his offer of peace.

Makes sense. In his own way, Henry's as much the Alpha of Sacre Coeur as I was to my patch of land and my empty cabin—and we both proved that again just his past month when another one of his vampires attacked my mate.

This time, I got to take his head, and Henry gifted Quinn a fang of her own so that she could feel safe walking around the woods that surround our home.

And if I purposely ignore the fact that she was running away from *me* when Nolan chanced upon her, it's because I have to. Remembering everything I put Quinn through while I was trying to kickstart the mating dance is a surefire way to bring that *thing* inside of me out again. It's been thirteen days, a new record, and I'd like to keep it like that.

Because not every supe is damaged—but I'm one of those who is.

Feral… When vampires give in to their bloodlust, they're rogues. When a shifter loses the balance between both of his halves, becoming more beast than man, we call it feral.

That happened to me. Only about a year ago, when the strain on my wolf being denied his vengeance became too much, something inside of me snapped. My wolf didn't care that Lucius was dead, only that *we* didn't kill him. He wanted to rip. To snarl. To tear flesh. To make beings *bleed.*

More than anything, though, he wanted to run.

Now that? That I could do.

Struggling against the desires of the thing I was when the beast came out—no logical thought, only urges and twisted emotions—I could run. I didn't think I would be able to outrun the ghosts of my family, the guilt of not being there to fight for them when the rogue appeared, or even the loneliness that had me nearly succumbing all the way to the *thing.* I wasn't try to outrun it.

I was trying to *distract* it.

Besides, when I lost control like that, I wasn't dwelling on what I lost, or what I couldn't have.

I'm an alpha. The Luna granted me all of this dominance so that I could take a mate, maybe lead a pack, but definitely create a family of my own. A new Wilder Pack. For more than a decade, it was a dream, but as though our goddess was punishing me for turning my back on her, on our people, she didn't help me find my fated mate.

She could have. During the ceremony that made an alpha wolf *the* Alpha, she rewarded her chosen leader with the names of their mate. Some even before that.

Not me.

I had no pack. No family. No *mate*—

—until the fateful day I ran hours and hours away from Sacre Coeur, living up to my name as I chased a sliver of happiness and peace, and I fucking *found* it.

When the feral wolf ruling me caught the scent of rainwater on the breeze during a sunny, summer day, the rage, the pain, the *ache* that tormented me became entirely focused on finding that female and, in whatever way I could, making her mine.

Fuck Fate. She wasn't the female the Luna might've meant for me, but I wanted her anyway.

So what if Quinn Malone, my gorgeous delta female, *did* have a fated mate of her own? Because she did. Damn it, she had *him*. The Beta of the Sylvan Pack. The bonehead who was handed Quinn on a golden platter by the Luna, only to reject her for another female.

I snort; I can do that now, since she chose *me*. He's an idiot. A she-wolf like Quinn… you fight for her. I would've. I *wanted* to. When I was working on trying to figure out how to get her to come home with me, to stay with me, just taking her wasn't my first idea. Though I had no idea how to approach a female, I thought I could at least introduce myself.

But then I realized that the feral would probably want to say *hi*, too—and his version would have me pulling her lush body beneath mine, rutting mindlessly because he was convinced she was his mate—and I couldn't let that happen. If Quinn met the feral before Chase, she'd never accept my pursuit of her.

Challenge the Beta, though? I liked that idea. Kill Reed and I'd prove I was the stronger male. That I could be the perfect protector for her.

Only… I watched her. I spent more time lurking around the wolf territory of the Sylvan Pack than I did in my own cabin during the nine months I stalked her, learning everything I could about the female who'd one day be mine.

All that time, she was waiting for her fated mate to give in to their bond. She wanted him to. He was wavering. I could tell. I saw it happen with a fated couple in my old pack. No wolf can resist a half-bond. Either you finalize it or you break it, and since Reed kept her dangling on a hook for so long without outright rejecting her, I knew it was because he was going to take my female when he realized he had no other choice.

I couldn't let him finalize their fated mate bond. Not with the only female I'd found who actually soothed the savage beast inside of me. Whenever I was near Quinn, hiding just out of reach of her senses, breathing her scent into my lungs, hearing her voice as she playfully talked to herself even as her own heart carried as much ache as mine… the *thing* stayed settled. Always watching, always hungry, sure. If I let up for only a second, he'd break free, but I was strong enough to hold him back.

I felt… not whole. Not yet. But like I would be.

I am now.

My hand—not the furry, twisted paw that's there when the beast is loose—is resting on the door handle to the cabin. I give myself a full body shake, trying to get rid of the vampire stink clinging to me, then let myself inside.

Two steps into the living room of our cabin and my cock is already twitching the second her intoxicating scent reaches me.

My home smells of rainwater, and it's all because of Quinn.

Tonight, that's not the only scent I pick up on as I stalk toward the kitchen, though it's definitely the first one that hits me. My beloved mate had shooed me out of the cabin a couple of hours earlier, telling me that it was her turn to cook for me again, and that I could finally come back when the sun started to set for the evening.

Now… it's not that she was lying. Not exactly. My wolf knows instinctively whenever someone is lying to him; another perk of being an alpha, since dishonesty is one of those dangers and threats we pick up on. A month now since we've become forever mates, I can forgive Quinn a lot of her tiny lies; after how our relationship got its start, she's earned it. She rarely does it anymore, not since she learned that—despite being a feral—I never lost the ability.

I don't know why she was surprised. It's common knowledge in the shifter world that alpha wolves can do that. Being a feral? That part of me—the *thing*—is so much closer to pure instinct and emotion than even my wolf. Because of that, the feral's more sensitive to it. So, though I've been able to keep the *thing* back for the most part after our mating, I can still experience the world as he understands it.

Plus, I know Quinn. My mate wasn't quite lying to me earlier this afternoon, but she definitely was up to something.

I didn't care. My gorgeous mate was offering to feed me, and I needed to go out and do some territorial markings to reinforce the borders to our land anyway. If it made her happy to tell me to go, I'd kiss the hell out of her, then jog out the door until she wanted me back.

Pissing around our territory isn't a hardship. It's a *necessity*. I'm thorough, taking my time, because the safety of my mate is on the line.

I'll never forget how fucking scared I was that I would be too late to get to her after she ran away. With her fear rushing through the woods to slap at me, the tang of her blood driving the *thing* wild, I knew my worst fear had come true: a vampire had gotten its claws on my female.

My only regret is that I only got to kill Nolan just the one time…

Now, I might've made Quinn my captive once, but I refuse to do it again. If she wants to visit the garden I planted for her, or take the drive into Sacre Coeur, or go for a run on our territory to get away from me because, Luna knows, I can be too much sometimes… if I have to piss circles on every tree, bush, and stick to let other predators know to stay away, I will.

For Quinn, I'll do fucking *anything*.

Luna, she's so damn beautiful.

Her skin is pale enough that it shines like moonlight. Her eyes are a perfect shifter's gold, without a single hint of insanity lurking in their depths. She's got this soft, soft black hair that spills down her back. When I bury my nose in its length, it's like I'm standing out in the middle of a sunshower. It smells of rainwater and heat, and it does more to soothe my feral side than anything else.

Except, of course, when she opens that soft body of hers up to me, giving me pleasure that I only dreamed of.

Sometimes I think I *am* dreaming. Even now, watching her as she finishes eating her dinner, I still can't believe she's mine.

My plate is already empty. Quinn says her cooking is passable, and she isn't lying when she says that. She doesn't realize that the meaning behind her meals—that she's telling me that she loves me, and my little delta will provide for her alpha mate in her own way—makes it the most delicious food I've ever eaten.

But, as she reminded me when we sat down together to eat twenty minutes ago, she prefers it when I cook. She doesn't like to do dishes, either, and she tells me that she expects them all washed up before we turn in for the night.

If the order came from anyone else, I'd be snapping my teeth at them for daring to tell me what to do. But not my mate, and that's because she *is* my mate.

It's bad enough being a dominant wolf. Going feral is like walking on a taut string of barbed wire with a bunch of prowling, hungry lions below you. It hurts like hell with every step you take, but when you know that what's waiting if you fall is a million times worse, you suck it up. A little pain is better than being savaged, and I've learned how to navigate that fine line. I might not use the chains I installed in the basement when I decided I had no choice but to steal my mate away from her pack, but make no mistake. I'm never completely free—unless I've got Quinn to rely on to keep me sane.

Being around her? It's more than just how the beast reacts to her, or how my wolf accepted that hers was his mate the first time he ever saw her. Though her lovely brindle wolf is a delta, she is no submissive.

Thank the Luna. I'd eat a submissive she-wolf alive…

I always knew I needed a female who would stand up to me, and once she realized that I was putty in her paws when it came to her, she never backed down again.

And, Luna, nothing in this world makes me go harder faster than when she jerks her chin up at me, golden eyes flashing, as she gives me a command that she absolutely expects me to follow.

Which I absolutely will.

She's my mate. I'll do anything she wants. Give her anything she desires. I'll buy her gifts, shower her with affection, plant her a thousand flowers so she knows that I love her more than anything.

If she wants to be the dominant wolf in our mating, I'll forever get on my knees for her.

And, since our mating, I've had that opportunity. It's the best.

Quinn tastes fucking *amazing* and, shit. I'm finished my meal and, already, I'm salivating.

My mate has the cutest little nick in her right eyebrow. She preened the first time I pointed it out so now I make sure to kiss it softly when we're cuddling after a mating, both my wolf and the feral too sated for me to worry about losing control during the afterglow.

Just then she's raising it in that habit of hers. "You've got that look again, you know," she says.

Busted.

Still, I try to act like I don't know what she means. "What look?"

"Your hungry look. Really, Chase? We just ate dinner. You even had seconds."

"Maybe I'm not hungry for food."

"Oh." Quinn's lips curve slightly, her eyes lighting up. "You in the mood for… dessert, baby?"

My nostril flare. Her rainwater scent is a soothing balm to my soul. But the rich musk of her arousal? It lights a fire inside of me. It's all I can do to keep from knocking the plates from the table, lifting Quinn up on top of it, and making her pussy my dessert.

I want that desperately. So much so that I wouldn't be surprised if I started drooling.

But this is Quinn's show. I knew she was up to something, and that mischievous expression on her face tells me that she's ready for me to discover what it is. The 'baby' seals it. My mate is full of pet names for me—something I've never experienced before—and 'baby' is my favorite.

I'm six feet tall, a hulking beast of a male even when Chase is in control, with enough baggage to fill a hotel, and she calls me 'baby' when she's feeling affectionate.

Affectionate, and *horny*.

"What have you got for me?" I ask.

I try to sound unaffected, to keep the game going.

I fail utterly, my voice dropping to a low rasp.

Though we never discussed it, I know that Quinn has a lot more experience when it comes to sex than I do; considering she was my first *everything*, it wasn't that hard to tell when she, at least, knew what she was doing. At sixteen, when most males were looking for a she-wolf to help them with their constant hard-ons and out-of-control hormones, I was busy burying the remains of my former pack. After that, my sole focus was on getting revenge. By the time I was a lone wolf, I was in my early twenties, I lived in a cabin bordering a Fang City, and I had no need for females.

Until, of course, I stumbled upon Quinn…

She darts out her tongue, playing at the corner of her mouth. Matching my rasp, letting me know that we're still playing the way that bonded mates do, she says, "A deal."

And… I'm lost. "What?"

Her golden eyes brighten. "I want to make a deal with you. There's something I've been wanting to do for a while now, and with the Luna almost full again, it's an itch I'm dying to have scratched. What do you think, Chase? You want to help your mate out?"

"You don't even have to ask," I tell her earnestly. "You know I'll do anything for you."

"Anything?" When I nod, she says something that would've had me on my guard if it was anyone else but Quinn: "Do you trust me?"

"Yes."

I don't even hesitate. With the bond stretching between us, I know that she's excited about what's to come next. And even if she wasn't? She's my mate.

I trust her with my life. I have to.

She *is* my life.

<hr>

I trust Quinn with my life. I… I'm just not so sure I trust her with the silver chains in the basement.

I glance at the length of chain stretched out on the floor.

The shackles are open, the key tossed in the far corner of the room.

She wants me to put them on. Willingly. Because she asked me to.

I will. For her, I *will*.

But first—

"Have I mentioned how much I love you?"

"Constantly, Chase, but if you want to again, I won't stop you."

Leaning over her, I press a quick kiss to the top of her head. Her scent wraps all the way around me, and though I'm a little uncertain when I straighten to see the chains winking up at me again, I'm ready to do whatever she wants me to.

"So. The chains…"

"Yup."

I place my hand on her shoulder, instinctively finding my mark near her throat. I stroke it with my thumb. "And this isn't just about you finally getting revenge on me for using them on you? Because I'm so fucking sorry, Quinn. I just… I wasn't thinking. The *thing* was."

"I've told you like a hundred times already," she says, patting me on my side. "It wasn't the chains that pissed me off. It was not getting a choice. The quicksilver, too, but remember: when I finally got to choose, I chose you, baby. There's no revenge between us. There will never be. So get that through your thick skull already, okay?"

Luna, I love it when she's forceful. "Yes, ma'am."

She rolls her eyes. "Don't be a dick."

"I thought you liked my dick," I tease.

"Oh. I do. A lot. In case you haven't figured it out, that's why we're down here."

Behind the zipper of my jeans, my cock jumps. It was

already as hard as it could get by the time I joined her in the kitchen. On our way down to the basement, I'd had to do a discreet adjustment, but now the poor thing is simply aching to get inside of Quinn again.

It's only been about five hours. An eternity to my poor libido.

"I'm ready when you are, Quinn."

She hold up her pointer finger. "Hang on. I said I wanted to make a deal first. You still up to it?"

Her voice has gone throaty. There's a promise of pleasure there I can't deny. "Of course."

"Here it us. We get naked, then you let me chain you up." Her fingers trail gently down my side, playing with the waist of my jeans before she steps away, reaching for the hem of her shirt. "I promise to make it worth your while."

Honestly? I'm a simple male. Even before my wolf splintered, turning into something more primal than he already was, I was never very complicated. I see things in black and white, what I want and what I'll take.

I want my mate. And Quinn? She had me at *naked*.

Flicking open the button on my jeans, I yank down the zipper, and quickly shuck them off. Since that's all I was wearing, I'm done before she's removed more than her shirt.

Quinn chuckles. "Eager, aren't you, baby?"

The truth is easy to admit.

"With you, yeah. Of course I am."

Smiling at my answer, she reaches behind her to unhook her bra. I bite back a moan when she removes it, showing me her gorgeous tits.

I swear, nothing feels better in my hands. My palms are already itching to feel their weight.

"Down, boy," she teases, and I'm not sure what she means

more: the way I was already reaching out to caress her globes, or how my erection is bobbing toward her.

"You're still not naked yet," I tell her in a mock growl. I show her my claws. Regular shifter claws, not the monstrosities I have when the beast is free. They're still sharp enough. "This is your deal, but I can help you with that."

"Hey, we can't all walk around in a pair of jeans and that's all, you know." She casts an appreciative glance over my bare chest, then to my jutting cock as she bites down on her bottom lip. "Not that I'm complaining, Chase. Not one bit."

If it was up to me, I'd go naked all of the time if it weren't for things like pesky public indecency laws holding me back. My whole life, I've preferred to stick to a pair of jeans and nothing else, especially since I might have to shift to my wolf at a moment's notice; as a feral, I just have an excuse now. Hey. You can only replace so many shirts and boots and boxers before you realize that they're all a waste.

Then again, as Quinn shimmies out of her jeans, then tugs her silky panties down past her hips, I have to admit that there's definitely some allure when it comes to my female's underthings…

Once she's finally undressed, she points to the floor. "You ready?"

"My heart is yours," I tell her, dropping down to a crouch, then kicking my legs out in front of me so I'm resting on my ass. I move my back up against the cinder block wall, sitting next to the chains. "So is my body. You can do anything you want to me."

"Oh, I'm planning on it."

Quinn picks up her jeans. She roots around inside of one of the back pockets before pulling out two scraps of familiar grey fabric.

"One of your old shirts," she explains. "The one that tore when I grabbed you. I found it in the closet and figured you wouldn't need it as much as I do. I hope you don't mind."

"Not at all."

Most of my clothes are at least a decade old. Once I went through my last growth spurt, a lanky shifter turning into the alpha he was born to be, I bought enough jeans and t-shirts to fill a closet and left it at that.

Jeans are sturdy. Cotton? Not so much.

As if she's thinking along the same lines as I am, Quinn says, "We gotta get you new clothes, Chase."

I drop my gaze to my lap, looking at my cock. It already has a drop of pre-come on it. "Can shopping wait?"

My mate giggles. "Sure thing, baby."

Dropping to her knees, Quinn uses the piece of fabric to scoot the silver shackle closer to her. She kisses my ankle, running her fingers over the skin, before wrapping it with the fabric. Just like I did when I brought my precious captive to the basement, she's wrapping me with a protective layer so I don't burn.

She attaches the one shackle, doing it quickly so that the silver on the outside doesn't burn her. She does the same thing to my other ankle, complete with the kiss and the caress.

Sitting back on her heels, Quinn smiles at her handiwork. "Perfect," she says, and I think she's talking about how she has me shackled—until she firmly takes my erection in her soft hand.

Unh. I don't think I'll ever get used to the shock of her willingly touching me like that. It's so damn *good*.

She starts at the base, stroking me from root to tip. It's a leisurely stroke, no real force behind it, but her gentle touch is already enough to test my sanity—and she's just getting started.

"These chains," she murmurs, and I can't tell if she's talking to me or to herself. "You trapped me in them. I trapped you that one time. I was thinking… maybe it's time we use them for something good. Something like *this*."

Tossing her hair over her shoulder, making sure my mark is on full display for me and my possessive wolf, she leans down, swirling her tongue over the head of my cock.

"Quinn." Oh, that feels even better, but I have to wonder: is she doing this because she wants to? Or because she's trying to prove something? This isn't the first time she's gone down on me, but the chains… I'm not so sure I understand what the deal with the chains is. "My mate. You don't have to—"

She cuts me off with a death grip on my cock. I strangle my groan as she squeezes the poor thing, pulling her lips away from my overheated, damp flesh.

"I know. I don't have to *do* anything. But… I love you, Chase. If this is one way I can show you, let me. Okay?"

I nod. "Of course."

"Good."

She lowers his head again, but not before I see her triumphant grin.

Mm. There really is nothing sexier than a confident female, except maybe *my* female as she takes my entire length between her lips again before slowly fucking me with her mouth and that wicked, wicked tongue of hers.

Consumed by her ministrations, I'm so turned on I can barely think straight.

I try anyway.

The chains are on my ankles. They don't stop me from patting her hair or caressing her cheeks as she sucks my cock.

The silver—even with the grey t-shirt protecting my skin from its burn—is enough to dull the feral's razor-sharp edge of need, but that's all it does.

Unless she decides to bite me, then dart away out of my reach, I can't figure out why this was something she wanted to do so badly that she actually arranged for just this scenario.

And that's when, after hollowing her cheeks, making me throw my head back with how good her tongue feels on my cock, she lets my erection slip out from between her lips with an almost audible *pop*.

I fight back the urge to grab her head and guide it back to my dick.

I was so damn close!

Could she tell? Probably. Quinn seems to know my body better than I do, and our mate bond would've told her that I was just about to erupt in her mouth.

"Quinn…" It's a plea. I don't even give a shit. I'll beg if I have to.

"I know, baby. But I want you to finish inside of me, okay?"

"Told you," I grit out, forcing my orgasm back. I was so close, and now that I know she's ready to mate, I have to hold on long enough to make it good for her. "I'm yours."

Tiptoeing over the chain, careful not to burn the bottoms of her feet, Quinn drops down over my lap.

Her eyes spark. "Got you right where I want you."

I hold out my arms, inviting her into my embrace. "I'm not going anywhere."

"I know. I've chained you to the wall to make sure of it," she teases.

Pressing up against my chest with one forearm while arching her back, she grabs my slick cock, then angles it so that our bodies meet. With a soft sigh, she pushes down on top of me.

The moment our groins touch, I exhale in pure contentment. Sure, my mate has me in chains, and my cock is primed to go off like a rocket, but there's nothing like that first connection when I know that the two of us are as close as two souls can be.

Well, except for when Quinn starts to ride.

Because that? That is fucking *magical*.

We've explored countless positions this past month. My wolf constantly grunts at me to take my mate from behind, but if I'm being honest? Nothing is as erotic as Quinn riding me, her tits bouncing in front of me, her beautiful face twisted in an expression of power and pleasure as my little delta mate dominates her alpha male.

As Quinn sinks down on top of my cock, again and again and again, I wonder for the millionth time how I got so fucking lucky.

I don't know, and if anyone tries to take her from me, I'll rip their balls off and make them eat them, and I won't even have to be feral to do it. That's my possessive instincts racing to the fore. I'll do it as a human, and I'll be wearing a predator's grin as I do.

This is my female. My mate. If the Beta of the Sylvan Pack was too much of an idiot to realize that, oh well. No matter where she goes, I'll follow. I'll chase. Let her put me in chains if she wants. I broke out of them once before to get to her when I sensed the vampire terrorizing her.

Her fear slapped at me over the distance. Even then we had some kind of undeniable tie. Now we have a bond.

If something happened at this very moment while I was shackled and Quinn was suddenly gone, I'd gnaw off both feet, then run on bloody stumps to get to her. That's how devoted I am to my mate.

That thought in mind, suddenly, I understand what she meant before.

It's time to use them for something good…

Obviously, Quinn has bad feelings associated with this set of chains. I used them to trap her, taking away her choice. She used them to shackle my wrist after I betrayed her by biting her the first time she showed any interest in me.

I get it. Now that we're fully mated, she needs to dominate the chains just as much as she dominates me.

At that realization, I can't hold back anymore. I'm going to come whether I like it or not. So, reaching between our bodies, I rub frantically at her clit, hoping that I'll bring her with me when I go over.

Thank the Luna, I *do*.

Once I'm completely spent and she stops gasping the pleasurable pulses from her climax, Quinn eventually climbs up and off of me.

My cock slides out of her as she moves away, though the sight of her ass wiggling seductively as she crosses the corner before bending over to retrieve the key to the chains has it stirring again.

It's a shifter thing. Just like how we have advanced regenerative properties, super strength, and phenomenal speed, I can get it up again almost immediately.

And why wouldn't I? I'm insatiable for my mate.

My cock is willing. My chest is still heaving from the rush of my orgasm. Just… give me a second, I think. I'll be completely ready for another round then.

Maybe I can convince Quinn to take it up to the bedroom. She did her thing with the chains. Now it's my turn to lay her out beneath me while we leisurely mate. For that, I must prefer a mattress to the hard concrete floor I'm currently sprawled out on.

Luckily, my mate seems to have the same idea. At the very least, she's dropped to her knees, head bowed over one of the silver shackles on my ankles, key clutched between her fingers.

She starts to slip the key into the notch on the shackle, pausing before she can turn it.

Quinn always points out my 'hungry' look. I should really begin to do the same for his mischievous expression.

She taps her chin with her finger. "You know… I did have to sleep down here for like three nights when you had me chained up after we first me."

Telling her that we first met nine months before she knew I was stalking her isn't smart. I don't, but that doesn't stop her from what she's thinking.

With a slight smirk tugging on her lips, she pulls the key back out.

I blink. "You're not going to leave me naked down here after you just made me come like a fucking fountain, are you? I want to get my mouth on you," I tell her, my voice dropping to a growl. "It's my turn. I want the dessert you promised me."

Through our bond, I can tell just how much that turns her on. My mate… she's such a tease, and I *love* it. "You drive a hard bargain, Chase. What else will you give me to free you from the chains?"

"Fuck the chains. If you come over here and sit on my face, I'll give you any Luna-damned thing you want."

"Good answer. Just for that, I'll let you loose first."

I wasn't kidding. If she wants to keep me down here in chains, I'd do it. For a taste of her, and because I owe her. I'll probably spend the rest of ours lives making it up to her—no matter how many times she tells me she forgives me—and I'll look forward to every second of it.

For now? My mouth is watering for her.

True to her word, Quinn sticks the keys back into the notch, releasing the first shackle. While I reach down to remove the fabric band she has around my ankle, she makes quick work of the second.

I rip off the second piece of fabric as Quinn gets back to her feet.

Now where does my mate think she's going? She said I could have my dessert.

I'm *starving* for it.

I swoop her up in my arms, squeezing her to me. My cock is back at half-mast and stiffening quick. It wouldn't take much to shift her so that I could get back inside of her where I belong.

But that's not what *I* want.

I'm a fucking alpha. A feral, too. What good is all of my dominance and strength if I can't use it to rip a delighted squeal out of my mate?

Bracing my bare feet against the concrete floor, I heft up my arms, lifting Quinn as high as I can. She's a smart female; she would know exactly what I was doing even if I hadn't already mentioned face-sitting to her. So, hooking her legs over my shoulders, she scoots until my pussy is hovering near my mouth, and my fingers are biting in her ass cheeks.

"You know," I murmur, the heat of my breath making her squirm, "I'd give you whatever you wanted no matter what. Not just because you unchained me."

She threads her fingers into my hair, jerking my head so that I'm perfectly positioned where she wants me.

Just now, this *is* what she wants.

"Yeah. I know," she tells me, her voice a purr that's somehow fitting for a she-wolf. "It was still more fun this way."

As I use the flat of my tongue to give her my first lick, groaning when I taste my seed mingling with her wetness, I have to agree with Quinn.

The chains. The head. The mating… now me pleasuring my mate for dessert after a delicious meal that proves she loves me as much as I'm a slave for the female I once had as my captive?

Oh, yeah. This is *definitely* more fun…

STOLEN MATES BOOK TWO
THE BETA'S BRIDE
INTERNATIONAL BESTSELLING AUTHOR
SARAH SPADE

THE BETA'S BRIDE

SARAH SPADE

ONE
CANARI

My brother might be the Alpha of the Sylvan Pack, but when he has something he has to say, Bishop usually comes to me.

He's not the only one, either. As the Omega, I have my own cabin in the heart of pack land, about a ten-minute jog from where the Alpha cabin is set. Unlike Bishop, I'm available for any packmate in need around the clock, and it's not hard to find me.

Of course, that's not why Bishop makes an exception to his rule of expecting his subordinates to go to him when he's available in the den.

In Hickory, I'm the exception to nearly *every* rule.

It's partly because—except for his beloved mate—I'm the only other Dupuis in Hickory; our parents are long gone, and we were the only two pups they had. More than that, though, it's my status as our pack Omega. I exist outside of the hierarchy, coddled and prized for the type of wolf that I shift into.

Which is why, when one of the deltas who serves on Bishop's pack council comes to my cabin to tell me that my brother wants to see me in his den, I'm surprised. I haven't been summoned by Bishop since the morning after his Alpha Ceremony eleven years ago when he told me that his fated mate was a she-wolf named Sofia Russo, and that she was coming to Hickory to bond with him.

That should have been my first clue that something was wrong.

My second? The fact that Tucker is the wolf who came to retrieve me.

If it was so important that I had to go to Bishop, I would've expected that he'd send his Beta. His right-hand wolf, West is the male that Bishop relies on more than anyone in the Sylvan Pack.

Plus, he's my chosen mate. We're not officially bonded—at West's request, we haven't performed the Luna Ceremony that would make our union unbreakable—but we've been in a committed relationship since we were nineteen. Five years now he's been my male, and with his possessive shifter instincts, he'd insist on escorting me to meet with Bishop.

Not that he's jealous of me being alone with the Alpha. Ew. Of course not. He's my *brother*, for Luna's sake.

But Tucker Madden? One of the wolves from our age group who used to sniff around my tail until I made it clear that I only ever wanted West? It doesn't matter that Tucker's been with nearly every unmated she-wolf in Hickory *except* for me. West wouldn't like me being alone with Tucker, even if it's on Bishop's orders.

So… that means he doesn't know, right?

I'm intrigued.

I shouldn't have been.

I should have thrown the door closed when I saw Tucker's toothy smile.

I didn't—and now he's holding the door to Bishop's den open for me. Once I stride past him, the short skirt on my sundress swishing as I move purposely toward my brother, Tucker nods at Bishop before disappearing.

We're alone. Me standing in the middle of the space when I realize that no one else is here except for Bishop. My big, brawny brother sitting behind his sturdy desk. His beard hides his expression from me; reaching toward him with my wolf, I can't feel anything as he blocks me from reading his emotions.

Bishop is the only one in the pack who can do that. His excuse is that he had a lot of practice since he practically raised me himself after our parents' deaths. Spending so much time around me as an omega pup, he developed a bit of a shield against my abilities. He doesn't often use it against me, but when he's trying to protect me—like usual—he has a habit of locking down around me.

Something's up.

When the Alpha is in residence, the den is rarely empty. Connected to the cabin that belongs to Bishop and his mate, the cozy space is a safe place. It's where any packmate can go meet with the Alpha and know that he'll listen to their concerns. Pack councils and meets are held in this room. It's always open when the Alpha's home, and I can't remember a time when I've walked inside of it and found Bishop by himself.

At the very least, the chair next to him usually seats the other half of the Alpha couple. But Sofia is notably missing, and Bishop looks even more stern than normal.

He waits until Tucker closes the door behind us before he lifts his big paw, gesturing at the empty chair opposite his desk.

"Canari. Please. Sit."

I still, my stomach going tight with instant nerves. My wolf chuffs softly, her head cocked to the side as she responds to my reaction. I can't help it. I think I'd been a little oblivious that this wasn't just a routine discussion with my brother until now, and I'm suddenly apprehensive.

I don't know what's worse, either: that it's just me and Bishop in the den, or that he called me 'canari'.

Canari. For as far back as I can remember, Bishop has had this little pet name for me. As we grew older, as he took on the mantle of responsibility, becoming Alpha at the young age of twenty-one, he didn't use it as often.

He's using it now, and I'm beginning to realize that something serious is going on.

Our parents died when I was barely a pup. I was five, Bishop ten, and while the rest of the pack gathered around us, making sure we wanted for nothing, Bishop did everything he could to take care of me.

Always the alpha, I think, giving him a small smile as I move forward and finally sink into the seat opposite of him.

Canari…

The tragedy of our parents' death turned Bishop hard, but I was too young to be affected by it. Oh, no. That came much later. But when I was still too naive to understand what losing my omega mother so young meant, I entertained myself by singing little songs I made up that—even then—I hoped would make my stone-faced older brother smile.

Back then, Bishop was still a pup himself, walking around with the weight of the world on his shoulders. A silly song from his younger sister was sometimes enough to remind him that the world wasn't such a dark place, and he developed the habit of calling me 'canari'.

Little songbird.

As fitting now as it was then, I still love to sing—and I live to keep my packmates content.

Even before I knew exactly what an omega wolf was, my instincts always led me to make someone feel better. Sometimes it was at my expense, but it didn't matter. I was born to make my packmates happy. To calm them, to soothe them, to keep them on the right side of going feral…

I was the official Omega by the time I was sixteen. Following Bishop's lead, I've devoted myself to the Sylvan Pack for years. It's what's expected of me, and I'm happy to do it.

Just like, if Bishop has a task for me, I'll do that, too.

When he doesn't say anything, just watches me with a scrutinizing look in his dark gold eyes, I decide to ask, "Where's Sofia?"

I love his mate. She's a sweet delta she-wolf from the River Run Pack, across the country from where we are, and the closest thing I've ever had to a sister.

He clears his throat. "She'll be here if you need anyone to discuss this with. If you don't want to tell me, I mean."

What? There isn't anything I can't confide in to my brother. From my first period to when I began a relationship with his best friend, he's always been there for me.

I make a face. "What are you talking about?"

"I had a visitor this morning. He came all this way from Darkwoods to meet with Helene Dupuis."

Wait… that's me. "Darkwoods?" I've heard of it before. It's the name of a wolf shifter pack territory. "The Gravetail Pack from Texas?"

I don't know a lot about all of the shifter packs in the

United States. I have no intentions of leaving the Sylvan Pack, so it's never interested me. I only know about Gravetail because they're our biggest threat. Only about a three-hour run away from Hickory in our fur, if they decide to challenge the nearest shifter pack for their territory, it would be us.

"That's right. Three wolves asked for permission to see you. I sent them away until you agree, but one of them... he won't be deterred. He's coming back tomorrow unless you refuse to see him."

"But... why?" They have to have their own Omega, and since that's my only worth as a wolf—and Bishop keeps me so protected, no one should know about me from off pack land otherwise—I don't understand. "Why would a Gravetail wolf want to meet with me?"

"You tell me, canari."

I open my mouth. Before I can repeat that I have no idea what he's talking about, a whisper of a soft, feminine voice flitters through my mind. It's as quick as the wind, almost as intangible, but I latch onto it before it vanishes as suddenly as it appeared.

I echo the sound out loud: *"Rafael Cruces."*

Bishop exhales roughly.

Me? I suddenly feel like I'm going to bend over and throw up on the hardwood floor of the Alpha's den.

When it comes to finding our Luna-given fated mates, our revered goddess doesn't usually whisper the name to any wolves except for an alpha. It's traditionally been her gift when a new Alpha takes over their pack. It happened to Bishop when the Luna whispered Sofia's name to him, and I heard stories about the same thing happening to our former Alpha, Xavier.

Other packmates—whether we're deltas, omegas, betas, or

even the elder gammas—recognize their fated mates more subtly. Eyes meet and, suddenly, the beginning of a mate bond is born between them.

Not me. The Luna just whispered Rafael's name in my ear, and I instinctively know that I'm meant for him.

Wait—

Cruces? "The Alpha of the Gravetail Pack is Luis Cruces, not Rafael. Right?"

Bishop nods. "Luis is the Alpha. His son is the Alpha-heir. He'll take over for his father one day, and when he does, he's asking that you accept him as your mate."

Because he knows my name.

Because the Luna whispered it to *him*.

Because he's my fated mate.

My whole life, I wanted to find mine. The one male meant for me, who would love me and protect me and keep me safe when I couldn't do it myself… the male the Luna would pick out as my perfect match, and who I would build a life with.

And then, at nineteen, I found my heart's mate. It didn't matter that the Luna didn't tell me he was mine. He *was* mine—

—but I'm not his.

That's what Bishop is telling me. For years, West put off performing the Luna Ceremony that would make us bonded mates because he was convinced that, one day, the Luna would tell us that we were fated.

We're not. And all that means to me is that there's a female out there who's more perfect for West than I am.

I take a deep breath, then ask, "Does West know?"

"No. When the Gravetail wolves came to ask for entry into Hickory, he was on patrol on the south side of our territory.

He knows that Rafael and his entourage were here, but not why."

"Because it's Alpha business," I murmur, my voice catching in my throat.

That's West for you. He knows his place is at Bishop's right hand, but he trusts Bishop implicitly.

Some of the gamma wolves who were part of Xavier's inner circle thought my brother was making a mistake when he handpicked West to be his Beta. He had the right type of wolf for the job, and could be coached to have the right temperament, but their close friendship isn't the reason why he ended up with the position.

His absolute belief that Bishop will always make the correct decision for the Sylvan Pack is what makes him the perfect Beta.

Bishop raps his palms on his desk. "It's not Alpha business, canari. It's *your* business. Rafael came to proposition you. You get the choice. You can reject him. Just because the Luna said he's yours, he only is if you agree."

That's right.

A mate gets to choose, and so stunned at this turn of events, I'm not sure what to do.

I don't ask my brother for his input. His own actions precede him. When the Luna told him Sofia was his mate, he didn't hesitate. He might not have crossed the country to meet her, but he did make a call out to the River Run Pack the day after he became Alpha. She accepted his proposal without knowing a single thing about him, and they were bonded the next full moon.

That was eleven years ago. Proving that the Luna knows what she's doing, they've been madly in love ever since.

But I'm already in love with another male...

Do I love him enough to let him go? Can I keep West, knowing that I'm depriving him of the chance to find his fated mate?

His true love?

And Rafael… I've never met him before, but if he's going to one day be the Alpha of the Gravetail Pack, a union with him would erase the threat to the Sylvan Pack. I'd have to leave Hickory, of course, but I'd be leaving my home knowing that my new pack would be allies with my old one.

Put that way, what else could I do?

"If I agree, would I have to leave with him today?"

"Of course not. Alphas only take their mate once they have control of their pack. With Luis still the Alpha, it could be years before Rafael is in a position to make you his mate. You'd stay here with me, under my protection."

I'd stay with Bishop and Sofia. But West…

"I'll meet with Rafael," I tell him. "But let me talk to West first, okay?"

My brother is careful not to give anything away with his expression. "You've made your choice then?"

I… I don't think I even have one.

"Yes."

Bishop reaches his palm out. Knowing what he wants, I place mine in his. "Don't worry about West. He'll understand. He'll do what's best for you."

I know he will. West loves me, but he's as equally devoted to Hickory as me and Bishop are.

"And I'll do what's best for the pack."

Bishop didn't tell West about Rafael. He told me he didn't, and I also trust him implicitly.

But my chosen mate knows. I'm one hundred percent convinced that he does. Why else is he standing outside of my cabin when I approach it, pacing nervously, his hands empty?

The pacing is unexpected, but not as much as the fact that he didn't bring a flower for me.

He always does.

It started when he became the Beta of the pack at twenty-one. Until then, we were inseparable. Friends since we were pups, our relationship turned serious when we were nineteen, the two of us always together. He had his own cabin, but since I was given the Omega cabin when I took the position in the pack, he spent all of his time at mine.

But then our last Beta retired, becoming a gamma, and Bishop offered the post to West. I was so proud of him, even if that meant pack duties and responsibilities kept us apart more than I liked.

That's when West started bringing me flowers. Whenever we were away from each other for more than a few hours at a time, he would pluck one of the wildflowers that grew on the outskirts of pack land and bring it back for me.

A reminder that he loved me, he would say, and that I was on his mind even when we were apart.

Not today, though. As if he was in such a frantic rush to reach me, he didn't stop for a flower.

When he sees me, he jogs right for me. Throwing open his arms, he's about to hug me when I dance out of his reach.

I've never done that before, but I have to. Touching West right now... I can't.

I just *can't*.

And he knows.

"Tell me it's not true, baby. Tucker said… he said that… *Gravetail.* He's trying to claim you as his fated mate. But that can't be. You're not his. You're *mine.*"

Next time I see Tucker, I'm going to encourage his wolf to lose his libido for a few days. When he can't get it up, maybe then he'll stop interfering in other packmates' matings.

A lump lodges in my throat. I almost invite West inside my cabin to break his heart in private, but I chicken out at the last moment. Having him near, surrounded by his sandalwood scent… this is already going to be so Luna damn hard.

Why make it even harder?

"I thought I was, West. But Tucker's right. I'm going to promise myself to Rafael of the Gravetail Pack."

"What? No! You can't do that. Didn't you just hear me say that you're mine? You always have been. You always will be."

Only I'm not. He might not see that now, but he will. One day, he will.

"We're both meant for others," I whisper, holding back my sob. "It's better if we leave it at that."

"Better? Better for fucking *who*?"

West's eyes are wild. Normally a steely, dark grey so unusual for shifters, they're the vivid gold of his wolf peeking through.

"For you. For me." For your future mate. "For the pack."

He hears something in my voice. I thought I did a good job holding back my ache, but he narrows his gaze on me.

West is looking right into my eyes, and though his type of wolf can't sense emotions like mine can, he knows me. He can tell how much it's killing me to do this, how much I'm already regretting this… and that only firms his resolve to push back against me.

"You don't have to do this. Screw the pack. This is about us. You and me, baby."

That's where he's wrong. A Luna-given mate is a gift. To refuse it is to insult our goddess. I can't do that. Just like I can't reject an alliance with the Gravetail Pack. And screw the pack? That's traitor talk. If Bishop heard him, I don't want to know how he'd react to that.

For so many reasons, I have to nip this in the bud. Least of all because of the tears welling up in my eyes.

"I'm sorry, West. My mind's made up. Don't make this any harder, okay?"

"I have to. I can't… okay, your mind's made up, Lane? How do I change it?"

I knew it would be rough, ending things with West. I didn't know it would be *excruciating*.

"You can't."

His jaw clenches.

"Weston, please—"

"I love you, Helene."

And that's exactly why this is as difficult as it is.

"I know."

But he'll love his fated mate more. That's why us shifters prize the idea of being blessed by the Luna to find that one soul. They're perfect for us, and when West finds his, he'll understand why I have to do this. For the pack, yes, but for him, too.

I want him to be happy. I don't ever want him to look at me and wonder: *what if?*

I don't want to look at him and think the same thing…

"For the sake of what we had, if you love me, then do this one thing for me: don't ever tell me again."

West runs his hands through his thick, dark brown hair,

leaving the strands to stand up on end when he drops his arms back to his side. He looks at me like I asked him to slit his throat for me, and while he'll do it, it's only because it's what I want.

But then he thins his lips. "I love you too much to let you go. You know that, too?"

Actually… I do. "But you're going to have to."

West opens his mouth. I see his fangs gleaming, much longer than their usual canine size. His wolf is riding him hard, and only his iron-tight control is keeping him from shifting on the spot.

I brace myself, waiting for him to argue.

He doesn't. With one more long look at me, he spins on his heel and stalks away. In between one footfall and the next, it becomes a run, then a sprint. Within seconds, West is gone.

And I'm free to dash inside and let out the sobs I struggled to keep in.

I'M ALL CRIED OUT, AND MORE DETERMINED THAN EVER TO GO through with my choice.

Maybe it's a good thing that West had to run away from me. I know I broke his heart—just like mine is shattered—but it's for the best.

Right?

When I hear the gentle knock at my door, I think it's Sofia. She stopped by about an hour ago, offering to sit with me while I worked through my emotions, but I respectfully asked her to come back later.

After making sure my yellow eyes aren't rimmed with red, my hair mussed from burying my face in my pillow as I sobbed, I straighten out my wrinkled dress and reach for the doorknob.

It's not Sofia standing on my porch.

It's West, and he's holding three wildflowers out to me: a brown-eyed Susan, a Shasta daisy, and a dandelion.

With a defiant expression on his handsome face, creased with lines that weren't there earlier and spattered with something that looks suspiciously like blood—but that's, hopefully, mud—West says, "You said I couldn't tell you that I love you. You didn't say anything about showing you."

That's West for you: determined and logical, and unwilling to ever give up so easily when he wants something.

That's how he convinced me to take a chance on him even when I always suspected that I wasn't his fated mate—and it's why I do something that I'll come to regret for years to come.

I accept the flowers.

TWO
SANDALWOOD

ONE MONTH EARLIER

andalwood.

I catch the alluring scent of sandalwood on the breeze filtering in through my open window before I catch a vague hint of honey peeking through the musk. Between the two of them, I know exactly who's heading my way—and what he'll be clutching between his fingers.

I don't have any excuse to send him away right now. After how rough the last two weeks have been, I'd have to be a heartless female to try. So when I hear his gentle rap at my door, I take a moment to settle myself, then pull it inward.

And there he is.

Weston, as gorgeous—and as untouchable—as ever.

On closer inspection, I can see the smallest of imperfections that hint at how tough of a time he's having. His dark grey eyes have faint purple shadows beneath them. His hair—usually cut short—is overgrown. His body is as muscular and lean as ever, but he looks like he lost ten pounds in the last two weeks.

His t-shirt used to fit his sculpted chest perfectly. Now? It hangs loosely.

As always, his wolf is torn. He wants to throw himself at my feet, begging me to run my fingers through his fur, while also having this urge to run off in search of something.

No. Not something.

Someone.

My heart breaks for him. Not for the first time, I'm so glad that he can't sense my emotions like I can other wolves.

He's hurting, but he smiles when he sees me. "Hey. Can I come in?"

Oh, West…

He's been so good. Since I asked him not to say 'I love you' to me, he's only slipped up a few times. No reason to use the words when the hundreds and hundreds of flowers he's brought me over the years send the message loud and clear.

Still tries to get an invite into my personal territory, though. No matter how I always gently refuse to let him into the Omega cabin, he always tries.

I'll give him credit. When I shake my head, he doesn't push. He just holds out the purple coneflower wordlessly until I accept it.

Because I will, and he knows it.

Despite its name, the petals are closer to pink than purple. Silky soft beneath the pads on my fingers, I murmur a soft, "Thank you."

He's quick. A shifter male is always quick, and a beta is only second to an alpha. His fingers shoot out, stroking a stray strand of my long, wavy hair. Tucking it behind my ear, he brushes his finger along the shell. "I picked this one on purpose. I thought it would look pretty in your hair."

My skin all but burns where he touched me. These fleeting caresses are so rare, and though I know I shouldn't, I treasure each and every one of them. When I finally leave Hickory, it'll be all I can cling to.

I haven't heard from Rafael since the day he walked into Hickory alongside the Beta of his pack and a pair of delta males. In front of his entourage and my brother, I pledged myself to Rafael as soon as he takes over as Alpha. At that moment, he went from my fated mate to my intended, and West officially became my ex.

He still refuses to accept that.

I always knew he was stubborn. Three years later, I know he's clinging to something we can never have at the expense of the future I sacrificed so much to give him.

By agreeing to mate Rafael when he's ready, I left West free to search for his fated mate. For nearly two and a half years, he refused. He wouldn't leave pack land on the rare chance he stumbled on his fated mate somewhere in the outside world. Level-headed when it comes to everything except his feelings for me, he figured that he was safe on pack land.

He was wrong.

Six months ago, he was sitting with me at dinner in the pack circle, trying to get me to eat food he chose just for me. It was a common occurrence, but what happened next wasn't.

Frustrated with my polite refusal, he glanced away. His eyes landed on the pretty delta in our age group who worked as the pack's stylist. At the same time, Quinn's soft gold gaze flickered West's way and *boom*. In an instant, I knew.

He found his fated mate. The only female meant for him.

His body jerked, surprise and *lust* twisting his features. Before that day, I was the only female he ever looked at like that, and as reality set in, I shoved my untouched plate away from me.

The sounds of the plate scraping across the outdoor table snared West's attention away from Quinn. He blinked, shaking his head, clearing it, then he smiled at me.

It was tight-lipped, but it was a smile.

He never smiled at Quinn. Not then, and not in the months since. He's saved all those crooked grins for me, and as much as I hate myself for treasuring them, too, I'm secretly grateful for them.

I just… maybe he should spare one for his fated mate.

It's been six months. He didn't quite reject her, but that's because—as Beta—he didn't have to. West just continued to act as if nothing had changed, and the whole pack followed his lead—all the way up until the moment Quinn vanished.

That was a few weeks ago. She went out into the woods on the edge of pack land despite a warning that the pack patrols thought we might have an unfamiliar shifter testing our borders, and the next time a sentry passed that way, all they found were a pair of two separate sets of paw prints in the dirt and the tattered shreds of the shirt and jeans Quinn had been wearing that day.

The consensus was that she was taken; definitely by a shifter, if not a feral. While West—at Bishop's command—led a search for the missing she-wolf, my brother made contact with the Gravetail Pack, checking to see if any of their wolves were involved. They weren't, and with Quinn blocking West from finding her through their mate bond, no one knows where she is now.

I like Quinn. I hope she's okay, and that she returns to Hickory. We never had much in common; she's a feisty delta who enjoyed mating as many males as she could before the Luna gave her to West, while she teasingly referred to me as Li'l Miss Pack Princess even before she found out her fated mate was ignoring her to spend time with me.

She put on a brave front, acting as though it didn't cut at her every time West picked me over her, but I'm an Omega.

I know exactly how much she hurt.

Just like I could tell that she would disappear into the woods to be alone so that the pity from the rest of the pack didn't make her pain even worse.

I tried. Reminding West once again that we both have fated mates waiting for us, I nudged him to accept Quinn. He refused. As he said, he would have me or no one, and six months after the Luna tempted him with his true female, he was still trying to convince me to reject Rafael.

I won't, and I only hope that West hasn't already lost his chance at forever with his fated mate.

"Any news on Quinn?"

I shouldn't have asked, and I regret it almost immediately. Even saying her name is like a stab right at the most vulnerable parts of this male.

In front of the rest of the pack, he refuses to let them see. He pulls on that emotionless mask of his, his "Beta" expression, and acts as though it doesn't bother him one way or another that his bond with Quinn Malone has a jagged edge.

But that's in front of the rest of the pack.

In front of me? I see past the mask, and not only because the Omega can tap into any packmate's emotion unless they purposely block us.

"No. Bishop is sure it's the wolf who's been sniffing around the last few months that took her. We just don't know why, though we can guess."

I can, too. No matter how sheltered I've been, when a rogue male shifter makes off with a pretty, unmated female, it's kind of obvious what he wants with her. Lone wolves want mates as much as the rest of us, and if he saw the opportunity to snatch one, he might have.

But if it *is* a feral… she's okay. She has to be. Even if she's purposely blocking West from finding her, if anything happens to her, there's no way she can keep him from finding out now that they have a thread tying them together.

Just like how, despite West wanting the whole pack to think Quinn is nothing to him, I know better. He loves me, but he never wanted to hurt her. Rejecting her would turn her into the pack outcast, the female not good enough for our beloved Beta.

Too bad that West accidentally gave that exact impression by avoiding her these last six months…

West is standing on my porch, one hand on the railing, the other reaching out for me again. I don't even think he's aware he's doing it. Part of his mind is on Quinn—where it belongs, I admit if only to myself—while the other…

He stumbles. Surefooted and confident, West doesn't stumble—but he just did.

I lay my hand on his arm to steady him. He's already recovered by the time I touch him, and I draw my hand back quickly once I see that he's standing straight-backed again.

Still, I have to ask.

"West? Are you okay?"

He rubs his chest with the heel of his hand. "Yeah. I'm fine."

Liar.

My wolf is right. Alpha wolves have the gift of knowing instinctively when a less dominant packmate is lying to them.

I'm no alpha, but as the Omega, I have a similar ability. No matter how well-intentioned, a lie rubs my fur the wrong way.

Only... I get the feeling he doesn't even know what he's saying.

Murmuring that he has to be going—and obviously distracted—West moves in to brush his lips against my cheek. If I wasn't already sure that something was wrong, that absent-minded action would've been enough to set off alarm bells.

I haven't kissed Weston Reed in three years. From the moment I accepted that I would be Rafael's mate, I couldn't. I couldn't change my past with West—and I wouldn't even if I could—but it was up to me to make sure that West knew we wouldn't have a future.

Collecting the flowers he brings me is one thing. I reject the food he tries to feed me, and when he tries to get too close, I always move just out of his reach. And while that doesn't stop him from trying to serve me at least once a week, even West knows better than to push my wolf on physical affection. He's only teasing both of us with something we can never have again.

But he kisses me, then jogs down the porch stairs before running off.

And as he heads in the direction of the Alpha cabin, I tuck the stem of the pink flower behind my ear, nestling the petals in my hair as I wonder what in the name of the Luna had just happened.

It doesn't take long before I know what caught West's attention.

Three days ago, he left Hickory with three members of

Bishop's pack council: Joey, Tucker, and Darrin. They returned late last night with a very subdued Quinn Malone nestled between them. West brought her to meet with Bishop, then escorted her back to her cabin.

He's basically been by her side ever since.

I want to be happy for him. If it wasn't for my visit with Sofia earlier this afternoon, I might have been.

They left on a rescue mission, but after Quinn explained what really happened, it turns out that she's one she-wolf who didn't want to be rescued. The feral who took her captive might have kept her in shifter chains until he could be sure she wouldn't attack him by drugging her with quicksilver and running away with her to his personal territory, but once she understood he was just lonely, she gave him a chance.

Sometime between plotting her own escape and West and the others showing up to bring her home, Quinn fell in love with her feral. She only came back with the four wolves who went after her because she was afraid there might be a confrontation between West and Chase, her feral shifter.

West is the sort of wolf who believes in doing his duty. It's why he went to retrieve Quinn when, for the first time since she was gone, he could track her through their bond; that's what happened the other evening on my porch. It's also why he decided to do the right thing and ask Quinn to accept him as her fated mate.

I was sitting down when Sofia told me that earlier today. At her urging, I was resting on the edge of my sofa, as though she thought I would take the news badly.

I refused to. How could I? Maybe I would've rather heard it from West himself, but for three years I encouraged him to go after his fated mate. I didn't have the right to be upset that he finally listened to me.

Instead, I wished him the best. Not to him, of course, since I haven't seen him since he left with the other three, but if there's one thing I honestly want, it's West's happiness—with or without me.

But just because I tell Sofia I'll be the first to offer West and Quinn my congratulations, it doesn't mean I don't mourn the future I could've had if the Luna hadn't decided to whisper another male's name in my ear. I do, and once Sofia leaves to return to Bishop, I curl up on the edge of my sofa, plug in my headphones, and lose myself in brokenhearted ballads and hopeless love songs.

No matter how loud the volume on my music player is, it does nothing to drown out the fierce wolf howl that rips through Hickory later that night.

I'm already tearing my headphones off, rising up to my feet before the echo of the howl finally dies down.

Even after it's over, something about the nature of the howl sends shivers down my spine. I'm not near enough to the source of the sound to get a good read on the wolf who made it, but I'm positive that it wasn't just any old howl.

That was a warning and a declaration all in one.

It also has an edge of insanity to it. Even if I didn't know that Quinn had spent the last few weeks in a secluded cabin far from pack land trapped with a *feral*, the pain in that howl would've clued me in.

Sofia told me that Quinn warned Bishop that the feral would be coming for her... well, no. That's not the right word for it. Warned implies that Quinn was afraid of her feral when the truth is that, in the time since she was taken, the feral male had courted her in his own way, and asked her to choose him as her mate.

Unlike me, she wasn't clinging to the idea that she had to

mate the male the Luna gave to her. She wanted her feral, but before Bishop could arrange to bring her back to him, it seems as if the feral has taken matters into his own paws.

He won't make it onto pack territory. Whether he's come for Quinn or not, Bishop won't risk allowing a raging feral to step paw in Hickory.

Just in case, I turn the lock on my door before retreating to my couch.

I go and grab a book from one of my shelves, cozying up with it. Since Quinn's return, I've been hiding out in my cabin. Call it cowardly, but even if I am the Omega, if she needs me, she can come to me like the rest of our packmates. I would never want her or her wolf to suffer from her time with the feral, but pack gossip says she's suffering more without him.

Besides, though she's never made it the pack's problem, Quinn's recent dislike of me wasn't something I could easily ignore. For her sake—for West's sake—I *did,* but while the rest of the Sylvan Pack thinks I'm some kind of saint, I'm not.

I'm hiding out, and I don't care if it's pretty obvious why.

Barely ten minutes after that fateful howl, someone is rapping at my door. It's not too late for a packmate in need to request a visit with the Omega so I don't question it. I just set my book to the side, straighten the skirt of my dress, and pad over to the front door to open it.

I don't know who I was expecting to find out there, but when I see West's smiling face staring at me from the porch, the difference between tonight and the last time I saw him is as stark as night and day.

He throws open his arms. "I'm free, baby. I'm finally free."

What—

Oh.

Oh.

Now I see it. The relief from both West and his wolf is obvious. It pours off of him, mingling with an emotion I'm far too familiar with.

Hope.

Oh, *no.*

I'm not quick enough. I start to wish him good night, telling him it's late, we can talk tomorrow as I begin to ease the door shut, but I'm not quick enough.

He grabs onto the doorjamb. He doesn't step inside of my cabin, but there's less than an inch separating the tip of his boot from the threshold. "Don't you have something you want to say to me?"

It's nothing he wants to hear.

He tightens his grip, knuckles gone white with the force. "I don't have a fated bond anymore, Lane. I'm *free.* All you have to do is reject Gravetail and we can start over. Neither one of us will have to worry about fate getting in the way. Quinn gets her feral, *he* can find a mate of his own, and we… Helene? This is fucking amazing. Why aren't you as happy as I am? This is what we wanted."

No. Getting out of mating Quinn Malone without being the bad guy, then convincing me to do the same with Rafael… that's what *he* wants.

West's gaze locks on my face. As an Omega, I can meet a dominant wolf's eyes directly and never have it be taken as a challenge. But, for the first time in a long time, I can't meet West's stare.

I look at the pale pink nail polish on my toes instead.

Over my head, West sucks in a pained breath. "You're still gonna go through with it, aren't you? Go to Gravetail… you still won't choose me."

Through the fringe of my eyelashes, I dare a peek up at

him. In a gentle tone, I remind him, "I never said I would. You know that."

"But I thought—"

I know exactly what he thought.

"Good night, West," I say softly. And then, before he can utter another word, I close the door. He pulls his hand away from the doorjamb a split second before it would've been closed on.

Just like I thought he would.

For the next few moments, I'm on one side of the wood, West standing motionless on the other. I don't move, either. Fingers pressed to my mouth, holding back my sob, I wait for him to go.

Only after I sense his wolf's reluctant retreat do I let the first tears fall.

THREE
ALPHA

NOW

y brother has been the Alpha of the Sylvan Pack for so long that I rarely remember a time when he wasn't.

Growing up, he was the Alpha-heir. Everyone knew that he'd take the reins one day from our former Alpha. Pack gossips used to whisper that Bishop would grow tired of waiting for Xavier to step down and he'd challenge him, but that's not like my brother at all. He's loyal to a fault, and wants nothing but the best for the pack. When he took over at twenty-one—back when me and West were sixteen—it was because Xavier knew it was time for the most dominant beast to be in charge.

And that was Bishop.

Nothing changed between us. If anything, he was even more protective of me once he took over the pack. Then he bonded with Sofia, and if I thought that he'd transfer his protective instinct over to her instead, I was wrong. Turns out Bishop Dupuis has enough to go around.

He treats her like she's precious—to him, she is—and Sofia adores her Alpha mate. Unlike me, it doesn't annoy her that Bishop's always there, breathing down her neck. A maternal delta, she accepts it as a sign of his love and devotion rather than a nuisance.

Today, when I'm once again called in to meet with Bishop in the pack den, Sofia is seated in a chair next to his. They're both behind the wide desk that takes up a majority of the space, heads bowed, whispering to each other.

Well, more like Sofia is whispering to Bishop as he grunts something back to her. Walking in on them, I can tell that—once again—whatever my brother has to tell me, my world's about to change for good.

Bishop nods at my entrance. Sofia smiles warmly.

"Helene. You finally made it."

"Sorry I'm late. Heather needed to sit with my wolf for a bit. I didn't want to leave her until she was feeling better."

Heather's one of the younger teen wolves. About sixteen and just budding into her maturity, she tried to attract one of the males in her age group. He romped with her in the woods last week, but Heather found out from another packmate that he mated another female last night. And while she understood that, without a bond, some wolves like to play the field, that didn't mean it didn't hurt the young female.

"Of course. Pack comes first." Tell me something I don't know. "But we're glad you could slip away. Your brother has something to tell you."

Yeah. I figured.

I don't blame her for speaking up for Bishop; after so many years as the Alpha female of the Sylvan Pack, Sofia's used to interpreting for Bishop. My brother's never been a big talker. Between West and Sofia, they know what every grunt, smirk, and scowl translates to. Most of the time, our packmates just need to feel his dominance brushing against their wolves to know what the Alpha is trying to tell them.

I don't need her to do that for my sake. He talks to me, and even if he didn't, I'm as good as the other two at understanding my brother.

Shoving his seat away from his desk, he widens his legs, boots still on the floor. Gripping her by the wrist, he gently tugs Sofia until she's sitting on his lap.

For a moment, it's like I'm not even here. When Bishop and Sofia are together, the rest of the world disappears.

As an impressionable teenaged she-wolf, I always thought their mating was the most romantic thing ever. An attractive alpha, Bishop could have had any female in the pack. Luna knows many offered, but he's stubborn, too. It's tradition that Alphas wait until shortly after their Alpha Ceremony to take a mate—like Rafael will do with me—and, the night he took over for Xavier, the Luna gave him Sofia's name.

That was that.

He never doubted that she would be perfect for him. He sent for her, and she accepted his offer of mating. They'd been together for eleven years since, and every year they fall deeper and deeper into love.

Watching their mating from a distance made me believe that all fated matings would be the same. It's one of the main reasons I agreed to bond with Rafael. Apart from what an alliance could do for our packs, maybe the Luna was right... maybe I'm meant to love him.

Just like West was meant to love Quinn—but he didn't. He couldn't.

And the doubts I've had about my own fated mating have only doubled, *tripled* in size since then…

I don't know what went wrong with their pairing. But Bishop and Sofia… that's true love right there. Fated or not, it doesn't matter. That's a decade of being partners, of loving and trusting one another… they had to work for their forever.

I did once. I thought I found it—and I lost it. I only hope the Luna knows what she's doing, and that I might find a sliver of happiness with Rafael that Bishop has with his Luna-given mate.

Patting the top of Sofia's hand, he glances down at her. "Let me talk to my sister, cher. Yeah? I'll let you know if I need you."

She presses a kiss to the underside of his clipped beard. "I won't be far."

She's his bonded mate. She never is.

As soon as Sofia slips out of the den, Bishop rises to his feet.

I sink even deeper into my seat.

"It's about Rafael, isn't it?" I guess.

He jerks his head. A nod.

Okay. I take a deep breath, blowing it out through my nose. I knew this day was coming. I mean, it's been common knowledge that I would have to leave Hickory for three years. I might have hoped it could've been a decade more, but as the Luna already proved to me, you don't always get what you want.

"He's getting ready to be Alpha?"

This time, Bishop shakes his head. And then he surprises me by announcing, "He already is. Had his Alpha Ceremony two Lunas ago."

What?

To make matters worse, there's something in the way Bishops says that so certainly, it's like this isn't news to him like it is to me.

"How long have you known?"

"A month."

"What?"

He nods again. "When I contacted the Alpha of the Gravetail Pack to see if they had any information about where Quinn had gone. Her mate was an outsider, and I thought he might be from Darkwoods. The male I got on the phone wasn't Luis. It was Rafael. He took over for his father the month before, canari. He's the Alpha now."

"Why didn't he tell you?" Because he would've gone through Bishop to get to me. "Why are you only telling me now?"

"It's one thing to take over a loyal pack. Xavier picked me to be the next Alpha so I never had any challenges. Rafael… he wasn't so lucky. His hold on his pack wasn't as strong as mine was after his Alpha Ceremony. He wasn't gonna bring an omega she-wolf into that mess. Not until he was sure he could protect you. He's ready now."

I understand that. It's for the same reason why Bishop would have kept that knowledge close to his vest. Why tell me when all I would've done is worry about what was going on in Darkwoods—and fret over my deadline to leave the Sylvan Pack looming closer and closer.

Because he knew how I would react—and what it would do to his Beta to find out that Rafael is prepared to take me as his mate.

It seems like a million years ago that we were having a similar talk. It was only three, but I remember it clear as day. Now, like then, my only thought is to ask:

"Does West know?"

"I told him this morning, canari."

A lump lodges in my throat. "Oh. Um. Okay. And he's doing all right?"

"He took off for the hickories as soon as he heard."

Well, that answers my question, doesn't it?

He's not doing all right at all.

West doesn't think I know what he does when he disappears into the hickories.

He doesn't know that *I* know that he shakes off the mantle of being the Beta, lashing out at the trees, using them to bleed, to hurt, to grieve, to *rage*… but I do because I know West.

And if there's anyone who understands what it's like to need to have a few moments to themselves to be something different than what everyone expects you to be… it's me.

Omegas don't get angry. Betas don't rage.

But sometimes… sometimes we *do*.

That's where he was when I was meeting with Bishop. This time, my brother gave his Beta an advance warning so he could get himself under control before he—inevitably—faced me again.

Which he does. Barely five minutes after I arrive at the Omega cabin, head whirling with everything Bishop told me, West comes racing toward me.

I'm on the porch. Hiding inside of my cabin would only make this harder, so I waited and tried not to gasp when he comes thundering up the stairs.

West is… *disheveled* is the only word I can think to use. His hair is mussed, sticking up on one side; it looks like he jammed his fingers through it, catching his claws on the strands and tugging them. Normally clean-shaven, his jaw is shadowed with the beginnings of a beard. His jeans have mud and—my wolf keens when she scents the rusty tang—West's blood spattered on them.

In his hand, he holds a wildflower. The stem is mangled, but the petals are pristine. No matter what hell he's been through, he made sure to bring me as flawless a flower as he could.

The Beta is the second-highest rank in a wolf shifter's pack hierarchy. The right-hand male to the Alpha, their type of wolf is characterized by a cool head and clear thoughts. That's the reason why he has his trips into the woods, working off the worst of his wild urges where no one can see him.

Only this time? He didn't leave them among the hickories. Like the wildflower, he brought them right to me.

"Helene." The pain in his voice as he utters my name nearly breaks my heart. "Tell me it's not true. Tell me you're not going."

There's a wild look in his eyes, gold and glimmering and *lost* that I've only ever seen once before: the day I told him that Rafael was my fated mate, and our relationship was over.

He didn't believe me then.

For three years, he held onto the hope that he could change my mind—and now time's up.

"I'm sorry, West." I'm so, so sorry. "I can't."

He falls back on his heels, my whisper a blow his powerful wolf couldn't dodge.

"So that's it? You're just… you're going? You're leaving Hickory. You're leaving *me.*"

My chest hurts. My eyes burn.

And still, I murmur, "Yes."

That one word is all it takes. As though the last three years of West holding onto the belief that I would change my mind and reject Rafael never happened, a sudden change comes over West.

"Well." Everything about him ices over. "I… Bishop told me. I didn't want to believe it, but you… you couldn't make it any clearer, could you?"

"West—"

He steps down. Shaking his body, his wild side falls away. Suddenly, I'm face to face with the Beta of the Sylvan Pack. "He's a lucky wolf. To have your loyalty after only meeting once. Then again, we all have our duty, don't we?"

I open my mouth. Close it.

Nod.

Because we *do*.

Without another word, he backs down the last few stairs. One last look, and then he walks away as if he'd only stopped by with a message from the Alpha.

It isn't until he's gone that I remember the flower in his hand. He never gave it to me. He was still clutching it tightly as he strode away.

And that, more than anything, lets me know that he's finally—*finally*—stopped chasing me.

He should've known this would be the outcome. After all, we're shifters. We live and die at the grace of our Alpha and the Luna. We have our duty.

And, whether we want to or not, we do it.

He's the Beta. No one should understand that better than him.

FOUR
QUINN

n the Sylvan Pack, West has a reputation.

Sometimes I wonder how big a role I played in forming it. While we were together, no one would ever have thought of him as cold or unapproachable. That only came after, and the shift was so noticeable because the only time he *wasn't* was when he was around me.

He's not cruel. In fact, as Beta, he's worked hard to earn the respect of our packmates. Most are drawn to a high-ranking wolf who acts as though he never loses control. It makes them feel secure in the power of the pack. They're content, knowing that, if the Alpha went on a rage-fueled rampage, there's at least one other wolf who can temper his, well, *temper.* They don't see his lack of visible emotions as a weakness. It's the opposite. He's strong, and there isn't a single packmate in Hickory who isn't loyal to a fault to West.

Still, there's no denying that—to those who don't know him as well as I do—the Beta is cold. Rational. He speaks in a clipped voice and takes nobody's shit. While no wolf wants to have to face the Alpha's dominant beast and explosive fury, those with a brain know that West might be icy cold, but he's just as dangerous.

In a shifter pack, *dangerous* is a good thing.

But while West has a reputation, I've always seen the other side of this male. The male who would slip a 'fuck' into every other sentence when he's excitable about getting his point across, with his wicked smile and his even more wicked fingers, and a scorching look that could make the right female nearly combust on the spot. The male who is stubborn and determined enough to push against insurmountable odds. The male who loves with his whole heart, who swallows his pain, who refuses to let anyone see it… but who couldn't hide it from me.

Until now. Until he sacrificed his fated mate.

Whether Quinn did the actual rejecting or not, if West had claimed her when they first recognized each other as fated mates, she would've had him. She never would've left to be with her feral shifter mate on a small patch of land across Louisiana. West would have been hers—but he isn't, and it's all my fault.

Not that he blames me. He doesn't have to. From the moment he came to me, telling me he was free only for me to remind him *again* that I wasn't, West…the Beta started treating me like I was like every other packmate in Hickory.

It's what I thought I wanted. For West to finally move on… it's what was best for both of us, and the pack.

Even so, I don't realize how much I'd miss having him near until he's gone.

No more stops at my cabin. No more wistful, puppy dog looks at dinner when I decline his offer to fetch me a plate. No more daringly whispered compliments, or visits to the hickories where West goes to blow off some steam before coming to me with a hole in his chest that I would give anything to be able to fill again.

No more flowers.

The flowers hurt the most. They shouldn't. I have no claim to West, and I'm just super selfish, taking his drawing back from me as a personal insult. It might have taken him three years, but he finally got the hint and left me alone—and I *hate* it.

I haven't spoken to him in two weeks. That's unheard of for us. Even if we couldn't be mates, West has always been my best friend. It's why I wouldn't reject him as brutally as another she-wolf might; I meant it when I told him that I never wanted to hurt him. I guess I just never expected it to be so hard when he finally became as cold and distant with me as he is with everyone else.

For the last few days, I don't even see him. I've taken to spending any of my free time on the porch of my cabin, hoping to get a glimpse of him. My wolf whines at his continued absence. My human side isn't doing too much better.

Not that the rest of the pack has any idea. The best thing about being an Omega? I can sense, read, and even manipulate other wolves' emotions, but I'm an expert at concealing how I truly feel.

They see prim, perfect Helene with her placid expression, bouncy blonde curls, and soft yellow eyes sitting on the porch, legs crossed beneath her dress, staring dreamily out into the comings and goings of the Sylvan Pack and have no idea that I want to rip every last hair out of my head.

But I can't. Like Bishop, like West, I'll do my duty for the good of the pack. And if I'm bitter sometimes at what being the perfect Omega has cost me, without West to see through my facade—one of only two in the pack who can—no one knows the turmoil inside of me.

Depending on which full moon Rafael wants to perform the Luna Ceremony, I'll be leaving for Texas soon. One week, maybe five… but it doesn't matter to West. It seems like he's already said his goodbye.

I finally asked Bishop if West was busy with pack duties. No. West asked for some time off from his responsibilities, and since he hasn't had any break since becoming the pack Beta six years ago, Bishop gave him all the time he needed.

Translation: he doesn't want to be around me, and he probably won't come back until after I've left to be with my intended.

I already knew that he's been spending most of that time off pack land. Though our bond might not be fated, it was forged from a lifetime of friendship, and five years of a committed relationship. I can't follow him through it—that only works with fated mate bonds, or those that the Luna blesses during the full moon—but I can always sense when he's away from Hickory.

Away from me.

And, honestly, I don't blame him one bit.

I FINALLY SAW WEST AGAIN THIS MORNING.

It was the fleetest glimpse. I'd sensed him returning to Hickory last night, too late to visit him at his cabin. I'd hoped that, maybe, he might visit me before breakfast. He didn't, and when I went to the pack circle to eat breakfast with some of my other packmates, he was already on his way out.

I saw him from a distance. No way I could miss the way he

moves, or how his body fills out his jeans. His wolf is like a beacon; even if I didn't recognize him from behind, the spark of his beta wolf sings to me. But he was gone before I could even think to go after him, so I grabbed some food from the communal serving dishes, then sat down.

Everyone wants to sit near the Omega. They want to be able to sense my wolf brushing up against theirs… but actually sitting *with* me? West was the only one who ever did.

Just because I'm on my own, doesn't mean that I'm apart from the rest of the community. As I eat my eggs, I can hear the latest gossip. Shifters are worse than little old human ladies, and by the time I'm finished, I discover that West isn't the only one who returned to Hickory last night.

Quinn Malone did, too.

I've been waiting for that. Last month, she followed that outrageous howl to the feral shifter who chased her all the way across Louisiana. After rejecting West, she went right to her chosen mate. They bonded during the next Luna, and Quinn moved into the feral's den near Sacre Coeur, one of the most infamous Fang Cities in the state.

According to rumor, as devoted as her male is, he's too untamable to join pack life. He's also an alpha, and we already have one. Quinn is still technically a member of the Sylvan Pack—she hasn't gone lone wolf or anything—though she's a packmate off of pack territory.

That's why she's visiting. She has her own cabin full of stuff that she left behind when she went after her feral. Last week, Sofia told me that Quinn asked permission from Bishop to bring Chase Wilder with her to gather up her belongings. Bishop granted it, and now they're here.

Hoping to avoid running into Quinn, I press my luck after breakfast when I go in search of West. I can sense he's still in

Hickory, but pack land is vast and I can't stray too far from the Omega cabin in case one of my packmates needs me.

I press my luck—and I lose when I cross paths with West's former intended.

In so many ways, Quinn Malone is my opposite. I'm wearing a pale pink sundress. She has on a silky-looking, dark red blouse and a pair of tight black jeans. My hair is long, wavy, and blonde. Hers is an inky shade, straight as a pin, hitting her shoulders. I look innocent; Quinn is a walking sex magnet. Her golden eyes dare you to challenge her, even though she's a low-ranking delta. She's feisty, too, and all but glowing with affection for her mate.

Being bonded looks amazing on her, and for the first time since the Luna told Quinn she was meant for West—and West made it clear she *wasn't*—the pretty delta smiles at me when we meet.

Then she flags me down, intent on having a conversation, and I can't think of a polite way to refuse.

"Helene, hi! How are you?"

Been better. "I'm doing great," I say. "You?"

"*Amazing.*"

Quinn's beaming. Even if she wasn't bursting with love, it's easy to see that her new mate has done wonders for her. For months, she ducked her head, avoiding packmates, hiding out in the woods to miss out on their pitying stares. West didn't mean to turn her into a pack outcast by rejecting their mate bond, but it happened anyway. This she-wolf was another casualty of the fallout from mine and West's relationship, and even if I'm walking into a mating I don't necessarily want, I'm glad that at least one of us is happy.

"Is your mate with you?" I ask. "I'd love to say hello."

"Have you met a male wolf before?" Quinn retorts, a tease

in her tone. "The only way I could get Chase to agree to let me come back to get my stuff is by promising I'd let him tag along."

I glance over her shoulder. She's right. I know male shifters, and I'm surprised when I don't see him lurking close by, keeping a watchful eye on his mate.

"Where is he?"

"Honestly? With West." I must have made a face because she laughs. "I know, right? But the Beta asked to talk to my mate. I told Chase to be on his best behavior and left them at my cabin. I also told them both I'd be really pissed if they got blood anywhere on my stuff so don't look so worried, Helene. They'll be fine."

Do I look worried? West wanting a chat with the feral shifter who came all the way to Hickory to challenge him for Quinn? Turned out he didn't need to—obviously, since Quinn chose Chase as her mate—but forgive me if I'm a little uneasy at *that* pairing.

When I change the subject, she lets me. She also doesn't ask me about West. Smart female. Just like everyone else in Hickory, she doesn't want to risk upsetting the Omega.

That doesn't mean she gives another wave and walks off to wait for her mate to track her down. The opposite, actually. For the next ten minutes, she talks to me like we're old friends. Which, technically, we are. Part of the same age group, until I became the Omega, I counted Quinn as one of my friends. She was always closer to West, but we were at least *friendly*.

And then she was picked by the Luna to be West's seven months ago, and the last shreds of our friendship were dead and gone.

That's one reason why I don't understand her obvious insistence on having this conversation. It delves into small talk fairly quickly. Quinn asks about Kara and her twins, the most recent pups born into the Sylvan Pack, and answers my questions about what it's like living outside of Hickory. She laughs off my shock that she's content living so close to a vampire community, and smirks when she shows me the vampire fang she has dangling off of a golden chain hanging around her throat.

A 'free pass', she calls it. I don't even want to know what that means, or how a she-wolf like Quinn got her paws on a vamp fang in the first place.

She looks like she's about to tell me when, in the middle of a sentence, the fang falls from her light grip. A smile curving her lips, she glances over her shoulder just in time for us to notice a dark-haired, tanned male stalking toward us.

Toward *her*.

She gives him a once-over as he reaches her. "No blood," she notes approvingly. "But no West, either. I hope that means you didn't gut West, wash off the gore, and now you're here to tell me we need to shift and run before the Alpha finds out."

She's teasing. The brooding look on her mate's face says that maybe… just maybe… she really isn't.

Chase nods, moving into her. "The Beta's fine. He just… he had a question for me about"—the feral's head shifts, eyes locking on my face—"something. Hello," he rasps. "You must be the Omega."

Feral or not, an alpha's senses are unparalleled. "Yes."

Quinn gestures at her mate's chest. "Helene, this is Chase."

Something about him is so familiar. Not his face. Handsome as he is, it's a different type of male beauty. West has a classic face, straight lines, symmetrical features, soft lips. There isn't an ounce of softness on this rugged male. His hair is shaggy, his dark gold eyes a warning blazing out of his face, his entire body a dangerous coil. Looking at him, I get the idea that he's only seconds away from attacking at any given moment.

And Quinn allows him to wrap his brawny arm around her waist, tucking her into his side.

Of course. Because she's the other half of his soul. The other half of his bond. In the entire world, she's the only one who'll never be touched by the feral's madness—and she has been since the moment he first imprinted on her a long time ago.

"I know you." It just slips out.

Definitely not his face. I've never seen his face.

But his wolf… I know him.

Quinn's eyes go from a bright gold to a burnished shade. "You do?" Swiveling her head to glance up at her mate, she says, "You never mentioned that you met Helene before."

Her overt jealousy rubs against me like sandpaper on my skin.

I thought that, after she rejected West, she'd get over her dislike for me. Our entire conversation, I was sure I was right. And she did—until she thinks about me having some kind of relationship with her chosen mate and, suddenly, all bets are off.

Oh, Luna. I have to fix this.

"Let me explain. His wolf… I recognize his wolf. I've sensed him before, always there and gone again before mine could reach out for him." With a delicate shrug, trying to assuage her blazing possessiveness and undeniable envy, I tell Quinn, "I never saw him, but my wolf knows his. She's happy to see how much better he's doing. It must be because of you."

Quinn gives her head a small shake, her sheet of hair

swaying over the tops of her slender shoulders. Her eyes brighten, her wolf ceding control back to her human side. *Phew.* "A mate bond does a lot to tame a feral," she admits.

Then, laying her hand on his arm again, giving it a gentle squeeze, she says, "And I guess you weren't as stealthy as you thought, watching me, if Helene Dupuis of all wolves knew you were skulking around, baby."

Not sure if that's meant to be an insult or not, I decide that it's time to take my leave. Especially since Chase is thrumming in place, watching me closely. I can only imagine what Quinn's told him about me. He doesn't like me being near his mate.

I'm happy to oblige.

Their stay in Hickory is a short-lived one. They'd brought Chase's truck to pack up as many of Quinn's belongings to take back to their cabin. Once it was full, they left, eager to make it home before night fell.

Reaching out for West, I notice that he disappeared, too. He must have left pack territory after his chat with Chase because, almost as soon as I walked away from the mated pair, I could sense that he was gone.

Again.

I tried one last time before I turned in for the night. I could've sworn I caught a hint of sandalwood on the breeze before I closed my window and crawled beneath my covers, but when I searched for him, all I found was the empty hole in my chest.

Ignoring the constant ache that has been my companion for far too long, I turned off my lamp and fell into a sleep where I dreamed that West was right beside me, and no other wolves could come between us...

FIVE
RING

fell asleep in my cabin. I'm one hundred percent sure of that.

I'd gone to bed early, waking up once when my wolf started yipping. Nothing seemed out of the ordinary, though, and after she settled back down, I slept through the night.

When I wake up again, feeling lightheaded and *off*, the first thing I notice is that I'm not in my bed. Mine is a lot softer than the mattress I'm laid out on, and my blankets are thinner.

The second thing I notice? My shifter senses are dull. It's like a hazy cloud has been dropped over my eyes, messing with my vision. My ears feel like they've been wadded with cotton. And my nose… I can't smell a thing.

Which leads me to the third thing: without scenting sandalwood, I don't notice that West is pacing at the foot of the bed until I pull myself up into a sitting position and he stops, swiveling on his heel, his dark grey eyes watching my every move.

"West…" I tap into my wolf, reaching out to make sure it's

him and not some kind of dream. And that's when I realize a *fourth* thing: my wolf is gone. Like someone's caged her, putting her somewhere I can't find her, I've been completely cut off from the other side of me.

That should've been enough to slap me wide awake—but it isn't. My head feels heavy, like I need to just lay back down and, when I wake up again, this really will have been another dream.

But then West speaks, breaking the illusion.

"How are you feeling, Helene?"

His voice is careful. Like he doesn't want to spook me, or give anything away with his clipped tone. And since I'm inexplicably cut off from my wolf, I can't use her to get a read on exactly what's going on with him—or me.

"I… I don't know. A little woozy. Confused. West… what am I doing here? What are *you* doing here? Where are we?"

He ignores each of my questions. Instead, he simply says, "The woozy feeling will fade. It's just a side effect of the quicksilver."

Wait—*what?*

I'm cut off from my wolf, but it's not inexplicable anymore.

"Quicksilver? You dosed me with quicksilver?"

"Injected you with it," he clarifies. "I needed you to be completely out, your scent undetectable, to move you. It was the only thing I could think to do. Wilder told me how to do it."

Wilder… Quinn's feral.

The same wolf who used a quicksilver injection to knock her unconscious and keep her docile when a trapped she-wolf would've gone for his balls or his throat to wake up and discover she's been taken captive…

Feeling so… so *human*, all I can do is curl my knees up to my chest. "Move me? Move me where?"

Again, he refuses to answer.

"Don't worry about that. We can talk about it when you're feeling better. I didn't expect you to be up so soon… and you're just woozy? Everything else is okay?"

Now that he mentions it, the side of my neck itches.

Purposely avoiding his stare, my fingers go right to the spot where I can feel the twinge. It's on the side of my throat, closer to the point where it meets the curve of my shoulder, but when I go to scratch it, I freeze.

My fingers find a curve of slight bumps. No. *Two* curves. One on top, the other on the bottom, a small bite.

It's slightly raised from my skin, too. Like it's a scar.

My stomach goes tight.

No.

It's a *mark*.

I swivel my head, dipping my gaze, panic rushing through me as I try to get a better look at my neck. I can't, and when I kick out my legs, ready to run for a mirror if I need to, West moves closer to me.

"Don't get upset. I can explain everything—"

Don't get upset? Too late.

I back away from him, desperate to get a better look at my throat. It's impossible, but I still try. Using my left hand to tug the collar of my nightgown away from my neck, I'm still trying to see what's there when the light from over my head flashes off of my hand, catching my attention.

I instantly freeze. Except for the fingers on my hand, that is.

They're trembling as I move them in front of my face.

There, on the ring finger on my left hand, is a simple golden band that wasn't there before.

I squeak.

West takes a step toward me. "Tell me, Helene, do you like my ring?"

He marked me with his teeth. That has to be what that scar on my throat is. But even knowing that he did that while I was asleep—that he injected me with quicksilver to make sure I *stayed* asleep—that's nothing compared to understanding that Weston Reed slipped a golden band on my finger.

"Why did you do this? Why am I wearing this ring?"

"Because you're my bride."

Bride…

Bride…

Bride…

I glance down at the nightgown I'd pulled on before I went to bed last night. White and lacy, in the right light it could pass for a racy wedding dress.

I refuse to acknowledge the ring. Calling me his 'bride'? That's simply nuts.

But the mark on my neck…

I point a shaky finger at him. "You bit me."

He smirks. "You kept it."

It's the smirk that does it. The ring… the bite… the quicksilver… I might not be able to reach my wolf, but that doesn't change what I am. I can't shift, but I can run, and before West can stop me, that's exactly what I do.

He could've stopped me. No doubt in my mind that he could've lashed out his hand, holding onto my bicep as I ran on wobbly legs past him. He doesn't. He lets me go.

Seconds later, I discover why.

It's not just the bedroom I'm not familiar with. Rushing

out of the room, tripping down a short hallway, flying through a small front room that has a couch and that's all, I have no idea where I am. This isn't West's cabin back home.

Obviously. Because we *aren't* home.

Throwing open the door to the cabin, it takes one glimpse at the trees surrounding us before it dawns on me what West had said.

To move you…

He didn't just move me into his personal territory. He's moved me off of pack land.

Because those trees? They aren't hickories.

This isn't *Hickory*.

He's taken me off of Sylvan Pack territory, and that means I have no idea where I am—or how to get home. A coddled omega who's never once set paw outside of Hickory, if I continue to run, I'll be lost in seconds. Trapped with West in an unfamiliar cabin, if I try to leave, I'm in even more danger than I would be staying with him.

And, Luna damn it, he *knows* it.

***

SHOCK AT MY SITUATION MAKES ME EASY TO CONTROL—AT first.

He lays his hands on my shoulders, guiding me away from the front door. He kicks it closed, then starts leading me toward the nearest open doorway. I let him, too. For a good few feet, I move along like a dazed fool until, suddenly, I sense the heat of his hands through my sleeves and can't stand it.

I shake him off.

West doesn't seem surprised. In fact, I get the idea he

expected me to shove him away almost as soon as he touched me.

I should have.

Instead, I cross my arms over my chest and tell him, "Bring me back."

"Helene—"

My lower lip is wobbling. "Bring me home."

His jaw tightens. "This is your home now."

No. It's not.

"You can't do this. I'm supposed to be going to meet Rafael—"

West's eyes flash. A glimmer of gold rolls over his gaze before the familiar dark grey color returns.

And suddenly I understand.

He hates Rafael. He hates a male he doesn't even know all because the Luna whispered the Gravetail Alpha's name in my ear.

That's why he's doing this. Why he followed Chase's lead, why he brought me to a place I can't leave… he's no longer trying to convince me to reject the mate bond I have with Rafael.

He's acting as if I already have.

West proves it, too, when he continues toward the entrance he'd been leading me to. He waits for me to follow, and when I don't, he moves until he's standing behind me. West doesn't quite touch me again, but because I don't want him to, it's so easy for him to herd me the way he wants me to go.

And that's right into the kitchen—

"What is this?"

"You must be hungry."

Of course I am. Or, I *was*… until I realized what West has done. I lost any appetite in an instant.

But this? He's gone *too* far.

In the center of the kitchen, there's a small round table with a pair of wooden chairs on opposite sides. The table is full. Save for two empty white plates, every inch of the space is covered with food.

Food that West prepared. Food he expects me to eat.

To an unmated shifter female, a meal like this has only one meaning: a proposition. By trying to feed me, West is saying: I will protect you, I will provide for you, and you'll want for nothing if I'm around. Accepting his offering is almost the same as agreeing that he has the right to do so.

Laying out this food, inviting me to eat… West is acting like I really *am* his bride.

But I'm not. I'm a she-wolf who has been pushed to the edge of her patience.

And I'd rather *starve* than let him think he can get away with what he's done to me even if I don't quite understand the extent of it yet. *This?* That's all I need to see before I turn on him.

Hanging a few feet back, his expression is one part expectant, one part hopeful.

I want to slap it off his face.

"How dare you."

"Lane—"

No. *No.* He's not going to call me 'Lane'. Not now. That's a nickname—a pet name—I'd allowed him to use when he was my lover. While my brother still uses my childhood nickname when he's in a protective mood, everyone else uses my full given name. I am Helene. West's Lane disappeared a long time ago, and if he thinks that he can call me by that name *now*, he's finally pushed me to my breaking point.

I'm an omega. We don't break. We don't snap.

We exist to keep our pack together, and to ensure that other shifters keep control.

Which is why it's probably such a shock to West when I lose *mine*.

I've been gently refusing him for years. He didn't respond to *gentle*. Maybe he'll respond to *this*.

I can't reach my wolf, but I'm strong enough without her help to grab the table by the edge and flip it over before West can stop me.

As the plates crash onto the floor, the tinkle of broken glass telling us that I smashed at least one, all of the food wasted as it splatters across the floor, I tuck a lock of hair behind my ear.

"Don't." The word is as shaky as the wobble of the table. "Don't ever try to feed me again. You might have me trapped in this cabin until you come to your senses and bring me home, but I'm not your mate. I'm not your *bride*. Right now, I'm not your anything."

He recoils as if I've slapped him. Then again, considering I've never spoken to him like that before, it's probably the closest I've ever come to purposely lashing out at him.

He deserves it. When he hangs his head, though his back stays straight and proud, I know that West understands that keeping me isn't going to be as easy as he thought—but I know him.

West wouldn't have done it any differently. He doesn't regret taking me. He only regrets that he hurt me in the process.

"Helene—"

No. I'm not listening to him.

Without a way home to Hickory, I'm stuck here. That doesn't mean I have to encourage his insanity.

Because he's insane. The West I knew… he's gone.

Replaced by a male so close to being feral, I'm amazed my wolf didn't pick up on the hints until now.

Sane shifters don't steal their mates. Chase Wilder is proof of that. And while his taking Quinn as the feral's captive might have worked out well for the both of them, I'm not Quinn. I'm Helene Dupuis, and I'm so sick and tired of everyone telling me what I'm supposed to do.

Bishop.

The Luna.

Rafael Cruces.

And now West...

When will it be *my* fucking turn to decide what to do with my life?

I don't know. Never probably, but even if I've done what I've supposed to for the last twenty-seven years, that changes now.

Without another word, I whirl away from West. Leaving the kitchen, I storm toward the bedroom I woke up in, slamming the door behind me so hard, the entire cabin shakes.

I don't lock it behind me. If I know West—and, after what he pulled, I'm honestly beginning to question if I ever really did in the first place—he'll see the closed door as a sign to give me my space. It always worked with my cabin; if I wanted to see him, I'd open the door, otherwise he'd sit out there until another packmate needed the Beta.

Let him sit out this door. Let him scratch at it and plead with me to let him in. He put me in this room. He wants to keep me as his Luna damn *pet*. Fine. But he can't be surprised when this she-wolf bites back.

Walking into the room, another burst of anger floods through me. Furious and not sure how to let it out, I turn my attention on the perfect target: the glass vase perched inno-cently on the nightstand by the bed.

It's stuffed full of wildflowers. As though West had spent hours gathering them before leaving Hickory, he brought them with him, leaving them in a water-filled vase right by my bedside.

I love you…

Before I can think better of it, I dash over to the night-stand, snatching the vase up with both hands. With an anguished shout, I throw it away from me, getting the tiniest bit of satisfaction when the vase smashes, water and shards of glass hitting the tops of my bare feet even from the distance.

It helped, but I need more. And while I don't have another vase to smash, there's something else I *can* do: I yank West's ring off of my finger with such force that the edge skins the bottommost knuckle.

Blood perfumes the air. I could give a shit. Rearing back my arm, I throw that next.

It *clinks* as it hits the far wall, echoing the sound when it lands on the hardwood floor. The ring wobbles for a few seconds before it goes still.

Good.

That done, I step around the glass, the flowers, the mess, and return to the bed. It smells of me—just me—but it doesn't matter. It's not mine, no matter how much West wants to convince me that it's going to be.

It's not mine, but trapped in this cabin with a male who must have lost his mind, it might as well be for now.

And that's when, curling up on the borrowed bed, burying my face in the pillow, I begin to weep.

SIX
TERRITORY

Crying helps me get a handle on my emotions. Sounds counterintuitive, but to an omega like me? It helps.

So does getting up and taking in the mess that I made.

It's so unlike anything I would've ever done that I can't help but smile at the wreckage of the room.

I don't know who this cabin belongs to. It's definitely a shifter shelter, but for all the time he snuck away from Hickory, he couldn't have built it by paw. Most likely it's an abandoned lone wolf cabin he found in the woods and fixed up to keep me with him.

Oh, well. Serves him right for me to destroy it bit by bit. That's what he gets for taking any choice out of my hands like that.

Mates get to choose. If both halves of our pairing don't agree with forever, there *is* no pairing. I never thought West would go this far. When I rejected his offer to be his mate, that should've been the end of it.

It wasn't. Taking cues from a feral, he drugged me and stole me, and when I think about the nerve he had to bite me while I was unconscious and slip a *ring* on my *finger,* I want to find something else in this room to smash.

Maybe then West will realize that, while I'm an omega, I'm still a she-wolf. We can't be tamed.

If I know him, he's expecting me to gloss over what he did. After all, I always have before. Almost like it's expected *of* me. Sweet Helene. Perfect Helene.

Prim, proper, Saint Helene, the pack princess.

Because that's who I am, isn't it? Not something I ever wanted to be, but, unlike when it comes to mates, I never had a choice about my place in the pack.

Before I was elevated to the rank of Omega, I was a pretty omega she-wolf with wide yellow eyes, wavy blonde hair, and a delicate human body. Even in my fur, my pelt matches the color of my hair; I'm small enough as a wolf that, from a distance, I could pass as a true arctic wolf, though in reality it's closer to blonde. I can't help my size, though. It's a shifter thing. Alphas are huge. Omegas... aren't.

Even if it wasn't my rank of wolf that led my packmates to protect and coddle me, being born as Bishop's younger sister would have. His dominance was obvious from puphood; so was his tendency to be protective of me. As soon as he figures out I'm missing, he's going to lose it.

And that's nothing compared to how he'll react when he discovers it's *West* who took off with me...

Now that he has me right where he wants me, West

can't stay away. It's barely been an hour since I left him alone in the kitchen before I can sense his wolf pawing at my door.

A moment later, there comes a knock.

I almost tell him to go away. I'm still so furious with him and I'm not ready to face him again.

But then I realize that a stubborn male who thinks it was a good idea to wolfnap me might not be put off by the silent treatment if I ignore him. This is Weston Reed. If I couldn't get him to stop coming around my cabin after I ended things with him, what makes me think that he'll back off now that he's convinced himself I'm his *bride* of all things?

"Door's open," I call out.

There. He can take that as an invitation, or he can hear the annoyance in my tone and realize he's already pushed me close to my breaking point.

His choice.

It's West. Of course he's going to take the opportunity to come face me again.

His gaze sweeps across the room. He sucks in a breath when he finds me sitting in the bed, legs tucked beneath me, propped against the headboard at my back. West's attention lingers on me for a few tense seconds—I can sense his wolf reaching for mine from across the room—before he tears it away.

Seeing me on the bed is too much of a temptation for him. I know exactly what he's thinking. There was a time when he was welcome to share it with me. For five years, he all but made my cabin—and my bed—his second home. He never would've doubted his welcome, and I would've already had my arms open to him.

Not now. My arms are crossed, wrapped around my chest, holding myself close.

He sees the shards of glass glittering on the floor, frowning at the flowers he must have picked specifically for me. They're nestled among the wreckage from the vase.

West swallows roughly. Out of the corner of my eye, I watch his Adam's apple bob. A muscle ticks in his cheek. But he's not angry. His shields are still up, making it harder for my wolf to get a read on his, but I guess I do know West after all.

He's not angry. He's *hurt*.

By taking his flowers and smashing them, I chipped a little more at his broken heart.

Because of course I did.

My wolf lets out a soft whine. As much as I want to hold onto my anger, I can't. Not when it's West. Time and time again, I admit if only to myself that he's the one male that could ask for me to bare my throat and I'd do it without a second's hesitation. To bite it, to mark it, to slit it… I want to give him everything.

Except forever.

I can't give him forever because, Luna damn it, it's never been mine to give.

"West—"

My murmur of his name seems to break the trance that had settled over him. He blinks once, banishing the hurt.

Beta West is back in action.

"I know you're angry with me… Helene." There was a split second's hesitation. He was going to call me 'Lane'. I know it. He was going to slip back into using his pet name for me… and he didn't. "You have every right to be. But, please, don't hurt yourself to get back at me."

Is that what he thinks I'm doing? "I'm not."

He frowns. "You don't lie to me. Not to me. Even if you

think the truth will hurt me, I have to know that you'll always be honest with me."

Yeah? Well, I needed to know that I could trust him. For so many years I did, and he threw that all away in one night.

He's looking down at the mess on the floor again, not letting it go. "Okay. So that vase… what? Slipped out of your hand? Ended up all the way over here?"

"Maybe it did."

"Or maybe you got some of your frustrations out by smashing the vase like you flipped the table?"

That's exactly what happened. Not like I'm going to admit that to him.

Not while he's pretending to be Beta West and not the Weston I've known my whole life.

When we first got together, I used to tease him that when he went all cold and logical, it was like he was a whole other male. I loved him no matter what, but I liked *my* West. Bright-eyed, smirking, who had a tendency to curse when making his points, and who felt every moment he didn't have me within paws' reach was a moment wasted. The wild lover, the protective shifter, and the male who loved me so Luna damned much that he brought me a token of his affection every time he saw me even after I had to reject his feelings for me.

When he gives me that knowing look, that haughty expression that he reserves for packmates who step out of line, I feel my fury rising again.

Omegas don't snap, but we can get angry. So many wolves seem to think that, as an omega, my purpose is to sit there, look pretty, and let my wolf work magic on theirs. We're the glue that holds a pack together, and just having an omega wolf near is enough to rein in any shifter teetering on the edge of losing control.

That's true. But just because my wolf encourages positive emotions in others, that just means that I'm a pro at recognizing the negative ones first—in me and my packmates.

As angry as I am, I'm also hurt by his actions—which is why I say flippantly, "It was just some flowers."

They're not. They never have been. In his way, every flower is another time he's told me 'I love you' without having to utter the words.

He bends lower, reaching for the nearest stem. "You can't honestly think…" His words trail to a close as he knocks aside a piece of glass, pinching his thumb and forefinger together as he picks something off of the ground.

Rising up from his crouch, his eyes search for my hand. When he sees that my fingers are bare of any jewelry, his face turns stormy.

I tilt my chin up at him. "What?"

"You took off the ring."

"Of course I did. I'm not your bride, West."

"Yes. You are." His bare feet crunch over the glass in his hurry to bring me the ring. He holds it out to me. "Put it on."

"No."

"Helene." He bites out my name. "Put the fucking ring on."

"It won't change anything. We're not married. We're shifters… we don't *get* married."

"If it doesn't mean a Luna damn thing, then put it on."

I shake my head, so ready to keep on refusing—until West does the one thing that assures that I'll give in to him.

He pleads.

"Please… it doesn't even have to be on your left hand. Just… I bought it for you. I want you to have it. Wear it for me, please."

Before I can take it from him, it slips out of his trembling grip. The ring lands on the mattress, bouncing beneath my folded legs.

West stumbles away from the bed. Already reaching beneath me for the damn thing, I don't notice that something is wrong until the aura surrounding his wolf seems to just *break*.

I glance up and over at him, gasping when I realize that it's not just his wolf that's breaking.

It's the male, too, and all because I threw away his ring.

I can fix this. Right? That's what the Omega does. She fixes broken packmates the same way Ginnie, our healer, helps when it comes to injuries that need a little more guidance to heal better.

He wants me to wear the ring? I'll wear it.

"There." I jam the ring on my finger, showing it off to him. "Happy now? It's on. Okay, West? It's on."

The ring might be back on my finger, but I was too, too late.

West has already let himself off the leash.

His features sharpen. Dark fur rushes out along the top of his arms. The seams on the collar of his t-shirt pop as his body hunches.

As shifters, we have two forms: one that mimics 'human', and another that mimics 'wolf'. Every now and then, when something interferes with our instincts, a rare third form appears. It's a partial shift. Half wolf, half human, it's more beast than anything—and it's the mark of a feral when a shifter gets caught in that shape.

It doesn't last. Thank the Luna. This twisted version of West falls forward, but he's not the one who hits the ground.

In a shower of torn jeans and his ruined t-shirt, he shifts to his wolf before searching for me with his golden shifter gaze.

His dark grey wolf dips his muzzle. His sleek tail is low, tucked between his back legs.

He's ashamed. As his wolf, there's no hiding his emotions from mine. Desperate and bursting with love for me, West is also full of shame which is exactly why he spins, claws scrabbling against the strewn material on the floor before he disappears out of the room.

Rushing forward, I slam the door closed and whirl around. The skirt on my dress flares around me, slapping into my thighs at the same time as I hit the wood of the door with the palms of my shaking hands.

I don't lock it, but not for the same reason as before.

If West really is on the verge of turning feral, it wouldn't matter if I did. My West would respect a closed door. That ferocious beast masquerading as the Beta of the Sylvan Pack?

A little thing like a lock won't stop him if he decides to come after me again.

After all, I think hollowly, looking at the golden band on my right ring finger, he thinks I'm his *bride*.

WEST DOESN'T JUST FLEE FROM MY ROOM. HE LEAVES THE cabin.

I know him; at least, I want to believe I still do. No way would West go too far, leaving me on this unfamiliar territory alone. Wherever he is, I have to believe he's near enough to keep me safe while also getting some control over himself.

He'll be back. I'm absolutely convinced of that fact. And since I don't know how long he'll be gone, I decide to take the chance to explore the rest of the cabin to get a better idea of the situation I'm in.

And who am I kidding? Though my stomach is tight with nerves, I haven't eaten since dinner last night. To keep mine and my wolf's energy up, we'll need to have something soon.

Food is a huge part of shifter culture *and* courtship. Whatever he thinks is going on here, he wants me to choose him over Rafael. If I ate the food he laid out for me when I woke up from the quicksilver, I would be signaling that I was interested in doing that.

Sure, I might have gone too far when I flipped the table, but he deserved it. Just like he deserves me sneaking into the kitchen, finding something to snack on.

He's cleaned up the mess from before. I refuse to feel guilty when I notice that the wooden table is sitting a little crooked. Instead, I go rooting through the cabinets, searching for something quick and easy I can throw together so that I'm feeding myself.

When I figure I can make an easy PB&J and top it off with some chips, it takes a second before I realize that everything in his cabinets is my preferred food, right down to the brand of peanut butter I like and the flavor of chips he stocked up on.

Happening on an abandoned cabin in the woods and possibly fixing it up for a den for him and his future mate… that's one thing. Tracking down some quicksilver to drug me… I'm blaming that on West's interest in talking to Chase when he showed up in Hickory with Quinn.

But that was only a few days ago. To set up this cabin *and* stock it with everything I would ever need or like… I'm beginning to think this wasn't a spur-of-the-moment decision like I thought.

This wasn't just because West found out that Rafael was ready to take me as his mate. Rafael's call was simply the catalyst to something West has obviously been planning for a while now—and I wish I had some idea how he managed to pull this off.

Too bad I wish I could claim the same ignorance as to *why*…

West wants me to do what he did: reject my fated mate and choose him instead. If only it was that simple. Then again, to West it is because he believes that I only agreed to mate Rafael because we're fated. That I promised myself to the Gravetail Alpha because a fated mate trumps a chosen mate.

In a way, West is right. When shifters are raised to revere the Luna, our goddess can do no wrong. But it wasn't the idea of *my* fated mate that pushed me to accept Rafael three years ago.

If I had a fated mate out there, that meant West did, too.

I'm selfish, but I'm not *that* selfish. Could I really stand between West and the female the Luna picked out for him?

He would tell me that I should've. As logical and clear-headed as West is, I've always been his one blind spot. He's loved me for so long that it never occurred to him that, one day, he might stop.

What would I have done if he started to wonder if his fated mate would've been better for him than me?

So I ended things with West, hoping I was doing the right thing. Of course, hindsight is twenty-twenty. Honestly, I probably should've known what West would do when the Luna finally did introduce him to his fated mate.

And maybe I would have if it hadn't turned out to be Quinn Malone.

Deep down, I always thought West's mate wouldn't be one of our packmates. She could've come from another pack, like Sofia did. She could have been human or even another kind of supe and maybe things would have been different.

But she wasn't. West's fated mate was a delta she-wolf we both grew up with, and while I'm sure Quinn would've been good to him—for him—if he had accepted their bond, West didn't look at her and see his future.

How could he? It was impossible when he was stuck in our past.

When I let him go, the idea of West refusing to take his fated mate never occurred to me—and then, seven months ago, it happened. He recognized Quinn in one moment, then completely ignored her in the next. He continued to court me, to treat me as his future mate, even knowing that I hadn't changed my mind.

I still haven't. That's what makes his actions since he whisked me away from Hickory so baffling.

Then again, if he really is turning feral? It makes sense.

West is logical. The Beta is rational.

Ferals *aren't*.

And now I'm trapped in a cabin with my former love who might just be one.

SEVEN
APOLOGY

He isn't gone long. A couple of hours at most, and when he steps gingerly up to the closed door, he stays on the other side without attempting to open it.

Unlike before, when he knocks, I don't offer an invitation to come inside.

He doesn't ask for one, either.

Instead, from the other side of the door, I can hear him take a deep breath before he shudders it out in relief.

"Thank the Luna… I could scent you when I walked back into the den… I wanted to believe it wasn't from before, but I couldn't see how you could still be here. I thought you would've left." He pauses, an anguished note finding its way into his voice. "You should've left me, Helene."

He's right. I should have.

"Where did you go?" I ask him through the door.

"For a run," is his clipped answer. Then, as if realizing how short he sounds, he sighs. "Sorry. It's just… we're not on pack land. You know that. It's just us. This cabin is our territory now. It wasn't really a run. It was a—"

"Patrol," I offer.

"Yeah. That's right. My wolf needed the release, and I... I needed to get myself under control."

I take in a deep breath. *Blood.* My nose isn't as strong as some of the more dominant wolves in the pack, but I know West's blood when I scent it. Tapping into my wolf, I spur her to search for his. Since he stole me away, he's been so careful to keep his shields up, a block between us so that I can't use my wolf against him.

It doesn't matter. This is *West.* No matter how tightly locked down he thinks he is, a part of him will always be open to me; not because I'm the Omega, but because he loves me. He wants to let me in.

And through the sliver in his shields, I can feel the echoes of the aches and pains wracking his body. They're half-healed, but it doesn't matter.

I know exactly how he got himself under control.

My lips tremble. Before I can let out a soft sob that he'll undoubtedly hear through the wood, I cover my mouth with my hands.

He can't see me, but he knows instantly that something's wrong. "Helene? Are you okay?"

I swallow back the sob. After what he did to me, I shouldn't care that he's still suffering so much. Pummeling the unfamiliar trees until blood streams past his wrists, his knuckles torn open, his claws filed down to nubs... it shouldn't hurt me as much as it hurts him.

It does, though. And it's even harder that he's right on the other side of the door, desperate for me, and he's only hurting himself more by putting me somewhere

where he can see me, scent me, *love* me... but never, ever have me.

A glutton for punishment or half-feral? Right now I'm terrified that he's *both*.

"Yeah," I lie. "I'm okay."

He lets me have the lie. "You were in the kitchen. You ate while I was out."

Even if I didn't leave the dishes in the sink, he would've known by my lingering scent. "I was hungry."

"I would've fed you. You know that."

I do. And I also know how he would interpret it if I ate his food.

"I can't let you do that."

I wait for him to tell me that I'm his bride again. Forget the fact that, for shifters, the closest thing we have to a wedding is the Luna Ceremony. Forget how I'm still promised to Rafael, and the longer West insists on keeping me here, the worse this is going to be for all of us. Sometime after talking to Quinn's feral mate, West decided I would be his mate—or no one's.

Too bad it doesn't work like that.

"You'd rather starve than stay with me?"

He would never let me starve. And I already proved that I have no problem going into the kitchen and feeding myself.

But whatever happened to the male I once knew—whether he's turned feral or this is a side of West I've never seen before—he refuses to accept that I can stand up for myself.

Of course not. I also showed him that, in one way at least, I have to rely on him. If West doesn't lead me back to Hickory, I'm stuck here. Sure, I could try to go out on my own and find a phone or someone who might help me, but I'm a wolf. I rely on pack only—and West is the only packmate here.

I need him to understand that he's making a mistake, and

not only because I can't even imagine what Bishop will do when he finds out his Beta took me to be his *bride*.

"I'm not challenging you," I say after a moment. "I'm asking you to stop this insanity. I want to go home."

"You can leave anytime you want. You're not my captive, you're my guest."

"A guest?" My voice comes out shrill. "I didn't realize guests were drugged and carried off without their permission. Because, to me, that seems like something you'd do to a female you *wolfnapped*."

"Okay. I admit I used the quicksilver, but I had to. Now that you're with me, I won't keep you in chains. If you want to leave me, go." I hear a *thud*. He didn't quite punch the wall outside of my room, but he might have slapped it. "You know I'll fucking follow you anywhere anyway."

I do know that, just like I know for sure that *West* knows I would never do that. It's not in me to abandon him, no matter how hard a time I'm having reconciling this dark, broken male with the handsome, sexy wolf who won my heart when I was nineteen. Especially since, when I close my eyes, all I see is the pleading Beta who, for the last three years, begged me to forget fate, forget the Luna, forget Rafael, and choose him instead.

I did that to West. This, too.

Me.

I never meant to. I made myself clear. Just like West, my duty is to the Sylvan Pack until the day I join Gravetail when their Alpha makes me his…

"But you won't bring me back?"

"When you agree to be my mate *and* my bride, I'll take you wherever you want to go."

An ultimatum. After what he's done to me, West has the nerve to give me an ultimatum.

"And what if I don't?" I ask.

"I told you, you can leave on your own whenever you'd like. You're not my captive, Helene. I love you too much... I would never hurt you. I did this for us—"

I glare at the door. He can't see me, but it makes me feel better as I tell him, "You did this for yourself."

"What else was I supposed to do? Watch you go to another male and be happy for you?"

Yes. That's exactly what he was supposed to do. If I'm strong enough to leave him for the good of the pack, he should've at least pretended to be happy. My wolf would know how he truly felt, but he could've *tried*.

When I stay quiet, he sighs. "I didn't want it to be this way."

"Me, neither, West. That's why you have to put an end to this."

I suck in a breath, waiting for his answer. He's a rational male. He has to know that he reacted impulsively, but it's not too late to fix it.

Right?

"West? Did you hear me?"

"Yes. But you know that I can't do that. I made my choice. Hate me for this if you have to, but I'd never forgive myself if I didn't give you one. Without the pack's pressure, without you being the Omega... you can choose—"

Choose?

I can't help myself. I throw open the door, cutting him off mid-sentence. "I already did. You know that."

From the way West's jaw goes tight, he does—but it doesn't matter. I didn't choose him, so it doesn't count.

That's what he thinks, and I realize that I'm not about to

change his mind anytime soon when West nods over my shoulder. "Enjoy the room. It's yours."

I shouldn't have opened the door. "Gee. Thanks. How generous of you."

"Well, I figured the least I could do was give you territory of your own in our den while you think things over."

Disregarding the part where he calls this cabin *our* den, I ask, "Where did you even get a place like this?"

"I found it. I claimed it."

I huff out a breath. My fingers lift to my neck, ghosting over the scar he left on my throat. "You've been doing that a lot lately."

"A wolf's gotta do what a wolf's gotta do, Helene."

Maybe that's so. But the Beta's forgotten one thing: I'm a wolf, too.

"You can't keep me here forever," I remind him.

His hand reaches for me. West is smart enough to pull it back before he lays it on my arm, but I can't sense how much he wants to.

"Forever is what I'm after," he says simply, "and it's worth whatever it takes to have it."

"Even if I hate you?"

West doesn't hesitate. "You'll never hate me."

He sounds so sure. So confident that's he right.

And, Luna damn it, I wish he wasn't.

He says I'm not his captive. Unlike poor Quinn, he's not keeping me in a pair of silver shifter chains to keep me docile. He doesn't have to. As an omega, I'm already as docile as I can be, and that's without the quicksilver slowly working its way out of my system—or the fondness for this male I'll never get over.

But that's exactly why I call bullshit. He doesn't need

chains or silver or locks to keep me right where he wants me. Without a phone—and I haven't found one yet—I can't contact Bishop and let him know that I need an escort back to Hickory.

If West isn't willing to guide me back, I'm as good as trapped, and we both know it.

Oh, I could hold my head up high and walk right out of his cabin. Between me and my wolf, I'm sure we can navigate the woods. What if I stumble upon a human neighborhood? Or, worse, a Fang City full of vampires?

I don't know where I am. I have no idea how to get back to Hickory.

I have no phone. No money.

And unless I can convince West to do the right thing and bring me home, I'm stuck here with him—which is exactly what he wants so why would he back down now?

Especially since it's not just my anger he has to answer to. When Bishop discovers that his loyal Beta not only abandoned the pack, but he also ran off with the Omega? With his beloved younger sister? What happens then?

He's risking his rank in the pack for me. He's all but challenging our Alpha *for me*.

Because he thinks he can get me to reject my promised bond with Rafael and choose him. If I do, everything he did would be worth it—to West.

But what about me?

<hr>

AFTER WATCHING WEST GO NEARLY FERAL, THEN OUR SECOND confrontation at the door that only solidified his stance that

I'm stuck here with him, I didn't think I would be able to get any sleep.

For a couple of reasons, too. I don't know how long the quicksilver he dosed me with kept me unconscious, and while I took a short nap earlier to sleep off some of the lingering grogginess—and avoid West's lurking presence—by the time it grows dark outside the cabin, I expect to lay awake all night.

I do for a couple of hours. But old habits die hard, and my traitorous wolf isn't on her guard when she's around West's. She feels safe, as though he will always protect her, and maybe his wolf would. But the human side of West didn't just cross the line, he tap-danced right over it, breaking both my trust and my boundaries.

I absolutely refuse to give him the chance to do it again.

Turns out, I shouldn't have worried. Around midnight, when I can't stand it anymore and climb out of my bed, I inch open the door. After easing my way down the hall and peeking out into the front room of the cabin, I find West curled up in his wolf form, snuffling on the couch as he rests fitfully.

He's always been a light sleeper. It's the protector in him. I almost expect him to catch me watching him sleep. Holding my breath, I wait for his eyes to blink open.

But they don't, and a part of me has to wonder if it's because he finally has me in the same cabin with him, even if we're in separate quarters.

It could be. The only times I ever saw him fully knock out was when we were in bed together. Then again, there's a good chance this is the first sleep he's gotten since made his move, sneaking my unconscious body out of Hickory without being caught by any of our packmates on patrol.

Or, Luna help him, the *Alpha*.

My heart thuds wildly when I think of my brother. I have

no doubt that Bishop will find me. He won't stop until he does, and I only hope West isn't so far gone that he decides to challenge him.

What makes it worse if that I can't guess how Bishop will react, either—and that isn't something I want to think about just then. So, instead, I watch West sleep and try to figure out how I should handle my ex while I wait for Bishop to track us down.

If I'm being honest, as I lean against the opening to the front room, part of me actually wants to shift to my fur and curl up beside West. Only knowing that he would see that as another victory gets me to turn away from him before returning to my "territory".

He wasn't exaggerating when he referred to this space as that before, and not only because I decided to claim it until I could leave. Once he said it was mine, I decided to go through every nook and cranny in the room. From the closet to the bathroom, and even the oversized dresser on the other side of the space, I searched it all.

I don't know what exactly I was looking for. Under the sink in the bathroom, I found a small brush and dustpan set. Since I didn't want to slice open my feet, I begrudgingly cleaned up the smashed vase and flowers on the floor. When I peeked in the closet and discovered three separate pairs of shoes all in my size, I snorted. That would've helped before I stepped on a shard of glass earlier.

That's not all that's in the closet. West has at least twenty dresses hung up inside there. Countless different colors and styles, they're all something I could see myself wearing.

Makes sense. West made it clear he has no intention of bringing me back anytime soon. Since it's just as obvious I won't leave on my own, I'll need clothes. He provided them.

Underwear, too. The first drawer of the dresser is full of panties in my size. Bras, too, though not as many; West knows that I'll never go panty-less, but bras are a different story. In the second drawer, I find boxer briefs and t-shirts for West. Silky nightgowns fill the third drawer, while the last has more jeans than comfortably fit in the space. Considering how quickly some shifters go through jeans—exploding them during a shift when they don't have time to take them off—I understand why he has so many. Doesn't stop me from cursing under my breath when I have a hard time closing it again.

See? That's exactly why I prefer dresses. Not only are they so much easier to shed before a shift, but I could probably fit all those simple shift dresses into this drawer and still have room left over.

I almost swap them. Before I do, I think about how West would react. Would he think that I'm actually making the territory mine? Not only am I imprinting on it, sleeping in the bed, but changing it around to suit me better?

With that thought, I leave the bottom drawer half open, then return to the bed.

I don't know how late it is when I finally fall asleep, but I've only been awake again for about twenty minutes when I hear a gentle rapping at my door.

I sit up, and his shifter's hearing picks up on the rustle of the sheets. He knocks again, calling out, "Helene? Are you awake? I have something for you."

Breathing in deeply, I check to see if he's bringing me food. When all I get is a lungful of sandalwood, I regret trying.

Throwing the blanket away from me, I call out, "If that's breakfast, no thank you."

"It's not. You can trust me."

Hmm. I'm not so sure I can.

However, I *am* curious to see what West's next move is. I so wanted to believe that everything he's done so far—from the quicksilver to running away with my unconscious body—was an impulsive reaction. He found out I was leaving before the next full moon and he panicked.

But then I searched the cabin. Maybe I could believe that he was lucky enough to stumble upon an abandoned lone wolf's den and make it his. But add in the stocked-up kitchen, the full dresser, the closet full of clothes specifically for me... he's been planning this for a lot longer than I ever would've guessed.

Still, despite myself, I'm interested to see what he's going to do now.

"Give me a second."

"Take your time. I'll be right out here."

Of course he will.

EIGHT
SING

Climbing out of the bed, I realize I'm still wearing the same nightgown I had on when I last fell asleep in my own bed. Even though I found the sleep clothes he brought for me in the dresser and the shift dresses in the closet, I didn't bother changing.

It's morning. The sunshine streaming in only highlights how my lacy nightgown does little to hide my body. Yesterday, I was too distracted to realize that West could see my nipples and the outline of my boobs.

Today? I'm not about to give him a peek of what he can't have.

And not only because I can't stop thinking of West in his wolf form, snuffling softly on the couch outside of my space, kicking his back leg out in an obvious nightmare…

Shaking my head, shoving sympathy for my ex out of my brain, I snatch the first dress I grab out of the closet, then march over to the dresser. I yank out a bra and a fresh pair of panties. I quickly change, kicking my used underwear and nightgown under the bed.

Then, only when I'm as decent as I can get right now, do I take a shallow breath—grimacing when the sandalwood washes over me again—and pull the door in.

West has a sheepish expression on his face. His hair is damp, patted flat with his palm. Unlike me, he's still wearing the same outfit as yesterday. The clothes are wrinkled from where he pulled them off and left them on the floor while he was his wolf, but he's made some effort to freshen up.

Probably at the bathroom sink, I figure. My earlier search of the cabin revealed it has two: one with a shower, one without. The shower—like the dresser full of West's clothes—is in the bedroom.

It's in *my* territory—and now he's pushing up against the edge of my space.

I narrow my eyes on him, making sure he stays on the other side of the threshold. "What do you want?"

In his right hand, he's clutching a small cardboard box only a little bigger than the one a phone comes in. He holds it out to me.

I don't take it. "What's that?"

"A gift for you. Well, really, it's an apology."

"I don't want an apology. I don't even want any explanation. I just want to go home."

"You know I can't do that. Not yet."

Right. Because my brother will have his throat if he waltzes back into Hickory without a good reason for what he did.

He offers me a crooked grin. It's not the smirk from yesterday that infuriated me, but an enticing smile that has me edging a little closer to him.

"Maybe this"—he jiggles the box—"will make staying here with me a little more pleasant."

Okay. Not gonna lie. He's definitely got my attention.

Not like I'm going to let him know that.

"You're going to spoil me, West."

"Nothing's too good for my bride."

Ouch. He just had to add that, didn't he?

I grip the side of the door, ready to slam it in his face. "You should go. Take your box with you, too. I don't want it."

And… there's that sheepish look again. Worse, I sense his panic and his frustration the same time his wolf lets out a pained cry, calling for mine.

Instinctively, I stay near him—and, again, that only assures West that he's doing the right thing, keeping me here in this hidden den.

His jaw goes tight, but his voice is gentle as he murmurs, "I'm sorry. Helene… I'm so fucking sorry, but I'm trying. Okay? And I know you're pissed"—yeah, *that's* an understatement—"but I need you to know just how much I'm trying. I want you to have everything you could ever want. My wolf… we need to provide for you. If I even think of stopping for good, I… I…*fuck*. Forget it. I'll give you the box later."

Luna damn it. I know exactly what West *didn't* say. If he thinks of stopping, his wolf takes a few steps closer to breaking. And if his wolf breaks, the man will shatter.

I shouldn't do it. I know better—but this is West. I can't let that happen to him no matter how mad I am at him.

"Wait. Come back here."

The flash of surprise on his face makes me regret my nasty thoughts. He wasn't trying to manipulate me. He was actually trying to walk away before I summoned him back to me.

Like always, he obeys.

Clearing my throat, I hold out my hand. Even as he drops the box into it, I tell him, "Another gift to make me forget my intended." Something that I can't do, no matter what. "Don't you think all those clothes were enough?"

Though his expression darkened at just the mention that I'm meant for another male, it's quickly replaced by a hint of pleasure as he looks me over, recognizing the new dress I yanked on. "You looked in the closet? What do you think? You like them?"

Saying 'yes' will only encourage him. That's the last thing I want to do right now.

I decide to go with a non-committal response. "You've always had good taste."

"It's easy when everything looks good on you."

I walked right into that one, didn't I?"

Scowling at him, I say, "You think flattery will help me forgive you?"

West has the nerve to give me that cocky grin of his again. Now that I accepted his box, he's in a much better mood. So much better that he actually decides to tease me, giving me a taste of the West I used to adore.

"Just being honest," he says. "Besides, I have the rest of our lives to beg for your forgiveness."

The tease falls flat as it hits me that: no, he doesn't. At best, he has until Bishop figures out where West brought me. If not then, I'll have to be gone by the next full moon.

I'm supposed to be in Darkwoods, Texas for either this Luna or the next. I'm sure Bishop will be political enough to explain away my disappearance if I don't show up, but I did a lot of thinking last night when I couldn't sleep. There's little more than a week until the next full moon, and if I'm still trapped in close quarters with West, I don't know what will happen between us.

It was bad enough when we were living together in Hickory. I had to fight every full moon to resist the urge to go to West. I never asked him, but I'm sure he struggled, too.

Why wouldn't he? He's considered us mates for eight years now, and moon fever is very, very real.

The sad thing is that West was the one who pointedly refused to mate on the night of the full moon. All because he wanted to wait until the Luna told him what he knew all along —that we were fated—we never spent the night together when the Luna was high over our heads.

It's so easy for shifters in a committed relationship to form a mate bond when the Luna is full. All it takes is claiming sex between two consenting partners, a mating mark, and the Luna's blessing for an unbreakable bond to snap into place. If West bit me on the night of the full moon during sex, I'd be his forever—but only if I wanted to be.

Our goddess wants us to form bonded pairs. It's a way to ensure that shifters continue as a species. Unlike our ancient enemies, we're not immortal even if we do have an extended lifespan. More pups mean more shifters, and there needs to be some sort of bond before a pair can procreate.

That's where moon fever comes into play. Already a lusty race, shifters go wild on the night of the full moon. Mature shifters will find it almost impossible to resist the urge to find someone to rut with. If they resist, the fever starts and, believe me, it's not pleasant. The only way I managed to get through it was because West was determined to wait. Later, I was the one who was waiting for my fated mate.

Will I be able to resist West if I'm still in this cabin with him when the Luna is high and he calls me his bride?

As shifters, we know instinctively each one of her phases. I have about a week to figure out what to do. Before now, the West I knew would respect that—in my right mind—I wouldn't want to fall into bed with him during the full moon. But what about a West who was pushed to steal me away from Hickory?

I don't want to think about it. So, shoving all that aside, I open up the box West gave me.

Popping open the cardboard lid, I see a small silver device nestled inside. Attached to it is a pair of wired headphones.

Oh… he didn't.

Playing dumb, I ask, "What's this?"

"It's for you. I meant to grab yours from your cabin, but in the rush of everything, I forgot. While you were sleeping this morning, I went out and got you a new one. Do you like it?"

Do I like it? Put it this way… "It's better than breakfast."

"So you'll keep it?"

Food has a special meaning to shifters that makes it so I can't accept meals from West without giving him the wrong idea. This music player, though?

I can take that from him.

"Yes."

"Thank the Luna." When I raise my eyebrow at him, already pulling the player out of the box, he adds, "I'm trying to do this right, Helene. I've already fucked up plenty, but even if the only way I can make you happy is by giving you something to drown me out, I'll take it."

He's not exactly wrong. We didn't fight often when we were in a relationship, but whenever West's heavy-handedness got on my nerves, I'd plug my headphones in and crank up the volume.

I've never left Hickory, but that doesn't mean I'm cut off

from the rest of the outside world. Music is my vice, and while I'm not very familiar with human artists, one of these charmed music players will have a variety of supe-only stations.

My favorite artist is a vampire pop singer. Vamps may be our enemy, but Callandra can *sing*. Already fiddling with the dial, I can hear one of her greatest hints—*I've got your blood in me (gimme more)*—blaring out of one of my new headphone's buds.

I smile, though it's short-lived when I notice that the guarded expression on West's face has softened.

"Helene?"

"Mm?"

"Sing for me?"

A pang gets me right in the chest. Silly Helene. How could I forget for even a moment that Weston Reed is a calculating Beta? He gave me the music player as a kindness, only to ask me for something in return.

A song.

My brother has always thought of me as his little songbird. Canari. But he's not the only one, is he?

As an omega, I've always been more sensitive than other shifters. There's a reason my type of wolf is so coddled and protected. A shifter pack follows the temperament of the Omega. If I get upset enough, Hickory becomes a powder keg ready to explode.

But I wasn't always the Omega. I didn't get the post until I was sixteen, and before then, the only one who cared how I felt was Bishop.

Or so I thought.

It happened back when my brother was seventeen. Already so big and fierce—even if he hadn't quite grown his beard in yet—when he discovered some of the shifters in my age group were making fun of me for singing my silly little songs to myself, he tracked them down and scared the piss out of them. Sending so many cruel little wolves running, there was one who stayed behind to comfort me.

The first conversation I had with Weston Reed was when a twelve-year-old beta shyly told me that he loved my voice.

Later, I could pinpoint the moment I handed my heart over to West to that day.

And that wasn't all.

My brother and West weren't close then. The age gap was too much, West twelve and Bishop seventeen. But that was about the time that my brother started keeping an eye on the young beta, taking him under his wing. By the time West was seventeen and Bishop twenty-two, they were closer than brothers.

Of course, that's why West waited another two years before he confessed his feelings for me. Torn between his loyalty to Bishop and his love for me, he kept his emotions to himself until he finally blurted out 'I love you, Lane,' and the rest was history.

Back then, he was so afraid that Bishop wouldn't think he was good enough for me. It took me reminding West that a mate gets to choose—not her overprotective older brother— before he stopped caring what Bishop thought about us.

Not that he had anything to worry about. If there was one male in all of Hickory that Bishop didn't mind courting me, it was West. Even after I agreed to mate Rafael, following in Bishop's footsteps, I think I disappointed him by not choosing West.

If I knew then what I know now… well, things could have been different.

But they're not, and me singing a song to West won't change that.

I press the 'off' switch on the music player, letting the wired headphones fall from my grip, trailing down past the edge of my skirt. "Maybe later."

"Of course. I'll be out front if you need me. And if you get hungry—"

I stiffen.

West notices. "Help yourself. Please."

"We'll see."

Smart wolf. He's learning. West knows that I'd rather go hungry than take food from him, and he's not testing me on it.

Good. It's about time West remembers that I'm not the delicate omega she-wolf the rest of the pack thinks I am.

NINE
TONIGHT

West holds true to his word. While the cabin he fixed up for us is 'ours', the bedroom is considered my territory. He leaves me to it, only knocking at the door to let me know he's left another meal just outside of it.

Another meal that goes untouched.

I'll give him credit. He tried to wait for me to go out and eat on my own. When I didn't, his wolf got the better of him. It was almost as if he was incapable of *not* trying to feed me.

The more he tried, the more I refused to eat at all. He might have considered the music player some kind of a peace offering. The way I saw it, it was more of a bribe. He wanted to buy my forgiveness. Since that wasn't going to happen—and I also wasn't willing to give him the music player back—the only way I could assert my dominance over such a powerful wolf was by controlling the one thing I can: my diet.

I'm already too slender to be considered a sturdy she-wolf. Another reason why my packmates have always treated me as

359

too delicate. Too breakable. I don't have many pounds that I can afford to lose, and by the third day of refusing to eat anything West brings me, my new dresses are beginning to feel a lot looser than they did when I finally changed into the first one.

All supes have a unique diet. Vampires are bloodsuckers, obviously, who survive on blood. Us shifters? We just need to eat a lot. Switching shapes requires a lot of calories, and considering I'm as much my wolf when I'm in my skin, shifters are constantly eating for two.

West knows it. The fourth evening, when I refuse *another* meal from him, he finally loses control.

I should've expected that. Just like how he flipped when he saw me without the ring, the constant stress of knowing I was slowly starving myself on purpose finally makes him snap.

He set out dinner for me about an hour ago. I sensed him leave again, going on another patrol, but when he returned and saw that the plate he left outside my door wasn't touched, he bangs on my door.

I'm hungry, but I'm not weak. If you ever wondered if a she-wolf could survive on spite, I'm living proof, and wouldn't that shock my packmates when they discover prissy Helene has some semblance of a spine?

Besides, I'm not actually starving, despite what West thinks. I'm not eating as much as I'm used to, but this is far from a hunger strike. I make sure to refuse the meals he leaves outside of my door like clockwork. Once West is on patrol or giving me a chance to leave my self-imposed cage, I grab a few things from the kitchen.

I have half of a loaf of bread under my bed, the chunky peanut butter I like, two bags of chips, a box of cookies, and a couple of granola bars. He might have bought them, but I stole them, and now they're mine.

He has to know I have it. Does that stop him from believing I'm going to wilt away like one of his wildflowers?

Not even a little.

Knock, knock. "Helene?" His raps come a little louder. "Open up. We need to talk."

"No."

"It's been two days since you opened this door for me. I want to see you."

I want to go home. "Go away, West."

"Let me in," he growls.

That growl rubs me the wrong way. I mean, does he really need me to spell it out for him?

"Are you here to take me back to Hickory?"

"What? No. I want you to eat!"

Not happening. Accept his food and signal that I'm interested in letting him take care of me? Let him think that he made the right choice by taking away *mine*?

I made my decision, and came up with my own plan on how to beat my former mate. I had to. It's been four days and no sign of Bishop or any of my packmates. For whatever reason, my brother can't find me, which I should've expected. If anyone could avoid being caught by the Alpha, it would be his Beta.

And if anyone could outlast West, it's me.

I did it for three years, and now I've done it for four days. With the full moon looming closer, I need him to realize that it's too risky to stay in this cabin together, but if he doesn't, the least I can do is barricade myself in my room.

Glaring at the door, I tell him in as cold a voice as I can manage, "I'm not hungry."

It's true enough. I just finished snacking on a stack of cookies before he came pounding on my door. Besides, if this is the only way I can show him how serious I am about going back to Hickory, then fine.

It's easier to remember how mad I am when he's on the other side of the door.

"Helene…"

"I said go away. In case you can't get it through your thick skull, I don't want to talk to you right now."

I expect frustration. I expect West and his "I know better than you" attitude to just ignore what I want—because he's good at that—and keeping knocking until I finally fling the door open just to get him to stop. If not that, I expect him to snarl some more, then storm out for another run.

But he doesn't do any of that.

He goes quiet. No more banging. No more growling. He waits a few moments, instead, gathering his thoughts.

Then, in a voice full of pain, he simply asks, "How much longer are you going to punish me?"

"Is that what I'm doing?"

It's definitely what I'm doing.

"Yes. I know you want to leave, but this is my one chance. My *last* chance. We both know it, and I… fucking hell, Helene. How can I convince you to choose me when you won't even look at me?"

"Choose you?" I glance down at the ring on my finger. The bite on my neck is permanent, but after his reaction when he saw me without the ring, that might as well be permanent, too. "Wow. For all your talk of choosing, I didn't think I was supposed to *get* a choice."

I don't know what hurts him more: my flatly conversational tone, or what I implied. I wasn't wrong, though. He didn't let me choose—and, in his next breath, West remedies that.

"Then reject me."

His voice is a ragged whisper. Because of that, I had to have heard him wrong. No way he said what I thought he did.

"What did you say?"

"Reject me," he whispers, his voice slipping beneath the cracks of the door. "That's all you have to do. Reject any bond we might have and maybe I can finally find the strength to give up on you. Then you can have what you want."

"And what is it you think that I want?"

"Me gone from your life."

It hits me like a sucker punch to the gut. Is that… is that really what he thinks of me? He already tossed at me that I could never hate him, so why does he think that it would make me happy to never see him again?

He might not be my mate, but he's always been my best friend.

I don't want to believe that I spent three years leading him on, or that I'm being cruel now by refusing to do what he just asked me to. The opposite, actually. As an omega she-wolf, his pain is my pain. I've done everything I can to blunt it, even knowing that we could never be.

But if I reject him the same way that Quinn eventually did? I'd break this male even more than I already have. If I let him go on believing that I want him gone from my life, I'd *crush* him.

All it takes is one-half of an intended pair to say the words "I reject you" and *mean* it for the promised mate bond to snap. When Quinn did, West was glad. He wanted Quinn to set him free. But if I do it… it won't work the same way because we don't have a mate bond.

That's the problem. We never had one, so if I make him hear me pointedly reject him, all I'm doing is ripping open the gaping wound in his chest and rubbing some salt in it for good measure.

My anger leaves me in a rush. It hits me then that, as mad as I am for what West did without my permission, I'm even angrier at myself for letting it get to this point. Three years ago, I could've admitted to both of us that I never wanted to lose him… and, now, I'm on the cusp of doing just that.

Because I couldn't say *yes* to the male I loved, and *no* to a stranger I had never met…

Folding in on myself, hugging my waist, I whisper back, "I don't want to hurt you."

"You don't think I'm hurting now?"

I know he is. "We can go home together. Talk this out with a more little distance between us than this den has."

"Reject me first." Stubborn as ever, West clings to his suggestion. "My wolf won't stop me from returning you to Hickory then."

Even if that was true… "I *can't*."

"I've never asked you for anything. Not like this. Not like you did to me. But if you ever cared… if you ever loved me… do this, and then maybe it won't hurt so fucking bad."

"West, you don't know what you're asking—"

"Yes, I do! Damn it, Helene. Reject me!"

"I told you. I *can't*."

His voice booms through the door. "Why not?"

"Because I wouldn't mean it!"

Even before the last word of my shout finishes echoing, the door is shoved open.

His chest is heaving. That's the first thing I notice. It's heaving, slicked with sweat, without any shirt in sight. He's got on a pair of jeans and nothing else. Fresh from his run in his fur, he yanked on his jeans and left it at that. Probably because he didn't actually expect me to look at him again.

I'm looking now.

His hair is mussed. His cheeks hollowed in a way that tells me he's seconds away from losing control. Arms hanging at his side, though his hands are curled into fists. No claws that I can see, but that doesn't reassure me.

He's looking at me with a hungry, yearning expression, but his human side is still calling the shots as he takes one step past the threshold into my territory.

I could stop him. I could tell him to turn around, to get off my territory, to leave me alone… he would listen. No doubt in my mind that he would listen if I told him to go.

But I don't.

I could blame it on me being what I am. I'm an Omega. It's not in me to watch another wolf suffer when I can do something to help them. When West acted as if he had the right to do what he did, I couldn't get through to him. He was too headstrong to listen, and I was too angry to get through to him.

Only now… so lost and vulnerable and aching, I couldn't stop my wolf from reaching out to him.

Even that doesn't explain what happens next. The only thing that does? Is that, in my own way, I just admitted to Weston Reed that I'm still in love with him.

I didn't say the words. I didn't have to.

"I love you."

It's been more than seven months since I heard those words coming from West. I didn't realize how much I missed them until he blurts them out, his grey eyes glimmering with another hint of gold as his wolf peeks through.

He stays a few steps inside the room, waiting for me to say that I can't stand to hear him tell me that.

I don't. Instead, I climb up from the bed, tiptoeing toward him as if I'm in a trance.

West doesn't move. As though eager to see what I'll do next, afraid to frighten me or that I'll change my mind and reject him after all, he stands like a statue.

I could have pushed him out the door and he would've let me. Instead, I move into West until his still-heaving chest brushes against mine, then wrap my hands around his waist.

It's the first time I've touched him in three years. I willingly walked into his arms.

I can't blame West for what *he* does next.

"I love you." He tilts my head back, chin up. His breath pants against my skin, hot and desperate and *him*. "I love you… I love you… I love you so fucking much."

His need assaults me from every side. How can any female resist?

I part my lips. Taking it as the invitation I meant it as, West swoops in. Stroking my tongue with his, kissing me frantically, our teeth clash as his fingers dig into my cheeks. Squeezing him tightly, I hang on as he kisses me with all the pent-up passion of a male who's been dying to do this for years.

Which he has.

In between kisses, he rests his forehead against mine. He needs every connection he can get. Foreheads touching, fingers still gripping me, our chests mashed together, and lower… through his jeans, he's thrusting his obvious erection against me.

"Alpha save me, but I can't stop. Make me. If you really don't want this… want me… tell me to stop. I'll do anything for you, Lane, even rip my fucking heart out of my chest and lay it at your feet."

"West—"

"Tell me." He gasps, lowering one hand from my face, clutching my side through my dress. The other lifts up, threading through my hair. The tips of his claws stroke my scalp, making me shudder. As out of control as West is, he's gentle as ever. Like I'm precious. "Tell me you don't love me."

Tell him I don't love him? Tell him I don't want him?

I part my lips again. The words won't come.

I'll always love West. Nothing he could say or do would ever change that. And, in his arms, feeling the heat of his body all around me, drunk on the scent of sandalwood and the musk of his heady arousal, I have the sudden urge to prove it.

This wasn't what I intended. When I climbed off of the bed and walked over to West... I didn't mean to end up with my hands in his pants.

But that's exactly what happens.

"Your turn," I tell him, my voice gone throaty. "Tell me you don't want me. Tell me to stop and I'll stop. But if you want to—"

That's all I have to say. Letting go of me just long enough to tear the button off his jeans, nearly yanking the zipper off in his haste to shove his pants down past his ass, West's erection springs free. I shift my hand, rubbing my thumb around the crown.

The muscles in his jaw clench. If I know West, this is the first time anyone has touched him like this since the last time I did. Already he's shoving his dick against my hand, even as he grabs both sides of my dress, hiking up my skirt to my waist.

I've still got my panties on. I don't even think about stopping to shimmy them off. The handful of seconds it'll take to strip might be enough for time for me to second-guess what I'm doing. Grabbing the soaked material, I jerk it to the side, then take hold of West's cock by the base.

It doesn't matter that it's been three years. Our bodies know each other in a way that even our minds can't comprehend. Working together, I angle West's cock toward me at the same time as he hoists me up off of the ground, urging me to wrap my legs around his waist.

One push. That's all it takes. One push and West is lodged partway inside of me.

It's been three years for West, but it's been three years for me, too. Luckily, between this angle, his strength, and the fact that I started getting wet the second I saw West standing there, shirtless and full of love for me... one push becomes two before I'm fully seated on West.

He gasps. As the connection between us sends pleasure shooting down my spine, I can't help but do the same.

I'm sure I'll regret it later, but for now? There's nowhere I'd rather be than in this cabin, with West lodged inside of me, his mouth going right back to mine as I plant my hands on his shoulders and start to ride him.

Because, if only for tonight, I can pretend that I won't have to say goodbye as soon as tomorrow.

TEN
ANYTHING

ust like I thought, last night was easy. The morning after?

Not so much—and it's all my fault.

The moment I open my eyes and realize that: a) I'm naked, b) I'm not alone, and c) my bedmate is also naked, I want to rewind time and go back to the moment before I let my heart and my pussy gang up on my common sense and beg for a do-over.

Because, yeah… I made a mistake. A big, big mistake.

It isn't even just that I slept with a male who isn't my intended mate. Until I bond with Rafael beneath the Luna's watchful gaze, it doesn't matter who I'm intimate with. Wolf shifters mate for life once a bond is formed. Before that? It's just sex.

Some females think like that. Following the more animalistic side of our dual nature, plenty of my unmated packmates find their pleasure in whatever male catches their attention. I was never like that. Between my type of wolf and my brother's rank, I was too coddled and protected to ever join the wolves in my age group out in the woods for some fun.

Until West.

Until I fell hard for him, and when we finally decided to mate each other, it wasn't just sex for either of us. It was a communion, the two of us becoming one, and I never wanted anyone else. Him, either. We were each other's firsts, and before the Luna whispered my name to Rafael, we were convinced we'd be each other's lasts.

If only we were. Things would've been so perfect, and I regret all those full moons that passed without the two of us performing the Luna Ceremony. So what if we were young? When it's right, it's right, and for me and West, it was *right*. We could've bonded as hearts' mates—as chosen mates—so long as the Luna blessed our mating.

So sure that, one day, we would wake up and the Luna would tell us that we were fated mates after all, West didn't want to settle for creating a bond. He wanted so badly to believe that we were meant to be. That there would never be anyone else for either of us. He wanted to wait until he recognized me as his, and I just wanted him to be happy.

He's not anymore. Weston Reed hasn't been happy a single day since he found out that I was meant for a future Alpha instead of him.

That's my fault in so many ways. I was the one who pushed for a clean break when I agreed to mate Rafael. If West had it his way, we would've kept up our love affair all the way until the night before I left to be Rafael's Alpha female. Only... I know him. West would never have willingly let me walk away. The way he *stole* me proves it.

As for me... I'm not so sure I would have found the strength to go if I held onto him 'til now.

Three years ago, I thought, if I ended it between us, he'd have time to find a female of his own. Even when the Luna took pity on him and revealed that Quinn *was* West's fated mate, he refused to give up on me.

On us.

And now that he's gone to the extremes, refusing to admit that we never really had a chance… when he decided to go *human* on me, determined to make me his bride even if I can't be his mate… when I spent the last few days trying to convince him to bring me back to Hickory, what did I do?

I fucked him.

Worse, I gave him *hope*.

I can't pretend I didn't. If it was just a quick romp to get it out of our systems, I should have kicked him out of my room the second he got me off. I was careful not to eat anything he's made me, and I've only invited him into my personal territory once. Last night didn't count since he basically barged in on me, but instead of telling him to go, I kissed him. I touched him.

I fucked him.

And then, as he murmured how much he loved me, how much he missed me, missed *us*… as he whispered again and again that he'll be the best mate I could ever ask for, I didn't remind him that he *can't* be. I didn't ask him to leave, or tell him right away that I made a mistake.

Lost in the familiar haze of being loved by West, I teased him when I noticed that we'd mated so frantically, my skirt was bunched up around my waist, my panties tangled, his jeans down by his knees.

Of course, West had to fix that. Always an attentive lover, he eased my dress off of me and removed my bra and panties before shucking his jeans so that they joined my clothes somewhere on the floor. Then, laying me down in the bed, he held me close until we both fell asleep.

I kept telling myself 'five more minutes'.

Five more minutes and I'll put an end to this.

Five more minutes and I'll explain to him that he has to leave.

Five more minutes and I'll tell him that that never should've happened…

I must have fallen asleep in his arms at four because the sun's streaming in through the window, it's morning, and we're still in bed together.

West is fast asleep. I'm on my side, curled into him. His body is turned toward me, his arm slung over my waist, tugging me closer. He's breathing softly, face buried in my hair.

His dick is hard. He's not inside of me anymore, but his entire length is cushioned between my thighs. His possessive grip on my waist isn't our only connection, either. My knees are bent slightly, my ankles kicking out behind me, while West has his leg laying over them.

I don't want to accuse him of holding me so tightly on purpose. It's been three years since I slept with West, but I haven't forgotten how he turns into a barnacle after he comes. As though afraid I'm going to slip out like a thief in the night, he's always had this protective instinct. He's never been the type of male to let go.

Looking back, that should've been a massive clue that, when I told him about Rafael the first time, he wouldn't readily accept that we were over…

West would never force me to do anything I didn't want to. What happened last night… it was so easy to forget that, during the next full moon, I might be in another male's bed. Surrounded by his scent, without Bishop's disapproval reminding me what I'm supposed to do, and the rest of the pack treating me like the Omega—just the Omega, never *Helene*—it was so Luna damned easy to forget that I can't have this male for my own.

So I took him and, at that exact moment, it was so... so *right*.

That was last night. This morning? The fact that a part of me doesn't want it all to end is a sure sign that I screwed up big time.

Okay. Deep breath, Helene. There's got to be a way to slip out of his hold without waking him.

Lifting his hand up by one finger, I slowly ease it away from my hip. Once it's settled on the sheet in front of me, I scoot backward a few inches at a time until his leg slips off of mine. West snuffles. I freeze, sure that he's stirring. His eyes stay closed, and I swallow my sigh of relief.

The same thing happens when I pull away from him enough that his cock isn't nestled between my thighs anymore. Missing my warmth, he reaches out for me in his sleep.

Here goes nothing.

I start to climb out of the bed. Turning away from him, I sit up, ready to place my bare feet on the floor to put some space between us.

Glancing down, I remember that I'm still naked.

If it was any other packmate, I wouldn't have cared. In a shifter pack, where our clothing never survives a shift, nudity is the norm. I don't often shift in front of others now, but as a pup, I did all the time. Long before the first time I ever mated West, we already knew what the other looked like in their skin.

All that changes when sexual attraction comes into play. There's a difference between seeing a male shifter go hard because the breeze blew the wrong way or tits in general set him off and knowing that he's looking at you, dying to stick his cock inside of you. When that happens, staying in your bare skin is basically saying: *yes, please.*

I don't see my dress from last night anywhere. West removed it. I have no idea where exactly he put it. There are plenty of others in the closet, but I'll have to walk over there to grab one.

The blanket, I decide. I'll wrap myself in the blanket to cover up and—

West snags my hand before I can snatch the edge of the blanket. Intertwining his fingers with mine, I'm stuck.

I glance over my shoulder at him.

He's wide awake. His eyes are a gentle grey this morning. Hair mussed from both our mating and my pillow, he's wearing a crooked smile—and nothing else.

In one practiced motion, he uses his hold on my hand to pull me toward him, guiding me to my back. West has done it so many times before that, like it's part of my muscle memory, I let him.

Mistake number two. I fall right open again. Taking that as his welcome, West doesn't hesitate to climb on top of me. His legs settle right into the cradle of my body. His arms bracket my head, pushing into the pillow beneath it as he peers down at me, pure pleasure turning his handsome features breathtaking as he smiles.

"Morning, baby."

Baby.

Oh, Luna. What I wouldn't give to be West's 'baby' again. If I thought hearing him call me 'Lane' was tough, his sleep-rough voice murmuring a pet name I haven't heard in ages has me wanting things I gave up three years ago.

I have a duty. Maybe it's not as important as being an

Alpha or a Beta, but an alliance with the Gravetail Pack can be an asset to the Sylvan Pack. No matter what I want, I gave my word. I promised to be Rafael's female.

He's waited for me for three years. What would happen if I reject him now for West?

They could be an asset, or they could be a threat. I'd never forgive myself if someone got hurt because I made the wrong choice. The time for me to refuse Rafael was three years ago when Bishop gave me the chance. And while I know my brother would back me up no matter what I decided, I don't know Rafael well enough to guess how he'd react to being rejected.

What if he challenged Bishop?

What if he challenged *West*?

I can't.

I just… I *can't*.

My palms go to his bare chest. With just enough force, I keep West from lowering himself completely on top of me.

Before I can tell him to get off, his chin dips. I know he's going in for a morning kiss and, right before his mouth finds mine, I turn my head. His lips land on my cheek.

I fucked him. No denying that. If pressed, I could probably explain away my lapse in judgment away as moon fever come early. The Luna is only a week out; the closer it gets to the full moon, the more our libidos will be in control. Unmated wolves will search for someone to rut with while mated wolves will be inseparable.

West considers us mates. Despite that being wishful thinking on his part, if I'm still in this cabin with him when the Luna is high overhead, I don't think I'll be able to resist him again.

We wouldn't be able to form a bond. With the one open

between me and Rafael, I'd have to reject the Gravetail Alpha before the Luna would bless a mating between me and West.

Will that stop us from falling back into bed again?

It won't—and that's just one more reason for me to find a way out of here as soon as I can without hurting West anymore. Even if Rafael is willing to postpone our Luna Ceremony until next month, I can't spend a full moon in this den with this male.

And not only because of what it'll do to West when I'll finally have to leave him for Rafael…

It nearly killed me to walk away from him the first time. For the sake of the pack—and for West having his chance at a happily-ever-after with his fated mate—I did, and I've paid the price every single day.

What will it do to me to walk toward Rafael, knowing that West is still somewhere behind me?

Right now he's on top of me. His sandalwood scent wraps around me and my wolf. The heat of his body is here. *He's* here.

And I can't have him.

I mourned our relationship once. I'm already doing it again, but West… he's thrumming with need. With pleasure.

With *happiness*.

Why wouldn't he? He got what he wanted from me. I initiated mating with him, and now he's basically buzzing in place, victorious and ready to make me his again.

Starting with the kiss I denied him.

Bracing himself on one arm, he lifts his hand, stroking the height of my cheek. His touch is electric. I jolt, but too pleased with himself, he doesn't notice.

"Lane? Something wrong with kissing me?" His lips curve, still riding high on his endorphins from last night. "If it's morning breath, you can tell me. I'll go brush and be right back."

Dropping his head again, nuzzling the bite mark on my throat, he chuckles. "Now that you let me back into your bed, it's fucking torture to leave it, but you know me, baby. I'll do anything for you."

West lifts his gaze enough that I can see the hope mingled with devotion written in his newly golden eyes. All strong emotions—and they're for me. "*Anything.*"

My heart squeezes at the same time as my stomach goes tight.

Okay. So it wasn't just the sex he wanted from me, was it?

Well, no. My brother might think I am, but I'm not *that* naive. I'm a fully mature female who's been mating since she was nineteen. Despite my self-imposed celibacy streak these last three years, I've had sex. Lots of sex. All of it was with this male right here, so I'd be an idiot if I tried to convince anyone that West's suddenly good mood didn't have something to do with me fucking him last night.

It's more than that, though, and I was being purposely obtuse by pretending not to know.

I love you… tell me you don't love me…

I couldn't do that. I also couldn't say the same words back to him, but I didn't have to. From the moment I moved into him, reaching for the button on his jeans before dipping my hand inside his underwear, I gave him the impression that I still loved him as much as he loves me.

I didn't stop him. I didn't correct him.

I didn't lie, either.

And, Luna damn it, I'm still wearing his ring. Wrong finger, yeah, but that doesn't seem to matter to West. I have his bite and his ring, and now I'm covered in his scent. Add that to the way his erection is nudging the top of my mound, the head of his cock searching for my entrance like some kind of heat-seeking missile, and he seems to think that last night wasn't just a one-time affair.

He took me away from my friends, my family, and my pack in a last-ditch effort to get me to choose him as mine before I went to Rafael. I'm still here. I could have left—and I didn't. After last night, West is giddy with victory.

He thinks he won when both of us have already lost.

Nothing has changed. Not really. I'm still supposed to mate Rafael, and while I couldn't reject West the other night, I can't bring myself to scorn the Luna and reject the Alpha of Grave-tail, either.

West is waiting for me to say something. To answer him. I wish I had one to give.

This is all my fault. I didn't want to lead him on; at least, not any more than I already have. It's not what I meant to do at all. In the heat of the moment, I justified it as one last time. If I'm going to have to spend the rest of my life with a male who isn't Weston Reed, didn't I deserve one final mating with him?

Selfish, Helene. Could I have been any more selfish?

This is the flowers all over again. I should have refused the first one he brought to me after I ended things. It just seemed so… so *harmless* back then. I wouldn't eat his food, and I didn't let him in my cabin, but if he wanted to bring me a flower, that was okay, right?

Wrong.

This is all wrong.

I shift my head, searching for him. "West—"

Eyes sparkling with a mixture of lust and love, he slips his hand between my legs.

It would be so easy to let him in again. Of course, it would only make things so much harder later…

I squeeze my legs together, stopping his hand in its travels. "West, don't."

There's no hesitation. The moment I tell him 'no', he immediately pulls his hand away.

"Sorry, baby. Don't know what I was thinking. You're probably still tender." A dark shadow passes across his face. I want to blame the morning sun dipping behind the clouds, but I know better. "I was too rough. I should've—"

I shoot my hand up to his face, caressing the edge of his jaw with the side of my thumb. "Stop that. Don't blame yourself." I'm the only one to blame. "I picked the pace. You weren't rough at all. Besides, you know I can handle anything you've got." It's probably the dumbest thing I can say at this particular moment, but to get rid of the darkness rising up inside of him, I add, "I always have."

He lowers his forehead, resting it against mine. "That's because you were made for me."

If only I was.

ELEVEN
SORRY

tell him I'm not tender—because I'm a shifter, and I'm *not* —but West wants to be careful. Since that also means that he doesn't push me to mate again, I go along with it.

It's a slippery slope. I go along with that, and when West kisses the top of my hair, then invites me to join him in the shower, I can't think of a good enough reason to refuse that won't force me to have to reject him so soon. We both need to freshen up anyway. The hot water in the cabin barely lasts through one shower, so I justify it by saying that neither of us should have to be caught beneath a cold shower spray.

He's gentle. Using his claws to scratch my scalp as he washes my hair for me, his body bowed over mine as the warm water streams over us, I realize that I made another mistake. Sex is one thing. But this? Showering with West is so much more intimate than anything that happened between us last night.

I try to tell him I can do it myself. Same with soaping up my body. Showering with him is one thing. Letting him wash me? I know I should stop him, but then he insists and I… I give in.

I do the same thing when it comes to breakfast. I'm too ravenous to even think about skipping out on the morning meal, and considering his worry over me starving is what started last night, I can't bring myself to say no to him cooking for me.

West, on the other hand, obviously thinks something monumental shifted between us after last night. Not only does he take my hand in his again, laughing as he leads me to the kitchen, pampered Helene gets to take a seat in the kitchen while West whips breakfast up for us. He serves me the thickest slices of bacon as an appetizer, watching as I nibble on them daintily before—with a satisfied smile—he finishes cooking the rest of the meal.

Every bite is a struggle. I'd like to blame it on my stomach shrinking over these last few days, but even I'm not that naive.

The food sits heavy in the pit of my stomach because I'm viscerally aware that I'm only putting off the inevitable.

I have to tell him. He needs to understand that last night was a mistake, and that it can't happen again. Letting him wash me, feed me… those are things a male shifter does for his mate. By allowing it, I'm giving him the wrong idea.

And, Luna help me, I can't seem to stop myself.

I don't want to hurt him. My omega nature got the better of me last night. I wanted to save him when he seemed to teeter too close to the edge, but instead of just being the Omega, the real Helene came out to play.

Helene loves this male. I couldn't deny it, and then… I got lost in the game I wasn't supposed to be playing at all. And now he's convinced I'm going to love him—to choose him— and I know I won't.

He doesn't. He has no idea. For the next two days, I get a glimpse of what life would be like if I *was* West's mate. As though that moment of connection between me and him—his wolf and mine—was enough to erase the last three years between us, he's the West I remember. Devoted and gentle, charmingly cocky, yet kind. He treats me like I'm precious to him. He kisses me. Cuddles next to me as we share my bed. He even starts talking about going back to Hickory and starting over there together.

I want that. The longer I let him have his fantasy, the more I wish I could just join him. Even knowing that I have every intention of crushing his heart again, it's like a repeat of the other night.

Five more minutes and I'll come clean.

Five more minutes and I'll tell him the truth.

Five more minutes and I'll watch my West shatter…

He admitted it himself. These last three years, he refused to give up on me—on *us*—because I never rejected him. I still can't. Time's running out, so I know I'll have to eventually, but what will happen to him then?

That's how I justify it to myself. And, yes, I know it's as weak an excuse as it sounds.

Because the truth of it all is this: I'm a coward. I'm a coward and I'm selfish, and I wish I wasn't those things just like I wish that I could abandon pack life and settle down in this cabin with West forever.

I thought about it. Last night, as West snored next to me, arm thrown over my nightgown as though he needs to make sure I'm close even as he's sleeping, I lied awake, thinking about just staying here. Once I got over my shock and anger at him bringing me to this secluded den, it hasn't been so bad.

It's peaceful. We don't have any pack politics getting in our way. No packmate coming to me so that I can make them feel better at the expense of my wolf. No Bishop standing over my shoulder, hinting at what I'm expected to do. No females throwing themselves at West because being the Beta's mate would be a coup for any of them...

But then I remembered that he's the Beta, a position he deserves and that he's perfect for. I can't ask him to give that up. I know he would—for me, he would—but what about the rest of Hickory? We have two more budding alphas in the pack. Nancy is the same age I was when I was made the pack Omega; she could easily fill my shoes. But West? He's the only beta wolf we have.

The Sylvan Pack needs him more than I do, and I've known that for a long time. He might think that my determination to do my duty to the pack by mating Rafael Cruces and forming an alliance with the Gravetail Pack is ridiculous. Maybe it is. But hasn't West sacrificed enough on his own to be our Beta?

Wearing that emotionless mask when he suits him, going out alone into the trees to let off some steam and hide his pain... he only does that because he's the Beta, and our entire pack expects him to be the level-headed one. The rational foil to Bishop's powerful alpha wolf... he's not allowed to lose control.

But he did. And that's another reason I seriously think about staying away from Hickory. The other night, I basically decided to stick by West so that Bishop and the rest of his pack council would never learn how close the Beta came to going feral.

In my own way, I'm protecting him. But I won't be able to do that forever, and I know West enough to know that he wouldn't even want me to try.

Besides, sharing a life with West again even if I could… those are only dreams. Silly dreams that belonged to me when I was still a girl. When our rankings in the pack meant nothing to two wolves in love…

That was a lifetime ago. What we're doing right now is trying to recapture that, but it's impossible. All I'm doing is prolonging the moment until the fantasy comes crashing down on the both of us.

Deep down, I'm sure he's aware that it's coming. Like he has been all along, West is in denial about our future. I can tell from the way he falls asleep, whispering his 'I love you's while I've barely said a handful of words in days. He can sense me pulling away from him even while I'm at his side.

There's no reason to keep doing this to either one of us.

He murmurs when I leave the bed. I don't even think he's conscious. Half-asleep, he senses the empty space next to him and reacts to it.

I tell him, "Bathroom," and that seems to be enough of an explanation for him. He probably thinks I'm just going to pee, then I'll be right back. Stopping only to get a fresh dress—and trying not to notice that there are so many more hanging up inside the closet, as though he never expects us to leave—I slip into the bathroom and take a quick shower.

West's disappointment to see me showered and dressed as soon as he wakes up is obvious.

"You got ready without me?"

I had to. In yesterday's shower, West started kissing my neck, making it obvious that he was preparing to take me up against the wall. I panicked and moved away from him so quickly, I nearly slid on the slippery floor. He caught me of course, teasing me for being clumsy, but I effectively killed the mood.

Last night, I told him flatly I didn't want to mate. That's all I had to say. Content to just curl up next to me, he kissed me on the forehead and fell asleep.

I already made up my mind to talk to him this morning. Waiting until after another shared shower would just make it so much worse.

"Yeah." I exhale softly. "We have to talk."

West's expression switches in a heartbeat. Slight disappointment turns to a panic he can't quite hide.

Oh, yeah. He knows what's coming.

"Breakfast," he announces, throwing the covers back. Unlike the night before, he slept in his jeans so I wouldn't be uncomfortable. He didn't even ask if that's what I wanted. He saw me stubbornly cling to my nightgown and, as always, followed my lead. "We can talk after we eat."

My stomach flip-flops. "I'm not hungry, West. And I don't think this can wait."

"You showered. Let me—"

He's looking for any excuse to put off the inevitable.

I don't blame him, but I have to stop this. "It's important."

"Okay. Of course. What's on your mind?"

How to begin?

Feeling fidgety, my she-wolf spurring me to pace, I climb up from my chair.

Big mistake. Big.

Huge.

West's gaze immediately dips, drawn to my bare legs for a moment before he slowly lifts his gaze—then stops. He sucks in a breath, and the panic rushing off of him becomes *need* even before he exhales.

What—

I follow his line of sight and, oh Luna, do I want to kick myself.

I'd been distracted when I grabbed my dress earlier this morning. Because of that, I don't notice until right this second that it's one of the shorter dresses in his collection. It barely skims the middle of my thigh, the skirt flaring at my hip, showing off my body.

I could deal with that. I've worn worse—and it's not like any of the dresses my former lover picked out for me leave much to the imagination—but it's not the length that catches West's attention like that.

It's the material of the dress itself.

It's made of some kind of sleek, white silk that, with the light streaming in through the window, might as well be see-through. It's not sheer, but it's close enough.

His lips part, mouth falling open. West doesn't blink. Lifting his hand, he wipes the corner of his mouth with the back of it.

The air goes heavy with lust. *His* lust. I managed to put off his attentions ever since the other night, but there's no denying that West already has me beneath him in his mind.

He takes a step toward me.

I throw up one hand, warding him off. The other wraps over my chest.

Another mistake. I pulled on panties after my shower, but decided not to bother with a bra. With my body type, they're not necessary. My boobs are small enough that it's not notice-able if I have one on or not—unless the dress I've got on is see-through and he can see the curve of my breasts and my nipples right through it.

His brow furrows when I cover myself. I'm not surprised. I've never hidden myself from him before.

"Lane?"

"Don't look at me like that."

"Like what?"

Like he's starving and I'm his next meal. "Like you're already mentally undressing me."

"You're right. Why do that when I can undress you myself? Then you can join me in the shower. Don't worry if you used all the hot water, baby. By the time we're done, we'll need to cool off."

"No, we won't because I… we're not doing that again."

I didn't think I had to spell out what I meant, but it seems like I do since West blinks before asking, "What do you mean?"

"It was a mistake," I blurt out. I wanted to break the truth to West gently, but with my wolf cocking her head, trying to understand why I'm refusing this male when we both want him, it comes out a lot harsher than I intended it to.

"I love you. You love me. Nothing that happens between us is a mistake, Helene."

He has no idea how much I wish that was true. "It doesn't matter. Whatever it was, it can't happen again."

West rocks back on his bare feet, like I shoved him away from me. He recovers quickly, face screwed up in determination. "Of course it can. You're my mate—"

"I'm not. And, I'm sorry, West… but I can't be. You know that. I've never told you otherwise."

He whirls from me, storming away. For a split second, I can sense his wolf throwing back its head, howling in despair. My rejection is an ache that cuts him deep, and I regret having to hurt him like this.

But then he turns to face me and I gasp.

Not only has he leashed his wolf so that I can't tell how

he's feeling, but West has completely closed off his expression. His eyes have a blank, stony stare to them, his lips thinned in a line.

This is the Beta. The second-most powerful wolf in Hickory, I'm looking at the calm, collected male who is responsible for steadying the Alpha and keeping balance in the pack.

The only clue that he's not in as much control as he wants me to believe is the rise and fall of his sculpted chest. It's heaving, hands curled into fists at his side. If he wasn't bare-chested, I never would've been able to tell that he's struggling to hang on to his control.

I hid from him. I guess it's his turn to hide from me.

"So… let me make sure I understand. What you're saying, Helene, is that you *lied* to me."

His tone is dripping with icicles. A total one-eighty from the heat that was there minutes ago, the last time he spoke to me like this was back in Hickory, when he was planning to steal me away from pack land.

What's running through his unpredictable mind now?

"West, no…"

"Not with words," he amends. What's worse, I wonder? The ice—or the newly conversational tone? "You wouldn't do that to me. But… you let me believe that I had a chance. I never did, did I?"

I can deny it all I want, but it doesn't matter what my intentions were. Only how he sees them… and he's right.

"If it wasn't for Rafael—"

"*Gravetail.*" That's a growl. "Why does it always come down to him?"

Because he's my fated mate. He's my intended.

And we both knew that when we fell into bed with each other.

"I wish it were different," I begin, but that's all I can get out before the rumble in West's chest tells me that that was quite possibly the worst thing I *could* say to him right now.

"It could be. Why can't you see that? It could be different. Reject him. We could be together then. Look at me. I did it. I gave up my fated mate. For you, Helene. I gave her up for *you*."

"I never asked you to do that," I argue.

"You didn't have to! I love you!" He throws his arms out at his sides. "This is what love looks like. It's sacrifice. It's pain. But, for Luna's sake, it's also the best fucking thing in the world when the one you love loves you back. And you… you *love* me. I know you do."

I do, and that's what makes this so hard. But I can't tell him that. Not now.

Not ever.

Instead, I say, "You didn't reject Quinn. She rejected *you*."

The distinction shouldn't bother me. I know it shouldn't. When I can't have West, it shouldn't matter who was the one who chose to sever their mate bond—but it does, because West ignored his tie to Quinn. She's the one who broke it to mate her feral.

West's eyes flash, the golden sheen rolling over his irises. Even more proof that his icy facade is still shattering. "I would have. I told you. For you, I'd do anything… I was just waiting for you to ask me to."

Is that how little he thinks of me? That, after pledging myself to Rafael, I would be so selfish as to ask West to give up his chance at a future with the female the Luna chose for her?

I sound wounded as I tell him, "I couldn't do that to you."

"So, what? I'm not supposed to ask you to reject Gravetail?"

West never has. Oh, no. He's only asked me to choose him over and over again, not understanding why I couldn't.

"I *gave my word. I promised.*"

"So break it. Isn't forever with me worth it?"

If that's all I was worried about, definitely. Maybe if I wasn't the prized omega she-wolf that Rafael has waited three years to claim. Maybe if it was just about me and West, without the Luna fiddling around in my life…

"I'm sorry."

"Sorry," he echoes. "Of course."

West is looming. I don't think he's even aware he's doing it. He'd rushed toward me, stopping short before he got too close, but his broad shoulders are hunched, his chin tucked to his chest. As a beta wolf, he's not as large as an alpha, but he still has a powerful build that usually makes my heart skip a beat.

I'm not afraid of him. I never have been. His looming isn't doing anything except letting me know that he's on the verge of losing control again.

The last time that happened, I lost my head and slept with him. And while I want to believe he's not acting like this on purpose, hoping for a repeat, I'm terrified that *I'll* be the one who uses it as an excuse to touch him again.

Curling my hands into loose fists, I hide them behind my back. Right now, I'd rather West see my boobs through the dress than the way my fingers itch to stroke his heaving chest.

I knew this conversation would go badly. Pity I underestimated just how big a disaster this turned out to be…

"I am. I know you can't understand just how sorry I am, but this is your fault, too."

"Is it?"

"Yes. If you hadn't taken me out of Hickory… if you hadn't *stolen* me… I've told you all along. I made my decision.

Good or bad, I made it and I stand by it. You're the one who wouldn't give up."

"Because I love you!"

"You think you do. Just like you think I'm some perfect pack princess. But I'm not." I sigh. "I can't be what you want me to be so I think that… I think you should go."

A rough shake of his head, and then, "I'm not taking you back to Hickory. Not yet. We can work through this. I know we can. Because I *do* love you. You can't tell me that I don't."

I can't do anything, can I? "I didn't mean Hickory. I want some space, West. Away from you."

He takes a step toward me. It's so opposite from what I just said to him that I growl under my breath. "This isn't the way we're supposed to end," he tells me.

Doesn't he get it? We ended a long time ago.

"You said this room was my territory," I remind him. "I'm asking you to leave it."

Especially since I *can't.*

TWELVE
FERAL

For a moment, I expect him to argue again. I don't know why. When we were in a committed relationship, we went nose to nose all the time. As much as he had the same urge to protect me as other dominant shifters, when it was just the two of us, he could see past my omega wolf and really see *Helene*.

And then I ended things with him, and over the last three years, he basically put me on a pedestal. He had this idea of what kind of female I used to be—that I *should* be—and he did everything he could to keep her.

It's time he remembers that I'm no Saint Helene. I make mistakes; big ones, obviously. I'm not perfect. I can't be controlled, and I'm not always going to do what he thinks I should. I'll make bad choices, but they're mine to make the same way the consequences are mine alone.

I think he's finally figuring that out. He doesn't argue, but he doesn't throw himself at my feet to beg my forgiveness, either. As if some of the luster of my shine is finally wearing off for him, he rips his gaze away from me and stalks over to the dresser.

Yanking open the second drawer, West grabs one of his t-shirts. I watch as he tugs it over his head, then heads for the door to the bedroom.

I don't say anything as he goes. I asked for space, but it's only fair that I give him the same—until I hear him snarl.

I tiptoe out of my territory, inching out into the front room of the den in time to see him glowering at a piece of string hanging from his clenched fist. With another snarl, he flings it away from him.

"Fucking shoelace," he bites out, talking more to himself than to me. "Had to snap off on me."

So that's what he's doing. He's putting on his shoes. He got dressed, and he's covering his feet. That's a sure sign that his human half is in control. Shifters go shoeless when they plan on shifting, so his wolf is definitely taking a back seat to whatever's going on with West right now.

Somehow, I don't think that's a good thing.

He leaves the shoe with the broken lace the way it is before jamming his foot in the other one. No socks, I notice, but he doesn't seem to care. He's in such a rush to get away from me that he doesn't bother with them.

He doesn't wear shoes inside. When he goes on patrol, he either leaves as his wolf, or strips outside. He stocked the cabin with plenty of clothes, but when I asked about his shoes, he admitted he had another pair that went missing from the outside.

It explains his need to do constant patrols around the cabin. Wild animals might make a nest in a pair of boots, but they won't run off with them. Anyone who would is someone West considers a threat to us.

Well, to *me*.

Pulling on his only pair of shoes means he's not going on patrol. But if he's leaving…

"West? Where are you going?"

He doesn't even look over at me. Rising up from the couch, he announces to the room, "You told me to leave. Did you miss the part where I said I'd do anything for you? You want me gone. I'm going."

I only wanted him out of the bedroom so I could sit and think in peace without his wolf tempting me to do things I shouldn't.

"Are you…" My voice is small, but I can't help it. "Will you be coming back?"

He laughs, but there's no humor in it as he makes his way over to the front door. "You know I will. I can't stay away from you." Jerking the doorknob, he yanks it open. His eyes never leave my face as he gives his head a rough shake. "Even if sometimes I wish I fucking could."

I'VE NEVER BEEN REJECTED BEFORE. WEST SLAMMING THE front door in my face after making his pronouncement? It's the closest he's ever come to rejecting me, and I don't know how to handle it.

And isn't that something?

Because I asked for space, I retreat to the bedroom. West's scent just about slaps me in the face. I should've realized that he'd imprinted on every inch of this room over the last few days. I didn't. Sandalwood hits me and my knees go weak.

My wolf wants to go after him. I do, too.

I don't. It'll only make the situation worse.

Instead, I return to my room. The first thing I do is exchange my see-through dress for a simple yellow shift dress —and a bra. After that, I try listening to music, but that doesn't last long; nothing puts you off listening to love songs than having to reject the male you adore. I think about reading the books he brought for me, but they're all romances so… yeah.

Eventually, I decide to curl up in the bed and think. I don't even pretend that I'm not breathing West's scent in from his side, or using it to soothe the jagged edges inside of me. West might have accused me of lying, but even if he thought I lied to him, I don't lie to myself.

I slept so badly last night that it isn't long before I knock out. Surrounded by West's scent, I can pretend he's here with me.

I don't know how long I was sleeping for when the sound of the front door opening jerks me awake. Unlike some shifters, my senses are weaker when I first get up. My wolf can tell that someone's near, and since no one is supposed to know we're here, it has to be West.

It's not.

I slip out into the front room right as a big, bulky male figure steps inside of the cabin. As my wolf goes from dozing to suddenly alert, she whines and snuffles through her snout as a dark, bitter, *rotten* scent slams into me, knocking me back a few steps.

He kicks the door closed behind him, blocking my only way out.

I can hardly believe what I'm seeing. At least a head taller than me and twice as wide, the wolf is nearly as big as Bishop —but there's something *wrong* about him. His shoulders are crooked, arms hunched forward. Those aren't hands hanging off the edge of his gnarled wrists— they're *paws*. His claws are long and thick and black, curving over knobby fingers.

He has no hair on his head. Completely bald up top, patches of fur stick out all over him. His chest is covered in thick brown fur, but so are half of his arms, and part of his neck. Fangs jut out of a twisted mouth. His expression is a broken snarl.

That's not the only broken thing about him, either.

It's *him*. His wolf feels fractured to mine, like someone took a shifter, broke him into a million pieces, but he's still walking around with thin lines running through him. Only… he doesn't want the glue to put himself back together. He likes being shattered, and uses it as an excuse to do what he wants—

Take what he wants—

And nothing can stop him.

Feral. I've recognized a twisted male like this before. Nowhere near as cracked as the male in front of me, Quinn's feral, Chase, had read as slightly fractured to me the one time I met him.

Quinn has kept him whole, though. His love for her… he was a feral, but he wasn't *lost*. He wasn't *insane*.

This male is, and he's focusing all of his madness on *me*.

"Well, well, well… and what are you doing in my den, little wolf?"

Suddenly terrified as I am, my first ridiculous thought is: how can he speak through a mouth full of fangs like that? His words should be as mangled as his jaw, but though his voice is rough and deep and ragged, I have no problem understanding what he said.

Figuring out what he means takes me a second longer.

My den—

Oh, no. Oh, no, no, no.

This wasn't a lone wolf's abandoned cabin that West found and renovated. It's a feral's *den* that he took over—and it looks like the male who owns it wants it back.

"Is it yours?" I squeak. "I'm so sorry. I had no idea. Here, why don't I leave and you… you can have it back?"

"Leave?" His dark yellow eyes glitter with insanity. "You ain't going nowhere without me."

What—

He flexes. There's no other word for what he does. His body tightens, then releases, but instead of shifting all of the way, he explodes out of the ratty jeans he had slung low on his hips.

I was staring at his misshapen body before. As the material of his jeans rains down on the living room floor, I can't help but lock on the massive dick swinging between his meaty thighs.

Before my eyes, it twitches, then starts to harden.

I swallow my moan of fright.

I thought me and my wolf could handle a feral. But an *aroused* feral…

"Let me go." I pour all of my wolf's calming energy into trying to convince the feral to stop this. "You don't have to do this. Let me go. Please."

In response, the feral reaches down, grabbing his dick by the base. He pumps it once, twice, then shakes his head.

"Nothing doing. You think I'd do that after all these weeks of watching that pack wolf sniff around my den? Pissing on my territory, marking it for himself… I knew he was hiding something in here. I just never expected to find a fresh female waiting for me. He left you, little wolf. He left you for me."

He didn't.

He wouldn't.

Too bad that doesn't change the reality of my situation.

He's moving toward me, treating me like skittish prey. I'm sure that's how I look, trembling in place as he continues to stroke himself. One wrong move and he'll be on me…

…so I'm just going to have to make sure the move I make isn't the wrong one.

Okay. I can't bolt for the door, but maybe I can hide somewhere else. In the cabin, there's a bathroom, a kitchen, this front room, and the room that I've made mine. Scared out of my Luna damned mind, my wolf seeks safety.

I run to my territory because, in my panic, it seems like the safest spot for me. Maybe I can smash the window and escape through it or… or…

I don't know. I don't know what to do, and I flee because it's the only thing that makes sense as the feral licks his lips and breaks for me.

He's quick. I pray to the Luna I'm just a little bit quicker.

Speed's the only thing I have on my side. I'm not like the other females in my pack. I'm not defiant like Quinn, or quietly strong like Sofia. I've seen Marcia challenge Tucker when he was getting on her nerves. She wiped the floor with him, and Tucker was ribbed for weeks over how easily Marcia's tiny brindled wolf kicked the much larger white wolf's ass.

And then there's me. The pack princess, there was no reason for me to learn how to defend myself. I have the same instincts all she-wolves do, but no idea how to use any of them. That's why I was raised to believe that I'd need a dominant male to protect me.

But I told the one wolf who would to go away because he —rightly—called me out for giving him false hope. Once again, prim, perfect Helene screwed everything up, and now I'm going to pay for it.

I bolt. He follows. Letting out a whoop, I realize that I messed up again. Male shifters love the chase. If he wasn't already planning on taking me before, he will now.

He's on me within seconds. Just as I cross the threshold to the bedroom, he grabs me by my waist, tossing me to the floor. My knees hit first, then my belly, then my chin. It's like I bounced before I slammed back on the hard wood. It rattles my head, jostling my teeth, but the pain is nothing compared to the fear racing through me.

It gets even worse when he launches himself at me. Covering my body with his, he uses his claw to rip through my dress, jabbing me in the side, yanking me up so that I'm on all fours beneath him.

No doubt in my mind what he intends to do with me. In this position, he's going to use that monstrous cock to rip me apart. And when he's done? He might decide to use his claws next.

Unless I shift first.

Despite shifters having two distinct forms, when it comes to mating, it's only ever done in our skin. That's just how it's always been done. Our wolves hunt, while our human halves fuck. If I shift to my wolf, he can attack me all he wants, but at least he won't force me to mate him.

He knows what I'm going to do. From the way I hold myself stiff for a moment, ready to shift, he can sense the change a split second before I can go through with it.

His laugh is closer to a bark. Rusty, *unused*, it skitters down my spine like nails on the chalkboard as he rears back, resting on his heels. Releasing me, he lays his massive paw on the middle of my back before trailing it all the way down the curve of my ass.

The instant he laid his paw on me, I froze. My she-wolf quails, tail between her legs, whining as the feral's darkness is a bigger threat to her than his oversized body is to me. His broken mind is terrorizing my wolf, making it hard for me to tap into her and give her control.

And then he speaks, and I realize it's pointless to even try.

"Go right ahead," he rasps. "You think going fur will stop me and my beast? I'm more animal now than you'll ever be. Wolves rut. Humans rut. I'll take you no matter what shape you are."

No.

I'd rather die than let this feral touch me like that. I've heard too many horror stories in the pack circle about broken male shifters who see a female and *take*. They'll mount her, breed her, *rut* like a wild beast if that's what their wolf wants. When they finish, some ferals leave the female as twisted as they are. She-wolves can be killed during the mating, or slaughtered when the feral is finished. Riding high on lust, they often go for blood.

Ferals are worse than rogue vampires. With a vamp, at least I know I'm dealing with an enemy. The feral is enough *wolf* to leave my wolf confused, trying to figure out why a fellow predator is treating her like the most enticing of prey.

If I thought letting him mate me would save me, I would let him. Shifters are built to survive, but this brute isn't anything like Quinn's feral. I'm meat to him. Flesh. I won't survive whatever he has planned for me, which means I have nothing to lose when I lash out with my heel.

I kick behind me. Hard. The feral curses angrily as something cracks. It might be my bone, but since I feel nothing except the adrenaline spurring me to get away, I take my chance to crawl out of his reach.

It was a good attempt. I'll die believing that because I only get a few inches away before he hooks the back of my thighs with his claws.

I didn't scream. All the way up until he dug his claws into me, dragging me back to him as he tore through my flesh, I refused to scream. I'm a shifter. A she-wolf. A *predator*. He didn't get to make me howl.

But that's not the only reason. If I screamed and West was near enough to hear it, he'd come for me—or what's left of me. I won't do that to him, but the choice gets ripped away from me when his claws slice through me, so deep he cuts through muscle and gouges bone.

"Ahh. Music to my ears." He digs deeper. This howl burns my throat raw but that's nothing compared to the fire racing down my legs. "*Yes*. Your screams are as beautiful as you are, female. If your pussy is just as good, I might think about keeping you."

Liar. He's having too much fun torturing me. The mating will only be another level to hurting me, and when he's done, he'll leave me in pieces on this floor.

And there's nothing I can do to stop him.

My vision starts to go hazy. With a grunt, he rips through my muscle, adding to my agony as he purposely yanks his claws out a different way than he latched onto me. Weak, I don't fight my latest scream, though it comes out as more of a whimper when a fresh wave of sandalwood hits me.

West.

Collapsing onto the floor, my last thought is of West before I'm drawn back to what the feral is doing behind me.

The bottom of my yellow dress is nothing but tatters as he

slashes it with his bloody claws. Fangs bite through my panties, tearing them off. Hot breath, *rancid* breath bathes over my skin. His mouth is right there—

—and then it *isn't*.

The feral's dark scent is overpowering, but when I gasp again, I still taste sandalwood—and blood—on my tongue.

The blood is mine.

The sandalwood is *West*.

He's *here*.

Somewhere behind me, I hear a snarl, then a massive *thud* as something large is thrown at the far wall. Without the feral pinning me down, I crawl a few feet away before rising up on my knees and climbing to unsteady feet.

My thighs are screaming at me. They're already healing, the skin stretching tight as I scurry over to the far side of the bed and crouch down behind it.

That's when the feral hops back up, the promise of murder turning his partially shifted features into something even more twisted than before.

Because he's looking *forward* to it.

THIRTEEN
HIS

Growing up in a wolf pack, I've seen plenty of challenges before. Blood is nothing new, even when you're a sheltered omega she-wolf. Neither is death.

But the idea that I might be watching West die all because he rescued me from a *feral*?

I don't interfere. The number one rule in any shifter challenge is that interference can be a death sentence to a bystander. Shifters aren't as ruled by bloodlust like vampires are, but in the middle of a fight to the death, I could distract West. He might strike out at me by accident. The feral could even use me against him.

I know what I'm supposed to do. Crouching behind the bed, ignoring the pain in my body as I watch the feral circle West, I send a prayer up to our goddess that I'll never doubt her wisdom again if only she'll spare West.

Because this is what I get. So close to disregarding the male the Luna gave me, rejecting my fated mate for the mate of my heart, I never told him how much I still love him with words… and now there's a chance I never will.

West is bristling with rage as he matches the feral step for step. That's all the emotion I can sense from him over the feral's lust for my body and West's head. Even as he taunts West, the feral is still sporting an erection that has me swallowing another moan of terror when I see it.

If the feral wins, that means West has to lose. I'll have to watch the male I love die, and then this cruel beast will attempt to use that monstrous dick on me.

I was scared before. That's nothing compared to the terror that hits me at that realization.

West jolts as the wave of fear rushes off of me. I didn't mean to do it. So focused on the threat in front of him, West had locked down his emotions like a cage: nothing getting out, nothing getting in—except, it seems, for my terror.

He's not the only one who senses it. Breathing in deep, nostrils flaring, the feral throws back his head and groans loudly, delighting in the scent of my fear. To my horror, his cock jerks, a small spurt of come exploding from the head. He didn't even touch himself. Bastard got off on knowing I'm terrified.

I've never felt so disturbed in my life. Covered in his scent and his claw marks, I didn't think I was dirty until I saw that happen. Though I don't want to distract West any more than I have to, a whimper escapes me.

West reacts.

The feral should've known better than to take his dilated eyes off of a threat for even a second. With his head still thrown back, West lunges forward, claws outstretched in front of him.

I gasp.

He swipes his claws from gut to chest. He starts low, digging all the way across the feral's bulk, left to right. The force of his hit sends hot blood spewing across the room. It slaps me in the face, landing on my cheeks, in my open mouth and on my tongue, my neck, even the bodice of my dress.

Don't throw up, I tell myself as the tang on my tongue tastes like poison. It's just a little blood.

Feral blood.

I gag, frantically wiping at my face and my mouth. It's an instinctive reaction. I don't think I could've stopped myself if I tried. And when I finally drop my hands, watching the feral gaze down at the hole torn through his chest, I wish I had kept my face covered.

Even worse, the feral digs his own claws into his gaping wound. Pulling them back out, he sticks his bloody fingers into his mouth, licking them clean. "Delicious," he hisses.

I don't know if he means his blood or mine. It doesn't matter. The taunt does something to West.

His earlier strike at the feral was calculated. Designed for a massive impact with the least amount of effort, he used the momentum of his swing to tear through the feral's body.

What happens next? Pure instinct.

Fangs bared, claws ready to rend, he falls on the feral.

The feral expected him to attack. I'd bet anything on it. But West is smarter than that. Instead of attacking, he dug his claws back into the wound, almost mimicking what that feral did to himself. Only West... he wasn't after the blood. He needed a good grip, and when he got one, he dragged the kicking, howling feral out of the bedroom and into the front room.

My legs are much better. Leaping up, I hardly feel a twinge as I follow after West.

He has complete control of the fight. Throwing the feral

to the floor, I hear a crunch, then a low snarl as the feral tries to recover. West doesn't even give him a single opportunity to turn the tables. The feral leaps, but West is ready for him. Kicking out with his boot, he catches the feral in his ruined chest, sending him flying out through the open front door.

Blood and tissue clings to the sole of his boot when he takes his foot back. He leaves a trail on the floor as he stalks forward, prepared to finish the feral off.

For me. He's doing this for me—but he doesn't want me to watch.

"Stay inside," he orders before he disappears out the door.

I almost refuse.

So what if I'm an omega she-wolf? I'm not as strong and fierce as most of my packmates, but I'm still a *wolf*. I'm not going to quail and hide while West fights a feral for me.

But then I realize… if he wanted to put down the feral in front of me, he would've done it in the bedroom. And maybe he didn't want to wash my territory in the feral's blood. Fine. The fight could've ended in the living room.

That's not where West tosses the feral. He brings him outside. Whether he's keeping death out of our cabin—not the feral's den, but *our* cabin—or he really doesn't want me to see what a Beta is capable of, I'm not sure.

He told me to stay inside, though. For West's sake, I'll listen.

I hear the rest of the fight through screams, grunts, and, finally, a death rattle. Hoping like hell that inhuman sound is coming from the feral, I drown it out by forcing myself to look around the front room instead.

Aside from the tracks of blood, there are strewn flowers everywhere. It looks like West had gathered enough to bring back a bouquet, but he'd dropped them to rush for the bedroom.

I can't go outside. Returning to the bedroom by myself… I can't do that, either. And maybe it's a trauma response because, suddenly, I need to clean up this space. It's West's and it's mine, and I can't stand looking at the scattered petals, broken stems, and bloody bootprints for a second longer.

Bending low, my thighs give a small shot of protest as I try to gather up as many petals as I can. Once I have my hands full of them, I think about dumping them in the trash—but I don't. That would require leaving the front room and I… I can't do that until I see West, whole and safe, with my own eyes.

I drop the flowers on the couch, then return for more. I'm just about done gathering them all when, out of the corner of my eye, a figure appears in the doorway.

My head jerks toward him, relief making me weak in the knees when I recognize the male standing there. Like the feral, he's now shirtless. His boots are gone, too. He's wearing a pair of black sweatpants. Considering he was wearing jeans when he went after the feral, he must have shifted during the fight, then dug for a shifter's cache outside.

Most dominant shifters have them. A store of clothes they keep near their territory for unexpected shifts, West must have kept a spare pair of sweatpants outside.

After what happened with the feral, no way would he return to me bloody and naked. Not when he's not sure how I would receive him.

Because he isn't. That much is obvious.

I swallow roughly, taking a few unsteady steps toward him. "*West.*"

"Don't."

On my third step, I stop walking. He bit out that word with such venom, I flinch like I've been stung.

Once he's sure that I'll stay away from him, he enters the house. Purposely avoiding me, he goes straight for the kitchen. I hear the sink turn on. It's hard to pick up the rushing water over the sound of my pounding heart, so hard that I don't even realize that it's off until he's back in the front room again.

His hands are clean; it never even hit me that they were bloody until I realize it's gone. His hair is wet; so is the hollow of his throat. Scratches and gouges, bites and claw marks cover most of the bare skin in front of me. That's something else I didn't notice before. So happy to see that he was the winner, I didn't care how he returned to me.

West obviously did. He'd gone straight to the kitchen to scrub. As I run my gaze over him, the injuries from the feral start to heal. He has one or two deeper gouges that might take a couple of minutes to heal, but the rest are nearly gone by the time he's looming in the doorway that leads to the front room from the kitchen.

Deciding that he only kept me away from him before because he was covered in the feral's blood, I take a hesitant step toward him again.

I'm prepared this time. When West shakes his head, I stop instantly even as I murmur his name in a questioning tone.

I didn't actually ask him a question. But West? He answers me anyway.

"You have to stay away from me. Don't you understand, Helene? I'm too dangerous for you."

Dangerous? He has to be kidding.

"You saved me—"

"From one feral," he says. Claws jabbing into his bare

chest, his grey eyes so dark, they're almost black, he whispers, "Who will save you from *this* one?"

I SAID IT BEFORE AND I'LL SAY IT AGAIN: I'M NOT AFRAID OF Weston Reed, no matter how tenuous his hold on his other half gets.

For days now, I've had the same fear. That, after three years of my silent, constant rejection, I broke him. That he turned feral, and it's all my fault.

I know better. Having come face to face with two feral shifters—one happily mated, the other a *terror*—my wolf was able to pick up on both the similarities and differences between them. It was instinctive. She did it all on her own, and it makes me absolutely positive that I know what I'm talking about when I tell West, "You're not a feral."

"No," he argues. "If you saw what I did to him... after that he tried to do to *you*... I'm *worse*."

"You're not—" I try again.

His jaw goes tight. "Lane, please. I'm barely holding onto my wolf as it is. I don't want to hurt you."

He would *never*. "I know you. You're *nothing* like that monster."

West's laugh is low and cold. "You sure about that?"

"You're not feral, West. *He* was feral. You're my wolf. My savior. My—"

Mate.

I don't say the word. The fact that I swallow it, keeping it to myself... it doesn't matter. He knows. He knows and, fisting his hands at his side, hiding his claws, West hangs his head.

"I love you." There's something in the way he says it... so

simply stated, like it's an undeniable fact. "I want you so badly, and I know I shouldn't. I know you won't choose me. But you love me. You love me, and I cling to that because when I think of not loving you, I can see myself turning into a fucking feral, too."

"West." I wait until he picks up his head, eyes meeting mine. "That won't happen."

Again with the laugh that makes me shiver. "You don't know that."

"I'm an omega wolf. Of course I do."

"You're too late, baby. I think… I think I might already be fucking gone." He lifts his hand, running it across his face. "I mean, I slaughtered him. *Slaughtered*. Not because he was feral, or because he accepted the challenge. This was his den. I recognized the scent. It was his territory… and I fucking *slaughtered* him because he thought he could take you from me."

"But you did that to save me. To *protect* me. You would've done the same for any threat to the pack."

His eyes were stone-cold, dark grey and vicious—until I say that. In an instant, they bleed over to blazing gold as he tosses his head. "I'd protect the pack to my last breath. But for you… I'd stay alive a second longer than anyone who tried to take you from me just so they would die knowing they failed. You're mine, Helene. Choose another male. Take another mate… it doesn't change a Luna damned thing."

Anguished hands digging in his hair, West sinks down to his knees.

"Are you listening? I'll always think of you as *mine* and treat you like you are. *Always*. And that's why no one is a bigger threat to you than me. Because, tell me, Helene… what happens when my wolf sees you as the one keeping us apart?"

I don't know what's harder to take: the icy-cold Beta or the broken male in front of me. He's not feral, but he's right when he says he's close.

He's also right when he points out that I'm the one playing games with him and his wolf. Not that he said it in so many words.

He doesn't have to.

Right then, watching West drop his face in his hands, I have to admit something I've always known: The Beta belongs to the Sylvan Pack. Weston Reed belongs to *me*.

And I'm losing him.

I *can't* lose him.

Just the idea that he might one day be out of my reach like that feral has me rushing toward him, joining him on the floor. When he doesn't jerk away from me, I take hope in that, clutching at his chest.

I want to tell him that that won't happen. That, no matter what, his wolf will never turn on me. But I don't get the chance. This close, West sees the blood covering my bodice, scents the feral on me, and begins to growl. "What did he do to you, Helene?"

Helene.

"It's just a dress." The words spill out in a rush. "Just a stupid dress that he ruined even before his blood splashed all over it."

"Take it off."

"West?"

"Take. It. Off. I can smell him on it. I… It has to go."

Fine. If I can't keep him with me with words, I'm not above using whatever I have to. He wants the dress gone? He wants me to strip? I don't know if he realizes that the feral already removed my panties, but I don't care. For West, I'll do it.

Resting on my heels, I grab the hem of my skirt, yanking the ruined dress up and over my head. Tossing it far away from me, I reach out, laying my hands on his bare shoulders.

He's in his sweatpants. Even though my panties are gone, I still have my bra on as I lean forward, holding tightly to him. There's absolutely nothing sexual about this, not even when he lowers his hands, running his fingers over the deep purple bruises covering my sides.

The feral must have grabbed me harder than I thought when he tossed me down, pinning me beneath him—and now West knows it.

"He marked you," he whispers. "I'd kill him again for these bruises alone."

"They're already healing."

"Where else did he hurt you?"

He sounds so much calmer than before that I don't want to answer him for fear that I'll start to lose him again.

With calm, though, comes clarity. "I scent your blood, too, Helene. I know he hurt you. Tell me. Please. I have to make sure you're okay."

Put like that, how can I refuse?

With a small nod, I pull back from West, shuffling on my knees until my back is to him. I'm playing with fire, doing what I'm about to do, but I fall forward, going to my hands and knees in front of him. I press my legs together so that my pussy is concealed from his sight, but there's no hiding my bare ass without any panties to cover it.

"My thighs," I murmur. "He clawed the backs of my thighs, but I wanted those marks gone so I healed them first."

West's hand ghosts over my skin. "That's right, baby. You kept my mark. Not his."

The possessive note in his voice has me rising up just

enough to push my thigh into his palm. "That's right, West. Only yours."

He doesn't point out that I'm lying to him. Maybe tonight I'm his, but the whole reason why he wasn't there when the feral found me was because I'd finally admitted that we couldn't keep this up. I still have an intended, but Rafael is a distant memory as West rises up on his knees, bending his body over mine.

He's still in his sweatpants. As though he wants me to be aware that he isn't trying anything like that feral did, he rubs the material of the sweatpants against the small of my back before he starts nuzzling my neck.

No. Not nuzzling.

Sniffing.

He's scenting me. Running his nose along the curve of my shoulder, down my back, near my armpit. As though he needs to know exactly where the feral touched me the most, he's checking every part of me he can.

When he reaches my waist, near the bruises, he stiffens.

"He grabbed you here," he says unnecessarily before he goes a little further south. When he skims down one of my bare ass cheeks, he growls, the vibrations enough to actually kickstart my arousal.

When the feral had his mouth on my pussy, I wanted to die. But when it's West just as close…

"You smell like him," he announces, his voice gone husky. "I can scent your heat and your cream, and fuck if it isn't delicious, but I smell him, too." Another growl. "I can't stand you smelling like that bastard."

Of course not. He thinks of me as his. Finding the trace of another male's scent on his mate? That's enough to turn even the most even-keeled shifter just a touch feral.

He's not a feral, but right when I thought I pulled him back from the brink, West is teetering on the edge of his control again.

His hands are on my thighs. He's still careful not to touch me too roughly, but he's not letting go. He's not moving his face, either. Just about burying his nose along my slit, I'm suddenly reminded that, while he has on pants, the feral *bit* my underwear off of me.

Just further proof that West is still in control. If he wasn't, I have no doubt he'd already be finding a way to get rid of the dark scent himself.

Actually, that's not such a bad idea.

QUICKSILVER

A shower would do no good. Neither would a bath. A male shifter's musk will only fade with time, or when another male overlays it with his.

Bracing myself in case he rejects me, I ask him, "Would you like it better if I wore your scent instead?"

"Are you asking me to mount you?" I'm not surprised that, over his need to erase the feral's markers, he sounds incredulous. "You told me that we can't mate again."

"I know. But… and don't feel like you have to… but if you want to use your mouth on me—"

"Feel like I have to? Helene, I haven't had a taste of you in three years. I never thought you'd let me get this close… and you say 'feel like you have to'? I know I've gone crazy. Have you, baby?"

Honestly? I'm not so sure.

The way I see it, the blood triggered his protective instincts. The scent of the feral's lust and musk overlaying mine? It's bringing out his possessive side.

As an omega, I need to rein him in. If I get a little pleasure out of it while making him happy, letting him replace the feral's scent with his own, is that so bad?

No. He's right. I think I have gone crazy.

"Never mind. There's got to be another way—"

"Uh-uh," West says, guiding one hand between my closed legs, easing them open. "I'm sorry, baby. You offered. I accepted. Unless you want to change your mind…"

Look at that. It took nearly losing me to a feral to finally realize that I should get a choice.

"I didn't. If you want to go down—*oh*."

Oh is right.

I thought he would at least flip me onto my back so that he could start licking me from the front. He, uh, doesn't. As though desperate to get his scent on every intimate part of me, he goes down on me from behind.

The heat of his palms scorches my ass as he spreads me wide open for his tongue. He licks and nibbles, not missing a single spot as he nuzzles the curve of my ass with his cheek, dips the tip of his tongue inside of my entrance, and does long, leisurely strokes on my inner thigh. He pays special attention to the spots on my thighs that had been torn open by the feral's claws, and when he's sure not even a single hint of a scar lingers, he finds my clit with his teeth.

This wasn't supposed to be about giving me pleasure. Honest. It was about soothing his wolf, letting him leave his mark on me. It was showing my gratitude for saving me from the feral… I didn't expect him to make me come.

But he does.

Tightening his hold on me, knowing I can take it, West doesn't stop until I'm squirming against his face, riding out my orgasm as he makes sure to gather all the moisture welling up at the entrance to my pussy as my legs began to shake.

Only then, when I come down from the high of my climax and West is satisfied that I smell like him—and he smells like me—does he finally release his hold on me. It's only for a few seconds, though, as he leaps to his feet, then swoops down and reaches for me.

Using his shifter's strength, he pauses only to check that the front door is locked and bolted before he carries me into the bedroom. He never once removes the sweatpants. There's no sign he expects or even wants any kind of reciprocation.

After returning from the bathroom with a damp towel, he makes sure this isn't a single speck of blood on me. That done, he climbs in behind me, tucking me into his chest, almost daring me to turn him away.

As if I could.

Between the shock of the feral's attack, my adrenaline crash, and West's gifted mouth, I'm half asleep by the time my head hits my pillow. Even so, as my eyes close, I can't help but dwell on this male.

I always knew I would need a strong mate to protect me, and whatever happens tomorrow, tonight West saved me.

And if I can find it in me to forsake the Luna's wishes, reject Rafael's claim to me, and choose West like I've wanted to do all along... I might just be able to save him, too.

SOMETHING'S WRONG.

That's my first thought when I slowly drift awake. Something's wrong. My head is heavy. My body almost disconnected from the rest of my consciousness.

Half asleep, I realize that this is what it felt like after he—
Quicksilver.

I clamp my eyes shut. My heart's already racing, thump-thump-thumping inside of my chest. My wolf is missing again, as if I needed another clue that I've been drugged, and I clench the sheets beneath me.

Don't panic, Helene. There must be a good reason why West pumped you full of quicksilver again. The feral. Maybe he wanted to make sure I had a nice, long, dreamless sleep after the feral's attack.

Without my senses, I can't find him. Forcing my eyes to open, I turn my head. Though West joined me in bed after he washed me clean, he's not here now.

I jolt upright.

There he is. Like we're having a do-over from the morning I woke up to find his ring on my finger, I'm alone in the bed and West… he's pacing again.

I call his name.

His head jerks my way, his expression so cold, I grab my covers for added warmth.

"What's wrong?" I ask, my voice a whimper. "What's the matter?"

I can't get to him. I don't know what he's feeling inside, but if it's anything like the ice in his steel-grey eyes, I probably don't *want to.*

"I thought I could keep you safe on my own."

Is that what this is about? I got a dreamless sleep, but West obsessed over the feral attack all night long?

"You did—"

"When I see you, I see Helene. I see sunshine and light. I see the best fucking five years of my life, and another three I wouldn't change for anything no matter how tough they were. Because I still got to see you. To hope. To think that maybe…"

"Maybe? West? You're frightening me."

He lets out a hollow chuckle that sends shivers down my spine. "I knew it was only a matter of time before I did."

That's not what I meant. "What's going on?" I ask again. "I think I missed something."

"I called Bishop."

Called Bishop… "There's no phone here. How did you call him?"

West dips his hand into the back pocket of his jeans. When he pulls it out again, he's holding a phone. "I had one for emergencies. I think you'd agree with me that last night was an emergency, Helene."

Helene, I notice. Not Lane.

Not anymore.

"What did my brother say?"

Instead of answering me, he has a question of his own. "How strong is the bond you have with the Gravetail Alpha?"

He doesn't use Rafael's name if he can help it. He never has, and I'm so used to it that I don't really understand what he's asking me for a moment as I try to figure out why he's bringing up my intended at all.

Wait—

If West never used Rafael's name, that's nothing compared to how he refused to acknowledge that I was Rafael's fated mate. That includes any kind of bond I might already have with the other male.

"You called for him. And I don't mean on the phone. You and your wolf… your soul cried out for *him*."

"What? When?"

"When the feral came after you. You called for him, and he felt it all the way in Darkwoods—"

Darkwoods. The name of the settlement where the Gravetail Pack claim their territory. And if he felt it, that means he knows exactly where I am…

At least, until West pumped me full of quicksilver.

No. I can't think about that. Not when West looks like he's seconds away from losing it, and all because my wolf wanted a male that wasn't him.

"I was terrified. Strong emotions reach down all kinds of bonds. Bishop probably felt my panic all the way in Hickory!"

West clamps his jaw.

"What about you?" I ask. "Last night, after you…" I can't even bring myself to talk about being intimate with West when he's looking at me like that. "You told me you felt me reach for you. That you were already on the way back to me before you heard me scream."

"I did. But it was just another way I convinced myself that you wanted me. I've been a fool for too long. It's not me. It'll never be me. And I'm only being a selfish prick keeping you with me when I know it's putting you in danger." He sniffs, tearing his gaze away from me. "Get dressed. We're leaving."

I should be happy to hear that. I should be fucking *elated*.

I'm not.

"Is that what's got you so worked up? You called Bishop and he ordered you to bring me home?"

Only a few days ago, I would've been ecstatic to hear that. I shouldn't need my brother to fight my battles for me, but if there was one soul who might get through to West to get him to see how reckless his taking me the way he had was, it's Bishop.

West is the Beta of our pack. More than that, he's Bishop's

closest advisor and most trusted friend. Except for Sofia and me, he's the only wolf who can look the Alpha in the eyes without immediately showing his throat. He would never challenge Bishop and every member of the Sylvan Pack knows it.

But that trust goes both ways. West is loyal to Bishop, and Bishop doesn't order his Beta to do anything. He doesn't have to. As though West is tapped into the Alpha's brain, he knows what Bishop wants done and always makes sure it *gets* done.

"Not exactly," he say.

"What does that mean?"

"I told you, Helene. *He* felt you. He won't wait until the Luna to have you safe on his territory. Your *mate*"—he spits out the word—"wants to be the one to protect you. Maybe he'll do a better job than I ever could."

What?

"I don't understand…"

"That's okay. You don't have to." West's nostrils flare. Still running on high alert since last night, he must scent something that my dulled senses can't. "They're here."

The little hairs on the back of my neck go up. "Who?"

West doesn't say anything.

"Luna damn it, West! I'm tired of you thinking you always know what's better for me than I do!"

His lips quirk up in a wry grin that doesn't quite meet the sad look in his dark grey eyes. "Then I guess you'll be glad to know that you won't have to put up with me anymore."

Darkwoods.

Fitting name, I think, as the Jeep I'm in goes off-road, tucking into a copse of live oak trees. Growing lower to the ground than my beloved hickories, their branches intertwined, they manage to block out the Texas sun.

It's late October, but with the sun shining down, you'd think it was still August. Once we disappear among the trees, the temperature drops a good fifteen degrees. Shadows are everywhere, too, and I don't see a single wildflower anywhere.

I'm in the lead Jeep with Francois, the Beta of the Gravetail pack. Behind us, there's another Jeep, with two other Gravetail shifters: Michael is the dark-skinned male, though I didn't catch the name of the blond. Too stunned that West was quick to pass me into their care, I'm lucky I learned the first two names.

He's not Rafael. I've only met the Gravetail Alpha once, but Rafael Cruces has bronzed skin, rich black hair, dark gold eyes, and a smile that never quite reached them.

I'm not surprised that my intended sent three of his packmates to retrieve me for him. He's the new Alpha of his pack. If he left Darkwoods, he's only inviting a challenger to try to move in on his territory while he's gone.

Maybe if I was his chosen mate, he'd risk it. But I'm not. I'm the fated mate that he imprinted on once three years ago, then was content to ignore until he became Alpha and pack tradition said he could finally mate me.

And, no, I'm not bitter about that at all. Why would I be? Up until the moment terror led me to cry out for help for anyone who could hear me, I purposely kept my bond with Rafael closed off. I would be his mate when the time came.

Now it has.

Besides, I made my choice, didn't I?

I falter in my step as that realization slams into me. I did. All this time, I've told myself that my future was out of my hands. That the Luna decided I would mate Rafael Cruces, so I would.

The blond shifter looks at me, eyebrows raising at my near-stumble. "You okay, Omega?"

I nod, and that's the last thing he says to me until he takes his leave from my side.

Dropping me off inside a small, cozy cabin that smells of cleaner and fresh air, the blond shifter tells me that the Alpha will come by to see me as soon as he can.

I thought it would take a few minutes, but I was wrong. I'm left alone in that cabin for about three *hours* before I hear a knock at the door.

Feeling spiteful and annoyed that I was retrieved and then abandoned, I almost refuse to answer. Of course, then that reminds me of how I almost did the same thing to West. Now, just like then, I huff out a breath and, like a good omega she-wolf, call out, "Come in."

I've never really paid attention to a male's scent before. With the exception of West and his unique sandalwood aroma, males just smell like *male*. I don't know what to think that my intended mate is no different.

It's been three years since I last set eyes on Rafael. As handsome and—yes, alluring—as ever, my wolf is torn between padding over to him to greet his and keening a lonely song because he isn't West. His hair is too black, his eyes not grey, his skin much darker, and his wolf… the level of his alpha dominance rubs my fur the wrong way.

Or maybe that's the way his eyes rove over me after a quick hello, lips curving down in a slight frown when his atten-tion snags on my—

My *neck*.

"Omega," he says in a tone more conversational than curious, "I see you have a mark."

Oh, no. I forgot about West's bite. None of the other three males seemed to notice it was there, but the moment Rafael walks into the cabin, approaching me where I stand up from my seat to greet him, it's the first thing he notices.

My hand flies to my throat.

Big mistake, Helene, since his eyes are now drawn to the ring on my finger.

My breath catches.

I didn't mean to bring it with me. If I was thinking, I would've left it back in the cabin with West. As it was, I only had enough time to pull out a fresh dress, grab some shoes, and use the bathroom before he was basically shoving me out the door himself.

Thank the Luna I'm still wearing it on my right hand. Rafael might not know the significance of a gold band on my left ring finger—Darkwoods is supposed to be as secluded from human communities as Hickory is—but what if he did? This way, it looks like a simple band that catches his attention, then loses it just as quickly.

Right. Because he's still looking at the bite on my throat in a way that makes me a little anxious.

I drop my hand to my side. "That? Oh, that's just a mark from a good friend. An old friend. That's all."

Not all marks are from mates. Most are, but some shifters carry scars like battle wounds. Lovers they had, then lost—kind of like me and West—or fights they're particularly proud of. I refused to let the feral mark me, but I wouldn't be surprised if West left a small scar somewhere on his lean body as a reminder of how he saved me.

Or maybe he wouldn't. Finally, after all this time, he was the one who wanted a clean break.

"Male, yes?"

He's an Alpha. If I lie, he'll definitely know. "Yes."

Rafael's brow furrows for a moment before he nods, smiling at me. "Ah, well. When I take you as my mate, I'll make sure to mark you on the other side. Then everyone will know that you have two males who have pledged to protect you."

Pledged to protect, he says, but not love.

Interesting.

"Anyway, my apologies for being detained. An Alpha's life is a busy one, yes? I'm sure you know. If not, you will surely learn once you're my Alpha female."

"Yes." It's a simple, non-committal answer and all I can offer him right now.

"I'm sure you want to start discussing our upcoming Luna Ceremony"—yeah, not quite—"but that will have to wait, dear Omega."

It will? Oh, thank the Luna. "I'm so glad to hear that. I was thinking… I'm here now. There's no need to rush."

His expression turns quizzical. Probably because my response was the opposite of what any intended would say. With moon fever as powerful as it is, coupled with the lure of the full moon when the Luna is out, most mates would insist on having the Luna Ceremony as soon as possible.

Not me. Not… now.

Besides, we waited three years. What's one month more?

Rafael clears his throat. "If that's what you want, then of course. The Luna is two nights from now, but if we wait, it'll give us more time to prepare for a Luna Ceremony worthy of the Omega. Still, that's not what I meant."

Oh? "What did you mean?"

"Trevor told me that we have a guest. He requested to meet with the Alpha and his intended, and I thought we could discuss our future after we do our duty."

The way he says 'duty' like that is a niggle that has my wolf cocking her head slightly, but the rest of me goes still when I re-run what he said through my mind: *we have a guest… requested to meet with the Alpha and his intended..*

Unless Bishop left Hickory to check on me, I can't imagine who it could be.

And then I catch the sandalwood scented drifting toward me on the breeze and nothing in this world could stop me from turning to watch as the blond shifter from before— Trevor, I guess—leads in a very familiar male.

"West," I breathe out.

Mere hours after he rejected me at last, he's here.

And I have no idea *why*.

FIFTEEN
RAFAEL

With a quick nod my way, he turns to Rafael, holding out his hand. "Weston Reed, Beta of the Sylvan Pack."

"Rafael Cruces, Gravetail Alpha."

West knows that. There's no way that he doesn't know who this male is. Considering he's hated the idea of Rafael for years, I never thought he would willingly step foot onto Gravetail territory. To offer his unwitting rival a nod, then shake his hand?

Someone pinch me because I must be dreaming—or, worse, this is some kind of terrible, terrible nightmare.

"What can I do for you, Beta?"

In his soft accent, Rafael sounds so polite. So pleasant. Almost as though he actually means it.

I hold my breath as West looks at a point just past Rafael. It's as close to eye contact as he can get with an Alpha who isn't Bishop, and probably more than he should dare while I'm still wearing his scent on my skin.

"I'm sorry I'm late," he says, and though he sounds apologetic, my wolf can sense how wild West's is behind his nearly locked-down shields. "I had a couple of loose ends to tie up before I could escort Helene."

Boots, I think, almost hysterically. He's fully dressed with a new pair of boots and a fresh shoelace. He went out and bought boots, then came after me...

I'm borderline freaking out, West cold and calm, while Rafael looks as though this is just another day in the life of an Alpha.

"Oh?" A tiny twitch of Rafael's lips. Part amused, part resigned. "I wasn't aware the Omega needed an outside escort. My Beta was more than capable of retrieving her for me."

"I didn't say he wasn't. But I did inform him that I would be following after her anyway... didn't he tell you?" I know West. He's not lying—obviously, otherwise Rafael would know—but there's definitely more to the story. "Frankie—"

"Francois," corrects Rafael.

West dips his head. "My counterpart, sure. He seemed to understand that my Alpha would want to know that Helene made it safe to Darkwoods. There isn't anyone he trusts in the Sylvan Pack more than me."

Oh, I think, breathing out softly through a pair of slightly parted lips. I'm trying to keep my expression as innocent as possible, locking down my emotions, but even so I have to admit: West is *good*.

Over the last three years, I've tried my hardest to keep some sort of distance between us. I had to, and that meant that I didn't always get to watch him act as the Beta for the Sylvan Pack. I must have missed out on a lot if this is just a sneak peek of what he can do.

No wonder he's such a pro at handling Bishop. While

every single word he just said was one hundred percent true, it's also pretty clear he didn't admit to a single thing at all.

Nothing concrete. Nothing definite.

Nope. He simply planted an idea in Rafael's head, and the Alpha runs with it when he says, "Oh. So... Bishop sent you?"

"Helene wasn't just our Omega. She's the Alpha's sister."

Another truth, and it didn't answer Rafael's question at all. Of course not. If West confessed to Bishop that he had me *and* that we were attacked by a feral, then West would be the last shifter in Hickory that Bishop would send to watch over me.

And that's even if my brother did. The whole point of accepting Rafael as my mate was because the Luna gave him to me, and that, as a future Alpha, Rafael would be strong enough to protect me. Sending a former packmate of mine as a... a *chaperone* totally undermines his dominance as well as any prospective alliance between our packs.

And both of these males know that, a sentiment Rafael echoes when he says, "I'm aware."

"Wouldn't he want to make sure that she arrived safely onto your territory? He knows you. He doesn't know your wolves. Omegas are prized and they need to be doubly protected. You sent your Beta. Bishop sent his."

"I guess that means you're just the male to watch over the Omega, aren't you?"

"I'm the Beta of the Sylvan Pack."

"So I've heard. Weston, you said." Rafael lifts his hand. I still don't get any emotion from him or his wolf other than his guarded nature, and I'm slightly surprised to see that his claws are out. Flicking at a stray lock of black hair that fell in front of his dark gold eye, he smiles again as it settles back among the thick strands.

There's no welcome in this smile.

"Have we met?" Rafael asks, lowering his claws back to his side. "I feel like we have. Your scent is very familiar to me."

Right. Because it's on *me*.

West keeps his stare on Rafael. He's much better at these inter-pack politics than I am because I glanced his way at Rafael's comment. I almost feel like I'm watching a game of fetch between pups, my focus is switching back and forth between males so quickly.

With the tension filling the small cabin, my omega she-wolf is just waiting for one of them to explode.

West searches Rafael's expression for a moment before he says, "Once. Three years ago when you came to meet Helene. We met then."

They did?

I didn't know that. I was under the impression that Bishop had purposely kept West away from his perceived rival.

Probably because I asked him to.

It made sense. After the way West reacted to hearing that I was ending our five-year love affair for a male I had never met, I didn't want to torture him any further by having him there when I met Rafael and his entourage for lunch the next day. Bishop must have because West was conspicuously missing during the meal and later that night.

I should've known better. He didn't join Bishop, Sofia, and me for lunch with Rafael and his Beta, but I wouldn't be surprised if he waylaid the Gravetail wolves on their way in or out of Hickory, trying to get his own read on Rafael. Like it or not, he'd spent years expecting that we would be together forever, and this male—and my fated mating to him—was the one obstacle standing between me and West having our own happily-ever-after.

Alphas have an earned rep for being calculating, but that's

nothing compared to a Beta who needs to be able to support the leader of the pack. To figure a way to win me back, did West go to Rafael himself to see what he was up against?

Is that why he's here now?

The tension in the cabin thickens, but it also becomes more noticeable as an awkward silence fills it. Reaching down, I fiddle with the skirt on my soft green dress. At West's urging, I grabbed three from the closet after I changed. Not knowing what I was walking into in Darkwoods, I took the dresses and my music player and that was all.

Well, except for the ring I forgot to give back—that, I realize as the fabric tangles around two of my fingers, I'm still wearing.

For a heartbeat, I think about taking it off. Would I give it back to West? Drop it in my pocket so I didn't have to explain? Since either of those options would catch Rafael's attention, I leave it right where it is.

And if West's gaze darts to my hand at the same time, checking to see if it's still on, that has nothing to do with me leaving it on…

Rafael clears his throat. My head jerks up in time to see that his expression is still as neutrally pleasant as before.

West is still watching me out of the corner of his eye.

"Three years," the Gravetail Alpha muses. "I would've thought it was more recently than that."

Right. Because it *was*.

Silly Helene. Reckless Helene. You realized that you smelled like West. Why didn't it occur to you that an *Alpha* would have easily noticed another male's musk all over me? His wolf should've taken one breath and scented it.

How long did it take him to match it to West's sandalwood scent?

One second? *Two?*

Honestly, it was bound to happen. I didn't bathe before I left the cabin in Louisiana. I still haven't. I'm covered in West's musk from when he nuzzled me, then licked me all over last night.

Thankfully, the quicksilver that West pumped into me has faded enough that I can get a better read on Rafael's wolf than I did when he first walked into this cabin hours after I did. Despite him showing off his claws before—and his comment from a few seconds ago—I don't sense any jealousy. There's no possessiveness coming from him. Unless he's found a way to fool an omega wolf, he really is as neutrally pleasant as he appears.

For now, I amend. Until he decides how he wants to handle an intended mate who smells of the Beta from her former pack...

To make matters worse, as soon as Rafael points out the obvious, West blocks me almost as effectively as Bishop does. Though he doesn't often, West is an old pro at leashing his emotions so that I can't get into his head when he doesn't want me to. The only way to figure out what the hell he's thinking is by asking him straight out.

Which I'm going to have to do.

Fixing my features into another deceptively innocent expression, I fold my fingers together in front of my skirt, hiding the ring with the pad of my thumb.

I turn to Rafael, ignoring how West's heat just about scorches my side as I shift away from him.

"Alpha." I make sure to address him the same way he's been addressing me: with his title. "Would you mind if I speak to the Beta alone for a moment?"

Rafael shouldn't say yes. Leaving his new mate alone with

a male whose scent is embedded in her skin? His wolf should be too possessive to agree to such a simple request. If I was bonded to him, his Alpha female, he wouldn't even *ask*. It's just understood that bonded mates are never left alone with unmated shifters who show an interest in them.

Only we're not bonded—and Rafael still isn't giving off any hint of possessiveness.

He nods, that lock of hair flopping forward again. "As you wish. I have some business to attend to at the Alpha cabin anyway. When you're finished here, won't you join me?" His gaze slides over toward West. "You too, of course, Beta. We can discuss any other messages from Bishop you might have for me then."

West nods, a single sharp jerk off his head. "We can do that. Right, Helene?"

Rafael isn't possessive.

West? He's bristling with the need to touch me.

Maybe being along with him isn't that good of an idea… too bad that doesn't stop me.

"Um. Yes. We won't be long."

"Take your time. Trevor will lead you to the den as soon as you're ready." He gives a tight-lipped smile before jerking his thumb over his shoulder, gesturing at a closed door. "And maybe you might want to freshen up a bit before we meet again. There's a bathroom right through there if you need one."

Oh, yeah.

I'm totally busted—and I'm not sure how to respond to Rafael's *lack* of a reaction.

I wait until Rafael is far enough away in the distance to whirl on West.

I don't know how to deal with my guarded new mate. But West? I know him. I know that he always does what he thinks is best for me and the pack, but by coming here, he's putting us both at risk.

He needs to understand that, just like I need him to give me one good reason why he's here—and not the story he spun for the Gravetail Alpha.

To me, it seems obvious. I hope to the Luna I'm wrong, but I can't see how I am. West doesn't want me to choose Rafael. Maybe he changed his mind after what happened with the feral, but seeing him here now… what do I do if he changed it again?

What if he's decided the only way to stop my impending Luna Ceremony is by challenging Rafael so that there's no one standing between us?

That's how shifter males do things. Their last resort—and sometimes their first resort—is to throw down a challenge. It could be until mercy, maiming, or death, but shifters settle things with their claws and their fangs.

But if West has really followed me to Darkwoods to challenge Rafael, it won't be until mercy. I know that as sure as I am that West made the decision to come after me on his own.

One of them will die. If West challenges Rafael, one of them will die. There's no getting around it.

I'm sure of that, too.

West is a beta wolf. While that means he's more dominant than nearly every other packmate in Hickory, the only shifter who might challenge and defeat an alpha is another alpha. Then again, I saw him *destroy* a feral. With the right motivation, I'm beginning to think there isn't a single male West couldn't defeat to keep me safe.

Would he be as aggressive to claim me?

He'd have to be. Rafael Cruces is a new Alpha. He only took over the pack at the end of summer. Two months, maybe. That's *nothing*. I already know that the reason he took as long as he had to send for me was because he had a few challenges already. He still has a lot to prove, showing his packmates that he's worthy of being their leader.

Plus, if West challenges Rafael over me, he'd be fighting for his right to make me his Alpha female.

But if that's why West is here, he would be fighting for his heart's mate—

No. That can't be it. It just… it *can't* be. If West really still thought of me as his chosen mate, the mate of his heart, then he never would've let me go this morning.

And he did. Without any fight. Without any remorse.

He watched me walk away, and now he's here and I want to know *why*.

I call bullshit on why he followed after me. But if that's not the truth, what *is*? I have to ask. I have to know.

Before I can even get a single word out, West speaks up.

"He called you Omega."

That catches me off guard. That was the last thing I expected him to say, though maybe it shouldn't have been. He noticed that, too? Of course he did.

West notices *everything*.

"It doesn't matter," I say quickly, answering him while also refusing to let him distract me. "When they're comfortable with me, they'll use my name. I'll be Helene then."

Following West's lead, I purposely try to keep my voice down. As a shifter, I know how far voices carry to supe ears.

Just because Rafael left us alone in the cabin, that doesn't mean he didn't also leave wolves posted nearby.

That's what a good Alpha would do, after all. And, look at that, the door might be closed, but the window isn't.

West purses his lips. "That's not what I meant."

I know it's not.

In a pack, using a high-ranking shifter's title is a respect thing. Normally, calling me 'Omega' is a sign that they're acknowledging that I have that post. Most of my packmates in Hickory know I don't like it. I'm 'canari' to Bishop, and 'Lane' to West, but everyone else calls me by my name.

Here in Darkwoods, I'm not the Omega. I'm sure they have one of their own already, and even if they don't—considering how prized and rare omega wolves are, not every pack has one—I can't be it. Despite my wolf type, as Rafael's intended, I'm not just another she-wolf. I'm the future Alpha female of this pack. They should be calling me 'Alpha' instead… but not a single Gravetail wolf has.

And West noticed that, too.

"Forget it. That's not important—"

"It's not?"

"No. What are you doing here?" I ask through gritted teeth. My voice is purposely low enough that only West can hear me, but in case any of Rafael's wolves are peeking in through the open window, I force my lips into a smile.

It doesn't fool West. He scoffs. "Lane… *Helene*. Please. You can't honestly act like you don't know why I've come."

I raise my eyebrows at him.

"Okay." He holds up his hands. No claws, I see, just swollen knuckles from broken fingers that haven't completely regenerated or healed yet. I guess I know what one of the "loose ends" West needed to wrap up was. "You need to hear it. Fine. You reached for this male, but you reached for me, too. Maybe you were right. Maybe it was instinctive, that the fear made you do it. But that's the thing. You still called for *me*. You still love me. I know you do. And I will never, ever forgive myself if I don't give you ever last chance to choose me."

And… there it is.

"West, please. Don't do this. Not now. You ended us this time."

"I didn't think there was an us."

Maybe there wasn't. But between his bite, his ring, the way I was the first one to initiate sex, and then everything that happened with the feral last night…

There might have been. If he'd kept me instead of throwing me at Rafael, there might have been.

"Doesn't matter. We were over before, and we're over now."

A rumble starts low in West's chest. In control, he silences it right away, but I know what I heard.

"West—"

"We will never be over. Not until you wear another male's mark over mine. Even then, I'll still hold out hope 'til my last breath that you'll change your mind. But that's where I went wrong last time. Thickheaded wolf that I am, I forgot that it's not just about what I want. It's your choice, Lane. It's always been your choice. I just… I have to witness you make it. That's all."

As I process what he just said, the corner of his mouth kicks up in a crooked grin. It's not that cocky smile I know so well, or the secret one who always shares with me when we're alone.

It's sad, and my heart breaks to see it.

Especially when he adds, "I'm not here to make things difficult for you."

I want to believe that so badly.

"Tell me, then: is this about you, or about me?"

He blows air through his nose. His wolf's aura brushes against mine; if we were in our fur instead of our skin, he would be rubbing our flanks together before going to his belly, showing his throat in the ultimate sign of submission.

To my wolf, but also to *me*.

"It's about you," he says at last. "It's always been about you. But on my run over... I realized that I made it about me for way too long. This is your choice, Helene. You have to make it, and I have to accept that. Whatever happens... I'm a beta, baby. My wolf needs to know when there's nothing left to fight for." Another small, sad smile turns his handsome features *devastating.* "I want you for forever, but I want you to be happy more. If Gravetail makes you happy, then so be it."

If only it was about which male has always made me happy. I could reject Rafael and run off with West right now—but I can't.

I'm also not sure that his motives are as pure as he wants me to believe. Maybe before he went so far as to *steal* me, I could have... but this last week didn't just change me. It showed me how much West has changed from the smirking, cocky twenty-four-year-old mate I once dreamed of forever with.

I don't know what he's capable of anymore, but regardless of what happens next, there's one thing I know for sure: I can do anything I have to for the sake of my pack, but only if West is still a part of it.

"So, just to be clear"—because my wolf insists on it as

much as my heart—"you didn't come here to challenge Rafael?"

West takes a deep breath. Exhales softly. "I won't lie and say I didn't think about it."

Oh, Luna… I bury my face in my hands. I *knew* it. "You can't. West… for me, please. You can't do it."

"Worried about your intended?"

A lump lodges in my throat. I force it down, and in a small voice admit, "I'm worried about you."

His jeans rustle together as he moves toward me. I don't look up, but I know instinctively where he is in the small room from my other senses.

"Don't be. I told you. I'm just here to keep you safe. I'm done hurting you. I'm done making mistakes. If this is what you want, you'll get it."

But what if it isn't?

Dropping my hands, I look up at him. I almost ask him that question. I'm so close… and then I say, "When are you leaving?"

Don't go. I wish I could say those words, too. They get stuck in my throat as I wait for his answer.

When he gives it, I'm not surprised.

"After the night of the Luna. I'll return to Hickory then."

So soon? That's the day after tomorrow.

"We're not having the Luna Ceremony," I tell West. "If that's why you want to leave already… Rafael agreed to wait until next month."

West's soft chuckle has an edge of pain to it. "You might not become bonded mates this full moon, but you know as well as I do what moon fever's like. If he's your mate, your wolf will need her male. One way or another, you'll finally have to make your choice. And when you go to him… when you go to his bed… you won't have to tell me you reject me. I'll already know."

He's not wrong. And even if I could resist Rafael, what if he can't resist me? An Alpha who finally has his promised female on his territory?

The Luna chose him for me. She'll want us to mate, and when I do, I'll lose West forever.

Unless I make a different choice.

SIXTEEN
DUTY

At my insistence, West promises that he won't tell Rafael about our history. He swears that he's here to watch over me until the night of the Luna—until he knows that I'm settled in with my intended—and then he'll go back to Hickory at last.

Rafael, I discover, is happy to please his new mate. Instead of refusing to let West stay in Darkwoods, he offers West the use of one of Gravetail's guest cabins. Proving that he's just as astute as I think he is, he makes sure to put West up in a cabin on the far side of his territory, but he allows him to stay.

I just wish I could understand *why* exactly West is insisting on waiting until I'm truly out of his reach forever to go. I don't know why he's torturing himself. Is this like how he would disappear into the trees and take out his frustrations on that towering hickory of his? Wearing his claws down to nubs, splitting open his knuckles, slashing and snarling until he could get control of himself again?

Based on his hands earlier, he did the same thing at the

feral's den before he abandoned it. Was that not enough? Is that why he chased after me? Watching me with Rafael is a new type of pain for West, is that it?

Beneath his Beta bravado, he's obviously hurting as much now as he has been since I admitted I was leaving—but I'm still selfish, too. Just knowing he's in Darkwoods is helping *my* wolf get herself under control.

I need it. I've only left Hickory once before today, and that was when West stole me away with him. Now I'm surrounded by a new pack and it's havoc on my poor wolf.

Gravetail is a little larger than the Sylvan Pack so that's seventy new wolves that mine has to learn. It's overwhelming, to say the least. That's not even counting the way Rafael's wolf keeps brushing against mine, recognizing instinctively that she's his mate while the male in his skin gives no sign that he's looking forward to spending forever with me at his side.

It's a good thing that just *sensing* West in the distance is enough to anchor my overstimulated wolf since I don't get to set eyes on him again after Rafael arranges for us to be separated. The rest of that first night in Darkwoods, my intended takes me on a tour of his territory before finally noticing that I'm flagging under the weight of all his packmates wanting to get a peek at the new Omega.

Not their Alpha's mate. Their Omega.

I don't even care. I just need to have a buffer between me and them. Rafael ends up escorting me back to the small cabin from earlier. After the Luna Ceremony, he explains to me, I'll move into the Alpha cabin with him. Until then, this one is mine.

Another Omega cabin, I figure, though I don't point that out.

The whole walk back across his territory, I dreaded Rafael

finally leaving my side if only because I thought he would expect a kiss goodbye from me. Silly Helene. I don't even get a backward glance after he bids me to sleep well.

With West's sandalwood scent lingering in the space, that's pretty much impossible.

The next day, the blond shifter—Trevor—is the male who returns to bring me to the Alpha cabin again. After some small talk where he tells me about his maternal delta mate, Claire, he asks me about my type of wolf.

And there you go. As it turns out, my suspicions were spot-on. The Gravetail Pack doesn't have an Omega of their own, though there are one or two younger pups in the pack who could grow up and take the position. Rafael hadn't mentioned it, but now that Trevor is more used to me, he's an open book. Whatever questions I murmur toward him, he answers, and that's how I learn that me being Rafael's fated mate is seen as a gift from the Luna.

I didn't need Trevor to tell me that. Rafael makes that clear when I spend the whole day—then part of the next—doing what's expected of an omega wolf. Joining Rafael in Gravetail's den, it's my job to meet with any of his packmates in need of an omega wolf's touch and company.

To be fair, I'm happy to be useful and glad for the distraction. The closer the clock ticks toward sunset, the more anxious I am. Tonight's the night of the Luna. I'm an unmated female with my intended within arm's reach. True, Rafael has been a perfect gentleman since we met. That doesn't do anything to quell the fire raging inside of me as the looming moon fever heats my blood up as the hours pass.

When I eventually catch myself squirming in the chair Rafael pointed out as mine, I have to admit that West is right. Alpha, Beta, or Omega, no one is immune to moon fever.

My body needs sex. More than that, I *need* a male. Nothing will cool this heat but a big body bowed over mine, thrusting into me before he comes inside of me. A mating mark isn't necessary, but I'm too far gone to think about getting myself off and hoping for the best.

I'm a she-wolf whose beast needs a mate. By the end of tonight, I'll be throwing back my head, begging to be mounted, and I won't be choosy about who it is who comes up on me from behind; my heart's mate or my fated mate, either one will do. My wolf recognizes that she has some kind of a bond with both males. It doesn't matter that I put my paw down about finalizing a mate bond tonight. When the moon is high, she'll want to rut, and whatever happens after that happens.

Because that's moon fever for you. Before, when Rafael was miles away and West out of my reach, I purposely handled my need on my own. Even with having both males tauntingly close I might have found the self-control to shut my wolf down. But then I think about what happened with West in the cabin and… yeah. I'll need *someone*.

And, for the first time in three years, my human half is wavering over who that someone is…

The only thing I can think to do is barricade myself in my cabin. Duck inside of the bathroom, maybe stand beneath the icy spray of a cold shower until I get through the worst of the fever.

And maybe that plan would've worked perfectly if Rafael hadn't invited me to have dinner with him in the Gravetail den after the last of his packmates leave.

I'm not sure what exactly his intentions are. Like in Hickory, the pack cooks will create the meal for us—I swear, I nearly swallowed my tongue when I thought he was suggesting that he cook for me instead—and bring enough servings that we could eat apart from the rest of the pack. It'll be private, and maybe that's not a good idea during the full moon, but how could I refuse?

Then again, even after agreeing to spend the early evening with Rafael, there's a chance I might have been able to resist my need until I could make it back to my new cabin. The reason for that is simple, too: I have absolutely no lust for Rafael. Handsome as he is, there's no actual spark between us.

No *desire*.

Sure, I won't be comfortable, but if Rafael doesn't push—and everything I've learned about him since I've gotten to know the Gravetail Alpha makes me certain he won't—we can get through the worst of the moon fever by distracting ourselves with food.

It's a good plan. Shifters are known for their fondness for three things: food, fucking, and fighting. I don't want to fuck Rafael. As an omega wolf, I would never fight him.

But food? I can eat. Besides, if he's eventually going to be my mate, I'll have to let him feed me sooner or later. That's what mates do.

I just never thought he would invite *West to* join us for our first private meal.

Dinner is as awkward as I thought it would be.

I'm used to eating in a communal space. That's how I've had every meal since arriving in Darkwoods, though I did grab my plate and scurry back to my cabin to eat alone if Rafael wasn't available to sit with me among the crowd. Whether on purpose or not—and I'm leaning toward *yes*—West ate at a different time from me. Fair enough. But when Rafael tells me that the three of us are going to eat together in the den by ourselves, I panic just a teensy bit.

It's easier when I see that the spread is still laid out buffet-style. It's traditionally how shifters get around the idea of food having a specific meaning to our kind of supe. It's not easy to accept a meal as a proposition to mate when we're each responsible for plating our own food.

For a split second, I'm afraid that West will try to serve me. At least once a week back in Hickory he did, doing whatever he could to show me that he still considered me his heart's mate. Knowing I was promised to Rafael, I always refused, and I'd have to do the same thing if he decided to feed me in front of the Alpha.

West doesn't—and neither does my intended.

Once we pile up as much food on our plate as we can to satisfy both our wolves and our human halves, we take our seats at a small rectangular table on the far side of the den. Unlike at home, where the Sylvan Pack den is set up more like an office, Gravetail has their den styled like a living room. It's connected to the Alpha's personal kitchen, has carpet beneath our feet, and a small dining area where the Alpha takes his meals if he's in a meeting.

I choose my seat first. No one offered me one, so I pull out the first one I reach, folding my skirt beneath me with one hand while balancing my plate in the other. Rafael places his plate at the setting on my right, West dropping down into the seat at my left.

While West and I are seated, Rafael moves away from the table as soon as he lowered his plate. Disappearing into the kitchen, I hear running water for a few seconds, followed by the cracking of... *ice*? It sounds like an ice tray.

I'm right. Water sloshes, something plopping into it, and Rafael returns carrying a large glass pitcher full of ice water and three glasses.

"If you get thirsty," he says, placing them in the middle of the table. Leaving us to pour our own drinks, he sits down and gets one for himself. Once he picks up his fork, the Alpha signaling that it's time to eat, we all dig in.

The food is delicious, but it's nowhere near the distraction that I need. I catch myself squirming again, moving just enough to rub my damp panties against my aroused clit. The moon fever has me hornier than I've ever been. That's not all, either. I'm so feverish, I can feel sweat beading up along my hairline.

Suddenly, the ice water makes perfect sense.

To get my raging hormones under control, I pour a glass and sip it as daintily as I can. Though it seems like Rafael's attention is on his food, I can sense him watching me from the corner of his eye.

West makes it halfway through his plate before he picks up his own glass. Bringing the rim to his lips, he tilts his head back, guzzling three-quarters of his ice water before he stops for a breath.

Luna help me, but watching his Adam's apple bob as he swallows the icy water? If I wasn't already turned on, that would have done it for me.

"What's the matter, Beta?" Rafael asks. His glass is still untouched in front of him. "Food that spicy? This might be Texas, but I thought you'd be used to the heat, you being from Louisiana."

"Food's delicious," West grates. He takes another gulp, his glass hitting the table with a *clink*. "Must be the Texas heat getting to me instead."

"It is a dry heat," Rafael says.

It's *October*, I want to scream, and it's the moon fever that's spiking our temperatures.

Well, mine. West's, too.

Rafael, though?

The Alpha is as cool as a cucumber.

The den is bigger than the cabin so the scent of my arousal isn't filling a small space, but it's obvious that I'm ready to mate. And Rafael turns his attention back to his plate.

Rafael does. West doesn't.

His grey eyes are flashing gold beneath the fluorescent lights as his nostrils flare, taking in the perfume of my obvious need. Sucking in a breath, he drops his freed hand beneath the table.

I can't see what he's doing, but I don't have to. Like I'm squirming, West is adjusting his erection.

Rafael scoops up his last forkful of rice, ignoring the two of us, until—

"Omega."

I jump at my title in his slightly accented voice.

Luna damn it. The rising moon already had me super twitchy, but his unexpected voice nearly has me jumping out of my skin.

Swallowing back my nerves, I tear my attention away from West, looking at Rafael. "Yes?"

"Forgive me for mentioning it, but I see that you keep stroking that mark on your neck. I hope it isn't bothering you."

I didn't even realize I was doing it. After I put my glass back down, I must have lifted my hand up to my neck while holding onto my fork with the other. Between the fever and West's reaction to it, I started absently fingering his bite.

Caught and unable to explain what exactly I was doing, I drop my hand to my lap. "I'm fine. Thanks for asking."

"Of course. Though… I've been meaning to see something. Beta? Would you mind showing me your fangs?"

Oh my Luna. He didn't just ask that, did he?

"I would actually," West responds, keeping his voice just as even as Rafael's. "Only my enemies and my future mate get a close-up on my fangs."

"I understand."

I'm sure he does.

West sets down his fork and knife. Folding his fingers in front of him, his turn to subtly flash his claws, he's still friendly as he points out, "If you want to know if that bite's mine, you can just ask. We're all friends here."

Rafael tilts his head in West's direction. Honestly, I'm beginning to think he's forgotten all about me.

"Our packs have an alliance, so I'd say we are. And I don't need to ask about the Omega's bite." Nope. Not when he knows that West's fangs would be a perfect match to that mark. "But if you'll oblige me… you mentioned your future mate. You don't have one now?"

A smart-ass wolf would point out that, if he did have one, he would be with her on the night of the full moon instead of playing nice with Rafael.

A shifter with a death wish might taunt the Alpha that the female he considers his mate is sitting with him at this very table.

But West… he just meets Rafael's curiosity with a flat stare of his own. "I had one once." He pauses. "Or I thought I did."

"Really?"

"The Luna gave me a feisty delta she-wolf," explains West,

"but it wasn't meant to be. She rejected me for her chosen mate."

"That's not very usual. Most shifters are happy to find and claim their fated mate."

Rafael's right. *Most* shifters are, so why isn't he?

That's something I have to ask myself. Since I've been in Darkwoods, Rafael has used his alpha aura to mute his emotions around me, but I'm a skilled omega wolf and he's not used to having me around. I've been probing, and if there's one thing I can say, it's that I haven't sensed any happiness coming from him. In fact, baiting West—if that's what he's doing, and I'm pretty sure it is—is giving him the most enjoyment he's had in days.

I can't help it. I frown.

West notices. Keeping his gaze on Rafael, he nudges my foot with his under the table, a silent show of support.

One touch. That's all it takes. One touch and I've been electrified. The moon fever comes back with a vengeance.

My soft gasp—that might have been a moan—is only covered up because West is answering Rafael's last comment with one of his own.

"That's true," he admits, agreeing with Rafael. "But it happens. I'd much rather have a female who wants me, who *chose* me, than one who's just doing her duty." Then, before I can really understand the meaning of what he said, he picks the pitcher up by the handle. "Your glass is half-empty, Helene. Would you like me to fill it for you?"

Good thing I finished eating. If I'd had food in my mouth when I finally got what West meant before offering to top off my water, I might've choked. Instead, I simply shake my head and push my half-full glass to the side.

Rafael pauses as West sets the pitcher back down. At first, I thought it was because of West's not-so-subtle offer to refill my glass, but then he shrugs. Like the rest of us, he lowers his utensils to his plate.

Dinner, it seems, is over.

Good. Maybe I can make it back to my cabin and put this behind me...

And then Rafael says, "We're shifters, yes? We all have a duty to our packs, don't we?," and I go still. For a moment, I even forget about how I want to go down on all fours to work off some of this lust riding me.

It's that word again. *Duty.* That word, and my reaction to it every single time Rafael murmurs it. It's hard to explain what I mean, though that's probably why it took me until right this second to pick up on it.

It's almost like, whenever he does, the thread tying my wolf to the Alpha is being tugged on. Like he's trying to tell me something even as West narrows his gaze on him.

He can sense something is up, too. Then again, from his obviously flushed cheeks, it might just be the moon fever affecting him.

"I'll do anything for my pack."

"Your pack," wonders Rafael, "or the Omega?"

I freeze. As the Omega, I'm used to being outside of the hierarchy. I'm prized, but I can also be dismissed. For these two to go back and forth, forgetting I'm here as the two biggest threats lock on each other... I'm used to it—and now Rafael's bringing me right back into the conversation.

"Me?" I ask. "Why would you say that?"

Ignoring me, Rafael keeps his attention on West. "I'm her intended. You were once her chosen... and she wears a mark on her throat that wasn't there the last time I saw her. Or the last time she was in Sylvan Pack territory."

West doesn't deny it. Instead, with a calculating look open on his features, he asks, "How do you know that?"

"You didn't think I would walk away from the Omega and not keep tabs on her while I was waiting to take over my father's pack? She was mine from the moment she agreed to be my mate."

That's not true. Well, no… it *is true.* That's why I ended things with my chosen mate three years ago. But if Rafael truly considered me *his*, he wouldn't just placidly ask about West's fangs. He'd be using his own to go for the Beta's throat for daring to mark me.

And that's without him knowing that, while I subconsciously kept the mark, I wasn't even aware that West had bit me until my fingers found the scar.

West shows some grudging respect toward Rafael. "That's what an Alpha would do."

"And a Beta can be quite clever with his words."

Okay. This isn't a challenge, but it's *something*.

I start to push my chair away from the table, intent to break up this intense conversation when Rafael smiles just wide enough to show off *his* fangs.

"Now that you've eaten at my table, why don't you do me a kindness, Beta. Tell me, what are you really doing here?"

"I don't think—"

"It's okay, Helene," West murmurs, his voice low but still able to cover up my panic. "I know what the Alpha is doing. It's his territory and you're his mate. He has every right… but I won't risk our alliance, Alpha. So let's leave it at that."

"You couldn't anyway. Our alliance is solid. We're not your enemy. Not under my father, and not under me. No matter what happens… nothing will change that."

No matter what happens…

Oh my Luna. Blame it on being so self-centered and involved with West, then watching these two go back and forth, but in the haze of West's soothing whisper and my muffled panic, suddenly everything seems to make perfect sense to me.

I turn to Rafael and, interrupting this *thing* he has going on with West again, I blurt out, "You didn't serve me dinner."

Now *that* caught his attention.

"What was that, Omega?"

"You brought the water"—and, yeah, I'm betting that that was more a way to point out that Rafael knows how me and West are suffering from moon fever...and he isn't—"but I had to pour it for myself."

Rafael's face goes blank. His dark gold eyes flare, turning molten orange, then fading back before I can be sure they really did, but the rest of his expression gives nothing away. "I didn't want to presume—"

He's a male wolf shifter. They *all* presume.

I'm supposed to be his intended. Spoiled and entitled or not, Rafael should've made my plate. He should've offered to feed his mate. He should've held out my chair. Poured my water for me. Not because I'm too prim and perfect to do it myself, but because he's a male wolf shifter. Taking care of his female is as ingrained an instinct as getting her under him.

Something else he hasn't tried to do at all. I'm not complaining, but it's suspicious.

Almost as suspicious as inviting West to have dinner with the two of us on the night the Luna will rise…

He knows. He knows that me and West were—and maybe *are*—a me and West, and he's talking about West's mate while pointing out the bite on my neck. He knows, but he's not doing anything about it except dance around the relationship I have with my Beta.

But why?

"You call me Omega," I say, working my way through this. "Like you need to be reminded of what I am. Of what I'll bring to your pack if you accept me as your mate."

"Helene—"

I ignore West. I'm on the verge of figuring something out, and if I don't do that now, I have the sinking suspicion that I'll live to regret it.

"You don't want to mate me." When the thread tugs again, a hint of relief traveling down the length, I know my suspicion is right. "Rafael… you're only going along with this because you think you have to."

West's hand jerks. He hits his plate, jostling it on the table. His fork falls, hitting the table with a loud clattering sound. I shocked him by being so forward and calling Rafael out.

I shocked West, but I didn't shock the Alpha.

"The Luna is out tonight. I can't pretend that I don't feel her pull. I'm not the only one in the den who is, either. But it isn't you, Rafael. I'm sorry, but it isn't."

He glances away from me, staying silent.

That's all the answer I need right there.

Alphas don't break eye contact. Like how peering directly into an Alpha's eyes can be construed as a challenge, an Alpha looking away is a sign of weakness to other dominant shifters.

I'm not a dominant she-wolf. I'm an omega.

And he doesn't have to say a word for me to know that my guess is one hundred percent correct.

I should know, after all. I feel the same as he does.

That's why I didn't recognize Rafael's cool behavior or his obvious resistance. I brushed it off, explaining it as him being overly respectful because I wound up on his territory so close to the full moon.

But that's not it, is it? I didn't recognize his hesitation and reluctance to treat me as his mate because he's acting the way I do: resigned to doing what's best for the pack, not for me. Accepting a mating that the Luna ordained instead of following my heart to the male sitting to my left.

Why not? If I could be in denial for three years, why wouldn't I ignore the same thing coming from my intended?

I know the answer to that. Because Rafael isn't my intended. Not really. He's a male who's only going to be my bonded mate because it's expected of him, and his pack needs an Omega.

But I need to follow my heart. It's something I should have always done, and I'm beginning to think Rafael's motive for inviting West to dinner wasn't as ulterior as I thought.

I'm going to need a male tonight. Just like West has been spurring me to do all along, Rafael was giving me a choice.

It's time I make it.

"Rafael—"

He knows what's coming before I say anything more than his name. It's the first time I've used it—following his lead, I'd kept my distance by referring to him by his title—and he closes his eyes for a moment.

When he opens them again, I see sadness and acceptance in the depths of his gaze.

"Your heart doesn't want me."

To my left, West straightens in his seat, waiting to see my reaction.

I give Rafael a small smile. "I tried. I really tried."

"I know," he says, matching my smile. "But it's always beat for the Beta."

He *does* know. He pointed out how he kept tabs on me earlier. No wonder he never tried to actually court me or trigger the mating dance between us. Deep down, Rafael knew he never had a chance.

"Omegas are the sunshine in our lives," Rafael adds. The smile fades away as he holds his hands out to me, palms facing up. "I can't dim your light, Helene."

Helene. He finally called me 'Helene'.

Shifting in my seat, I place my palms against his.

West growls. Even knowing it's a challenge to the Alpha, he can't help it. He's always acted like a bonded male, possessive and protective, and now that Rafael has acknowledged my love for West, it's just the sort of reaction I was expecting.

Rafael, too.

"I just need one touch. To make sure it takes… one touch and she's yours."

Not yet. I can't be—not until I do this.

Squeezing his fingers, I send a silent 'thank you' down the thin bond stretching between Rafael and me. Thanks for his understanding, and thanks for making my choice clear at last.

Then, in a slightly shaky voice, I murmur, "Rafael Cruces, I reject you."

And the relief that blasts me from all around tells me I made the right choice for all three of us.

SEVENTEEN
LUNA

When I rejected Rafael, I didn't know what I was going to do next. As much as he wanted an omega she-wolf for his mate, I was right when I thought he was only doing it out of a sense of duty. Now that I freed him, it didn't seem right to stay on his territory.

Proving that he truly is a good male, he offered us sanctuary for the night. As a favor to me and to Bishop, we could stay until the full moon was over. Then we could leave with his assurance that the proposed alliance between our packs would be even stronger for us not mating each other for noble reasons instead of being trapped together forever when I loved another male—and Rafael barely knows me.

I almost agree. One glimpse over at West, though? He might have managed to keep the worst of the moon fever at bay while we played nice with Rafael, but now that I'm no longer the Alpha's intended?

The Beta wants his bride.

Just in case my wolf didn't already sense the need and

longing and pure desire coming from him and his beast, West reaches over the table. While Rafael gets up, busying himself with clearing the plates so that he can avoid glancing over at us, West takes my right hand.

Gripping the golden band on my ring finger, he eases it off. Then, with a look that dares me to refuse him, he swaps my right hand for my left. As my heart thuds in my chest, the moon fever continuing to make me so very hot and wet and *achy*, Weston Reed slips his ring back on my left hand.

I could've taken it off. I could've told him that nothing changed between us just because I finally realized that I couldn't go through with mating Rafael.

I could've *lied*…

I don't. With a small smile, I lift my hand to my lips, kissing the band. West's eyes glimmer gold. The air becomes thick with arousal, both his and mine.

Rafael slips out through the kitchen.

Before I jump West and decide to mate him on the Gravetail Alpha's table, I rise up from my seat. He does the same. As one, we reach for each other's hands. Fingers intertwined, we head out of the den.

The Luna's watchful gaze bathes our skin as we slink out of Darkwoods. I keep waiting for reality to sink in. For regret to shove aside the lust, but it doesn't. With every step, walking side by side with West, I'm more sure that I did what I was meant to do. That the Luna's not upset with me for rejecting the male she gave me.

She just wants what's best for us. Even if it's not what she thought it was.

When I murmur that to West, he nods and says, "I've been trying to tell you that all along, baby. She just wanted you to choose the right male for you."

I squeeze his hand. "I did. It might've taken a while, but I did."

He ducks his head, stealing a quick kiss that does nothing except make me think that maybe we are far enough away from Rafael's den that we can mate *now*.

"I would've waited forever for you. You know that, don't you, Lane?"

I do. And because it really isn't all that far from Rafael's personal territory, I press my palms to his chest. "Can you wait a little longer?"

His eyes are still a blazing gold.

Oh, yeah. The moon fever's got its claws in him and *good*. How did I ever think I'd survive tonight without finally bonding myself to this magnificent male?

She knew. Our goddess knew, and now both me and West do, too.

He tilts his chin up at me. "How much longer?"

My tongue darts out, licking my bottom lip. "Depends."

"Yeah? On what?"

"On how long it takes for you to catch me."

It takes him a second to understand what I meant. Probably because West thinks he's dreaming, that Helene Dupuis would never lead him on such a chase, but if that's the case? Then he forgot all about what it was like when were still together.

Shifters love to run, but shifter males? They crave the chase.

In a flurry of material, I go from my skin to my fur. Because he wasn't expecting it, West has to knock away the scraps of fabric before it dawns on him that I'm already getting away. My blonde fur rustles from the renewed gusts that signal the force of his shift, but I'm already pouring on the speed.

I just had to make sure he was chasing me first.

It's an old shifter game. The run gets the blood pumping, the chase ramps up the anticipation, the adrenaline, and the need… and the capture leads to an explosive coming together. So long as both runners agree to the stakes, if the male is quick and clever enough to catch his female, he gets to mount her when the run is done. If he doesn't, he goes home with his tail between his legs, and his hand the only action he'll get.

No self-respecting she-wolf will ever fuck a wolf in his skin who can't handle her when she's in her fur. Doesn't matter that I'm an omega without a single ounce of dominance in me. I'm still a shifter and—especially beneath the full moon—there are just some instincts I can't deny.

West, neither.

The instant he tears off after me, body arrowed, tail streaming behind his grey wolf, there's no doubt in my mind that West isn't just playing the shifter game.

He's playing to *win*.

I could make it easy for him. If it was just any other night, any other run… I might pretend to trip over a paw or stumble into a rabbit hole. Anything to end the run quickly so I could shift back and find my male ready to claim his prize.

But this isn't just any other night. It's not even just the Luna, either. Sex tonight was inevitable; realizing I've never gotten over Weston Reed and now never will… that was unexpected, but still feels right. As I bound ahead of him, leaping over a bush, weaving between the trees… I put everything I am into this run. When he catches me—because I know he will—he's getting everything.

When we ran off of Gravetail Pack territory, performing

the Luna Ceremony wasn't even a thought in my mind. The more I run, though, the more I realize that he's treating this primal chase like it'll earn him forever at my side.

And it will.

With the Luna over our heads, spurring us to get as far away from Gravetail territory before we shift back to our skin and become one, we run and we run and only knowing that, in the end, I'll get everything *I* need—including her blessing—has me hoping that West will find a way to catch me before he can't.

I shouldn't have worried. A beta wolf who has never wavered in his belief that I was meant to be his mate, nothing will stop him from claiming me now that I've chosen him. Relying on his wolf's instincts, he knows exactly when to make the right move to end this chase at last.

All shifters have an innate sense of where one shifter territory begins and another ends. Agreeing with me that we need to be as far away from Darkwoods as we can before we give in to the moon fever, he follows at a close clip behind me for about fifteen minutes after we leave the outskirts of Gravetail Pack land behind us. The chase has become more of a side-by-side run, with West waiting for an opening to take.

I'm still not making it easy for him, but I don't have to. Full of lust and love and need that burns me even hotter than moon fever, he proves that he kept most of his beta speed restrained until he's ready to overpower me.

And he does. Closing the gap between us, springing off of the earth with his powerful back legs, he launches himself at me.

I zig, but he accounted for me trying to make my escape. He twists mid-air, tackling me, bringing me to the dirt. But since West will never, ever hurt me, he uses his momentum to roll with me instead of flattening me against the dirt.

Once we stop moving, I end up beneath him on my belly. Of course I do. He won the chase, and I'm his prize.

I shift to my skin. After letting out a victorious shout as his wolf, West does the same. His naked body curves over mine; big and heaving from the exertion he used to catch me, his feverish skin nearly sears my back.

His hands drop to my naked waist. After nuzzling the back of my neck, his nose brushing aside my mussed hair to breathe in my scent, he uses his gentle grip on my sides to lift me up. He has his knees perched on the outside of mine, his hard cock nudging the small of my back as he eases me up so that I'm on my hands and knees.

He shifts his position. His cock bobs, slapping my right ass cheek. His breath goes heavy, mine more of a soft wheezing moan as West releases his hold on my side. His hand slips between us, taking hold of his cock.

Panting my name, he positions the head of his cock at the entrance to my pussy; as wet as I am, I take it easily. Back when we were first together, I would never let him just mount me and mate me. I expected him to worship my body, tasting me as thoroughly as he did when he was trying to erase the feral's scent.

I used to love pleasuring him with my mouth, too. There's something about a dominant male shifter being so vulnerable, putting his dick so close to my pair of sharp fangs… it gave this omega power in a whole different way that I missed almost as much as being able to be honest with my feelings for this male.

After the Luna Ceremony is done, I'm going to spend as much time as I want reacquainting myself with West's gorgeous body. I've missed it these last three years, and the other night was as frantic a mating as this one promises to be.

I can't freaking wait.

Which is why I nearly snarl when he pulls his hips back, taking the head of his cock with him.

"Say no," he pants, his remaining palm a scorching brand on my hip. He kneads the flesh with the tips of his claws. I'm not even sure he knows he's doing it. "If you don't want me as your forever mate… if you're not choosing to bond to me… say no. We don't have to do this tonight… I'll wait forever if I have to… but if this isn't it for you, baby, tell me no."

Ah, West… I'm never going to tell him 'no' again—and it's time he knows that.

Arching my back, inviting him to mount me again, I whisper in a ragged voice, "*Yes.*"

One push. That's all it takes. Once he has the crown nudging at my slippery opening again, he makes sure he's in then *shoves.* Just one rough push and he's fully seated inside of me, his groan resting against my back, one hand reaching around to take a handful of my bare tit.

He stays like that for a moment, as though double-checking that I want this. That I want *him*. In the heat of the moment, I don't want to think that I'm the reason my heart's mate doubts his welcome.

Sex with West was never the problem. It was the emotion that came with it, and my insistence that I do what was right for the pack. But following my heart… becoming the other half of the Beta couple as I remain the Omega… *loving* West… that *is* what's best for the pack.

The pack, and me, too.

I rock back and forth, guiding him. Taking the hint, West begins to move. Just like I did, he starts out with rocking, short, shallow strokes that show how desperate he is to keep the connection with me.

But there's more to finalizing a bond. We need the Luna's blessing—which I sense we already have—and for him to finish inside of me. At the same time, one of us needs to mark the other. If we do those three steps during the night of the full moon, we'll create a bond that nothing can break.

I need that. I need that more than my next breath.

My orgasm is already creeping up on me, thanks to the moon fever. I'm so sensitized, one good tweak of my clit would have me going off like a rocket. But as much as I'm drowning in pleasure, I need to make this forever.

I made my choice. Now it's time for West to make me *his*.

He's thrusting harder now, chasing his own climax the way he'd chased me over the shadowy woods. I can sense the turmoil mingling with his pleasure. Torn between making this mating last and forming our bond, he's just pounding away.

My fingers dig into the dirt, clutching the grass, holding my position so that West can control this mating; I did the last time, back in the feral's den, and tonight's his turn. I know him, though. When his pants turn to throaty moans, his motions going so quickly, I'm pulling grass out with my fists, I know it's almost time.

I have to risk letting go with one hand to grab my sweat-soaked hair, scooping it up and tossing it over my shoulder. Then, once I've resumed my position, I gasp, "Weston… mark me."

This is the most important part of the ceremony after hoping for the Luna's blessing. One mate must mark the other, and while my wolf will want him to wear her mark eventually, tonight we both agree that he needs to mark us first.

He's hesitating. I know exactly why, too, and I refuse to let his mistake come between us.

I'd already forgiven him for marking me while I was drugged with quicksilver. He wasn't in his right mind, and even if I chose to mate Rafael, it would've been a reminder of the male I loved and lost. I thought that there must have been a reason I subconsciously kept the bite West gave me and there is: because I loved him, and I wanted to wear his mark even when I couldn't allow myself to think so.

Now I want to be wide awake when he bites me so that I can keep it for real.

Bracing my weight on one elbow, I grope behind me, trying to find the middle of his back. As sweaty as he is, West is also pretty slippery. I'm determined. Slapping him lightly, I do what I can to guide him down toward me.

He goes because I want him to, even as he says, "But… you already… I did before, Lane."

"Then do it again." My eyes flutter closed, groaning under my breath as his latest stroke sends a jolt of pleasure through me. I back up into him, taking more.

Taking everything.

And then, "Please, West. This time… this time I *want* you to mark me."

That's all I have to say.

Sinking his fangs into the mark that's been on my throat for little more than a week, giving me the bite I begged for instead of one I never asked for, West slams his cock all the way inside of me, bucking his hips up so that there's no separating us at that moment. He only removes his fangs from my throat in time to throw back his head and howl as he finishes inside of me.

His howl pushes me over the edge. That, or the absolute

pleasure of his bite invigorates every Luna damned nerve in my body… either way, I squeeze him tight as I come crashing down around him.

Legs shaky and arms weak, I press my feverish forehead to the earth. Breathing in deeply, I smell dirt and grass, sandalwood and *mate*. That last one has another rush of energy and need rolling through me as I get my second wind and eagerly push my ass back against him.

He's still hard.

Well, of course he is. This is the full moon—this is our Luna Ceremony—and West won't go down until our goddess does.

And I look forward to every moment of what's to come.

ANY HOPE THAT WE CAN STUMBLE ONTO PACK TERRITORY without drawing attention to the whole pack dies a quick death almost immediately after we cross into Hickory.

Thank the Luna that West stopped at one of the countless shifter caches that he keeps hidden on the land just outside of Hickory. As Beta, it's his responsibility to make sure the pack is prepared. For any wolf that might stray too far from Sylvan Pack land and find themselves in need of a quick change of clothes after they shift from fur to skin, he has them all over within ten miles of Hickory.

Finding a pair of sweats and a t-shirt that fit West is pretty easy. Since he's the one who stashes them, it only takes two tries. Finding me a dress takes a little longer. We go through four caches before he pulls out a light blue shift dress that's a little loose, but covers what counts.

He insisted on searching until he found one. I would've

been content pulling on anything, but West knows I prefer dresses and he refused to let me settle for anything else.

Of course, then I tease that my mate just wants to be able to throw my skirt over my head and have access to my pussy. West liked that idea so much that he had to give it a try and… yeah. There's a good chance one of the Hickory patrollers might have heard us long before our approach.

And the one we run into? Oh… he's not happy to see us at all.

Joey stamps his boot against the earth as we stroll up on him, my right arm wrapped around West's middle, his left arm nestled around my waist. "Luna *damn* it! Of all the points of entry to Hickory, you just had to pick the part I'm patrolling."

West nods at the delta male. Nuzzling my head with his cheek, he pauses, then lifts his right hand. Plucking something from my wild hair, he shows me a leaf.

Lovely. Not only do we smell like sex and the outdoors, but one of my brother's devoted deltas just saw me with a leaf in my hair.

For some reason, West thinks that's hysterical. Laughing as he flicks the leaf to the grass, he says, "Good to see you, too, Joe."

Joey isn't looking at West anymore, and not just because— good mood or not—daring to meet the Beta's stare for too long isn't a good idea.

Oh, no. He's goggling at me.

More notably, at the fresh mark standing out on my neck.

I see his nostrils flare, as if double-checking his senses.

It's not just the scent of sex he's searching for. From the moment our bond snapped into place, our entwined scent isn't just embedded in our skin from our last mating. Until the day I die, I'll smell a little bit like sandalwood.

I'll smell like my mate.

"Ah, *shit*, West. You marked Helene? You *mated* her? Do you want Bishop to rip off your head and punt it like a football? Because when he finds out what you did last night, he's going to rip your head off and punt it like a football!"

No. He isn't.

I roll up West's sleeve. Four delicate slash marks—pure white, like the bite on my neck—stand out around the curve of his bicep. Tracing them lightly with the points of my fingernails, I smile as West can't keep from shuddering beneath my touch.

"It's okay. I marked him, too. Do you think Bishop is going to rip my head off?"

Poor Joey. I shouldn't tease. As the Omega, I'm the peacemaker, not the instigator. I can't help myself, though. When he pales beneath his ruddy complexion, staring at my mark on West's arm, I think: *sometimes it's just too easy.*

Blinking away his stunned expression, he jerks his head. "Of course not, Helene. But… this is still bad."

"Why?" West tightens his hold on my waist. "You said something about us crossing on the part you're patrolling. What's that about?"

"Ah, Luna. I almost forgot." He lets out a rush of air. "Bishop wants to see you. Both of you."

I glance at West. We knew this would happen sooner or later once we decided to return home… "Okay. We'll go right now."

Better to get it over with.

"Not together, you aren't." As West starts to argue, Joey holds up his hands. "Sorry, but Bishop gave us his orders. If either of you came back, we had to bring you directly to his cabin. If you came back together, we had to separate you."

What?

"But we're bonded," I try to explain.

Joey's not hearing it. Already shaking his head, he interrupts with a quick, "And Bishop's the Alpha."

He's also my brother, but Joey has a point. Before now, West would've been able to get away with disobeying a direct order from Bishop so long as he had a good reason; Beta's prerogative, unless it's a challenge. Me? I could pull the Omega card or the little sister one. Either way, Bishop would give me what I wanted.

Do I want to test him right now? After everything that's happened since I saw him last?

No. I don't.

Neither does my mate.

Huffing out a breath, he nods. "Fine. You're right, Joey. Alpha's word is law."

"You taught me that," Joey points out.

"Yeah. I did, didn't I?"

EIGHTEEN
FLOWERS

t's kind of strange, being treated like a pack enemy while surrounded by the hickories that have watched over me my whole life.

And maybe that's being a little melodramatic. Their wolves reach out to me, welcoming me home, even if their human halves are acting a touch more apprehensive.

That's not because of me, though. It's the Beta.

It doesn't matter that we're mated, or that we're wearing each other's mark. All my packmates know is that their Beta went rogue, running off with the Omega, and something like that is enough to shake the stability in any wolf pack.

So I go with Joey. West is taken in another direction by two deltas: Kevin and Philip.

Hoping to get this over with, I expect Joey to lead me straight to the Alpha cabin. To the den. He doesn't. On another of Bishop's orders, I'm taken straight to Ginnie, our pack healer. Only after she looks me over and assures Joey that I'm perfectly healthy does he escort me to the Alpha's den.

To my surprise, when I enter, Bishop is alone.

Bishop is rarely alone when he's in the den. There are official reasons why, of course. And the fact that, when he's in the den, it's usually because he has a line of packmates who need to meet with him.

But the biggest reason? He's so protective of his mate, he prefers to keep Sofia close by as often as he can.

I don't blame him. What happened with our parents… it affected our lives in so many ways. Bishop grew up with an insatiable urge to protect those who are important to him. My dad failed to protect my mom. He never forgave himself for it, and in one attack, we lost both of our parents. He died shortly after she did of a broken heart, leaving Bishop to pick up the pieces.

It affected me, too. For as far back as I could remember, all I knew was that, if I couldn't protect myself, I would need someone to do it for me.

And I did. In a Beta who destroyed a feral threatening me, I found him.

But where is he now?

"Where's West?"

The look on Bishop's face tells me that I should know the answer to that question.

If I did, I wouldn't have asked.

As his mate, I should be able to follow West through our bond—but the lingering echo of Rafael's bond is tripping me up. Closing my eyes, when I reach deep inside of me, I see the shadowy Darkwoods on the other side. Unless West went back to Gravetail territory without me, I'm picking up on Rafael.

No matter how many times I try, he's all I can find. At first, I wondered if the Luna took back her blessing. Panicking a little, I ran right to the bathroom in Ginnie's cabin, swooping my hair out of my face to get a good look at the mark on my throat in her mirror.

Pure white. A mating mark, and not just a scar my subconscious had refused to heal.

Rafael never bit me. The most he did was take my hand and kiss the top of it. No. The mark meant I was West's bonded mate, only without a bond currently tethering us together. It's like he's been cut off from me since arriving in Hickory.

Only one substance in the world could do that to a pair of bonded supes.

Silver.

"Oh my Luna, Bishop! You put my mate in chains?"

"What did you expect me to do, canari? He *stole* you."

I can't deny that. "Yes, but—"

"Ah… there it is. *But.*"

"Exactly. *But* he's my mate."

"He is now, isn't he?"

"Bishop… what's going on? I mean, I *know* what's going on… but why did you separate us? Chains? Yes, he stole me, but he had his reasons."

And I can*not* believe I'm justifying everything West did to me. But I'm a shifter, after all. A she-wolf. We see things differently, don't we?

But, as Alpha, Bishop sees things in his own way, too.

"A mark of a good Alpha is ceding control," he says. At first, I think he's changing the subject, until he adds, "It's like Quinn with her feral. For nine months that stray sniffed around, waiting to make his move. If he took any longer, I might've grabbed him by the scruff and dropped him off in front of her. Only reason I didn't is because, technically, she was still West's intended. But we all knew that wasn't gonna happen, didn't we? Good thing, too. If she hadn't gone off and mated her feral, who knows how much longer before West would've gotten the nerve to make *his* move."

Hang on…

"You knew, didn't you?" I guess, only it's not a guess. It's something I should've realized when Bishop never found me. "You knew he took me?"

"Not at first. The quicksilver was smart," Bishop grunts. "I wasn't expecting that. I knew he was planning something when he spent all his time working on the cabin, but I figured he might be going lone wolf on me. When you were gone, I knew he had you. I might have had to find a backup Beta if it wasn't for his constant phone calls, checking in with me."

I blink, stunned. "West told you? What… everything? So you knew after I was gone? And you still let me with him?"

A nod.

"Why?"

"He's my Beta," Bishop said simply.

And even when it seemed like West was going off the deep end, Bishop trusts him.

Just like I do.

Well, maybe not as much as I do, considering—

"So why the chains?" I ask him. "If you were on board with this insane plan of his, why did you separate us? Why did you chain up my mate?"

"Maybe because I'm the Alpha?"

"Bishop…"

"What? I had to let West do what he had to. No matter what, I knew you were safer with him than anyone else but me. Only you… You're my kid sister, canari. You're all grown up… you're bonded now… but you're still my little sister. I had to make sure this was what you wanted."

"Mates get to choose," I remind him.

"That they do, but Omegas are different. They always have been. Too often they do what they think is best for others instead of being selfish like the rest of us wolves."

"I *am* selfish—"

"For an Omega," he points out. "You wanted West. A true she-wolf would have followed her heart and told Rafael to fuck off three years ago. But you didn't. You accepted his offer for the good of the pack."

"It wasn't just the pack," I confess. "If I had a fated mate out there, so did West. I didn't want to keep him when he might have wanted another female more than me. It wouldn't have been right."

"Fair enough. But… remind me? What part of that makes you selfish again?"

This is Bishop. He'll never see any of my flaws. I stopped arguing about that one a long time ago.

"Besides," he adds, "from the time West was a pup, he's only had eyes for you. Believe me. When he started sniffing around your tail, I tried scaring him off like all the other boys who wanted you, but he was the only one who ever stood up to me. Twelve and scrawny, he didn't back down in front of an alpha… why did you think I made him my Beta when he filled out some?"

"Um, because he's your best friend?"

Bishop snorts. "He's my best friend because I liked how he treated you and, apart from you and my cher, he's the only one who puts up with my shit. None of this… *yes, Alpha, no, Alpha, let me lick your boots, Alpha…* crap I get from other packmates. He stood up to me for you, canari. Even if he wasn't a beta, he'd be my right-hand wolf. Just like he's always been meant to be your mate."

He says that with such certainty, it's all I can do not to stare up at him in ill-disguised shock.

It takes a second for me to find the words, and when I do, I nearly shout them at my brother. "If you wanted me to end up with West so badly, why didn't you say something?"

He shrugs, big shoulders moving up and down. "Couldn't. You had to be free to make your choice."

My choice… that's all I ever wanted.

Tears well up in my eyes. They're happy tears, though, and I make sure to soothe Bishop's wolf before he can worry that he's made me cry.

Lips twitching beneath his beard, he throws open his arms.

I rush around his desk, flinging myself at him. Wrapped up in my big brother's bear hug, I shudder out a sigh of relief mingled with just enough apprehension to catch his attention.

My wolf soothed his, but the other half of Bishop can't be fooled.

"Oh, canari…" He strokes my hair. "What aren't you telling me?"

I shake my head.

"There's something. Go on. You can tell your big brother."

Alphas know when those weaker than them are lying straight to their face. But Bishop? Considering I've learned to get around that talent of his by never outright *lying*, he's learned to pick up on my tells. Even if I'm not fibbing, he knows when I'm hiding something from him.

Like now.

Pulling away from him, I glance up. An alpha's stare is so powerful, I let myself fall into it as I admit, "I still feel Rafael. The bond snapped when I rejected him, but it's like… like he's still holding onto it for some reason. Still holding onto his claim to *me*."

Bishop frowns. I don't like that frown one bit. "Have you told West?"

And risk him deciding to challenge Rafael? "No."

"You should."

"I can't. What if he doubts my bond with him? We're mates… no one can change that. But I never expected to still sense Rafael after the Luna was over and I do. I shouldn't… and I don't want West to think I'm not committed to him."

The time for those doubts is long gone. Especially since he never doubted me. I was the one who kept him at arm's length. Now that I have him, what will it do to me if he's suddenly the one having second thoughts?

Reaching down, Bishop takes my hands in his. "You're an omega, canari. I don't think you know what it's like to be around a wolf like yours. It's like the sun shining after a rainy day, so bright and warm. It's easy to get addicted." He pauses for a moment. "I thought West was. Addicted to you."

Maybe he is. "He loves me." I believe that with every fiber of my being. "He loves me for me, wolf and all."

"I know he does. And if you decide to tell him about Rafael or not, that's your choice. But you've already made your choice when it comes to your mate. It's about time I congratulate him."

Releasing my hands, Bishop stalks over to the door to the den. Shoving it open, he sticks his head out of it.

"Bring me Weston," he bellows.

Oh, boy. *Weston.* Bishop's using West's full name. Considering my brother is the one who started calling a twelve-year-old Weston by the shortened version of his name in the first place, I'm not sure that's such a good sign.

He said he wanted to congratulate him, though. Then

again, he put him in silver chains. That's almost as bad as West dosing me with quicksilver.

Hmm… come to think of it, maybe it'll do West some good to find out what it's like to be cut off from his wolf.

Not for long, of course, but maybe just a tiny taste…

It's not much longer. Less than five minutes later, I sense him again. Our bond springs back to life, so strong and powerful, it shadows the faint echo of the one I have with Rafael. As though he was worried for me while *he* was in chains, he sends a reassuring pulse down our tie, followed by one of pure love.

I return it, then sit down again, waiting for his arrival.

It's only a few more moments before the door swings in again.

Sofia enters first, smiling at me before—like two magnets being pulled together—she drifts right into Bishop's embrace. She kisses the underside of his bearded jaw, laying her hand possessively on his chest. Both of them stay standing.

West enters the den next, rubbing the raw patch on his right wrist. I wince. The silver must have bit through his skin.

I didn't feel the pain through our bond before because the silver would've tamped it down. Not only does the mineral cut us off from our wolves, but it also keeps us distanced from our mates in all ways.

"Oh, West…"

He spares me a grin before he turns to Bishop. Any humor slides off of his face, suddenly serious as he addresses the Alpha.

"It was worth it. If only to know Helene was mine for a single night, it was worth it."

Bishop raises his eyebrows. "You fixin' to find a way to break the bond with my sister, Weston?"

"What? No. That's not what I—"

"After all the trouble I went to to give this mating my blessing, you want to back out now?"

West jaw goes tight. "Never," he bites out a split second before understanding slams into him. "Blessing?"

Bishop grunts. "That's right."

We didn't need his blessing, but Luna… does it feel good to have it. From the pleasure reaching me from my mate, he agrees.

"Welcome to the family, West," Sofia says warmly.

Bishop lays his palm over the curve of her ass. "Ah, cher. He was *always* family."

ONCE BISHOP—AT SOFIA'S URGING—DISMISSES US FROM HIS presence, I grab West's hand and lead him outside. It's already healed from the silver, though I can sense how much he needs to remind himself that we're truly mates. Being cut off from me so soon after our Luna Ceremony has left him rattled.

We need privacy.

Turning to glance up at my mate, I ask, "Should we go to your cabin or—"

"Yours."

Whoa. Okay. That was quick. "My place it is, then."

West has a cabin of his own. It was a gift from his father when he became Beta. Up until then, he still lived at home with his parents. A lot of unmated delta shifters do, so it made sense that he didn't move out until he had a much higher rank in the pack.

While we spent a lot of time together in mine, when we wanted privacy, we went to his since it was further from the heart of pack land.

We want privacy now—so why wouldn't he want to return to his?

I don't ask him. Then again, I don't *have* to.

"I'm sorry for snapping, baby. It's just…" He exhales roughly. "I haven't slept in my bed in three years. Not since the last time you were in it with me."

Oh, West. Three years?

As if he feels the need to explain, he continues, "I would curl up on my couch as my wolf. And that's when I wasn't sleeping on your porch."

"You didn't…"

He nods.

Wow.

West's determination to get me back was the biggest open secret in the pack—but that's something I didn't know. He spent so much time outside of my cabin, the sandalwood lingered. I just… it never occurred to me that he would much rather sleep outside on my porch than in a bed without me.

And it had to be the porch. I haven't let him step foot inside of my home since the day I broke things off with him…

So he closed off his bedroom, a shrine to our relationship. Was what I did any better?

I squeeze his fingers. "Come on. Let me take you home."

That's all it takes. West leans down, nuzzling his bite on my throat, then lets me lead him toward the Omega cabin.

As we walk inside my territory—*our* territory—West pauses. I glance over in time to see his nostrils flare. His lips part, sampling the air.

I freeze.

I didn't think it was that obvious. At least, I didn't until West says, "That scent…"

Busted.

Brushing my shoulder with his palm, almost as though he's incapable of passing by me without even the quickest connection, he moves toward my bookshelf. I have six thick leather-bound albums tucked in between all of the paperbacks and hardcovers in my collection.

He unerringly reaches for the first album. Looking over his shoulder, waiting for me to nod, he turns his attention back toward the album. He flips it open.

I fiddle with the hem of my skirt nervously.

West sucks in a breath. "Helene…"

"Yes?"

His gaze searches me out again. This time, the dark grey glitters with gold. "Is this what I think it is?"

An album full of hundreds and hundreds of pressed wild-flowers? Because that's exactly what it is. Just like the other five still perched on the bookshelf.

I smile at him. "What did you think I was doing with all the flowers you brought me?"

EPILOGUE

SIX MONTHS LATER

April in Louisiana is gorgeous.

The warblers sing their songs during the spring migration, the wet season is still on the cusp of arriving, and the wildflowers that dot the forests surrounding hickory are in full bloom. It's nowhere near as hot and sweltering as it'll be come June, but as the temps reach seventy during the day, I pull on another sundress and sit on my porch, enjoying the cooler breeze in the early morning.

At least, that's what I do when I'm not helping Sofia and West keep the pack from acting out because Bishop is off territory.

Whoever said that, when the cat's away, the mice will play only did because they didn't know anything about wolf shifters. From the youngest pup to the oldest gamma, the moment the Alpha steps paw off of immediate territory, they get the itch to rebel.

It's a shifter thing. A pack is at its best when there's no doubt who the leader is. We need a concrete hierarchy, each one of us intimately aware of where our place in it is. Alpha's at the top with the Alpha female, followed by the Beta, the Alpha's inner circle, the gammas, and then the deltas. As always, omegas are set apart from the rest of the pack, though I'm still closer to the top because of the way my type of wolf has power over those on the bottom.

That's why, on the rare occasion that Bishop has to leave Hickory, I have to be on my guard, calming any wayward packmates who might feel lost without their Alpha to lead them—or talking down those whose wolf go feral enough that challenging the absent Alpha seems like a good idea.

I'm in charge of their emotions. As Bishop's mate, Sofia's presence is a reminder that one-half of the Alpha couple is still imprinting on the pack and our territory. And West… our Beta will do whatever he has to to protect Bishop's position of power.

It's not as though any of us expect our fellow packmates to lose their mind and rise up against Bishop. We don't. Bishop has all of our loyalty and has since he became Alpha a decade ago. Doesn't matter. Shifters respond better to routine, and when something changes it, it's up to the rest of us to keep life in Hickory going smoothly.

It's been six months since West ran off with me and we returned as bonded mates. Losing the Beta and Omega at the same time was a hard blow to the pack's stability that we only recently got under control. Seeing us together, sensing our mate bond… it helped, but it also inadvertently gave some other packmates the really wrong idea of what's acceptable when it comes to a mating.

West is the Beta. As Bishop's right-hand wolf, he should've

known better to put his own needs before those of the pack. When he did what he wanted anyway and Bishop didn't punish him publicly for it, some other wolves thought that meant our Alpha condoned what West did.

As if. The only reason my brother kept his reaming out of West behind closed doors was because he thought of it as a family matter first, and a pack matter second. That was Bishop's mistake. Too busy thinking like my older brother, he forgot that impressionable packmates were watching.

We discovered that around Christmas, four months ago. When Reese disappeared with Lux, leaving only a vial of quicksilver behind in her cabin as a clue that he'd followed West's lead, Bishop shifted on the spot when he was told, roaring so loudly that there wasn't a single wolf in Hickory—wild or shifter—who didn't submit at the sound.

Including his Beta.

Not that I blamed Bishop at all, but I almost missed my first Christmas as a mated she-wolf because his solution was to send West on his own to track down Reese and Lux. West wasn't allowed to come back unless he brought them with him so Reese could explain himself, and Bishop could make sure that Lux wasn't forced into doing anything she didn't want to.

I know the two younger wolves. Both in their early twenties, neither one had met their fated mate yet, and though they weren't in a relationship when Reese made his move, that wasn't for a lack of trying on Lux's part. She'd been trying to attract the black wolf for years. Too thick to notice, he pined for her from a distance until he decided to follow his Beta's lead and whisk her off of pack land to proposition her.

It didn't matter to the Alpha that Lux was ecstatic that Reese both chose her, then stole her away to shower her with his attention. Bishop put his paw down at the beginning of this year: anyone who brought quicksilver into Hickory would be punished, and the next wolf—male or female—who forgot that mates get to choose was going to be banished from the pack.

No ifs, ands, or buts.

Desperate to get back to me, West ran them to ground in three days. He told me later that he burst in on them in the middle of mating; with the whole cabin smelling like wolves and sex, it wasn't the first time they had mated, and he missed the grunts coming from beyond the door until it was too late. Reese is a delta. Normally, he would be no match for the Beta, but, normally, he didn't have his naked female beneath him, his cock buried balls-deep inside of her.

Poor West. While nudity is no big deal in a pack, that doesn't count mating. He saw more of the younger wolves than he ever wanted to. Then, to add injury to insult, my mate got a nasty bite to his arm when Reese pulled out, shifted to a wolf, and lunged at West in a bid to protect his female.

Served him right, Bishop said later, lips twitching in the closest thing he did to a smile.

Reese and Lux are bonded mates now, and no one has defied Bishop's latest law since then. He was a little worried they might when he had to leave—not gonna lie, so was me and West—but, so far, everything's run as smoothly as possible.

I never left Hickory before West made off with me in the middle of the night. My brother, though? As Alpha, sometimes he has no choice. At the very least, he has to travel to the annual Alpha meeting that takes place every July. And then there are those times when the Alpha collective—the ruling body for shifters in the United States—needs an Alpha to do their duty.

That's what happened a couple of days ago when Bishop was summoned to the Northern Winds Pack in the Northeast.

Turns out that the fabled Luna-touched female who could break bonds with the touch of her finger is *real*. A she-wolf who lost her fated mate because of the other female went to the Alpha collective with her complaint, and they decided to put Elizabeth Howell on trial. Twelve Alphas had to go meet with the female and see if she was as big a threat as the other she-wolf claimed.

Bishop was one of them.

Sofia might be the Alpha female of our pack, but her wolf is a maternal delta. When she heard that Bishop would have to interrogate a shifter who could *break bonds*, she was understandably worried. Only Bishop assuring her that the she-wolf's "gift" wouldn't work on a bond as strong as theirs kept Sofia from making it even harder on him to leave her behind.

He promised he'd be back within the week. It's only been three days since he left, and I can't wait for Bishop to return so that I can have West to myself for more than a few minutes.

I knew what I was getting into when I mated the Beta. His loyalty to Bishop and our packmates makes him attractive in a different way than his sexy smile and his handsome face. He's devoted to Hickory, even if I'm the only female who's ever held his heart in her paws.

Without Bishop here, West is acting as the de facto Alpha. He still spends the nights in our bed, but he's either sitting in the den, mediating any pack squabbles, or strolling around our territory, letting the other wolves see him and know that a dominant wolf is in charge during the days while Bishop is gone.

As for me... Sofia is obviously struggling without Bishop. She doesn't want anyone to see it, but I'm the Omega. I don't *have* to see it to know that her wolf is keening inside of her chest, calling for her mate. When I'm not busy with another packmate, I'm sitting with her, soothing her wolf's loneliness with my presence and my wolf's calming nature.

And, okay, maybe I tell her a few of my favorite childhood stories about Bishop to cheer her up.

It's early evening now. The sun is streaming through the hanging leaves of the hickories on the edge of our land, and it's even warmer than it has been lately. As shifters, we run hot to begin with. The dress I'm wearing today is a simple light blue shift dress covered in a daisy print that reminds me of the flowers that my beloved mate still brings me whenever we're apart.

West has brought me three Shasta daisies alone since Bishop left. I've pressed each one of them in my latest album —except for the one from earlier this morning. That one I have tucked behind my ear, nestled in my loose hair.

Sweat wells at the base of my neck as I go for a stroll further away from the pack circle. Careful not to jostle the daisy, I swoop my hair over my shoulder, slicking the moisture away with the back of my hand. Sofia is visiting with Kara and her rambunctious twin pups this evening. After spending the last hour alone on my front porch, an open invitation for any of my packmates to visit with me, I decided to stretch my human legs and take a walk.

And if I so happen to cross West's path while he's out on patrol? I'm sure that'll be just a happy accident…

Oh, who am I fooling? Earlier, I followed my end of our bond to West. Instead of sitting in the den like he has been, he was up and moving. Figuring he was meeting with another packmate, I left him to it—until Sofia slipped away from my cabin and I felt a tug as West moved further from the center of pack territory.

By the time I decided to go search for my mate myself, I knew exactly where he was. I just... I wanted to double-check *why*.

Since our mate bond snapped into place, finalizing with the Luna's blessing, West has regained complete control over his wolf. He doesn't sneak off to take his frustrations out on the trees in his private clearing anymore. He no longer returns to me smelling of sweat and blood. He still disappears there to find me flowers, but his trips are as quick as they are frequent.

Still, three years of watching him suffer and convincing myself that it was for the best has broken me in a way that I'm still coming to terms with. I was so sure I was right, that the Luna wouldn't have sent me Rafael's name if we weren't meant to be, that I ignored my own heart and tried my best to push West away. The whole pack knows how well that worked out, and while my only regret is that it took me three years to realize that I did have the choice, that I could tell the Luna that I chose West instead, I never want West to feel like I don't love him with every inch of me, body and soul.

Because I do. I always have.

And he finally knows it.

I had to stay away from him for so long that, sometimes, I have this urge to go to him. Back when I was meant for Rafael, I had to lock myself in my cabin to resist it.

West is my mate now. He's mine whenever I want him to be.

Thank the Luna.

When the enticing scent of sandalwood fills my nose, then my lungs, I break out into a jog. A smile is already curving my lips as I weave around the trees, anticipating the moment when I'll see that first glimpse of his cocky grin, his steely eyes, and the possessive look that has always belonged on West's gorgeous features.

Because he's mine now, but I've always been his.

He's just rising up from a crouch when I break into his clearing. He moves easy, shifting on his heel, turning to face me as soon as I come to a standstill.

The sun silhouettes West, soft golden light bathing him as he holds the purple coneflower in his grip out to me.

"You didn't have to come to me, Lane, baby. I was on my way to you."

I laugh. Confronted with the smolder in his gaze and the love for me he no longer has to leash, I stumble a few steps toward him, drunk with joy and pure affection for him. Six months after I stopped pretending that he hasn't ever been the only male for me and I still go giddy when West looks at me like that.

"Maybe it's time I do the chasing for once," I tease, regaining my footing as I move toward him.

"Never," he says, the heat in his voice making it clear that he's not angry. He's reminding me of the promise he made to me that fateful day in Darkwoods. "You're worth every step I take to you… after you… *with* you, my mate. You don't ever have to— *whoa…* Lane. You okay?"

His tease turns to panic as, between one footfall and the next, my knees buckle. Quick as my mate is, he's in front of me in an instant. Wrapping his arms around me, he catches me before I can fall forward into the dirt.

I clutch his chest through his t-shirt. West uses his impressive strength to lift me easily, setting me back on my feet before he cradles my head with one hand, the small of my back with the other. He's panting my name over and over again, a spark of fear traveling down our bond.

It's his fear, and I realize that something's wrong.

No. Not wrong.

Different.

For six months, I've dealt with an echo of a bond that was impossible to ignore. I told Bishop that I hoped it would fade in time, but it hasn't; if anything, I felt Rafael tugging me harder in the months since I rejected him than he ever did when I was standing right in front of him, trying to sense any kind of love from him. He never loved me. Even these last few days, when shadows of my former bond with Rafael were almost stronger than the unbreakable one I shared with West, I only sensed loneliness and need, never *love*.

My mate knows about it. I couldn't hide it from him, and I told him about it shortly after we returned from Gravetail territory. He swore that it didn't change anything, and I believed him. Rafael clung to me because I was an omega she-wolf, not because I was his mate. West understood that, and he never asked me about it again.

When I nearly collapse, it doesn't even occur to West that my tiny spell could have had something to do with the phantom mate bond. But it did. I'm not so sure what happened —or even *how* it happened—but that's what's different.

It's *gone*.

Somehow, some way, the whisper of a bond I had with Rafael has vanished, leaving only the one I have with West. Shining like a beacon inside of me, it's the most beautiful thing I've ever seen.

"West." My claws unsheathe on their own. I only realize that they have when I accidentally slice through his shirt, cutting him enough that the tang of his blood slaps the last of the haze from my head. "West!" A laugh bubbles up and out of me as I release my hold on his chest. Instead, I throw my arms around his tapered waist. "Oh my Luna, *West!*"

He's running his fingers through my hair, holding me close. At the sound of my laughter, the spark of fear brightens and I realize that I'm worrying him.

I pull away just enough that I can tilt my chin and meet the concern written in every line of his handsome face. "It's gone," I breathe. "It's finally gone."

"Gone?" Concern turns to confusion turns to undisguised *hope*. "You mean—"

I nod, beaming at him.

"Gravetail? He's *gone?*"

"It just happened. It's like… I don't know. This weight on my shoulder was lifted," I explain. He should understand. When Quinn rejected her mate bond with West, he told me that's exactly what it felt like. "That's why I almost fell. I wasn't expecting it and—*oh*."

I wasn't expecting *that*, either, though I probably should have.

West's relief—with an added dose of love for me for good measure—slams into me a split second before he reacts. With a whoop, he lifts me off of the ground, whirling with me until we're both dizzy and now West is laughing with me. He lowers me again, cupping my chin with his palms so he can tilt my head back, taking my mouth in a claiming kiss that swallows our laughter.

We're both breathless by the time he breaks the kiss, tugging me back into his tight embrace. Even as he starts to lead me over to his favorite tree—marked with gouges from his claws, dotted with old blood, and covered in the scars that

West healed on himself during my continued rejection of him —I know exactly what he wants to do.

Every full moon since the all-important one we spent together outside of Hickory, he leads me to his personal territory, positions me up against this tree in one way or another, and takes me as if it's our last time together.

It's not. It'll never be. Nothing can separate us again, and if he needs for us to build better memories in this clearing, our sex christening the ancient hickory instead of his pain, I'll brace my arms against the stripped bark, arch out my back, and invite him to take what's his whenever he needs it.

Like right now.

I'm already sopping wet by the time West lowers his hands to my waist, already gripping the fabric of my sundress, inching it over my hips. Breathing the same air, his lips on mine, West groans into my mouth when he takes a deep breath and catches how thick my arousal is.

He dives back in for another kiss, backing me up against the tree as he strokes my tongue with his, nipping at my bottom lip with his fang. He's panting, but I can still make out his words as he grates, "Luna knows you've always been mine. If I had to share you to keep you, I would, but…"

West groan turns even huskier as he slips his claw-free hand between our bodies. His eyes blaze when he realizes that, when I set off in search of him earlier, I left my panties behind. He drops his mouth to my neck, already fumbling with his jeans as he adds, "But, baby, I'm so fucking glad I don't have to."

I press my palms against his chest, enjoying the feel of his thundering heart. It's such a heady realization, knowing that it beats only for me—and that it always has.

That's not all, either.

His heart is mine. His body is mine.

His *forever* is mine…

Then again, it's only fair.

As West lifts my thigh, guiding me to wrap my leg around his waist before he frantically pushes his cock inside of me, I let out a throaty moan, burying my hand in his hair. He hasn't turned me to take me from behind; probably because he wants to steal kisses in between thrusts. Fine with me. My human side adores face-to-face mating, and I clutch a few strands of his thick, perfectly-styled hair as I hold on and let him take me for a ride.

The evening sun is shining down on us. The soft yellow light glitters against the gold ring on my left hand.

I grin, thinking of the matching one West has on. I thought about ordering one for him. I was too late, of course. He had the matching band in his sock drawer, only slipping it on his ring finger after we first returned to Hickory as bonded mates. He wants the whole world to know—human and supe—that he belongs to me.

Like West, I'm proud to wear his bite and his ring. Wedding or no wedding, I'm not only his mate. I'm the Beta's bride, and when a shifter says *forever*, they mean it.

Me and West are it, 'til death do us part.

SNEAK PEEK OF PREY

You think that I would've gotten used to being bombarded by good-looking guys since I've been in Winter Creek—and then there's this guy.

When I first met Tristan, I thought of him as beautiful. Remy was striking.

My savior is just my type.

I didn't think I had one until now. None of my boyfriends had anything in common except a tendency to use me for sex and fun before moving on. I've been attracted to all kinds—and some women, too, not gonna lie—but I've never understood the phrase "love at first sight" until right this very second.

It's just because he saved you, Fallon, I tell myself. That gut punch of attraction is gratitude. The sudden possessiveness I feel for a man I just met is simply ridiculous.

Right?

I mean, I can't even pinpoint what exactly it is about him that has my palms going sweaty. About five years or so older than me, he has a sharp jaw and high cheekbones that are contradicted by a lush mouth and dark eyelashes that almost look like he's had them done. They frame a pair of amber-colored eyes, too orange to be hazel. Unlike the other two guys I've met in town, he's not clean-shaven. He has a five o'clock shadow that develops into a closely-cropped beard that covers the knife's edge of that masculine jaw. It suits the slight scowl on his handsome features.

Because he's totally scowling now that I can see his face.

That doesn't bother me. More than that, I get the feeling that I *know* him and the scowl is pretty much his default expression. That we're not just strangers who met in the weirdest of circumstances… and it hits me why I feel like this: I've seen him before. Only just a flash, and Tristan distracted me from staring then, but—

"I know you."

He straightens in his chair. "You do?"

"I, uh, yeah. I think I saw you in the town square a couple of days ago."

On the edge of the square, when I shivered because I felt like someone was watching me only to see a guy standing there on his own, nodding at Tristan.

"Possibly." He returns to his slouch, glancing at a point over my head instead of meeting my eyes. "I was there."

Translation: I don't remember seeing you—and if I do, it doesn't matter regardless.

Fair enough. I'd gotten so used to Tristan's flirting and Remy's not-so-subtle interest—that I will never return now, thank you very much—that I think it went to my head. Just because those two were interested in the new girl, it didn't mean every guy in Winter Creek was.

Maybe it's better that the man who saved me doesn't seem to know what to do with me.

Yeah, well, I don't, either.

"Anyway, I guess I should thank you." Obviously. "For the woods. And, um, bring me to—"

"My hunting cabin," he supplies.

I take the excuse to tear my gaze away from him, glancing around the room instead. Hunting cabin, he calls it. He isn't wrong. Opposite the chocolate-brown couch I'm perched on, there's a fireplace just behind his seat. There's a single wooden table next to him, a door to my right, and light brown walls covered with stuffed animal heads and weapons.

I notice a mounted stag's head—which, while creepy, is at least understandable—and an honest-to-God's wolf mounted opposite of the stag that has me doing a double-take. An ax is resting on pegs over the fireplace, a crossbow is pinned next to the stag head like it's part of the trophy, and he has lines of arrows posted on the other side of the bow.

Okay, then.

I feel a little bit better now that I notice them. I've got no shot when it comes to using a bow and arrow, but if I can wrangle that ax down, I have some way to protect myself if I have to.

"Anyway, you don't have to thank me," he adds, dragging my attention away from the sharp, silver edge of the ax back to him. "Anyone else would have done the same."

His matter-of-the-fact attitude has me momentarily forgetting about the weapons.

Anyone else would've helped me? Considering it was my grandmother and a dude who made it obvious he wanted in my pants who trussed me up in the first place, I doubt that.

I shrug, leaving it at that.

My savior allows it. Nodding at me, he says, "Besides, I'm more interested in hearing how you ended up tied to a tree in the first place."

I should've been expecting this. Of course he'd ask.

"What?" I offer him a crooked grin. "That sort of thing doesn't happen in Winter Creek often?"

AVAILABLE NOW

PREY

WOLVES AND WITCHES AND CURSES, OH MY...

I never believed in the paranormal mainly because I never had any reason to—at least, not until I received a telegram from a grandmother I didn't know existed, inviting me to a small town that was nearly impossible to find, full of shifters and witches that shouldn't be real.

Of course, I didn't know that until *after* I agreed to visit her in her secluded home.

When I pull into town, I almost regret my impulsive decision to take this trip. Bordered on all sides by rivers and mountains and dense forests, Winter Creek is a trap. Once you get in, it's just as difficult to leave. No one has cars here or internet service, and my own phone is a glorified paperweight as soon as I step off the train.

Speaking of the train... I discover too late that it arrives on its rickety tracks once a week if you're lucky. And, of course, there's the small matter of the curse.

Turns out there's a reason why my grandmother finally got in touch with me for the first time in twenty-five years. In Winter's Creek, there's a curse involving a coven of witches, the feral wolf who haunts the dark forest, and a woman from seventy years ago who looks enough like me to convince my grandmother that I'm the only one who can break it at last.

When I refuse, I discover that my grandmother isn't just the head witch of Winter Creek—she's the one responsible for the curse that's kept the town in stasis for the last seventy years. To break it, she's willing to do whatever she has to, including sacrificing me to the big, black wolf that's been lurking in the shadows, watching me since my arrival.

Because the beast in the woods is hungry, and I'm the perfect prey...

Prey* is the first in a new rejected mates/fated mates series featuring Fallon Witt, a human woman who doesn't know anything about the paranormal—until she's thrown headfirst into it. While partly inspired by Beauty and the Beast, it also has elements of Little Red Riding Hood—though, in this series, the big bad wolf is the hero, and the grandmother is the true danger in the woods of Winter Creek...

COMING SOON
THE ALPHA'S HEART

Bishop Dupuis is the new Alpha of the Sylvan Pack.

A powerful wolf shifter raised to follow his duty, when the revered Luna—the wolf shifters' goddess—whispers the name of his fated mate into his ear following his Alpha Ceremony, he has no doubt what to do next: send for the female and offer to mate her sight unseen. After all, if the Luna says the little cher is supposed to be the Alpha's mate, who is he to decide otherwise?

On the other side of the country, Sofia Russo is growing tired of her place in the River Run Pack. She loves her job as one of the pack's teachers, molding young pups, but all that does is remind her that she's never had a mate. Her wolf is choosy, and none of the males in her territory have caught her attention. So when she discovers that she's the fated mate to an Alpha from Louisiana, she jumps at the chance to go.

And then she meets the towering, bearded Bishop with his grunts and his snarls and his fiery gold eyes and she nearly flees all the way back east...

For Bishop, it's love at first sight. For Sofia, she can't understand why the goddess would give her such a terrifying male—until she gets to see beneath his Alpha nature and realize that she couldn't ask for a better male.

Because she's the Alpha's heart, and he's the other half of her lonely soul.

KEEP IN TOUCH

Stay tuned for what's coming up next! Follow me at any of these places—or sign up for my newsletter—for news, promotions, upcoming releases, and more!

Website
Newsletter

ALSO BY SARAH SPADE

Holiday Hunk

Halloween Boo

This Christmas

Auld Lang Mine

I'm With Cupid

Getting Lucky

When Sparks Fly

Holiday Hunk: the Complete Series

Claws and Fangs

Leave Janelle

Never His Mate

Always Her Mate

Forever Mates

Hint of Her Blood

Taste of His Skin

Stay With Me

Never Say Never: Gem & Ryker

Sombra Demons

Drawn to the Demon Duke*

Mated to the Monster

Stolen by the Shadows

Santa Claws

Bonded to the Beast

Fated to the Phantom

Stolen Mates

The Alpha's Heart*

The Feral's Captive

Chase and the Chains

The Beta's Bride

Wolves of Winter Creek

Prey

Pack

Predator

Claws Clause

(written as Jessica Lynch)

Mates *free*

Hungry Like a Wolf

Of Mistletoe and Mating

No Way

Season of the Witch

Rogue

Sunglasses at Night

Ain't No Angel

True Angel

Ghost of Jealousy

Night Angel

Broken Wings

Of Santa and Slaying

Lost Angel

Born to Run

Uptown Girl

A Pack of Lies

Here Kitty, Kitty

Ordinance 7304: the Bond Laws (Claws Clause Collection #1)

Living on a Prayer (Claws Clause Collection #2)